# City of Daggers

## The Iron Teeth: Book Two

Scott Straughan

ISBN: 978-1-7750029-4-9

*I dedicate this book to my readers. I couldn't have gotten this far without the support of those first few brave/bored story lovers who were willing to give me a chance.*

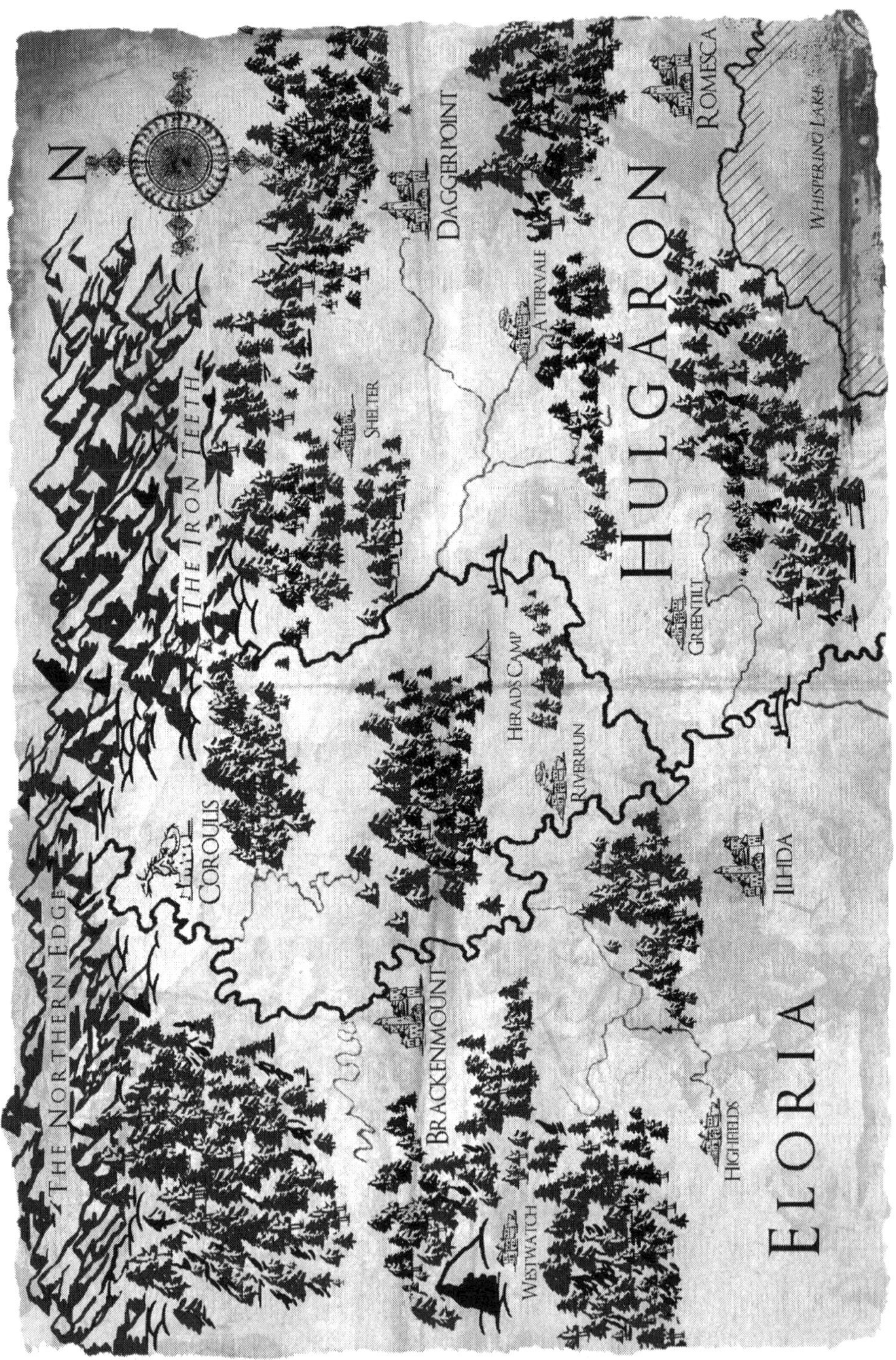
N
The Northern Edge
The Iron Teeth
Coroulis
Shelter
Daggerpoint
Attervale
Romesca
Whispering Lake
Hulgaron
Herads Camp
Riverrun
Greentilt
Brackenmount
Westwatch
Highfields
Ilhda
Eloria

# *Part One:*
# *Along Twisted Paths*

# *Chapter 1*

The hobgoblin stared down at his target with beady hate-filled eyes. Green trees lay behind the lanky warrior. Sunlight reflected off the axe he was holding as he raised it above his head. The motion was smooth and full of vicious intent, waiting to be unleashed.

"Arrrgh. Die!" he suddenly screamed as he swung his axe down with all his might.

The muscles in his back burned as he guided the sharp edge toward his defenseless target. The blade bit into the soft flesh of the log and cleaved right through it. Two equally sized pieces of wood flopped down onto the ground with a hollow thud, leaving the axe head embedded in the stump beneath it.

"Meh, that time wasn't too bad. You're still putting too much effort into your swings though. Just let the axe fall, and you don't need to yell every time," the old human ranger, named Saeter, remarked casually from where he was seated several feet away.

Blacknail gave him an annoyed look as he tugged on the axe handle to free it. "Screaming makes the axe hit-ss harder and faster."

"Maybe, but you're scaring the neighbors," the old scout replied.

Blacknail looked around. Their neighbors were all hardened outlaws and members of Herad the Black Snake's bandit company. Most of them were used to the hobgoblin in their midst by now; a little yelling wasn't going to alarm them too much. It wasn't like he was burning down the camp again.

"Why am I even doing this? It's boring and making me hungry," Blacknail whined.

The hobgoblin had to suppress the urge to snarl and spit as a sudden wave of anger rose within him. The rush of energy made his teeth ache. Living among humans required he constantly fight his violent urges.

Yelling while chopping helped him suppress his rage, and it was one of the few ways to do it that wouldn't annoy his chieftain or require him to dig any graves. Digging was hard work, and he preferred to avoid it.

"Chopping wood is great for your back and will help your swordcraft. Plus, it's getting damned cold out at night, so we need the wood," Saeter remarked.

Blacknail felt like asking his master why *he* wasn't chopping wood, but he suspected he already knew the answer. Besides, his master was right; it was getting bloody cold out.

Over a week had passed since the attack on Herad's camp by the knights that had come looking for the ghouls Herad had wiped out. The days had been steadily getting shorter as autumn grew older. The smothering white of winter would soon descend upon the North.

Blacknail wasn't really used to staying above ground when darkness descended, so the cold bothered him. He used to live in the sewer under a city to the south, before he'd been imprisoned and placed in a merchant caravan. Saeter had been the one who had freed him when Herad's bandits had attacked the merchants.

There hadn't been a lot of perks involved in living in a mucky cramped sewer, but it had stayed warm in the winter. Of course, he'd only been a little goblin back then and not a magnificent hobgoblin. One night, after joining the bandits he'd fallen asleep a goblin and then several days later he'd woken up with a taller body and a sharper mind. The transformation had been a surprise to him, but Saeter said it was just something some goblins did.

Blacknail set a new piece of wood on top of the log and raised the axe above his head. With a grunt of effort, he brought it down again and continued his work. Chopping firewood was annoying, but it did supply him with a steady stream of stuff to burn. Blacknail loved feeding fire until it grew huge and roared wildly. The dancing red and orange flames were so pretty. They made him feel like laughing and clapping his hands together.

"Do we have enough twine?" Saeter asked the hobgoblin

while he idly whittled away at a wooden figurine.

"We have-ss enough for all the snares and to tie up the wood-ss," Blacknail replied dryly.

His master was clearly just looking for something to keep him busy. They always needed more rope and twine, but creating it was a chore. It had to be carefully twisted from specially prepared plant fibers. Ugh, it was annoying even to think about!

"Then I guess you can take a break now and grab something to eat," the old scout told Blacknail.

The hobgoblin smiled and set the axe down. All right, he was super hungry! What did he want to eat? There was plenty of dried meat and leftovers around, but he felt like gorging himself on something fresher. Blacknail stared past the nearby tents and log buildings toward the forest beyond them. Yes, he was definitely going to go out and get his own food. It was time to go hunting.

As Saeter kept whittling away beside his tent, Blacknail stalked off toward the woods. He pulled his hood over his head and slipped through the bandit camp. No one gave him a second glance as he made his way to the edge of the trees.

Unseen, Blacknail stepped through the thick bushes at the edge of the clearing and disappeared into the shadowy forest beyond. The sun was high in the sky, but its light was blocked by a smothering maze of branches and leaves. The hobgoblin took a second to look around. Even this close to the human camp there could be dangerous creatures lurking around. Nothing moved in the green canopy overhead or on the forest floor. The only sounds were of birds singing and the faint rustling of leaves by the wind.

Satisfied he was alone, Blacknail sniffed the air and began to circle carefully around the camp. He crept slowly through the underbrush and tried to camouflage in with his surroundings. The prey he was looking for kept to a certain schedule that made them predictable. He knew almost exactly where to find his midday meal.

Sure enough, after a few minutes of sneaking through the bushes, he detected the telltale shuffling sounds of movement ahead. The cloaked hobgoblin dashed over to a thick brown tree trunk and pressed himself up against the bark. He then peeked out around it. His prey was in plain sight a few dozen feet away, and Blacknail had arrived at exactly the right time. The hobgoblin smiled wickedly to himself and licked his lips hungrily.

The forest was incredibly dangerous and full of hungry beasts that would like nothing better than to devour humans and hobgoblins alike. Blacknail had run into more than a few of these while out with Saeter. There was also the possibility of another tribe of humans attacking the camp by sneaking through the woods. Thus, Herad had sentries posted around the perimeter of her base.

That was what lay before Blacknail, a human sentry, and he was eating his lunch. The delicious smell of roasted meat and gravy rose from the plate in front of the man. A torn-off chunk of bread lay next to it. Blacknail sniffed the air again, and the delectable aroma caused his stomach to gurgle in anticipation. Soon, it would be his.

The sentry was leaning against a tree trunk while he took a bite out of the bread. He held the plate in front of him as he lazily surveyed the forest out of the corner of his eye. The man was obviously more concerned with eating than watching, and thus deserved what was coming to him.

"Mmm, I love bread with herbs in it. I need to get some more of this," the sentry mused to himself between bites.

From behind the tree, the hobgoblin withdrew a good-sized stone from one of his pouches. He squinted as he took in his surroundings and roughly measured the distance between the sentry and himself. Then, Blacknail whipped the rock off into a nearby clump of tall thickets.

There was a loud rustling sound as it tore through the branches and a muted thud as the rock hit the ground and rolled. The sentry twitched and spun around toward the unexpected noise. His eyes were wide as he scanned the bushes for any signs of a threat.

He was also looking in the exact opposite direction of Blacknail. This was a fact the hobgoblin took full advantage of as he closed in.

The sentry was frowning in concern as he warily watched the

bushes. Without looking down, the man carefully placed his plate of food on a nearby log. He then took several wary steps over toward the bushes. His hand rested on the hilt of his sword. "If there's someone there, come on out!"

Behind him, Blacknail silently prowled closer. The hungry hobgoblin put on a sudden burst of speed, hopped over a rotting log covered in moss, and grabbed the plate. It was his!

"Huh, weird," the sentry remarked to himself as he studied the bushes.

With his prize in hand, the hobgoblin turned and hurriedly scuttled behind a nearby tree and away. He clutched the meat-covered plate to his chest as he ran. There was no stopping him now!

The sentry relaxed when nothing emerged from the bushes and attacked him. With a happy little sigh, the man turned and started walking back to where he'd been eating. Suddenly, he let out a frustrated yell.

"No, what the hells! Where did my bloody food go? This is the second time! What keeps taking my damn lunch? Ack, I'm bloody hungry!" the shocked scout swore in disbelief.

Blacknail giggled to himself as he cheerfully hopped back through the forest and toward camp. He was the sneakiest and cleverest member of Herad's band for sure! Taking food from sentries was the perfect crime. No matter what happened, they were supposed to stay on guard, so they couldn't give chase. They also couldn't complain about losing their food to anyone, because doing so would be admitting that they hadn't been paying attention on watch.

It wasn't an actual crime though, and it definitely wasn't thievery. Blacknail wasn't a thief. He and the sentry had been engaged in a contest of skill, with the food being a prize for the winner. That was nothing like stealing. Blacknail would have given the man something if he had been spotted, but he hadn't been.

The hobgoblin took a seat atop a large stone on the edge of the woods. From there, he could see into the camp but he was still mostly out of sight. The brown of his cloak and the green of his skin made him blend in with the forest. Swiftly, he began slurping down his meal.

When the last bit of food had vanished into his stomach, he belched and started to plan his next move. He wasn't quite full yet, so he needed to get more grub. Luckily, he knew where to get some. Blacknail got up and headed over to meet with Varhs. The man owed him a huge favor and had promised him tasty treats. The young—at least next to Saeter—bandit scout had taken a goblin as a pet. The wretched little thing was named Scamp, and he was a stupid greedy little thief.

After a few minutes, Blacknail arrived in front of Varhs's tent. The young scout was sitting in front of a firepit and frying up some eggs. They crackled and cooked on top of the pan he was holding above the flames. Scamp was tied up beside him and curled up close to the fire. There was a content look on the goblin's dreaming face. Blacknail didn't like it.

"Ah, I thought you might stop by," Varhs remarked when he looked up and saw the hobgoblin.

A while ago, the goblin had stolen some magic crystals and raised a huge ruckus. Blacknail had heroically tried to catch him, but the little bastard had still managed to annoy Herad. As a result, she had wanted to get rid of Scamp.

Out of the goodness of his heart, and for the promise of a lot of treats from Varhs, Blacknail had agreed to become responsible for training the ugly runt of a goblin.

"I see Scamp still-ss hasn't run away," the hobgoblin observed aloud.

The goblin in question woke up and yawned. He noticed the hobgoblin, and a sulky expression appeared on his face. Blacknail didn't like it.

"My little buddy wouldn't do that. He's a loyal companion and a great sniffer. He just needs some discipline," Varhs remarked as he petted Scamp affectionately.

Saeter had almost never petted him when he had been a goblin! Blacknail would have to remember to give Scamp a good kicking later when Varhs wasn't around. He was obviously spoiled rotten, and it would be for his own good.

"About-ss that training..." Blacknail slowly drawled.

"Yes, you can have some food. I have a spare egg here and some honeyed fruit tucked away," Varhs told the hobgoblin with an obvious hint of amusement. Blacknail frowned at the man's words. Apparently, he had gotten predictable. That wasn't good. Well, whatever. It couldn't be helped, if it was about tasty treats.

Several minutes later, the hobgoblin was once again walking through the camp with food in hand. He licked his lips as he sucked on the last bit of sugary fruit in his mouth. It was delicious! However, he was still kind of hungry. Should he go find Geralhd? That man was almost always easy to get food out of, and he tended to have good stuff.

Blacknail decided against it. Saeter would be looking for him; they had practice soon. His master was teaching him how to shoot a bow, and it hadn't been going all too well.

"There you are. What took you so long? Don't make me wait for you," Saeter huffed as Blacknail arrived back at the spot where their tents were set up next to each other.

"Sorry, master," the hobgoblin replied as he grabbed one of the bows that were laid out next to Saeter's tent.

Now that lunch was over, the camp was becoming busier. Herad's minions were getting back to work. The sounds of wood being sawed and hammered filled the forest clearing. It hadn't been long since the bandits had set up here on top of the old abandoned farmhouse, but a lot of work had been done. Most of the bandits had moved out of their tents or lean-tos and moved into log cabins.

Several more buildings were still being constructed in the clearing. Winter was coming, and this was the North. Tents were fine for the other seasons, but the snow and cold would be deadly in the winter. If Herad wanted most of her minions alive come spring, she had to make sure they were prepared. Food, firewood, and clothing all had to be stockpiled.

Log cabins and barracks weren't the only thing being built either. Defenses also had to be constructed. Wooden watchtowers had been assembled near the entrance to the camp. Barricades were being built to stop not only attacking monsters from the forest but also people approaching from the road. Herad had plenty of human enemies.

Off to one side of the clearing, there was an area that was still mostly empty. That was where Blacknail and his master headed. They had set up a series of targets there yesterday.

"Just take your time and stay focused," Saeter reminded

Blacknail.

"No problem-ss, this is easy," Blacknail replied cheerfully. The hobgoblin was good at everything, so he obviously couldn't be bad at archery. All those misses and injuries from last time were nothing but flukes.

"Just remember that you have to retrieve any arrows that go astray, so no more shooting at birds," Saeter reminded him with a glare.

"They looked tasty..." Blacknail muttered to himself in frustration.

"You get more than enough to eat! I'm surprised you're not completely round by now. Focus on learning to shoot, you big green idiot," Saeter harshly replied with a scowl.

With a sigh, the hobgoblin strung his bow and nocked an arrow to it. His master didn't need to call him names, that was mean. Besides, he was still much thinner and prettier than a big fat pink human, and that was unlikely to ever change.

The steel point in front of Blacknail's eye pointed right toward the red circle that had been painted on the piece of board he was aiming at. With a confident smile, the hobgoblin let the arrow loose. There was a muted thrum as the bowstring vibrated and the projectile whizzed through the air. The arrow raced toward the target and flew right past it without coming within five feet of it.

"I could hit-ss it easily with a rock from a sling..." Blacknail muttered in disappointment.

"Well, I don't feel the need to stay here and watch this travesty. Just keep shooting until you get a feel for it, if you ever do," Saeter told the hobgoblin. The old human scout then shook his head and wandered off.

Blacknail took his time lining up his next shot. There was no point in rushing, now that Saeter was gone. He would tire himself out, and it was still early in the day; he had other jobs to do later, like sword training with Vorscha. Life with Saeter was basically a never-ending series of chores, so you needed to know how to pace yourself.

The hobgoblin's next arrow also flew off into the grass without going near the target. Blacknail eyed the bow in his hand skeptically. There had to be a trick to this. Maybe if he screamed threats really loudly while shooting or if he pretended the target was Scamp...

# *Chapter 2*

"All right, that's enough, fall in you two," Vorscha shouted to Blacknail and Khita.

The hobgoblin and the young redhead were going through a simple two-person sword form. When they heard Vorscha's command, they immediately stopped, sheathed their practice blades, and started walking toward her. Both of them were sweating and panting after almost an hour of hard practice under the large woman's supervision.

"All right, it's time for something a little different. If you two keep repeating the same stuff, you'll both develop bad habits," Vorscha explained.

"Great, I'm ready for the real stuff. No more babying around," Khita exclaimed excitedly.

Vorscha threw Khita a skeptical glance. She didn't seem to agree, and she was the expert on the subject, so Blacknail thought she was probably right. Vorscha was one of Herad's most trusted lieutenants and one of the most skilled fighters in the camp.

"All right Geralhd, get up here," Vorscha called.

The smaller man was sitting off to the side of the patch of trampled grass that Vorscha had claimed as a training arena. At the sound of his lover's voice, he looked up from the book he was reading with a startled expression.

"Who me?" he asked in surprise. Geralhd didn't look or act like much of a fighter. He was shorter and less physically imposing than Vorscha or most the other men in camp.

"Ya, you, loverboy. Come over here," Vorscha told him with a bemused roll of her eyes.

Geralhd stood and put his book down on the crate he had been using as a seat. Then he reluctantly dragged himself over to join Vorscha and her students. Vorscha gave him a quick smile of greeting, and looked over both Blacknail and Khita with a thoughtful expression.

With Vorscha and Geralhd side by side, it was easy to compare them. Vorscha was unusually large for a woman and taller than Geralhd. She wasn't masculine looking though. She had a shapely body with more than its fair share of curves. She also had short, curly brunette hair and there was almost always a cheerful grin on her face. Geralhd was a bit skinny for a human male and wasn't very physically imposing. He usually wore fancy clothes, and his brown hair was currently pulled back into a ponytail.

"Right, so Blacknail, you'll be sparring with Geralhd," Vorscha announced as she held out her practice blade for Geralhd to take. "Don't let him fool you. He's not as useless as he looks."

"I will watch him carefully, and he will not fool me," Blacknail replied and smiled in anticipation. He had nothing against Gerlahd—in fact, the man frequently gave Blacknail treats—but he seemed like an easier opponent than the people Blacknail usually sparred with.

However, Geralhd looked more than a little unsure about fighting Blacknail. He stared blankly at the sword in Vorscha's hand for a few seconds before reaching out and taking it.

"Are you sure this is a good idea? It might be too much of a challenge for a beginner like him," he asked Vorscha confidently.

"Go easy on him then," she replied as she smirked in amusement.

"Hey, what about me?" Khita interjected irately. The young redhead had an annoyed look on her face, and her arms were crossed in front of her. She was clearly annoyed at being ignored.

"You can go sit over there and wait your turn," Vorsha replied dismissively.

She gave the much smaller woman a shove in the direction of the crate Gerahld had been sitting on. Khita scowled but did as she was told. She grumbled to herself the entire way over though.

"Now, the rules will be the same as when you spar with Khita. I'll give points for knocking your opponent off-balance and for touches. I expect Geralhd will be more of a challenge for you than Khita though, Blacknail. He has a somewhat different style," Vorscha explained.

"Hey now, not everyone is a former mercenary. I learned swordplay from a proper dueling master, even if I wasn't a very good student," Geralhd remarked as he swished his sword playfully through the air with one hand.

"I understand, mistress Vorscha," Blacknail replied as he narrowed his eyes and observed his new opponent.

With a quick smile, Geralhd took a few steps back and brought his blade up to assume a stance. Blacknail took a stance as well, but there was a frown on his face. He didn't recognize the stance Geralhd was using. It was very different from any he had seen before. He wasn't even holding onto his sword with both his hands.

"Are you ready, Blacknail?" Geralhd asked the hobgoblin.

"Yes-ss, I'm ready," Blacknail answered lazily and let his posture loosen.

Without warning, the hobgoblin sprang into motion. He lunged forward in an attack designed to take full advantage of his hobgoblin speed, but Geralhd was already slipping to the side. The hobgoblin's attack passed him harmlessly by, and Geralhd's own blade sliced into Blacknail's way.

Blacknail's eyes widened in surprise, and he had to immediately duck under the unexpected counterattack in order to avoid walking right into it. The startled hobgoblin recovered and quickly took a step back so he would have time to figure out what had happened. He had never seen a move like that before.

"Hmmm, you're very fast," Geralhd remarked thoughtfully.

"And you're sneakier than you look," Blacknail replied with a nod of approval.

"Umm, thanks?" his amused opponent replied as he carefully circled around the hobgoblin.

When Khita fought, she was energetic and daring, and when Vorscha fought, she was graceful yet unstoppable. Geralhd was like neither of them. He was constantly moving but always watching as well.

Blacknail took a small step forward. His opponent stepped to the side and slightly adjusted his stance. The hobgoblin took a step back, and Geralhd moved again as well. Blacknail frowned as he realized his opponent was preparing to counter his moves before he even made them. He didn't know what to do about that, so he decided to just rush in. Blacknail started another lightning-fast attack, but this time when Gelalhd moved to deflect his blow, he was ready. He shifted the angle of his blade and swung again. His first attack had been a feint to set up his second.

Geralhd grimaced but managed to block the second blow. Blacknail launched a series of rapid-fire slashes, in an attempt to knock his opponent off-balance. However, a frantic-looking Geralhd managed to avoid or deflect all his blows. Growing impatient, Blacknail felt a spike of anger and stepped forward to try another attack, only to have Geralhd meet him halfway and bat his blade down. The man then delivered a solid blow to Blacknail's shoulder while he was off-balance.

"Point for Geralhd," Vorscha announced.

"Damnations-ss!" the hobgoblin hissed as he let his blade drop. He should have been able to block that. There was no way he was a worse fighter than Geralhd.

Sensing his control was slipping, Blacknail focused on his breathing, and his anger began to subside. Usually, swearing like his master and the other bandits helped him quench his fury, but this time it hadn't been enough. In the past, he had allowed his rage to take control, and he had paid the price. He wasn't going to make that mistake again. Just thinking about it almost made him angry. He also hated losing. However, what really annoyed him was that unlike when he was fighting Saeter or Vorscha, the fight with Geralhd had actually been close. If he hadn't lost control and grown angry, he might have actually won.

"That's one point for me and zero for you," Geralhd bragged as he smirked at the hobgoblin.

"Enough talking, start round two," Vorscha interjected loudly.

"I'll get-ss you back, little man," Blacknail told Geralhd as he raised his blade again and took a stance.

The unconventional bandit and the hobgoblin fought for several more rounds. Blacknail lost the first few, but then he managed to adjust to Geralhd's style and win two bouts. He simply overwhelmed Geralhd's ability to predict him by constantly changing the direction of his attacks.

Eventually after both combatants grew exhausted and sweaty, Vorscha called a halt to the sparring. Seeing the other two were done, Khita got up and walked over.

"Huh, I thought you'd be even worse than that," she told Geralhd.

Geralhd wasn't insulted though. He gave her a smug smirk. "If I was actually a terrible duelist, I wouldn't be here or a wanted man. I would be dead at that bastard Byron's hands. Instead, I did the world a great service and put that thrice-damned son of a whore in an early grave," Geralhd replied cheerfully.

"You shouldn't brag about not being terrible at something, aim for excellence instead. You need to practice as much as Blacknail, and I don't know how you can think your petty vengeance was worth exile," Vorscha told him with obvious disapproval.

"It wasn't petty. Byron hurt my family and ruined my sister's reputation. Beating him in a fair duel, and running my blade through his heart as I looked him in eye, was the best moment of my life," he replied.

"And having a murderer for a son didn't hurt your family?" Vorscha replied dryly.

"Dueling may be illegal in Eloria, but it's still considered an honorable way to end a dispute. So I might be a criminal, but I didn't dishonor myself. Besides, if I hadn't done it, I never would have met you," he replied with a suggestive grin and wink at Vorscha.

"Oh, I make it all worth it, do I? Stop trying to deflect, you silver-tongued demon. Sometimes I swear you're pigheaded enough to be a noble, instead of just a merchant's son," Vorscha remarked with a smile.

"Ha, I bet your bounty is really tiny though. Only the real dangerous criminals get good bounties," Khita told Geralhd in a condescending tone.

"It's three silver, but don't worry, I have a plan to increase it. I'm going to murder a whole bunch of innocent villagers and dump their bodies in front of the nearest bounty office," Geralhd remarked sarcastically as he glared at Khita.

"Huh, I was right, that's almost nothing," the young woman countered.

"It's enough to get me hanged by total strangers if I don't watch my back. It's also more than you have, since you're the only one here completely without one," Geralhd replied.

Khita looked around for a second and frowned, but she smiled when she saw Blacknail.

"Blacknail doesn't have one either," she told him.

"You are once again proven ignorant. He has one. All hobgoblins have a bounty of five silver on their heads. For some reason, people dislike having them as neighbors. Their bounty can even get higher if the local peasants find something to blame them for. I figure if he keeps hanging around with us, his bounty will rise quite a bit. He might even become famous, or infamous anyway," Geralhd explained.

"A high bounty isn't a good thing," Vorscha added with a frown.

"Oh, what's yours then?" Khita asked with obvious interest.

"Doesn't matter," Vorscha replied stiffly.

"I can answer this question," Geralhd explained with an amused glance toward Vorscha. "She got a price on her head when the count that was employing her refused to pay her mercenary company its due. Instead, he decided it would be cheaper to just trump up some charges and put a bounty on her head, a quite spectacular five gold bounty at that."

"It wasn't even a tenth of what he actually owed my company," Vorscha replied in disgust.

"I could buy a mansion for that much!" Khita exclaimed in surprise.

"Well, a half-decent house anyway, as long as it was fairly small," Geralhd corrected her.

"One day, I'm going to get an even bigger bounty than that. Everyone will be terrified of me," Khita announced proudly.

Geralhd gave her a doubtful look, and Vorscha frowned in concern.

"That's enough talking, Khita. It's your turn to spar with me," she told the younger woman.

Vorscha and Khita then started sparring, and predictably, the larger woman dominated the other inexperienced fighter. After they finished training, Blacknail went to rest in his tent for a few minutes before getting back up. Now that he was done being trained, it was time for him to do some training.

As Blacknail wandered through the camp, he passed groups of bandits that were working or loitering around. None of them paid him any attention, and he soon arrived at his destination, the tent that belonged to Varhs. Most of the bandits lived in log cabins now, but several of the scouts still stuck with their tents, and Scamp was tied up outside of this one. Of course, the goblin could have gotten loose by chewing through the rope, but that would have led to punishment. Blacknail had been the one to tie the goblin up, and he had made it very clear he would rip the little fellow's eyes out and eat them if he tried to escape. The rope was simply there to remind the forgetful goblin that he wasn't supposed to move.

Scamp whined pathetically as Blacknail approached, but the hobgoblin was completely without pity. Scamp deserved to be tied up. He was an undisciplined menace that constantly stole things and got into trouble.

"Shut up," Blacknail barked as he looked around. He wasn't impressed by what he saw.

Today, he had given Scamp the job of scrapping a pile of rabbit skins clean so they would be ready for drying. Blacknail hissed angrily as he noted the goblin's poor progress, and Scamp flinched at his reaction. The hobgoblin knew the lazy little runt was just trying to get out of work by acting pathetic though. Varhs may have let him get away with that, but there was no way Blacknail would.

"No food-ss for you until you're done!" he reminded the goblin before turning and walking away.

The routine over the next few days was much the same. Blacknail worked on all the tasks he was given and gave Scamp work similar to that which he had done himself when he had been a goblin. Eventually, Blacknail wasable to get Scamp to act at least sort of disciplined. He even began letting Varhs take the goblin out for walks, as long as the scout promised to be stern with the goblin. The man was probably lying, but Blacknail didn't care that much. He had grown bored with yelling at Scamp already.

After a week had passed, Blacknail was having a bite to eat with Saeter at their campsite at the edge of the bandit encampment. They had just come back from hunting, but their meal was interrupted by the arrival of another bandit.

"Herad wants to see you. She's calling a meeting," the large, muscular man told them. He was one of Herad's personal bodyguards.

"I doubt she actually told you she *wants* to see me," Saeter huffed as he stood up.

"Close enough. Just follow me," the bodyguard replied indifferently before walking back the way he had come.

Saeter grunted sourly, but he did as he was told and followed the other man. Blacknail hadn't technically been invited, but no one had said he wasn't either, so he quietly shadowed his master. He wanted to know what was going on. Herad was the leader of the bandits, so if she was calling a meeting, it was probably important.

Saeter soon reached the old farmhouse Herad used as her headquarters and stepped inside. Blacknail waited a minute, and when the coast was clear, he took up position outside one of the windows. The bushes there concealed him from view, and his sensitive ears could hear everything being said inside perfectly, although a human would have had problems.

"Tomorrow I'll be leaving for Daggerpoint with several dozen men. As I told you before, Red Dog will be staying here to command in my stead while I'm gone, and Vorscha will serve as his second," Herad told her minions.

Blacknail snuck a quick glance through the window before ducking back down. Herad was seated in a simple wooden chair, and a matching table had been placed in front of her. Everyone else was standing in a loose group before her.

"I can't say I like the idea of you leaving with so few men. We have powerful enemies in Daggerpoint," Red Dog replied.

"I agree. Werrick has sworn to kill you, and his men will easily outnumber yours if he's in town," Vorscha added.

"So what? That's always been the case. Four dozen is about what I've taken every time before this. It's only recently I've even had more, and when we arrive, the first thing I'll be doing is recruiting. I know somewhere I can get some trustworthy men," Herad replied.

"The rookies will need supervision to make it through the winter, and they won't be up to the march north either," Saeter remarked to Red Dog.

"True, I guess that does limit how many men you can take," Red Dog admitted with a frown.

"Everything in life is a gamble of one sort or another, but enough of this. I didn't call you here to question my decisions," Herad told them coldly as she stared up at them from her seat.

"Yes, mistress," Red Dog immediately replied and snapped to attention. He was a bit of a boot licker.

"On top of my personal guard, I'll be taking you and Mahedium with me," Herad told Saeter.

"Why me and the mage? He's gonna be slow, and I'm not much use in a place like Daggerpoint," the old scout replied with a frown.

"Oh, you're wrong as usual, old man. I'll have a use for you there. Your name still carries weight in certain circles, if only the gods know why, and that will help me drum up some muscle," she replied smugly. "As for the mage, he asked to come and promised it would be worth my trouble. He wants to try digging up some fellow black spell-slingers to trade notes with."

"Well, Daggerpoint is probably his best bet for that. There's usually one or two mages around, and they won't be guild members, but anyone he finds in that pit is likely to be just smart enough to know which end of a staff to point at the enemy. Despite what they claim, you don't need too much in the way of brains to be a combat mage," Vorscha commented.

"He thinks it will be worth his while, and who knows, maybe he's right," Herad replied in a dismissive tone.

There was then a squealing sound as she pushed her chair back and got to her feet. After a brief look at her lieutenants, she walked over to the nearby window. The hobgoblin hiding outside heard her coming. He quickly scampered over to a bush off to one side and went very still.

"I'll leave early tomorrow morning with the dawn, so make sure you're all ready. When I return, no one will be able to challenge my claim on this territory, and that's just the beginning!" Herad announced to the air outside the window. She then turned back around. "When I get back, I expect this place to be fit for a queen, so no slacking off. Now off with you lot. I have stuff to do, and I'm sure you have your own concerns."

After her dismissal, everyone quickly left, lest they annoy their boss. As Red Dog walked out the door, he threw an uncertain look back over his shoulder. He seemed unsure about how serious Herad's command about fixing the place up had been, but if she noticed his concern, she didn't bother to enlighten him.

Blacknail continued to sit in the bush outside the window for a few seconds until everyone was out of sight. Just as he was about to get up, he heard something from inside the house.

"Soon, it will all be mine! They will all bow before me," Herad whispered lovingly to herself before chuckling hungrily in anticipation.

Soon, the chuckle died down, and there was only the sound of breathing from inside. Very carefully, Blacknail got up and crept away. He was reassured that Herad was confident in her plan, despite the others' doubts. The more powerful the tribe of bandits grew, the higher his own position could grow, so Blacknail approved of her ambition.

She was obviously looking forward to victory a lot too. Blacknail got like that sometimes. Standing over the corpses of your enemies felt so great. It felt like someone was tickling your brain, and you just wanted to keep on smiling...

The hobgoblin sped around the building. He had to get back to the campsite before Saeter started to question what he had been up to. As he moved, he watched the camp for people who looked to be paying him too much attention, and he thought about what he had just heard.

Mistress Herad had mentioned Saeter would be going with her, but no one had mentioned him. Blacknail found himself wishing he could go with Saeter to this human place called Daggerpoint. Things had begun to grow boring around the camp, and he kind of wanted to see a human city again. He had lived in one for years as a goblin and roamed the streets at night after all.

With the clothes Saeter had given him, Blacknail didn't think he would have too much trouble doing similar things again. Only now, he could think of much more exciting things to do after dark, and he knew he could find tastier things to eat than garbage. The city would be full of targets that weren't part of his tribe, and thus he would have no reason to hold himself back. It would be nice to finally let loose. Discipline was important, but that didn't mean he could never have fun.

Blacknail shivered in eagerness as he pictured it. He could almost already taste the blood.

# *Chapter 3*

No one had said it directly, but from listening to people talking, Blacknail swiftly came to the conclusion he wasn't invited to join Herad's expedition. That wasn't going to stop him though. He was looking forward to visiting a human city again too much to let a simple lack of permission get in his way.

So as night fell and everyone went to sleep, he started scheming, and he quickly came up with a foolproof plan. The best way to make sure he was included in the party sent to Daggerpoint was simple; he wasn't going to ask. If no one knew he was there, they couldn't tell him to go back.

The next morning, when Saeter was getting up to get ready to go, Blacknail was nowhere to be found. The hobgoblin had woken up even earlier than usual and had quickly made his way out into the woods, as if he were checking the snares or hunting.

However, he had no intention of doing his usual routine. As soon as he was out of sight and safely hidden in the forest, he stopped to make sure no one else was around. Blacknail then stealthily crept through the bushes around the edge of the camp.

When he got to the road, he selected a nearby tall tree that overlooked the area and scrambled up it. The bark of the tree was gray and rough, but once he got up into the branches, it was easy climbing. Scaling trees took a lot less effort since he had become a hobgoblin because his limbs were so much longer.

Once he was a couple dozen feet up, he stopped and hid on a particular leafy branch that gave him a good view of the surroundings. Then the hobgoblin simply waited for the expedition to leave.

It only took a few minutes for something to happen. Unseen up in the tree, Blacknail watched Herad, Saeter, and the rest of their group pour out of the camp and head down the road. As he watched, he caught a brief glance of red hair. Wait, was that Khita? They were taking that useless human whelp and not him! Why? The hobgoblin glowered down at them from his leafy perch.

When they were out of sight, Blacknail smiled gleefully again though. He'd show them how sneaky he could be. It was time for him to put his plan in action. He hastily climbed to the ground and hurried back through the woods to the far end of the camp. Once back in the clearing, he calmly walked over to his campsite and packed up some of his things. If he had done it beforehand, it would have alerted Saeter. There was no way his master would have missed something so obvious. That done, he picked up his bag and once again strolled over to the back of the camp. He got a few odd looks, but no one said anything. Not that a lot of people usually struck up casual conversations with him anyway.

Once back in the woods, he headed toward the road. By this time, Herad's group had quite a lead on him, but the hobgoblin could keep track of them by their scent. Even if they left the road, he wouldn't have any trouble finding them. As Blacknail jogged in pursuit, the scent grew stronger until he knew he was almost upon them. Forewarned, the hobgoblin slowed his pace. It would be very bad for him if he was spotted now.

The forest was thick and green on both sides of the road. The occasional hill or curve limited the vision of anyone following the trail. Blacknail saw one of those twists up ahead. It would hide him, so he hurriedly ran over to it and peered through the bushes at the road ahead. The bandits he had been tracking were right there.

Herad was leading the way and dressed in her usual attire of dark leather armor. Blacknail really didn't want to be caught by her. The bandit chieftain wasn't a large woman, but her frightening fighting skills and ruthlessness kept all the other bandits in line. Blacknail had seen her cut down the disobedient and the stupid several times. Her dark eyes didn't show a hint of normal human weaknesses like mercy or honor. That was why she was one of Blacknail's favorite people.

Saeter was walking directly behind Herad, and the rest of

the bandits were following him. They all had long-hooded travelers' cloaks meant for keeping people warm and dry. Their supplies and camping gear had been loaded into large backpacks like the one Blacknail was wearing.

A few moments later, the group disappeared behind another turn in the road, so Blacknail crept after them. He moved cautiously and kept his senses alert in case they left a scout behind or came to a sudden stop. He kept careful watch on Saeter in particular. If anyone was going to spot him, it would be his master.

As they walked, Blacknail grew excited. He loved the act of stalking! It filled him with eager energy and just felt right, like he was doing what he was meant to. He didn't mean his tribe any harm, but it was still exciting to fool them. He was truly a skilled hunter!

After a few hours of trudging down the dirt road, the humans suddenly came to a stop. They froze as a loud cracking noise reverberated through the forest. A second later, it happened again, and then again. The forest was now full of the sound of cracking tree branches and the thud of heavy footsteps. Blacknail dropped low and hurriedly scanned his surroundings as the barrage of noise echoed from every direction. His long ears perked up as a surge of panic ran down his spine. What was going on? He didn't see anything.

Suddenly, a tree down the road fell and crashed to the ground. As the ground shook and leaves flew up into the air, several massive brown creatures appeared from out of the greenery. They were easily the largest creatures Blacknail had ever seen. They were far taller and bulkier than even the troll Blacknail had encountered. Like trolls, they had two thick legs and two long arms, but that's where the resemblance ended. The creatures were easily three times as tall as any man, many more times as heavy, and covered in thick brown hair. Most of them moved ponderously on all four limbs, but every once in a while, one would rear up onto its back legs and walk around that way for short distances. It would then reach up into nearby trees and rip branches down. Their arms ended in truly impressive claws as long as swords that shredded the wood effortlessly.

Blacknail was too far away to get a good look at their blunt faces, but two large curled horns rose from their heads. The beasts brought the leafy branches they tore from the trees to their mouths and chewed them. That meant they were either eating some very slow and stupid tree rats, or they were plant eaters. The hobgoblin vaguely remembered his master mentioning something like them, but he had forgotten their name.

Feeling extremely curious, Blacknail used the distraction the creatures were creating in order to move closer to Herad and the others. He wanted to hear what they were saying. Carefully, Blacknail slipped into the bushes at the edge of the road. He stealthily made his way right up behind the position the bandits had taken. They had stopped on the road a fair distance from the giant creatures, and were talking amongst themselves as they watched the beasts. Blacknail managed to get within two dozen feet of the humans. That was more than close enough for him to hear everything they said, even with all the noise the beasts were making. He had good ears.

"...ogres will move on in a bit. We just have to be patient. There's no reason to leave the safety of the road. Right now, they're watching us. If we all stumble into the forest, we might spook them, and that could end badly," Saeter was telling Herad.

The bandit chieftain was looking impatient, and not completely convinced by Blacknail's master's words. She was scowling at the ogres, and her hands were on her hips. She looked like she wanted to single-handedly kill the beasts that had dared slow her down—which Blacknail would have enjoyed watching—but then she sighed in resignation. "Fine, tell the men we'll be resting for a bit. We'll be doubling the pace when the way is clear though, to make up for lost time."

Saeter nodded and moved to fulfill her orders. He moved slower than usual and didn't make any loud noises, probably as not to spook the ogres.

As Blacknail's master had suggested, the bandits simply held their position and waited for the ogres to move away from the road. The minutes passed by, and the ogres continued to move ponderously from tree to tree so they could eat the leaves and fruit. Every once in a while, one would turn toward the bandits and give them a curious or wary look, but they didn't seem too concerned by the presence of humans. That was definitely a good thing, because Blacknail didn't think even Herad could take on several of the gigantic beasts. It would be like a goblin trying to wrestle a large man; the goblin would without a doubt end up stomped flat.

As Blacknail was beginning to relax, a deep roar suddenly pierced through the ogre's racket. Instantly, the giants all stood up on their hind legs and looked alarmed. They scanned the forest as it grew eerily quiet in every direction. Even the birds went deathly silent, and Blacknail's fear returned in full force. He knew deep down he had just heard the primal call of a massive predator.

"Hells... a drake," whispered Saeter as all the bandits around him grew stiff with fear.

"It's not close, right?" one of the other bandits asked him fearfully.

"Shh, shut your trap."

Another louder roar filled the air. The sound seemed to ricochet through the trees and caused a shiver to crawl up Blacknail's back. His instincts were suddenly screaming at him to find a nearby hole and disappear down into it. If he hadn't been worried about losing sight of his master, he might have listened. Holes in the ground could be quite comfy and safe.

Saeter seemed to be listening intently, and he was now staring at the forest behind the ogres. After a moment, he whipped around and urgently warned Herad. "Shit, we need to move. Now!"

Before he could get a response, the sound of splintering wood and the unmistakable boom of a falling tree echoed through the forest. None of the ogres had moved, but now several of them flinched, and Saeter immediately started running back down the road the way his party had come.

"Fall in and follow, or you're dead meat!" Herad commanded everyone before taking off after the scout.

With a scared snort, one of the ogres dropped down on all fours and started to flee. After a second of hesitation, another ogre quickly joined it. Then with a chorus of alarmed huffs and snorts, the rest of them took off in pursuit of the first two. They were headed almost directly toward where several of the bandits were still standing. That didn't last long. The remaining bandits immediately spun around and joined Herad in retreating out of the stampeding beasts' path. Several of the humans looked like they were screaming and shouting in fear, but Blacknail couldn't hear them over the thunderous noise of the running giants. The ground was shaking beneath him and he could see the leaves of nearby trees shaking.

The vibrations were so strong, they made running more difficult than usual, which was bad because the ogres were headed in Blacknail's direction. The hobgoblin had wasted no time; he had started running as soon as Herad had. On all fours, he scrambled through the trees at the side of the road after his master. He whipped through bushes and tore up dirt and leaves as he ran. He could hear the ogres growing closer, and he didn't want to find out what they thought of hobgoblins.

A bright red fox red suddenly burst out of a nearby thicket and began racing alongside the hobgoblin. They both gave each other surprised looks, but neither stopped running or even changed directions. Blacknail heard the sound of splintering wood behind him and redoubled his pace. His heart was beating frantically in his chest. Being near the stampeding ogres reminded him too much of when he had been a little goblin, and beneath the notice of larger creatures.

Then the thud of heavy footsteps started to die down. Blacknail gave a relieved sigh and let himself slow down. The fox that had been running beside him sped off into the trees. Now the noise of the stampeding ogres had almost completely faded, and the forest no longer seemed to be shaking. Blacknail leaned against a nearby tree trunk and sucked down a few quick breaths. Gradually, his heartbeat returned to normal. He was tired after such a hard sprint but glad to still be alive. Not being crushed was good.

Once he had recovered, Blacknail stood back up and went to check out the road for signs of his tribe. He glanced around a tree at the forest's edge and saw that Herad and her minions seemed fine. They were recovering from their own mad sprint, and Saeter was motioning everyone off the road and into the ditch beside it. Blacknail smiled after he saw everyone was all right. He would have hated it if they had decided to turn around and go back to camp. He wanted to see Daggerpoint!

Just then, there was another loud boom. Blacknail whipped around to look a fair distance up the road toward its source. He was just in time to see a massive green shape bound out of the trees and across the road before disappearing into the forest on the other side. It hadn't been an ogre; it had been much larger and faster. Blacknail gulped as his stomach twisted in fear again. The hobgoblin had only got a quick look at the creature, but unlike an ogre, it had obviously had a long neck and tail. It could only have been a drake, one of the rulers of the forest that Saeter was always telling him about. The most dangerous creatures you could run into, and likely the last.

Both Herad's group and Blacknail stayed still and hidden for the next while. Only after several long minutes had passed did the bandits get up and resume their trek to Daggerpoint. Blacknail followed them as closely as he could without being seen. He really didn't want to be left behind right now.

Much to everyone's relief, no more drake screams were heard, and the rest of the day was fairly uneventful. It began to get dark, but Herad kept pushing them to keep going. Blacknail was starting to wonder if they were even going to stop for the night when they came upon an abandoned stone building at the side of the road. Even in the dark, it was easy to see it was in poor repair. It bore signs of once being an impressive building, but there was an obvious hole in the roof and one of the walls had collapsed. It would still be a much safer and dryer place to sleep than outside though, so the bandits all headed inside.

As Blacknail moved to follow them, he noticed signs of other long-decayed wooden buildings among the grass and bushes. They must've been the remains of an old, sizable human settlement, but now only the one large building remained to remind travelers that a flourishing village had once stood there.

The hobgoblin could see and hear much better than the humans in the darkness, so he had no problem creeping up to the building in the dark. The bandits were setting up camp and building a fire for the night. The light from the flames served only to hinder the humans' night vision and make his approach easier.

The hobgoblin slipped up beside one of the outside walls. He watched and listened a while through a small hole that gave him a clear view of the inside. It was pretty boring stuff though. The only thing even remotely of interest he learned was that the building was called a temple, and it was supposed to be good luck or something. Soon the bandits started going to sleep, and that was really tedious to watch, so Blacknail moved away. He had to figure out where he was going to rest for the night as well. He hadn't brought his tent, but he had brought a pair of blankets. Carefully, Blacknail explored the area around the temple.

Crumbled stone bricks and thick bushes surrounded the old building. A few dozen feet away, through the darkness, the thick growth of the forest loomed. The hobgoblin didn't want to move too close to the dark woods. He had no idea what might be lurking out there. He could hear crickets chirping and leaves rustling, but it was what he couldn't hear that worried him. He had been reminded earlier that no matter how experienced you became, the forest always contained new unseen dangers. Besides, he felt much safer closer to Saeter and the bandits than out there. He couldn't get too close to them though, or he would be seen.

After a few frustrating minutes spent circling the temple, Blacknail noticed firelight flickering through a window near the roof of the building. With a surge of excitement, the hobgoblin began to climb his way up to it. The old weathered stone walls were easy to grip; he just had to watch out for loose bricks. Once up there, he found a shadowy ledge that was concealed from both below and outside. It was the perfect place to sleep, so Blacknail laid out his blankets.

He briefly glanced down at the bandits and Saeter. They were gathered around their fire and most of them were asleep. Saeter appeared to be on watch though, because he was one of the few still up and about. Blacknail's master was drinking something from a cup while seated on a piece of rubble. He was looking outside into the darkness through one of the building's doors, but then he leisurely turned and looked up toward the hobgoblin's hiding spot.

Blacknail leaned into the shadows and held his breath, but Saeter soon turned back to the door. He didn't appear to have seen anything because the old scout was still relaxed and casually took another sip from his drink. Blacknail cautiously turned away and lay down on his spread-out blankets. As the light of the flames below flickered over the roof above him, the hobgoblin gave a silent yawn and closed his eyes. It didn't take long for sleep to overcome him.

# *Chapter 4*

Herad's group was out and moving early the next morning. They continued their march north as the light of the dawn peeked over the trees. The bandits remained on guard, but they encountered nothing more interesting than the occasional passing traveler that day. Herad ignored them and had her men do the same. She had places to be and better things to do than rob peddlers and peasants. No one who had anything worth stealing traveled alone in the North.

When night came, Blacknail usually slept up in a tree just out of reach of the light of the humans' fire. From there, he could keep his eyes on them and enjoy some protection from anything that might be lurking in the night.

The next day, they passed several more abandoned villages but no occupied ones. This confused the hobgoblin. Who had created all these villages, and why had they been destroyed? Had some monster from the forest leveled them? On the third day, they encountered a walled human settlement, but Herad and her minions passed it by without entering. Blacknail considered scaling one of the walls in the night and seeing what was inside, but thought better of it. He would have plenty of time for that when they got to Daggerpoint.

The scenery began to change as they continued their journey. The gray and white mountains that rose on the horizon started to grow ever larger. The terrain also became much rougher, and the road began winding up hills and along tall, rocky cliffs. The steeper terrain was harder to traverse, so the bandits grew tired and their progress slowed. At one point, they had to cross a rickety wooden bridge over a river. The river was extremely wide, and its frothy white waters roared as they swept down from the distant mountains. There was no way anyone could possibly swim across the raging waterway, so one by one the bandits carefully crossed the bridge. After everyone else was out of sight, Blacknail crept over to the bridge and made his way across it unseen.

That evening, while his human tribesmen were setting up for the night, it finally occurred to Blacknail to wonder how long it would take to reach Daggerpoint. He probably should have figured that out before he followed Herad north, but there was no going back now. He hoped it wasn't too much longer, his feet were getting more than a little sore. All Blacknail could do was lazily circle the humans' camp as he once again searched for somewhere safe to sleep for the night. Row after row of trees lay in every direction. Their shapes were indistinct and murky in the dark of night.

As he was creeping through the shadowy woods, Blacknail heard a noise out on the road. At first, he thought one of the bandits had slipped past him, but then he dismissed that as unlikely. Cautiously, he went to check it out. He was fairly sure it wasn't anything too dangerous, but you could never be too sure out in the wilderness. Once Blacknail had pushed his way through the dark brush, the road became clearly visible through the trees. The moonlight was shining down on the pale dirt of the road so strongly, that it almost seemed to be subtly glowing, and what Blacknail saw there surprised him. Two humans were walking along the road and headed for the light of the bandits' campfire. Feeling curious and rather bored, after several days by himself, the hobgoblin decided to investigate.

Although their outlines were clearly visible, thanks to the pale road beneath their feet, the details of the two humans were indistinct in the darkness. However, they didn't appear to have any obvious weapons, so Blacknail flipped his hood up to conceal his visage and walked out of the bushes. He heard a gasp of shock as the people he'd approached flinched back away from him. Since he wasn't trying to scare or murder them yet, the hobgoblin quickly raised his hand in a human gesture of greeting.

"Hello, I won't harm you," he announced in his best imitation of a human voice.

"Who are you? Are you from the fire?" the larger one, who

smelled male, asked him.

"I'm a friend, and I'm not from the fire. They're bandits and bad people. They'll take your stuff and kill you," Blacknail replied.

The two humans glanced at each other. They seemed very unsure, and suspicious of Blacknail. The hobgoblin didn't know why, he thought he was doing a very good impression of a human.

"How do we know you're not the bandit. You could be trying to lure us away from safety," the man replied.

Blacknail hesitated and scowled. The stupid humans didn't even know when someone was trying to help them. How could they not trust him? He was always very honest.

"I could take you to get a look at them?" he offered. If these humans were going to be so annoying, then Blacknail was just going to leave them, or kill and rob them himself. Maybe they had interesting shiny things he could take.

The pair leaned close and whispered to each other for a few seconds. Then the shorter one, who smelled female, spoke up. "No, that's fine. We hoped to find safety at the fire, but deep down we knew finding refuge there would be too convenient. It was unlikely at best that anyone friendly would be out here. Thank you for the warning."

The woman, and that's definitely what she sounded like, looked tired and miserable. The man reached around her shoulders and pulled her closer into a reassuring hug.

"We shouldn't complain since we're lucky you were here to warn us. I don't suppose you have somewhere safe to rest for the night?" he asked.

Blacknail thought it over. He had been scouting the forest for a while, looking for somewhere to rest. In that time, he had discovered a small cave. He had initially disregarded it because it was too big and open for one person, but with three people, they could set a guard. "I found a cave earlier. You could rest there."

"That sounds better than staying out here in the dark. If you don't mind me asking, what are you doing out here, and what's your name?" the man asked him.

Blacknail hesitated as he tried to figure out what the right answer was. He knew his name was odd for a human, so he said the first name that popped into his head.

"I'm... Saeter, the man. I was out hunting when I saw the fire, so I snuck up and spied on them. I'm very sneaky." Blacknail was rather proud of his lies. How could the humans not believe him? They were perfect. This was turning out to be a rather fun break from all the walking.

"Right... well, let's see this cave of yours," the man replied.

With a nod of agreement, Blacknail led them through the woods, away from the bandits and down an incline. There, the cave mouth was visible in the exposed rocky side of the hill they had just come down. However, it was too dark to see inside now, at least for a human.

"Is it safe to light a lantern, do you think?" the man asked Blacknail.

"Yes, there's no one to see it here," the hobgoblin answered confidently.

The man reached into his bag and withdrew a small, metal hand lantern. It smelled of ash and oil to Blacknail. With a flint and steel, the man quickly set the lantern wick alight. It took a few seconds to catch properly, but then their surroundings were lit by the small flickering flame. When the light was held up, the inside of the cave was revealed. It only extended a little more than two dozen feet past the narrow gash in the rock that served as its entrance. However, there was plenty of room for three people inside, and it served as shelter from both the wind and observers.

"It's going to be awfully dark inside there when we snuff the lantern," the woman remarked.

"You set up. I'll get some wood for a fire," Blacknail told the pair. He was struggling not to hiss or mangle his words.

"That'll be very dangerous in the dark," the man observed aloud. He sounded more than a little concerned.

The hobgoblin shrugged and started walking back toward the road. "I'm very sneaky," he replied as he disappeared into the dark.

Blacknail wasn't stupid. He wasn't going to wander the woods looking for dry wood. That did indeed sound like a good way to get killed, and it was totally unnecessary. He just had to borrow some wood from Herad's group. They were all the same tribe, so it was kind of his wood anyway.

By this point, most the bandits had drifted off to sleep, except for the two men on watch. It was thus a simple feat for Blacknail to creep up through the blind spot created by some of the tents, and make off with some of their wood and tinder. They had a fairly large pile of wood piled up against one tent. It was now substantially smaller though, and it amused Blacknail greatly to wonder what they would think when they noticed it was missing. He almost considered waiting around to see their faces, but that could take forever and would be dangerous.

When Blacknail got back to the cave, he saw that the pair of humans he had saved from the bandits had finished settling down for the night. The woman was lying down on a low rock ledge. Her rough traveler's clothes were placed beside her, and she was between a pair of thick blankets. In the light of the lantern, her shoulder-length blondhair and plain-looking face were visible. The man had set his own gear down and unpacked his blankets on the ground close to her, but he was standing guard inside the entrance of the cave instead of resting. He had short brown hair, a weathered face, and a few days' growth of facial hair. His posture was tense and stiff as he gazed out into the darkness, but he relaxed a little when he saw Blacknail approach carrying a heavy load of wood.

"I'm glad you're back, Saeter. I was getting worried about you. Where did you get that wood? It looks like it was split with an axe," he asked.

"I knew a place to get it," the hobgoblin explained as he walked inside.

"Ah, a huntsman's cache. You must travel through here a lot. We were truly fortunate to run into a good man like you."

Blacknail just gave another shrug and began setting up the fire. He was pretty great, but he wasn't a man. He smelled much better for one thing.

The fire was kept small and set up near the cave's mouth so smoke could escape and it would serve as a barrier against wild animals. Blacknail was careful to face away from the man so the shadows concealed his face as he worked. Once done, he withdrew into the far corner of the cave where the shadows were deepest and started setting up his own sleeping place. He didn't want his new friends to get a glimpse of his green skin. As he was working, the man started talking again.

"I'm sorry for not introducing myself earlier, Saeter. I'm Rickas, and that's my wife, Selstia. We're travelling north... for our own reasons. Thanks again for helping us. I wish we had some way to repay you, but we don't have much."

"Got any cheese?" Blacknail asked hopefully. He really liked cheese.

"Er, yes. I have a small piece left. You're more than welcome to it," Rickas replied uncertainly before digging through his pack and tossing Blacknail a small package.

The hobgoblin caught the cheese. He could already smell its poignant scent through the cloth it was wrapped in. Cheerfully, he unwrapped it and then slowly savored its sharp taste. He had eaten all his cheese days ago.

"Well, Saeter, um... I can tell Elorian isn't your first language. What is your native tongue?" the man asked the hobgoblin.

Blacknail froze in the middle of eating. There was more than one human language? Why? He didn't know of any other languages. What was he supposed to say? Luckily, Rickas noticed his hesitation and interpreted it in his own way.

"I'm sorry if it sounded like I was prying. I was simply trying to make conversation, but I see now that you are a private person," he said apologetically.

"No problem. Do you want first watch?" Blacknail responded in relief.

"That's fine with me. I'll wake you when my watch is over," Rickas said.

"Good, but just call out 'Blacknail' to wake me. Don't get too close. I'm a private person." Blacknail placed his sheathed sword against the wall in a very obvious gesture.

Rickas looked confused for a second, but then nodded in understanding. "Ah, I see, that's a code word of some sort? Anyway, I assure you that we're no threat to you, and I'll do as you ask."

Blacknail sat down and leaned his back against the wall. He had placed his blanket beneath and behind himself to serve as a cushion. His form was still completely concealed by his clothes, hood, and the shadows, and he wasn't too concerned about the humans sneaking up on him as he slept. He was a very light sleeper when he wanted to be.

The next morning, Blacknail woke early and went out scouting. When the rest of his tribe had gone down the road, he headed back to the cave. After a brief talk with Rickas and Selstia, they parted ways. The pair once again thanked him profusely for all his help.

The hobgoblin rather liked all the praise they were giving him. He was glad he hadn't let them wander into Herad and that he hadn't killed them either. As he sauntered off in pursuit of Saeter and the others, he heard the pair talking to each other.

"I know he saved us, but he's still creepy. Neither of us got a look at his face the entire time we were with him. He was always completely covered by his clothes, and he never got close to us. That's quite odd," Selstia murmured to her husband.

"True, but he probably has his reasons. Maybe he's a wanted man or is scarred. Why else would he hide his face and live out here?" Rickas replied.

"What about his voice?" she countered.

"He probably has a damaged throat or was hiding his voice as well."

'Maybe, but there's still something off about him. Something different..."

"What, you think he was secretly one of the forest people? Like in the myths where travelers stumble upon a mysterious stranger who helps them out or tricks them? You didn't accidently promise him our firstborn, did you?" her husband asked teasingly.

"I know you're joking, but I can't help but think that you just might be right. It would certainly explain a lot," Blacknail heard Selstia say before they were out of his hearing range.

Blacknail would have liked to stalk his new friends for a while and hear more of their conversation, but he was in a rush. Herad and his master had gotten quite a head start on him now. He broke into a light jog so he would catch up to them before they got too far ahead, but Herad must have been pushing her minions hard, because even after an hour had passed, Blacknail had yet to catch a glimpse of them. He would have worried, but the scent of their passing assured him he was still on their trail.

As he jogged down the forest road, Blacknail came across a break in the trees. On one side of him, the forest was replaced with thick, heavy bush. There were only a few scattered young trees growing up through the bushes. Without the heavy tree cover to stifle it, the hobgoblin felt the wind around him pick up. Its caress cooled him off and felt refreshing as it blew under his clothes. Blacknail looked around and saw what looked like a collapsed building deep within the clearing. It reminded him of what Herad's base had looked like when he had first seen it, but with more bushes. This whole area must have once been a human farm that was now slowly being swallowed by the forest.

After continuing his jogging until he was about halfway through the clearing, a rustling noise caught Blacknail's attention. It was probably a rabbit or something, but to be sure, he slowed his gait and focused on listening for a second. The sound of several more things moving through the bushes alongside him reached his ears. That wasn't good. Rabbits didn't move in packs and stalk hobgoblins. Feeling a surge of acidic panic work its way up from his gut, Blacknail picked up his pace and gripped his sword hilt. If anything decided to jump him, he was going to give it a face full of steel. That would discourage most of the things that lived out in the wilds... but unfortunately not all of them.

The sounds moved closer, and Blacknail noticed the leafy bushes begin to tremble as something ran through them. Whatever these things were, they were clearly not afraid of him. He sniffed the air for a hint of what was approaching, but the wind was blowing in the wrong direction. All he could smell was green trees and dry earth. Suddenly, up ahead of him, the shrubs shook as something launched itself out of them. A shocked Blacknail had to throw himself to the side to avoid the stone projectile that whirled past his head. He landed on all fours and hissed in alarm as a creature stepped out of the bushes and cut off the road in front of him. He had never seen one before, but he knew without a doubt what it was.

His opponent answered his hiss with a screech of challenge. The figure wore a dirty hide loincloth and brandished two crude stone axes high above its head. Its skin was green, and two horns rose up from its unruly gray hair. It was a hobgoblin... and it had brought friends. Shrieking goblins began to emerge from hiding all around Blacknail until he was completely surrounded and couldn't escape. The goblins waved rocks and crude stone-tipped spears in his direction. Their eyes were filled with hate and cruel excitement.

"Human shit," Blacknail swore nervously from where he was crouched on the ground. He had accidently stumbled into the territory of another hobgoblin.

# Chapter 5

Blacknail was very badly outnumbered. He quickly drew his sword and dropped his pack on the ground, as furious goblins encircled him. The green swarm was shrieking and waving their crude stone weapons. It would have been comical, if not for the mad gleam in the goblins' eyes. The goblins didn't earn more than a brief glance from Blacknail though. His eyes were locked on the hobgoblin that stood in front of him. If he looked away, it would be a sign of weakness, and one he couldn't afford.

The other hobgoblin's crude loincloth did little to conceal its body, so it was obviously male. It glared evilly at Blacknail, and it growled as it raised its axes threateningly. The weapons looked to have been made from pieces of chipped stone that had been secured to fire-hardened branches. They were obviously crude weapons, but still very dangerous looking.

Out of the corner of his eye, Blacknail observed the goblins around him. They hadn't attacked him yet, but when they did, they would swiftly overwhelm him. They might be small and weak, but there were a bloody lot of them, and they seemed quite angry. His best bet was to deal with the hobgoblin quickly and hope that would scare the goblins into submission. Of course, the other hobgoblin was noticeably larger and older than Blacknail. Several long, pale scars decorated his exposed skin, and a particular nasty-looking one ran down his left eye. However, his most distinct feature was his black horns. Both of them were over half a foot long and branched like small antlers. They were impressive, and Blacknail found himself more than a little intimidated by them. His own horns had never really had a chance to grow because he had taken to filing them down. They might look imposing, but horns made disguising himself and wearing hats impossible. Still, he really wished he had a pair of horns now.

Blacknail hissed angrily and waved his own weapon around as he took a step toward the hobgoblin. He needed to make this a challenge between the two of them. There was no way he could defeat the swarm of goblins as well as their hobgoblin leader.

"Hey, stupid tree head! You're ugly, and I'm going to cut you up," Blacknail growled as he took another step forward. He knew the other hobgoblin couldn't understand his words, but he didn't need to. There was no way he could misunderstand Blacknail's tone of voice and body language.

The two hobgoblins postured and growled at each other for a few seconds as they slowly moved closer and began to circle each other. The watching goblins' howls of anger turned to excitement. They were now eager to see the two hobgoblins fight. This made Blacknail smile. He had succeeded in making this a one-on-one fight for dominance. After stepping forward again, Blacknail suddenly turned his movement into a full-out lunge. He slashed violently down at the other hobgoblin with the intent to kill and end the fight before it had really begun. Unfortunately, his opponent reacted faster than anyone Blacknail had ever fought before. The enemy hobgoblin easily hopped back out of the attack's range, and instead of counterattacking, he simply eyed Blacknail's sword suspiciously.

Blacknail frowned as he realized his enemy was far from stupid and knew how dangerous Blacknail's sword could be. That changed things slightly. Before he could think through the implications though, the other hobgoblin attacked. One of his stone axes hurtled towards Blacknail's head as his opponent swung it. Even while surprised, Blacknail knew better than to try and block it. The axe was heavy, and the horned hobgoblin was bigger and stronger looking than him, so he slipped to the side and out of the way. Immediately, the second axe was swung at Blacknail as well. The horned hobgoblin jumped forward and swung it down at him. Again Blacknail tried to slip to the side, but as he was readying his counterattack, the other goblin threw his first axe.

Blacknail was caught off guard and flinched as the axe

hurtled toward his face again. He jerked his sword up in a desperate attempt to deflect the savage projectile, but he only managed to graze it. The axe bounced off his weapon and smashed into his shoulder. The weapon didn't hit edge-first, but it still cut into him, and it definitely hurt a lot. Blacknail let out a hiss as pain ripped through his side. The attack left only a small cut, but his arm was beginning to numb from the impact. He needed that arm!

As he sized up his opponent anew, Blacknail growled loudly. It was a bluff. The horned hobgoblin was hanging back and watching Blacknail for any sign of weakness now. Around their small patch of road, the goblins were jeering and chattering excitedly. Things were still relatively even though. Blacknail's one arm was injured, but his opponent had lost a weapon. Rather than show weakness before his opponent and the watching goblins, Blacknail attacked again. He unleashed a flurry of quick slashes at the horned hobgoblin's body and hands. His opponent countered by stepping back and trying to smash Blacknail's blade aside with his own heavier weapon.

Blacknail's lightning-fast slashes drew blood and opened several small gashes on his opponent's arms and ribs. He smiled victoriously as the scent of his enemy's blood filled the air. However, Blacknail's sore arm suddenly flared with pain and his last slash faltered. His opponent seized the opportunity and brought his axe down on Blacknail's blade. The stone edge of the hobgoblin's crude axe shattered, but the impact shocked Blacknail's injured arm, and it went numb. He lost his grip on the sword, and it was ripped painfully from his grasp.

The horned hobgoblin shrieked joyously and dropped his own damaged weapon. As Blacknail was still reeling in pain, the other hobgoblin leapt and tackled him to the ground. Blacknail was knocked onto his back as his opponent landed on his chest. The horned hobgoblin straddled Blacknail, reached down, and began to viciously strangle him. Blacknail coughed as his throat was forced closed, and he lost the ability to breathe. He tried to wriggle and escape, but it didn't work. The feral hobgoblin grinned gleefully down at him as he choked the life from him. Blacknail felt himself grow light-headed and weaker as he futilely tried to suck down air. With his opponent's superior strength and weight, it was nigh impossible for Blacknail to get free. So he didn't try. Instead, he reached under his cloak with his good hand and drew his dagger. Then, he brought it up and savagely stabbed the horned hobgoblin in the side under the ribs. Then he did it again, and again. Then he did it one last time to make himself feel better.

His opponent coughed, and blood splattered all over Blacknail's face. Unceremoniously, Blacknail pushed his now twitching and weak opponent off. The horned hobgoblin flopped sideways and hit the ground as Blacknail rose to his feet and wiped his face clean with one of his sleeves.

"Fair fights are for idiots," Blacknail hissed before spitting on his fallen opponent.

Around him, the circle of goblins had gone silent and were now staring at Blacknail intently. Blacknail repressed the urge to fall over and glared back at them with as much menace as he could muster. The air was full of tension for several long moments, and then the goblins suddenly broke out into shrill screams and rushed forward. Blacknail almost fell over in surprise, but then he realized he wasn't under attack. The goblins were yelling in excitement, obnoxiously loud excitement. They pressed against him as they tried to reach out and paw the victor of the duel. Blacknail would have pulled away, but they came at him from every direction at once. He was jostled and pushed as the swarm seemingly tried to swallow him. Surprised, Blacknail tried to shove through them and escape from the mass of unwashed goblins. The little critters had really dirty hands. Blacknail didn't know what they had been touching, but he knew he didn't like the fact they were getting it all over his clothes. One of the goblins broke away and stepped over to examine the pack Blacknail had dropped earlier. The hobgoblin saw him and growled menacingly as he tried to get free from his new admirers.

"Mine! Back, you little thief," he barked angrily.

The swarm of goblins around him scattered as his furious yell startled them. They retreated from him and began running around and yelling as well. Since they all choose different directions to go in, the swarm devolved into utter chaos as goblins began smacking into each other and yelling random nonsense. Blacknail ignored them and knocked aside any goblins in his way as he lunged toward his pack. The goblin that was riffling through the contents of the backpack saw him coming and quickly ran off into the nearby bushes. Blacknail briefly checked to make sure nothing was missing before quickly snatching his bag up. Then he patted himself down to make sure none of the goblins from earlier had stolen anything, and of course they had. He was missing a dagger and a pouch.

"Little thieves, bad goblins," he hissed as he scanned the nearby goblins for signs of his stuff.

He saw his pouch in the hands of one of them and moved to grab it back. He was too slow though, and the thief slipped away into the bushes at the side of the road. Blacknail growled and immediately followed the goblin. He swatted branches and plants out of the way as he pursued his target through the thick scrubland. His arm was still sore though, and he was quickly growing tired. This feral pack of thieves was beginning to really annoy him.

He followed the goblin until he stepped out of the bushes and into the ruins of an old human house. It looked to have once been fairly large, but it had crumbled away long ago. Only an uneven square of cracked bricks a few feet high remained to mark where the house's exterior walls had once stood, but the ground between the ruins was still packed hard enough that only a few small plants and grass grew there. The result was a small clearing, and the place reeked of goblins. As the hobgoblin looked around, he spotted a pile of ashes and burnt stones that marked the location of a fire pit. It had clearly seen recent use. Other signs of goblin activity, such as tracks and small animal bones, littered the area as well.

Blacknail heard the bushes behind him shake, and he glanced back over his shoulder to see several goblins emerge from the greenery behind him. They cringed and lowered their eyes submissively when he threw a glare their way. He ignored them; they weren't a threat anymore. Goblins such as these feral pipsqueaks would never pick a fight with a hobgoblin such as him. Their natural place was below him.

Now, Blacknail just needed to find his pouch so he could get going. Every minute he wasted here, the rest of his tribe got farther and farther away. He scanned the surroundings for signs of the thief and quickly spotted what looked to be the entrance to an old basement or cellar hidden among the rubble. He smiled and headed toward it. That was probably where the thief was hiding. The rough stone and mortar walls of the stairway were still intact, but the steps had long ago shifted and eroded. This made the walk down the ruined stairway treacherous. Luckily, Blacknail had both very good night vision and excellent balance.

It took his eyes a few seconds to adjust to the dark, but when he made it to the bottom of the passage, he got a good look at the goblins' den. It was a large room big enough to hold dozens of people, or many more goblins than that. Like the stairway down, the old cellar's walls were rough stone with mortar holding them in place. The room had obviously originally been constructed by humans. The floor was packed earth, but Blacknail was unsure if it had always been that way or if the dirt had built up after it had been abandoned. Signs of goblin habitation were everywhere. Collected bits of feathers, wood, and human trash were scattered around the floor, not to mention several insects that buzzed around among the garbage.

The only sources of light were the passage behind Blacknail and a small tunnel some of the goblins had dug in the far wall. Goblins always had more than one entrance to their dens, so they could flee from predators or bigger goblins. Over in one corner, there was a flattened pile of dried plants and bits of cloth. It looked like the horned hobgoblin's old bed to Blacknail. He sneered at it; his bed was much better.

The hobgoblin then noticed his pouch on the ground beside the rear tunnel. He quickly jumped over and scooped it up before another goblin could appear and make off with it. He felt relief wash over him when it was back on his hip where it belonged. He was glad he didn't have to spend any more time looking for it.

Just then, a feeling of dizziness overcame Blacknail, and he realized he was starting to feel tired and sore from his earlier fight with the hobgoblin. That didn't surprise him; he had kind of gotten the shit kicked out of him. His opponent had got a few lucky blows in. Unsteady now, Blacknail moved over to the grass bed in the corner and sat down. He needed a moment to rest, and this den was probably safer and more comfortable than anywhere else he could find. As the hobgoblin surveyed the room around him, his throat suddenly tightened and he was overcome with a feeling of homesickness. It wasn't quite the same, but the cellar definitely reminded him of the sewers he had grown up in. That seemed like a lifetime ago now, even though it had only been several months. So many things had changed.

A twinge of pain went through his arm, so Blacknail removed his cloak and shirt to get a better look at it. The cut had already stopped bleeding, but there was a really nasty deep purple bruise forming around it. Blacknail winced as he examined it. The gash was really going to start hurting once the rush from the fight wore off. He was not looking forward to that at all. That stupid, feral hobgoblin, with the all-right-looking horns, had really gotten lucky during their fight.

Carefully, Blacknail began to clean and wrap the cut using supplies from his pack. By the time he was done, his earlier excitement from the fight had completely worn off. Blacknail yawned as fatigue from the struggle and all his traveling caught up to him all at once. He decided to take a quick nap, just for a bit, so he had some energy for the road. With a little rest, he would probably be able to move faster anyway.

Lazily, Blacknail took out his Flybane and began applying it. Once he had applied enough to keep the bugs away while he rested, he yawned again. Then, he laid his head down on his pack as if it were a pillow. He would just close his eyes for a second so he could rest better...

Sometime later, Blacknail woke to the grumbling of his stomach. For a second, he wondered why he was so hungry, but then he sniffed the air. The hobgoblin quickly sat up and looked around. Several goblins were cautiously loitering around the den, and they had apparently laid out a spread of food for him. A collection of berries and nuts were piled on some leaves in front of him, and that wasn't all. They had also placed a dead rabbit there and returned his knife as well. Blacknail eyed the nervous-looking goblins, and sniffed the food warily. It smelled very good, better than the dried human food he had been eating on the road. Maybe this tribe wasn't so bad after all. They certainly knew how to treat a hobgoblin, unlike most humans.

Blacknail quickly scoffed the berries and nuts down, which left the rabbit. He grabbed both it and his knife as he headed up above ground. Goblins scattered nervously out of his way when he moved. As he climbed the slippery passage upward, he was alarmed to see it had grown darker. Hopefully it was just some cloud cover. Quickly, he jumped outside and looked up at the sky. The sun was starting to set; he had slept for almost the entire day.

"Damnnation-ss and rot!" he cursed in frustration.

He would never be able to catch up with the rest of his tribe before night now. That left him only two options. He could either take his chances and sleep alone in the forest by the road, or stay here for the night. There were also his injuries to consider. The smell of his blood would draw predators to him like flies to shit.

With a resigned sigh, Blacknail placed the rabbit carcass on a nearby rock and went to gather some wood. Several goblins trailed after him. It didn't take long for him to gather up quite a bit of wood. The area was full of it, and as he worked, more and more goblins joined him. In the beginning, only a few of them silently followed him around, but as he gathered up pieces of wood and tinder, they began to whisper among themselves and copy him.

Within a few minutes, almost two dozen goblins were running everywhere and collecting fuel for the fire. An amused Blacknail soon stopped doing the labor himself and instead headed back to get a fire started. As he worked to light the tinder, goblin after goblin appeared to drop loads of twigs and branches at his feet. Soon he had far more fuel than he needed, and a roaring fire.

As the flames roared higher, even more goblins appeared to see what was going on. Blacknail counted about three dozen of them, which was probably the entire tribe. There were several small goblins and pregnant females among them. They must have been hiding from the unknown hobgoblin when he'd first arrived. He didn't blame them. Goblin leadership transitions were often bloody, even without throwing hobgoblins into the mix.

Since Blacknail didn't care about the young goblins in the least, he ignored them and started skinning the rabbit. He enjoyed eating the furry critters raw, but after so many days on the road, he felt like hot food. In fact, he felt like more than just rabbit. Had he seen a pot below? Blacknail wandered back down into the den. His memory was right, and in one corner of the room, there was a large, blackened steel pot. The humans must have left it behind when they deserted the village, and the goblins had claimed it when they moved in. Among the trash, he also found several wooden mugs and bowls.

The hobgoblin grabbed all the stuff and dragged it up to the fire. Working quickly, he grabbed a large branch and stuck it into the ground at an angle so it leaned over the fire. Then he propped it up by placing one rock under it and another atop the buried part. Now he needed water and some other ingredients. Blacknail turned to the closest goblin and repeated the word his old tribe had used for water. The goblin tilted his head to the side and gave Blacknail a bewildered look. This goblin was obviously an idiot. The hobgoblin sighed and began to lap up imaginary water from his cupped hands. It was more than a little embarrassing. This was really beneath his dignity. The goblin just continued to stare at him with a confused expression.

However, another goblin off to the side made an excited sound and rushed over. This goblin's eyes were wide with recognition, and he began to gibber excitedly. He was an average-sized goblin with a slight blue cast to his skin and a few strands of gray hair on the crown of his head. Blacknail made a shooing motion towards the bushes. His eager helper ran up to the border and looked back to see if the hobgoblin was following. Blacknail went after the goblin and trailed him for a few minutes until they came to a small, bubbling creek.

After scanning it carefully for any signs of danger, such as giant snapping turtles, Blacknail approached the stream and took a drink. That done, he filled the two cups he was holding and gave one to his guide. When they got back to the den, the hobgoblin tried to explain what he wanted to its little green residents. After several embarrassing failures, Blacknail managed to get the goblins to start filling the pot using the bowls and cups. Soon after that, he had them bringing him wild carrots and other common herbs. He chopped up all the ingredients and threw them all into the pot, and then he hung the pot from the branch above the fire and waited for it to boil. About an hour later, the pleasant aroma of stew filled the air above the goblin den.

After Blacknail had finished eating, there was still a lot of stew left, so he offered it to the goblins. Tentatively at first, but then with eager excitement, the tribe began taking mugs and cups of the stuff and drinking it down. Judging by their excited murmuring, and the brawls that broke out over bowls, they really liked it. Several goblins tried to drink directly from the pot, but they stopped after Blacknail kicked the closest one across the clearing.

As the sky darkened and the stars began to come out, Blacknail found himself sitting around a fire with an entire tribe of goblins. They scampered around energetically and chattered incomprehensibly among themselves. It reminded Blacknail of his life in the sewers but was also disturbingly different at the same time. He had changed so much. He couldn't even picture himself as one of the little green runts that were running around him. It wasn't even that he was a hobgoblin now; life with humans had changed him. As he stared at the feral goblins, Blacknail realized he no longer saw the world the way this tribe did. They had such tiny short little viewpoints. They were just focused on simple things like food and shelter. When they saw the road at the edge of their domain, what did they think? Did they wonder who had made it or where it led?

Blacknail sighed as he realized a simple life like this would never satisfy him anymore. He couldn't believe he had ever wanted to return to the sewers. He would stay here for the night, and in the morning, seek out Herad and the rest of his tribe. Humans had much better food anyway.

# *Chapter 6*

Blacknail grunted in annoyance as he watched the fire. It was too late to try and go after his master, but he had recently woken up from his earlier nap so he wasn't going to be able to fall asleep anytime soon. He didn't really want to sit around and watch a bunch of dirty goblins gulp down stew either. Even Blacknail couldn't believe how messy they were.

The hobgoblin was used to doing chores when he had spare time, so out of habit, he looked around for something to do. His gaze stopped on the pile of wood. It shouldn't be left out in the rain, so he decided to build a shelter for it. He got up and began to construct a lean-to against the remains of one of the nearby brick walls. He used some of the larger branches the goblins had brought him and tied them together with twine to form the roof. When he was done, Blacknail stood back and admired his handiwork proudly. The goblins behind him murmured in appreciation. The hobgoblin froze as a realization hit him. What in all the hells was he doing? Why was he building these little green pests anything?

With a disgusted grunt, Blacknail sat back down by the fire. He slouched over and rested his chin on his palm as he gazed into the flames again. For a few minutes, he enjoyed staring at the crackling dance of the blaze, but he quickly grew bored. He had depleted some of his stock of rope earlier, so he decided to replace it. He walked out into the bushes by the road and began to gather plant fibers. When he returned, the goblins had not only replaced all the wood he had used up but actually made the pile substantially larger. Blacknail ignored them and began to twist the fibers together to make rope. As he worked, several of the goblins copied him. The hobgoblin gave them a disdainful look. As if they would be able to do it properly! It had taken him weeks to learn to do it, and he was a genius.

A few minutes later, when Blacknail next looked up, he saw several of the goblins working together to make near-perfect rope. He felt his jaw grow slack and fall open in shock. That wasn't possible; there was no way these feral little runts should be able to do it so easily!

Then, Blacknail remembered the other hobgoblin's axes. They had used similar cord to keep the stone heads attached. Obviously, the goblins had already known how to make twine. That made sense. They had probably practiced for years to manage the feat, while under the threat of strict punishment. Still, maybe they weren't as dumb as they looked.

It was some time before Blacknail grew tired. Before then, he'd managed to make two more lean-tos, replace all his rope, and construct a door for the goblin den's entrance. He'd made it from more branches and tied it down using twine and stakes. He was planning on sleeping down there anyway, so having a door directly benefitted him. He obviously hadn't done it for the goblins. That would be stupid...

Several nearby goblins were playing with their new door as they squealed in excitement. Blacknail shooed them away, flipped the door open, and went down into the den. Once down there, he scowled. It was dark inside. Even with the door open and goblin night vision, he was having some problems seeing. That wouldn't do. Blacknail walked around the room until he found a section of the wall where the stones were crumbling. Using the deceased hobgoblin's axe as a hammer, he opened a small hole there. Then, he shoved a nearby goblin into it and forced the gibbering runt to dig its way to the surface as he motivated it with pokes from his sword. His fireplace was thus completed!

It only took a few seconds to fill the newly dug shaft with wood, and light it with a burning branch from the other fire outside. Blacknail removed the goblin first, of course. A burning goblin would undoubtedly make a truly hideous amount of noise.

With the light from the fire and the help of several eager goblins—they were eager not to get kicked—Blacknail was able to clean the place up a bit and lay out his blankets. The final touch was to scatter Flybane around to ward off the bugs. With that done, Blacknail had created a comfy place he actually wouldn't mind sleeping in. In fact, it was actually pretty nice. Moving around so much had caused his wounded shoulder to start aching again, so Blacknail lay down on his blankets and went to sleep. Just before he slipped unconscious, he thought he felt several warm bodies cuddle up next to him. It could have been a dream though. He was definitely alone when he woke up.

As the sun was peaking over the tree tops the next morning, Blacknail threw open the new trap door he had built and stepped outside to greet it. He had everything packed and was ready to continue his journey to Daggerpoint. He couldn't wait to hit the road! Feeling fully rested, the hobgoblin made his way through the bushes and back onto the road. He was going to have to travel quickly if he was to have any chance of finding Herad and the others' trail, so he immediately started running.

However, as he was about to leave the bushy scrubland behind him, Blacknail heard a shrill screech fill the air. He looked back over his shoulder to see a flock of harpies circling the goblin den from high up in the air. They looked mean. Blacknail then heard the unmistakable yelp of a terrified goblin. That wasn't his problem, but he hesitated and grunted in annoyance as he watched the harpies circle. Harpies were dangerous predators. They resembled huge birds except they had claws on the ends of their wings, and mouths full of teeth instead of beaks.

Stupid, bloody, feral, good-for-nothing goblins, it served the runts right for attacking him! So what if they got eaten by harpies? The hobgoblin took another step forward but then froze. He was totally not responsible for them just because he had killed their chief. That wasn't how it worked!

Blacknail fought to keep walking away, but he couldn't take another step. He let out a long, resigned sigh and turned around. Swiftly, he raced back to the clearing in time to see one of the circling harpies dive. Below it, a goblin was desperately attempting to scramble through the bushes toward the entrance to the den. It didn't look like it would make it. Blacknail was prepared though. He had already pulled out his sling, and he immediately sent a stone whirring toward the diving harpy.

His hasty shot missed, but it definitely caught the raptor's attention. The sound of the stone shooting past it startled the harpy and caused it to abandon its dive. Instead, it fluttered in the air for a second before winging its way across the clearing. The goblin it had been aiming for reached the trap door and slipped under it. The other harpies that were still circling above began to screech angrily. Blacknail eyed them warily as he pushed his way through the scraggly bushes and back toward the den. When he burst into the ruins of the old home, one of the flock detached itself and dove toward him.

The hobgoblin saw the harpy coming and whipped another stone at it, and this time it hit. The harpy squawked in pain and dropped from the air. There was a loud thud as it smashed through the bushes and into the ground. Blacknail gave the mangled body of the downed raptor a brief look-over. He was fairly confident it was dead. That had been quite the lucky shot, or maybe he was just super skilled? That only left five more harpies. Blacknail hoped they would give up now that they knew how dangerous he was. He was really strong and fast after all! They wouldn't gain anything from attacking him.

Suddenly, the air above him was filled with the furious screech of vengeful harpies. Moving as one, the entire enraged flock descended upon the hobgoblin. Blacknail swore as his eyes widened in alarm. Maybe that hadn't been a lucky shot after all... A surge of panic rushed through Blacknail as he sprinted for cover. He could hear the harpies descending upon him, so he quickly measured the distance to the den's entrance as he ran. It was obvious he wouldn't make it, so he swerved and threw himself aside at the last moment. The first four harpies missed and blew past him in a gust of wind, but the last one caught the edge of his cloak with its hind claws. The furious raptor began to slash at Blacknail with the long claws on the end of its wings. Luckily, its efforts were hampered by the hobgoblin's clothing.

Blacknail rolled and ripped his cloak off, with the harpy still attached to it. He then drew his dagger and stabbed at it. The flailing creature slipped away from him, so he only managed to graze it. That was when the other harpies swung back around and whipped past him once more. The hobgoblin tried to roll out of the way again, but this time, one of the raptors managed to slash him across his back as it flew past. The cut stung, and Blacknail could feel his clothes grow damp as blood seeped from the gash.

The hobgoblin's roll ended as he hit one of the nearby crumbling walls. He placed his back up against it and brought his dagger up in defense as he climbed to his feet. Bleeding and tired, Blacknail prepared himself to face the winged terrors again.

The first harpy rushed at him. Blacknail grabbed his cloak from off the ground and swung it at the creature. Instinctively, the surprised harpy gripped the long piece of fabric, so Blacknail whipped the cloak around and sent the raptor hurtling off into the nearby brambles. The other three harpies that were still in flight dove at him, so Blacknail flipped over the wall at his back. This forced the furiously squawking raptors to fly over him harmlessly. Blacknail smiled mockingly at the stupid feathered beasts. They weren't so tough.

That was when the first harpy that had attacked him pounced out of the bushes and onto his back. Blacknail shrieked in pain and tried to throw the creature off, but it had its claws dug in deep. As he futilely tried to reach around and stab the harpy with his knife, it suddenly and unexpectedly released him. Blacknail rolled through the dirt and hissed in pain, but the urge to survive raged through him and drove him to act. He landed on his feet with his dagger up and spat loose feathers from his mouth.

"Stupid man-faced birds, I'll cut you all up!" the hobgoblin roared. He had expected to immediately have a face full of furious harpy, but it didn't happen. It soon became obvious why. A goblin had shoved a spear up the raptor's ass.

A wave of angry shrieking goblins was rushing out of their den and were in the process of finishing off the two grounded harpies. Several of them were mercilessly stabbing each of the flailing raptors with stone-tipped spears. Several more rushed over to Blacknail and surrounded him protectively. They waved their spears and jeered at the three harpies that were still flying around. The now very outnumbered winged beasts apparently didn't want to keep fighting. They twisted in the air and started flapping toward the woods. A few seconds later, they let out one last angry shriek before disappearing into the trees. Blacknail let out a deep sigh of relief as the goblins around him began cheering at the top of their lungs.

The fight was over. Blacknail grunted in pain as he awkwardly tried to stand up straight. That fight could have gone a lot better... There was no way he was going to be able to start after Herad and Saeter now. He had to clean and patch all the new wounds he had gotten. Not to mention, he wasn't exactly feeling up to a long run.

Oh well, it wasn't all bad. At least he had a safe place to sleep and recuperate. Of course, it was full of annoying little runts that were being way too loud right now. He kind of, but not really, owed them one though. So he could also use the time to teach the goblins a trick or two. Just so they could survive without a hobgoblin around to look after them.

After getting a nearby goblin to grab him some more food and patching his wounds, Blacknail went straight to work. The most important thing was that the goblins were able to protect themselves. That way he could leave without having to worry about them being attacked as soon as his back was turned. If the harpies came back, the goblins would need slings. Even a small goblin could do a fair bit of damage with a sling, and they worked well against flying targets. Then again, a rock to the face worked well against almost everything. He didn't have nearly enough cloth to make slings though... How else could he do it? Well the goblins had shown they could make twine, so maybe he could use that.

Less than an hour later, the hobgoblin was laughing excitedly as he launched a small rock across the clearing using the twine sling he had just made. It had worked; he truly was a genius! Immediately, Blacknail grabbed several nearby goblins and forced them to make twine. He had to smack them a few times to keep them from slipping away, but once they knew what he wanted, they went to work. The gray-haired goblin that had guided him to the creek was there, and Blacknail didn't have to hit him at all. That was an impressive amount of intelligence for a goblin.

When Blacknail had enough twine, he got the goblins to watch him make another sling and use it. The weapon apparently impressed the goblins, or maybe they liked mimicking the hobgoblin, because soon the air was full of flying rocks. That also meant the ground was soon littered with fallen goblins who had welts and bumps decorating their heads after being hit by stray projectiles. Looking back, that outcome should have been obvious to Blacknail, and even he had to dodge the occasional rock that shot past his head. He couldn't figure out which goblin, or conspiracy of goblins, it was that kept doing that. His plan to discipline them by giving them all a good kicking also failed. There were too many of them, and the little runts were quick when they wanted to be.

"Stupid ungrateful idiots," he muttered to himself as he stared suspiciously in every direction.

Clearly, Blacknail had to rethink his strategy. How did Herad control so many bandits? She had lieutenants like Saeter and Red Dog! Could he train a goblin? The gray-haired goblin had shown something that mimicked intelligence... kind of. He was also standing right beside Blacknail, which placed him within easy reach. With his mind made up, the hobgoblin began instructing the gray-haired goblin on how to use a sling.

"You boss goblin now," the hobgoblin told his wide-eyed follower.

"You boss," the goblin repeated.

Blacknail sighed. Well, language wasn't important anyway. It was time for phase two of his goblin-proof plan. Blacknail handed Gray Hair a spear and had him go around smacking the other goblins with it. If they tried to fight back, Blacknail gave them a solid kick, and that was that. Thus did Gray Hair rise in the pack hierarchy.

After repeating the process two more times, Blacknail had trained himself some loyal lieutenants. Now, if the stupid tribe of goblins didn't do as the hobgoblin wanted, it was his lieutenants' problem, because he would take it out on them. That was much less work for Blacknail to do. Smacking goblins around started out fun but swiftly grew tedious if you had to keep doing it forever.

The hobgoblin's plan worked flawlessly, because he was a

genius. Soon, Blacknail had the goblins under his, almost, complete control. He kept them very busy while he recuperated. With the help of his new lieutenants, he managed to force most the goblins to practice slinging stones. This time no one got hurt, except the stupid goblins that deserved it.

Next on the list was fortifying the den some more. First, Blacknail started constructing some more stone axes. He copied the horned hobgoblin's simple design. A sharpened stone was wedged into the split top of a length of wood and wrapped in twine. He had goblins use the axes to cut down saplings. The work went quickly with two dozen goblins all working together, especially since if one of the goblins wasn't working fast enough, they got poked by one of the hobgoblin's spear-wielding lieutenants. Blacknail knew how to motivate goblins.

The wood from the saplings was used to reinforce the trap door and to add two smaller trap doors to the back tunnel and the fireplace. With the leftover poles, he was even able to make himself a raised platform to sleep on. It was good to be chief.

Once that was done, Blacknail taught the goblins how to make snares and how to use them to catch rabbits and squirrels. This greatly increased the amount of meat the goblins caught, so Blacknail cooked stew again that night.

After a firelit feast under the stars, Blacknail and the tribe withdrew underground. The room below was barely recognizable now. The flickering orange light of the fireplace illuminated the old cellar. Thanks to the den's new doors, the fire also warmed the cold stone walls of the chamber. Most of the trash had also been removed, and the place now smelled of Flybane instead of goblin... stuff. The less he thought about that, the better.

From his place on his newly constructed bed, Blacknail yawned and snuggled into his blankets. He felt good enough that tomorrow he would probably be able to hit the road again. For now though, he wanted to enjoy this rare moment of comfort.

He was just about to fall asleep when he heard a goblin approach. He opened his eyes to see a female approach and begin to lick his face. She was tall and skinny for a goblin and had short black hair. Blacknail found her attractive, and he smiled in anticipation as blood rushed to his lower regions. It had been quite a while since the last time a female goblin had shown interest in him. Blacknail rolled over and sniffed the female. Lust built up in him as he took in her aroma. He growled in appreciation, and his heartbeat quickened. As he was about to mount her, two other female goblins moved over and began to lick him as well. Blacknail's smile grew even wider. He was definitely enjoying being a hobgoblin, and was without a doubt glad he'd come back to help this tribe.

His master and Herad would be fine without him for a few days. How dangerous could this place Daggerpoint be?

# *Chapter 7*

The morning sunlight shone gently on Blacknail as he jogged. He'd been very busy yesterday. The hobgoblin had been so busy, he hadn't even had time to hunt. Instead he'd made the goblins he'd been staying with bring him food and water, while he was busying. Thus, a satisfied grin was plastered across the hobgoblin's face as he headed down the road. He was feeling quite cheerful. This was despite the fact that he had no idea where he was going or what he was going to do when he got there. It sure was a nice day out though!

Herad and her men's trail had long since faded, and it wasn't like Blacknail could stop and ask for directions either. His clothes had been torn apart by his recent scuffles and didn't serve as much of a disguise anymore, unless he was trying to disguise himself as a hobgoblin wearing rags.

This left him with two options: turn back toward camp and hang out with Red Dog, or continue on down the road and hope it led him to Herad before winter came. He chose the latter. Red Dog was no fun, and he was pretty sure if he followed the sound of screams, Herad would be close by. She was funny like that.

Whenever Blacknail heard or saw someone approaching, he would slip into the woods and hide among the trees. He didn't want to draw any attention to himself or get delayed any more than he already had been. It wasn't like the passing humans had anything he wanted anyway. He hadn't wasted the time he had spent recuperating with the goblin tribe. His backpack was stuffed full of fresh supplies. Before leaving them, he had smoked quite a few strips of meat and collected several handfuls of nuts and berries. This meant he wouldn't need to stop to restock for quite awhile and could thus keep moving the entire day. Hopefully, that would help him make up for some of the time he had lost.

The forest on both sides of the road was full of birdsong and the occasional snapping of twigs as creatures scurried through the underbrush. Most the trees here were covered in long pointy needles instead of having leaves. The ground itself was uneven and rocky. It had only the thinnest amount of soil on it, and large sections of jagged stone were exposed. The rocks reminded Blacknail of broken bones erupting from torn flesh, so they made him a little hungry.

"Harpy teeth-ss and damnation!" Blacknail suddenly growled angrily as he took in the sight before him. He had just run around a curve in the road.

The road ahead forked; it split in two, and both parts went in completely different directions. Blacknail had no idea which one he was supposed to go down. He tried to find some sign or scent of his tribe's passing but was unsurprised when he discovered nothing. There were too many footprints going in every direction. As he circled the crossroads for what must have been the tenth time, he suddenly detected a noise. It sounded a lot like heavy footsteps, especially those of horses. Quickly, Blacknail slipped into the nearby bushes before he could be seen.

As he watched from his hiding place, a group of humans came down the road. There were about three dozen of them, and they all wore heavy packs. Their clothing was more than a little faded, but it still seemed oddly colorful to Blacknail. Red and blue of various shades decorated their outfits. Among their number, there were three men and two women on horseback. Blacknail could already smell the foul beasts, the horses not the men. Their mounts also seemed to be carrying a lot of baggage. He had seen their like before on missions for Herad. These humans were traders. When they got to the fork in the road, the travelers started heading south the way Blacknail had come from. The hobgoblin eyed them carefully. They seemed to know where they were going. Perhaps he could somehow arrange to get this useful bit of information from them?

The hobgoblin waited until they had passed him by and then began to stalk after them. It wasn't hard, since they weren't exactly moving quickly or being all that observant. Blacknail easily slipped through the bushes behind them unseen. Seriously, what was up with their colorful clothing?

None of the human merchants seemed too dangerous, but there were way too many of them for Blacknail to overcome alone. In broad daylight, his torn clothes wouldn't disguise him so approaching them was also out. That left him with only one option. He had to somehow get one of them away from the rest of the herd. That way he could get some answers out of them. How could he do that though? Humans such as these tended to stick together. They were cowards.

The hobgoblin slipped into the trees, picked up speed, and soon got ahead of the traders. A plan was starting to form in his head. When you baited animals, you used food. So what did humans value instead of food? The answer was shiny coins, and Blacknail had some of those. Once he was a fair bit ahead of the human party, the grinning hobgoblin left the cover of the trees. He raced to the edge of the road and placed his open coin pouch beside a patch of thick bushes. He hid himself nearby and smiled eagerly in anticipation as he waited for someone to fall into his clever trap.

It didn't happen. The stupid bloody humans were obviously blind because not one of them noticed the pouch. Not a single one of them! After they had all passed by, the grumbling hobgoblin emerged from hiding and started running ahead of the humans so he could try again. This time, Blacknail placed the pouch somewhere more obvious, and scattered a few coins around it decoratively. Then, after a second of thought, he tied the pouch to a bit of string. That way he could draw his prey in even closer. With his trap set, the hobgoblin once again hid himself nearby and waited. A human had better notice the pouch this time, or he was going to get really mad!

As the traveling merchants were passing him by for the second time, a man that was walking at the back of the group happened to glance in the right direction. His eyes went wide in surprise as he noticed the pouch, but he quickly looked away. Nonchalantly, the man began to slow his pace and fall to the back of the group. Blacknail smiled excitedly from his hiding spot; that was perfect! Some suitable prey had noticed the bait. It was a greedy idiot.

Once the rest of the merchants had moved past the coin sack, the man hurriedly walked off the road and toward the pouch. With a wary glance back over his shoulder to make sure none of the other merchants were looking in his direction, the man made his way over to the bushes. He smiled greedily as he reached down to pick up the unexpected windfall. Right before he could pick it up, however, the pouch seemed to slide deeper into the shrubs. The man frowned and took a step after it. Then he froze as his eyes went wide in realization. Coin pouches didn't usually move themselves. It was, however, much too late for him. Off to one side, Blacknail suddenly lunged out from the bushes. Before his prey could even blink, the hobgoblin was behind him with a dagger pressed firmly against his throat.

"Don't-ss fight or talk-ss," Blacknail whispered as he pulled the terrified man into the bushes and completely out of sight of anyone on the road.

"What... oh gods, you're not human," the man whispered with obvious terror as he visibly paled.

"Stupid man-ss, that's obvious. I will ask-ss questions here, not you," Blacknail replied viciously and pushed the now shaking man into the woods.

Once they had gone a few feet farther in, Blacknail stopped and looked the trader directly in the eyes. The man flinched and whimpered. Blacknail had to fight a sudden urge to smack some sense into his prisoner. Then he had to fight the urge to stab him.

"Which way is Daggerpoint?" the hobgoblin asked the man as he pulled the knife tighter.

"What, you can talk?" the stunned man replied.

Blacknail sighed. Why was this man so stupid? With his free hand, Blacknail grabbed the man's shoulder and squeezed until his sharp nails drew blood. His prisoner whimpered in pain before gasping.

"Still obvious, answer-ss my question!" Blacknail growled.

"It's north! Daggerpoint is north of here," the man whimpered.

"Again, that's obvious. Back the way-ss you came, which road would you take?" the hobgoblin asked scornfully.

"Uh, the left! It's the left road."

Blacknail considered this answer for a second. How did he know the man wasn't lying?

"I'm going to tie you up, and go-ss capture another human. If he says different from you-ss, then you will both die," Blacknail explained untruthfully. That would be way too much work.

"It's left, I swear!" the man repeated.

Blacknail thought he was probably telling the truth. The whimpering man was obviously a coward, and he had no reason to lie anyway.

"Take off your clothes then lay facedown on the ground," Blacknail commanded as he took a step back and drew his sword.

The man stood there for a second with a startled expression, but when Blacknail waved his sword at him, he immediately began getting undressed. When the whimpering man was naked and lying on his stomach, Blacknail picked up his clothes and addressed him.

"Look up and I stab you," Blacknail warned him.

The hobgoblin immediately began creeping silently away. After he was a fair distance away, he broke out into a run. Honestly, he had really wanted to stab the dumb human, but it would have broken Herad's rules. The man was a merchant, and he had been told to rob but not kill them. That way he could rob them again later. It made perfect sense to Blacknail. That human merchant had been so stupid, Blacknail could probably rob him several more times the same way. In fact, the hobgoblin was already considering several ways to improve his human trap. He could place the pouch over a covered pit. That would mean a lot of digging though. Oh, he could place it beside a giant snare like the one Saeter had used on him! No, that would be way too noisy. He obviously needed to knock them unconscious somehow...

With a new set of clothes and another pouch of shiny human bait to add to his own, Blacknail headed toward the left fork in the road. He was relieved that he had managed to get back on his tribe's trail without too much of a problem. It had even been more than a little fun. He was certainly a genius among hobgoblins! A few hours after heading down the left road, he had to stop again. He had arrived at yet another crossroads. He growled in frustration. How many bloody roads did humans need? He probably should have asked the man about the entire way to Daggerpoint...

Blacknail spent quite a while circling the area futilely. The time he was wasting frustrated him, and he began to growl and hiss to himself. He couldn't just choose a path and follow it though, he could end up anywhere. He had no choice but to wait for someone to come by, hopefully before tomorrow. It grew dark before any other travelers appeared, but much to Blacknail's relief, eventually some did. Disguised by the darkness and his new outfit, Blacknail was able to simply approach this group and ask directions.

The humans turned out to be a pair of hunters returning to their camp. When he asked them directions, they were more than happy to help him out, but they warned him Daggerpoint was a vile den of thieves and murderers. For his own good, they didn't want to tell him how to get there. After a brief conversation, he managed to convince them though. He told them he needed to find some of his tribe—or family, as humans called it—who had headed there and who needed his protection. Khita was likely dragging Saeter into danger right this moment. What would they do without their favorite hobgoblin to look out for them?

The huntsmen thus gave him detailed instructions on how to get to Daggerpoint and wished him luck in finding his family. Their instructions were rather long. Apparently, there were more than a few crossroads between the hobgoblin and the city. The world sure was a large place.

After a heartfelt thanks and friendly wave goodbye to the two helpful men, Blacknail wandered off to find somewhere to hole up for the night. The huntsmen had offered to let him camp with them, but Blacknail hadn't thought that would be a good idea. They seemed far more observant than the last pair of humans he had spent the night with, and also more dangerous.

The hobgoblin eventually found a good hollow tree to sleep in and drifted off. The next morning, he was up and on his way to Daggerpoint. He traveled that way for several days, and actually made fairly good time. The white-tipped mountains in the distance grew larger and larger as he followed the road north. Then at last, the hobgoblin arrived outside the city of Daggerpoint, or at least he hoped it was Daggerpoint. He didn't see any actual dagger, with or without a point.

Blacknail stood upon a hill that looked down at the valley below. The city stretched out through the valley below him. It was an ugly place and noticeably smaller than most of the other cities Blacknail had seen before. Both the city he had grown up in and Riverdown had been much bigger. Of course, he had only seen Riverdown from a distance. Other than that, the first thing he noticed about the city was they used a lot of wood, forests worth of the stuff. The wall that encircled the city was made completely from lumber, and practically every building he could see was as well. The stone most other cities used to make buildings was almost nowhere to be seen.

Near the center of the settlement, there was one large fancy house that stood on the tallest hill in the valley. It was much larger than any of the other buildings and stood entirely alone. At the base of the hill was what looked like some sort of fence, and the only greenery in the entire city lay within it. Blacknail thought the large house would be a good place to look for Herad. She always took the largest building as her own whenever she moved somewhere.

All the other homes and other structures seemed to be placed haphazardly. Blacknail couldn't see a single straight road that lasted more than a few hundred feet. Everything seemed randomly placed and hastily built. All these features made Blacknail think the entire place could be set aflame by one well-placed fire, he was even briefly tempted to try it. He should probably find Herad and Saeter first though. The fun stuff would have to wait until later.

The hobgoblin scanned the city walls as he looked for a way in. The road he was on ran down the hill and through a gate in the wall. Two men stood outside the gate and briefly looked over everyone who entered. They didn't appear to be checking everyone too carefully or going through their stuff, so Blacknail briefly considered just walking through but decided not to risk it. It wasn't like he would be able to casually walk the streets during the day anyway. He would instead wait for night and scale the walls. They didn't seem very hobgoblin proof, but then again, few things were.

Blacknail sat down to relax. He pulled some snacks out of his bag and chowed down on them as he watched the city from his hillside lookout. He could be patient when the reward was great enough. Several hours passed, and the sky above him darkened, but Blacknail didn't budge from his lookout point. For a while, light shone out of most the buildings in the city, but soon most of it died until only a little remained, and the valley grew dark. The hobgoblin looked on as the city gates were closed and the guards withdrew.

The night air was crisp and the moon was high in the sky when Blacknail finally descended the hill and approached the walls. As he strolled along their lengths, he ran his fingers over their rough, dry exterior, and he smiled as his claws found purchase in the timbers. He continued walking until he found a spot where the other side of the barrier was both dark and silent. Then, with an eager smile, he dug his nails into the wood and began to climb. His lean-but-muscled body made the ascent hardly any effort at all, so soon the hobgoblin was perched atop the wall. His cloak rippled in the wind as the breeze blew in from over the dark forest behind him. He looked down to see several squat ramshackle buildings separated by a dark alley. Beyond them stretched a seemingly endless maze of wood and stone.

Despite its rundown appearance, even at night the city was alive with noise. Off in the distance, Blacknail heard a chorus comprised of the clatter of footsteps and human voices raised in both fear and joy. As he listened, a shriek of pain filled the air from only a few streets away. It sure sounded like the people inside were having a lot of fun. The hobgoblin couldn't wait to join in, so he smiled and began to climb down into the alley. He was very glad he had made the journey north and not stayed in the camp. This place seemed like it was going to be exciting! There were so many wonderful treats waiting to be plucked and trapped here. It made him feel all tingly inside just thinking about it.

Blacknail reached the ground and began walking out toward the street. The alley around him was piled high with refuse, but he didn't mind. Ahead of him, flashes of warm light could be seen as doors and shutters were opened and closed off in the distance. The hobgoblin scanned the nearby buildings. Several of them seemed in bad repair and were probably abandoned. Humans sure liked abandoning buildings. Well, it made it easy for him to find somewhere safe to sleep, so he wasn't going to complain. No one was going to be able to find him in this twisted, wooden, human hive. It would be like trying to search for a single mimic in an entire forest, and just as dangerous for the searchers.

Also, unlike out in the forest, there were no dangerous beasts here. The wooden wall and the thick human stench behind it kept them out. In this city, there were just blind, deaf, and stupid humans. Blacknail chuckled darkly in amusement. Well, there had been no dangerous beasts in the city. Now there was him.

# *Part Two:*

# *Den of Beasts*

# *Chapter 8*

The city smelled of humans. That was no surprise to Blacknail. It was a scent he knew well, but its intensity was still almost overwhelming. The dark alleys and city streets reeked not only of human sweat and urine but also of their blood and shit. The smell made Blacknail grimace in disgust as he slipped through the shadows along the edge of the street and past the other pedestrians. He stayed away from the light that shone out from nearby buildings. Even goblins knew better than to shit where they lived. Were the humans just lazy, or were they too afraid to go outside?

The black gloom of night lay thick over the city as Blacknail searched for some sign or scent of his tribe amongst the torrent of other odors that filled the streets. Try as he might though, he couldn't detect anything. Mingled among the foul and the vile, there were, however, some other more pleasant aromas. They were smells he couldn't quite place but were familiar nonetheless. Some of the scents were somewhat like stew but even more... varied. Other smells reminded him strongly of bread or some of the treats Varhs and Geralhd had occasionally brought him. However, these were so much more full and fresh in their aroma. It brought back bittersweet memories of his life before he had been taken from the sewers.

The sound of nearby whispering tickled Blacknail's ears. He looked over to see the shadows shift at the entrance to the alley he was about to walk by. There was movement within. Suddenly, figures dressed in rags burst from the alley and toward him. Some of them were quite small so Blacknail kicked the closest one away and growled at the rest. Only then did he get a good look at them. They were human children, and they were now fleeing in every direction. The larger female he had knocked over quickly got to her feet and scrambled away as well. Blacknail smiled smugly to himself as they fled. The pests may have looked like they were running past, but the hobgoblin hadn't been fooled. He knew they'd been targeting him, most likely for theft. Goblins played similar tricks on each other all the time. A good kicking was always the right answer.

Since the children were no real threat, the hobgoblin moved on. His recent actions had caused some attention to be focused on him, but not too much. No one had died, and he hadn't made too much noise. The humans of this city seemed to value their privacy, which suited Blacknail just fine. He was even far from the only person out and about in a hood and cloak. Most of the passersby were alone or in small groups, but occasionally a larger group of armed humans would pass by. Anyone who got too close to them was hassled and shoved around. Blacknail had examined a few of these human packs from a safe distance. They wore no uniforms or other marks of identification he could see. He had even seen two of the groups meet and exchange insults and threats. They hadn't actually fought though, so while they weren't friendly, they weren't enemies either. Blacknail suspected these were warriors from different tribes attempting to gain status through displays of might and bravery. However, since it was easy for him to avoid these large groups he decided to move on.

The hobgoblin wandered the sprawling streets of the city for a while without finding anything of too much interest. He did, however, pick up two tails. Blacknail didn't look back, but he had definitely been hearing the same steady sound of footsteps for the last few minutes. That was interesting; he wondered who they were. Blacknail suddenly swerved and walked into a dark alley to his left. There were a lot of dark alleys to choose from in this place. He crouched behind a pile of junk and waited. Just as he had planned, two men soon stepped into the alley. They walked quickly toward his hiding spot as they scanned the shadows for signs of him.

Blacknail observed and frowned in disappointment. He didn't know these men, and they didn't smell of anyone he knew. They were probably just a pair of random stupid humans. With a sigh, the hobgoblin rose from his hiding spot and confronted the men who had been following him.

"There he is!" the smaller one barked as he spotted Blacknail.

His companion whipped around and pointed a long dagger at Blacknail's face. The hobgoblin tilted his head to the side lightly and gave him a quizzical look.

"Give up your coins or we'll..."

Blacknail tuned him out and sighed again. These men were just boring thieving humans and no one important. They didn't even have swords or look tough at all. Oh well, it was to be expected. Thieves were the lowest of the low after all. The hobgoblin raised the sling he was holding at his side and launched a rock at the talking idiot's face.

There was a loud crack as the stone smashed into the man's forehead and tore a bloody gash across it. The injured mugger staggered and began to collapse. Before he hit the ground, Blacknail was already moving. The hobgoblin shot forward, drew his sword, and slashed at the second man.

"Wha?" the man said as he fumbled for his own dagger.

Blacknail's blade cut deep into his shoulder before his target could manage to draw his weapon. The man screamed shrilly in pain as his arm went slack, and the dagger fell from his limp fingers. The disabled man tried to pull away from the hobgoblin, but Blacknail took a step after him and silenced his annoying blubbering with a second heavy chop to his neck. Blacknail then pulled off his right glove and leisurely reached down. With a satisfied smile, he tore the unconscious first mugger's throat out with his bare claws. The man's flesh felt nice and squishy between his fingers as he squeezed. It was too bad humans didn't taste that good.

The grinning hobgoblin took a few seconds to listen for the signs of anyone approaching. However, it was soon apparent that no one was headed over to check on the source of the brief scream, so Blacknail began rifling through his attackers' clothes for things to take as trophies. He found a few shiny coins, and pocketed their daggers as well, before leisurely continuing on his way down the alley. He could tell no one was coming, so there was no reason to hurry.

A few minutes later, Blacknail stepped back out onto one of

the main streets. At this time of night, there were only a few other people around, and none of them were looking his way. As he started walking deeper into the city, his stomach gave a rumble. Killing things usually made him hungry. There were still some nuts left in Blacknail's pack, but all the exotic smells around made him hungry for something more. The hobgoblin wanted to sink his teeth into something new and tasty. Thus, Blacknail followed his nose in the direction the most delicious aroma was coming from. Soon, he found himself moving closer toward one of the more crowded and well lit areas of the city. Cautiously, he looked out from a shadowy alley to see what was going on.

The street was wider here and stretched quite a distance in both directions. It was well lit by bright torches and the open doorways of buildings that lined the street. What had to be hundreds of humans were walking around as they shouted, yelled, and did other annoying things that were too loud. Most of them wore rough, cheap clothing and bore visible weapons, but not all of them.

Blacknail also saw quite a few human females dressed in next to nothing, and some similarly garbed men as well. He thought they looked more than a little cold. Scattered around the street were several other humans in much nicer and more colorful clothing walking around too. Usually, they were surrounded by more than a few tough-looking escorts. They seemed to be higher status humans with their own warrior underlings.

The hobgoblin still didn't see anyone he knew, so he looked past all the rather fatty and oily humans to see where all the wonderful smells were coming from. The most potent of the aromas seemed to be leaking from several large well lit buildings with open doors. The problem was that lots of people were coming and going from them. Light and crowds of humans in close proximity were something the hobgoblin planned on avoiding.

Some of the smells were coming from booths or smaller buildings with far less people in them. Those looked far more promising. Hesitantly, Blacknail stepped out of the shadows and onto the dimly lit street. He forced himself to casually walk past all the loud men and woman around him. As he moved, a few of the tough-looking men gave him glares, but they ignored him when he moved out of their way. Some of the skimpily dressed men and women looked him over curiously, but after he failed to meet their gazes, they lost interest as well. No one appeared to notice anything off about him, so Blacknail relaxed and even began to enjoy himself.

Ha, he was so tricky! All these stupid humans didn't know he was right there in front of them. This was too easy. All it took was a cloak and the humans couldn't see him, and they sure couldn't smell him either! As he walked past a pair of chatting humans, he sniggered in amusement. One of the women threw him a rude glare but kept walking. This only caused Blacknail to snigger harder. He was so amazing! Now he just had to find some food and then locate his tribe.

The hobgoblin scanned the nearby wooden booths. They were covered in delicious-looking treats, but at least one human was watching over each of them. Blacknail grinned smugly; that didn't seem like it would be a problem. The hobgoblin did a quick walk down the street and back to pick a first target. Eventually, he settled on a booth being operated by a fat man that appeared to be selling some sort of meat pastry. Their spicy and meaty aroma made his mouth water.

Blacknail watched the man carefully for a few minutes from the across the street. When he had the man's mannerisms down, he made his move and began his walk by the booth. The fat man watched him approach from the corner of his eye but seemed unconcerned. Blacknail was just another random person on the street. As he reached the booth, the fat man looked up and away from the hobgoblin, toward a scantily clad woman who was walking by. Instantly, Blacknail's hand shot out and grabbed several pastries. Quick as a striking snake, the hand withdrew out of sight and back beneath his cloak. The hobgoblin picked up his pace ever so slightly and swerved to disappear into a nearby alley before the man even noticed anything was missing.

Once safely out of sight within the alley, the hobgoblin stuffed his face full of meat pies. They were so very delicious! Ugh, he couldn't eat them fast enough. They were too good.

Blacknail began coughing and choking as he fought down the urge to throw up from eating too quickly. That didn't stop him from devouring the last succulent pie as he shivered violently in excitement though. The delicious taste was worth it.

After a few more dashes out to liberate food that wasn't being used, Blacknail had filled his stomach. He took a brief rest to let his stomach settle before continuing on his quest to find his tribe. It quickly grew even darker out as the hobgoblin searched the quickly emptying streets. Eventually, all the lights went out and all the humans disappeared. Blacknail cursed as he stood alone in the middle of a completely empty cobblestone street. During his search, he hadn't managed to find any trace of Herad or the others. Well, at least he was in no danger of starving to death...

With a tired yawn, the hobgoblin decided to abandon his hunt for now and find somewhere to sleep. After thinking it over for a minute, he thought the best place to look was the area where he had first entered the city. Most the buildings there had been empty and abandoned. They were also a little worse for wear, but he didn't care. As long as they kept the rain and wind away it was fine.

Blacknail's cloaked form slipped silently through the now pitch-black streets. The sky overhead was heavy with unseen clouds that blotted out the heavens' light. Even the hobgoblin had some difficulty seeing where he was going. However, his nose worked fine. Soon, Blacknail was back where he had started earlier that night. He selected one of the nearby houses as his territory for the night. The one he had chosen was a squat wooden structure with a small upper floor. There was a hole in the roof, but it was still mostly intact and would serve as a shelter. It was also the house that smelled the least of humans and rot. Unfortunately, it also smelled strongly of rats, so Blacknail went around and urinated on the walls to mark the territory as his own. That would keep them away while he slept, and if not, then he would simply not have to look very far to find some breakfast.

The stairs to the upper room had collapsed, but Blacknail had no trouble climbing up using its remains. Once he was on the second floor, he found the driest corner and set up his blankets. With that done, he looked around and gave a satisfied nod. No humans would be able to sneak up on him while he rested there, and the rats probably couldn't either.

When Blacknail woke up the next morning, the sun was at its peak in the sky. So it wasn't really the morning at all anymore. No rats, dogs, cats, or humans had disturbed his sleep. The hobgoblin got up and looked out of the nearby window. It only gave him a good view of the nearby empty alley, but he could see the sky as well. It was cloudy overhead and the sun was hidden, but it was still far too bright for him to be comfortable going out.

Of course, his only other option was to stay in the ruined house for hours until it got dark, and see if the rats ever showed up. After thinking it over, Blacknail decided he would be fine exploring the city as long as he stayed away from people. Daggerpoint was a maze of shadowy alleys and narrow streets, so it wouldn't be that hard to keep out of sight. Besides, he smelled something delicious and really wanted to taste it.

Blacknail slipped his cloak back on and hopped down to the first floor. After looking around to make sure no one was nearby, he crept carefully outside and into the sunlight. He then decided the first thing he was going to do was find some breakfast. Hopefully, he would stumble across some clue to Herad's location as well. So Blacknail started wandering the alleys and back streets of the city. He saw a few people around, but he kept his distance from them, and they stayed away from him as well. The people of Daggerpoint weren't very friendly.

Once, Blacknail accidently walked past a man covered in rags who was crouched under a ledge without seeing or hearing him. When the man unexpectedly spoke, Blacknail jumped in surprise and dashed away. It wasn't his proudest moment, but that was how Blacknail found himself standing outside the back of a large, colorful building. It was only two stories high, but it was still one of the tallest buildings around. It had a solid stone-and-mortar foundation and was solid wood above that. Unlike all the other buildings around, it seemed in good repair and looked freshly painted. Most importantly, there was a rather interesting aroma wafting down from one of the second-floor windows, and there didn't seem to be anyone nearby.

Intrigued, the hobgoblin gave a quick look around before slipping over to the wall and beginning to scale the outside of the building. His claws found purchase easily enough, and it didn't take him long to reach the window ledge. He hung below it for a few seconds and listened, but he didn't hear movement in the room on the other side.

Reassured, he slowly raised his head over the windowsill and looked within. His first thought was that the room on the other side was rather fancy looking. In fact, it was the fanciest room he had ever seen. The walls were dark red, and luxurious wooden furniture lined the room. A huge, carved wooden canopy bed dominated the center of the chamber. Red curtains hung from the bed's canopy, and it was piled high with ruffled sheets and pillows. However, Blacknail was focused on the wooden stand just on the other side of the window. There was a silver platter and a jug of water on top of it. The delicious aroma he smelled was wafting up from there.

With an eager growl, Blacknail climbed through the window and crept quietly over to the tray of food. He eyed it critically for a second. There looked to be some kind of cheese, slices of red meat in some sort of sauce, and bits of fruit on it.

They all looked tasty, but the cheese smelled so good, he began to drool. He reached for the food with a happy smile on his face, but the smile slipped as he suddenly heard the sound of sheets shifting.

"What's going on here?" a sleepy but smooth voice asked from behind him.

Blacknail jerked back in surprise before quickly pulling his hood down farther and turning away to hide his face. He looked out the corner of his eye toward the source of the unexpected noise. He was just in time to see the mass of blankets and pillows on the bed be thrown aside to reveal the form of a completely naked human female with long dark hair. The sheets slid down her body as she gracefully pushed herself off the bed and stood up, before glaring suspiciously at Blacknail. Much to the hobgoblin's surprise, she didn't betray a single shred of fear at his presence.

Luckily, she didn't appear to have a plate in her hands. The last time Blacknail had surprised a naked woman, she had smashed his nose with a plate. It had hurt a lot.

# Chapter 9

Blacknail stared nervously at the woman who had appeared behind him. She was definitely completely naked... yet she was looking him over without a single hint of fear. The hobgoblin found that to be more than a little unnerving. She was in a room with a cloaked intruder while totally undressed! Why was he the anxious one?

"You're definitely not a customer. You'd never get in the front door; your clothes are too rough looking. My first guess would be a burglar, but who would be stupid enough to rob this place? Maybe you're a fan? Although, that also seems unlikely," she asked with a thoughtful frown.

Blacknail considered drawing his blade and killing her but quickly discarded the idea. She wasn't a physical threat, and the worst she could do was make some noise, which was what was most likely to happen if he did attack. Instead, he snatched up the plate of food and prepared to make his escape. The food was what he was here for anyway.

"Make no sounds, woman. If you make noise before I leave, I'll kill you," Blacknail told the woman as he took a small step back toward the window. He spoke as clearly as he could.

The woman smiled at his remark and stretched herself out provocatively. As she arched her back, her sizeable chest heaved. "Since you apparently came in here without knowing who I am, I'll introduce myself. I'm known as Luphera, and surely you wouldn't want to hurt a harmless woman like me." She pouted playfully.

Blacknail suddenly found himself growing quite uncomfortable. He was feeling things he wasn't used to feeling about humans. There was something so very attractive about the sinuous way this human moved. He wanted to lick her...

Wait, what?! Blacknail shook his head to clear his thoughts. What was he thinking? All humans were pink and fatty. He must still have some of the female goblins' scent on him, and it was confusing him. He took an unconscious sniff of the air in the room, and his nostrils were flooded with a weird flowery scent. As he fought a sudden urge to sneeze, a realization hit him. It wasn't the leftover scent of a female goblin that was confusing him, it was the sweet floral scent! It smelled somewhat similar to a female in heat.

"You've intrigued me, you mysterious stranger. I don't get much in the way of excitement these days, and even for a thief you're oddly covered up. Not to mention your voice is just so chilling. It sent a shiver down my spine," the woman told Blacknail as she hugged herself and shuddered theatrically.

Blacknail froze as he was about to take another step back. Against his will, his eyes were drawn to her trembling body. The dark-haired woman grinned smugly as she noticed his reaction.

"Are you ugly, is that why you cover yourself? You needn't worry. I can assure you I've been with uglier men. I've seen it all: scars, deformities, and pockmarks. You get used to them after a while, so these things don't turn me off. In fact, they can be exciting in their own way. Why don't you put that food down and come over here to amuse me for a while. It's early enough in the morning that we won't be disturbed."

Blacknail was beginning to get a strange headache. He really wanted to stay and stare at this female for a while, yet at the same time, he also felt an overpowering need to jump out the window and flee as quickly as possible. The woman noticed his hesitation.

"No? How rude, you're making me feel unattractive. There must be something you want though, beyond a plate of food. I deal in more than just sex, you know. My clients also come to me for secrets and gossip as well. Maybe we can play a game? I'll answer one of your questions, and then you can answer one of mine," she offered him.

Blacknail found himself nodding, and he wasn't completely sure why. He wanted to find Herad and Saeter, but he suspected it would be very dangerous to stay here. Unfortunately, leaving would require him to take his eyes off the woman.

She smirked at his gesture of acknowledgement, then twirled around and leisurely strolled back over to the bed. Once there, she sat down and leaned back in a relaxed manner with her slender legs tucked up beside her. Blacknail had to bite his tongue to fight the urge to sit down next to her. The scent was really messing with his head.

"Ask your question then," she told him.

Blacknail hesitated for a second before answering. He really wasn't sure this was a good idea.

"Is Herad in-ss this city?" he eventually asked.

The woman raised a finger to her lips and looked thoughtful for a second. "The Black Snake? That's an odd question for a petty thief to ask. You just get more and more mysterious. I can't figure you out, and it's actually rather infuriating. However, since you asked, I'd be more than happy to answer," Luphera told him. "Yes, Herad the Black Snake is in the city. Her arrival a few days ago was big news, and her activities lately have shaken the city. There will be blood in the streets soon, I think."

A cool surge of relief washed through Blacknail, and he broke out into a pleased grin. He hadn't been certain he was even in the right city. For all he knew, there were dozens of human cities in this area. Actually knowing he was so close to his goal removed a weight from his back he hadn't even known he'd been carrying. Plus, the blood-in-the-streets thing sounded fun.

"Oh, it's my turn to ask a question now! Let's see, what should I ask? Well, since you've been terribly discourteous by not introducing yourself to a lady, why don't we start with your name?" Luphera told him with playful disapproval.

The first thing that occurred to Blacknail was he should leave now that he had his answer. The second was he should lie. Yet another part of him didn't want to displease the woman. Besides, he still needed to learn exactly where Herad was. It was becoming a big confusing city full of the weird distracting smells.

"My name is Blacknail," he answered reluctantly.

Luphera let out a deep sigh and collapsed onto her side across the bed. She gave the cloaked hobgoblin a pouty frown.

"That doesn't help me at all. Could you be any more confounding? You're making me so curious! I just can't stand it. Go ahead and ask your second question."

"Where in the city is Herad?" he asked her.

"I don't know. I could get the answer for you of course, but I'd have to get in contact with some of my people. I don't think you want to wait for that," she replied.

Blacknail frowned. If she didn't know where Herad was located, there was no point in sticking around. Now that he knew he was in the right city, he wanted to get right down to finding his mistress. The scent in the air was making him drowsy and really clouding his thinking. He had to leave now, or he didn't know what he would end up doing.

"I'm leaving." He grunted as he spun around and walked over to the window.

He didn't turn back in her direction until he was climbing out. Luphera was giving him a thoughtful look. When she saw him looking, she sat up and smiled at him again, in a way that perfectly exposed her bare chest.

"Must you leave? I'll just die of suspense if you leave me hanging like this. I had such great questions all thought out too! I don't get many unapproved guests, so please feel free to climb back through my window anytime, Blacknail the mysterious. I'll have someone leave a tray of food out, and then we'll continue our little game," she told him with a wink.

"Maybe." Blacknail tore his gaze away from her and forced himself to climb down the side of the building. He immediately found himself wishing he'd said something more interesting, and he wasn't sure why.

Fortunately, the fresh air outside cleared the haze from his head. Once down on the ground, he hastily slipped away down a nearby alley. Right before he was about to turn the corner and head out of sight though, he glanced back to see Luphera standing at her window grinning smugly at him. Her expression reminded the hobgoblin of a cat that had found a mouse to play with. He picked up his pace, if only to counteract the part of him that still wanted to go back and see what would happen.

Once he was safely away from any possible pursuit, Blacknail relaxed and started wandering the city again. It was still light out, so like before, he stayed away from other people. He stuck to the back streets and used his sensitive hearing to make sure no one snuck up on him. Just as he was beginning to despair of ever finding Herad anytime soon, he came upon a familiar scent. It smelled... annoying, or more specifically like Khita. Blacknail smiled; he had never been happier to smell the greasy scent of a human.

Eagerly, the hobgoblin began tracing her trail deeper into the city. As he moved through the winding streets, it soon became apparent she wasn't traveling alone; a man was accompanying her. Blacknail couldn't place him, but he smelled sort of familiar, so he was probably one of Herad's men.

Blacknail pulled his cloak tighter as he followed the trail past a pair of talking men. When he skulked past them, they didn't do more than glance his way. Soon, however, the scent led him out of the back streets and into one of the city's main roads. Blacknail peered around a shadowy corner as he weighed his options. In front of him was a bright street full of people walking and talking amongst themselves. It was lined with stalls, and even a few horse-drawn carts were carefully making their way down it. Of course, this being Daggerpoint, almost everyone Blacknail saw was tough looking and armed to the teeth.

The hobgoblin didn't really want to go out there. Not only would it be much harder to conceal himself while out in the street, but Blacknail was also pretty sure it would be much harder to follow the scent. There were a lot of people, food, and garbage out there. Not to mention the horses, which were horrid stinking beasts. He was also sure to draw unwanted attention to himself if he went around with his nose against the ground. Humans didn't usually do that in his experience.

With a sigh, Blacknail stepped out into the street. He didn't really have a choice; it wasn't like he could stay in the alley all day. If someone saw him, he would just have to run away very quickly or hope they wouldn't care he was a hobgoblin. Of course, every human he had ever met had cared about that quite a lot...

As he clutched his cloak tightly to himself, Blacknail hurried down the street. Khita's scent had been fairly fresh, so he scanned the nearby crowds for her as he walked. A man that was walking by suddenly veered into Blacknail and knocked him aside.

"Out of my way, shorty!" the man said as he walked by.

The hobgoblin was pushed sideways, and almost jumped out of his skin in surprise. He had to fight down his panic and resist the urge to draw his sword. Murdering the man in the middle of the street would probably draw attention, even in Daggerpoint. At least he thought it would...

So Blacknail ignored the rude human and quickly moved on. Besides, the man had somehow managed to drop his coin pouch into Blacknail's hands. As he hurried away, the hobgoblin scanned the crowds. He didn't see Khita or anyone else he knew anywhere, so he hissed in frustration. Who knew Khita could annoy him without even being around?

The crowds were beginning to get to Blacknail and make him feel squeezed from every side. There were so many humans around. Their stench and noise filled the air. It was suffocating. He needed to get away and catch his breath, so he made a break for a nearby alley.

Right before he slipped away, he threw one last look back and froze. There they were! He saw Khita, and What's-His-Face, the bandit. They were across the street looking over some things at a stall. As he watched, they broke away from the stall and headed toward a nearby shop. As Blacknail stepped out to follow them, he noticed a group of five men look up from a booth down the road. They stared after Khita for a few seconds and then moved toward where she'd gone. The hobgoblin's eyes narrowed as he watched them with sudden interest. They were definitely moving like hunters after prey—with eager steps and a coiled focus Blacknail knew well. He was thus willing to bet they weren't friendly. This was a problem. As annoying as Khita was, she was still part of his tribe, thus an attack on her was an insult to him. Plus, if she was killed, he wouldn't be able to trail her back to Herad or kill her himself some day. Blacknail thus needed a plan. Taking out five large fighters was well outside his abilities. He was very dangerous and they seemed like normal stupid humans, but five was still probably too many for him.

Khita and her companion spent the next few minutes

moving from stall to stall and down the street. She had always claimed the city was her natural environment, but Blacknail was unsurprised to see she seemed completely ignorant of the fact that almost half a dozen hostile-looking men were trailing her. Of course, those men were in turn completely unaware they were being stalked in broad daylight through the busy city streets by a hobgoblin, but that wasn't their fault. Blacknail was just amazing at everything.

Suddenly, Khita and her escort headed off the main street and down a back alley. The leader of the thugs barked an order at his minions, and the group split up. The leader took one of his men and rushed ahead, while the last three continued to follow Khita. Blacknail grinned with vicious glee as he watched them separate. This made the odds much better. The hobgoblin stalked after his new prey. His former nervousness faded away and instinct took over as the excitement of the hunt warmed his skin. The mobs of chattering people around him stopped being possible enemies and instead became part of the camouflage that hid him from his quarry. Life was now so simple for him. Nothing else mattered but the chase and its inevitable end. All he had to do was outwit his opponents, and then he would get to taste their sweet blood, metaphorically.

As the three slower moving bandits slipped into the alley, Blacknail was right behind them. He crept along without making a single noise but the quiet beat of his excited heart. He tracked them more by sound than sight as he slipped from shadow to shadow and hid behind trash and the occasional crate. The men didn't seem too concerned about being followed though, because Blacknail never even saw them look backward to spot a tail. They were typical stupid humans who thought they were safe in their city, but they weren't. Blacknail had to stifle a vicious cackle. This was too easy!

As they moved into a particularly dark alley that was surrounded on all sides by tall rough-looking wooden buildings, one of the men fell behind the others a bit. Blacknail sensed an opportunity and made his move. He glided forward and silently closed the distance. As the other two thugs turned a corner, Blacknail descended upon the unsuspecting third man's back. Blacknail's target must have heard or felt something because for a split second he slowed and began to turn his head. That was the wrong thing to do. Before the man even managed to turn around, Blacknail had a dagger against his throat. An unnoticeable moment later, blood poured from the man's neck as Blacknail's blade slid across it. The thug began to choke and stagger as red seeped down his body, but Blacknail wasn't looking. He had already bounded after the other two. He had to kill them before they noticed their herdmate was gone.

The hobgoblin could hear his preys' footsteps, so he knew it was safe to turn the corner. He rushed around it and saw the other two thugs. They were peering ahead as they walked, intent on keeping up with Khita.

"I hope Balstein lets us have some fun with the redhead before we kill her," one of the thugs whispered to the other.

The only reply he got was a stern disapproving look as the other man shushed him. Apparently, they actually thought they were being stealthy or something. Blacknail almost sniggered in amusement at the thought. They were about to learn what being sneaky was really like. It would be a very brief lesson.

The hobgoblin put on a burst of speed and reached out to grab the back of the first man's shirt. The thug jumped in surprise as Blacknail pulled him backward and then rammed a dagger up under his ribs.

"Oh shit, what the hells!" the second thug cursed as his companion staggered forward and fell.

His eyes were wide with alarm, and he reached for the dagger at his side. However, Blacknail was already drawing his sword, and he was faster. The blade came free in one smooth motion, and the hobgoblin immediately violently slashed at the man. His opponent managed to dodge under the blow though and draw his own weapon. Blacknail's second slash was blocked by a hastily raised dagger, so Blacknail stepped forward and kicked the man in the chest. The thug was sent flailing backward and hit the ground hard. Sensing his opportunity, the hobgoblin stepped forward and stomped on the man's hand.

The man shrieked, and the dagger slipped from his grip. Blackanil grinned and hissed savagely as instinct took over. He dropped his weapon and jumped on the thug. As he landed, he grabbed the stunned man, and to make sure he stayed that way, he headbutted him. There was a quiet crack as the hobgbolin's forehead smashed into his opponent's face. The movement also placed Blacknail in just the right position to tear his prey's throat out with his teeth. The man flailed weakly beneath Blacknail as the hobgoblin bit down on the flesh of his neck and tasted the iron of his blood. A few seconds after his prey stopped struggling, Blacknail sat back up and sighed happily as he licked his lips. He had ended up sampling human blood after all. They didn't taste all that good, too fatty, but there was nothing like catching your own food.

Unfortunately, he knew he didn't have time to savor his victory. He had to follow Khita and make sure the two thugs who were left didn't kill her. Blacknail had gotten a good look at the men, and he didn't think odds favored Khita. The bandit leader looked dangerous, and Khita just wasn't. Thus, Blacknail took a quick second to loot the bodies of their weapons and baubles. Then he hurriedly cleaned himself off and restarted his pursuit.

As he caught sight of his tribemates, they came to a stop. Blacknail snuck up closer to get a better look at what was happening. He crouched and hid behind a barrel that was up against one of the nearby dirty alley walls. Up ahead of him, at the other end of the alley, the two other thugs had stepped out from a side street to cut Khita and the other bandit off, and they'd brought reinforcements. They'd somehow managed to find another man and a tall lanky woman to back them up. Blacknail hissed in annoyance. Why did they think they needed so many warriors? As far as these stupid humans knew, they had already outnumbered their prey by quite a bit. Weren't two more fighters kind of overdoing it?

The leader of the thugs had a nasty scar across one eye and looked particularly dangerous. There was an eager gleam in his eyes, that Blacknail didn't like, as he drew his sword and pointed it at Khita and her companion. The hobgoblin's two tribemates drew their own blades in response.

"What do you think you're doing? We're part of Herad's band and under her protection," Khita's companion told them confidently.

"Oh, we know. That's why we're going to kill you. We serve

the Wolf, and Werrick wants your bitch of a leader dead. I figure killing you two is a good start. Besides, no one is going to miss a few grunts. People stumble over the corpses of weak fools in Daggerpoint every day," the scarred man replied.

Then, he lunged forward and slashed at Khita with his sword. The young woman attempted to block the blow but wasn't fast or skilled enough. Her sword was sent flying out of her hands, and she yelped as the blade whirled past her face.

Blacknail hissed in frustration. Even if he thought he was a good enough fighter to turn the odds around, and he wasn't, he was still too far away to reach them in time. Surprise attacks were very different than face-to-face sword fights. He wouldn't be able to get a clear shot with his sling either. There was nothing he could do beyond what he already had. As he watched, two of the other thugs moved to attack Khita's nervous-looking companion. Their leader grinned savagely as he stepped forward to finish the now unarmed young woman off. As his blade slashed toward her, Khita's eyes went wide with fear.

# *Chapter 10*

"Shit!" Khita swore as she threw herself out of the way of the blow at the last second.

She rolled awkwardly over the dirty cobbles of the road but somehow managed to escape unharmed and land in a low crouch. As her attacker delivered a follow-up slash, she scrambled backward, and the blade grazed her shoulder. The wound bled profusely but looked shallow. Khita wasted no time in drawing her daggers and snarling at her attacker. The scarred man apparently wasn't impressed though, because he gave her an amused smirk.

"Ha, what do you think you're going to do with those tiny little—"

Before he could finish, Khita whipped one of her daggers at his chest with an overhand throw, and the startled man had to dodge to one side. It only took him a second to recover, but that was all Khita needed to draw another dagger and put some more distance between them.

Blacknail took advantage of everyone's preoccupation to clamber up the side of the wall beside him. Once up on the roof, he laid low and began to inch his way closer to the fight. If he managed to get closer, maybe he could end the fight with a sneak attack.

Khita's companion was warding off his own attackers with defensive swordplay but was slowly being pushed back. Neither he nor his opponents seemed too eager to close in on each other. Khita threw a glance at her comrade as she took a few more steps back and looked at the empty alley behind her. Her scarred opponent continued grinning smugly and didn't bother chasing her.

"Don't even think about running. I have men positioned to

cut you off the second you try it. You're trapped here," the thugs' leader bragged loudly enough that it echoed down the alley.

He then smiled viciously and looked expectantly at the end of the street. Everyone else followed his gaze as well, including Khita. Several seconds went by... and the man's smile slipped from his face.

"That means you should come out, you bloody idiots!" he shouted in an exasperated tone.

Several more seconds went by as everyone stared toward the end of the alley. No one moved, and the only thing anyone heard was background sounds from the city. Nothing happened, and no one appeared from around the corner of the street. Eventually, the silence was broken by the sound of snickering.

"Are you ever right about anything?" Khita asked the scarred man with a roll of her eyes.

"Shut up and run!" the man who had been fighting beside her said and made a break for it.

Khita took his advice; she quickly threw another dagger at the enemy closest to her and then took off as well. After a brief moment of shock, their attackers gathered their wits and ran after them in pursuit.

"Where in all the hells are the others?" their leader asked sourly as he ran.

None of his men had an answer for him. Blacknail knew, but he obviously wasn't telling.

Instead, the hobgoblin watched the action from his rooftop perch. Unfortunately for Khita, it looked like the tallest of the thugs was a good runner. He was quickly closing the distance between him and his quarry. As the humans ran down below him, Blacknail sighed in frustration. Stupid Khita couldn't even run properly. He wasn't about to let her, or What's-His-Face, die though. Her death would waste all the effort he had already put into saving them. So Blacknail drew his sling and sighted on the fastest of his tribe's enemies. As the weapon's crack filled the air, he ducked out of sight again.

A scream of pain rang out below and was quickly followed by a crashing sound as the man he hit tripped and rolled into a pile of large wooden crates. Blacknail sniggered in amusement from his hiding spot. Humans had such terrible senses...

"Bloody fucking hells!" the hobgoblin heard his target swear between grunts of pain.

It sounded like it hurt a lot, which was good. The tall man's noisy crash had distracted and slowed his fellows as well. The scarred man was livid and red with rage as he turned toward his fallen subordinate.

"You bloody idiot! How'd you manage to trip over yourself? Now we're going to lose them. What's wrong with you morons? First, the others apparently get lost somewhere and now this!" their leader growled angrily.

"I didn't fucking trip, boss. Look at my leg! It's a bloody mess. Something hit me," the downed man replied between labored breaths.

"As if! There's no one here but..."

Blacknail had stopped listening. Once he'd confirmed his tribemates had gotten safely away, he'd rolled over the roof and climbed down the other side of the building. He had to follow Khita and the other man back to their base before they got too far ahead of him, so he dropped back onto the street and raced around the shabby building at the corner. Once he reached the entrance to the side street, he caught their scent again, and he took off after them. He was tired of wandering the city. He wanted to find his master already!

By dashing frantically, and ignoring the stares of the people around him, Blacknail closed the distance enough that he could hear his quarry. Their running footsteps stood out in this quieter part of the city, so Blacknail was able to follow from a street behind. They led him to a large sturdy-looking building located right against the eastern section of the city wall. It formed a compact compound with several smaller buildings that surrounded it. As he closed in, the hobgoblin smelled the scent of familiar people. The rich earthy tones of the forest still clung to some of them. This was definitely the right place.

Blacknail's ears suddenly twitched as the sound of voices he recognized reached them. One of them was just Khita, but the other was definitely Herad. He'd found her! The hobgoblin grinned happily as he realized his long journey was finally over. The sound of the conversation was coming from a nearby window, so he bounced joyfully over to it. Then he looked around to make sure he was unseen and stopped to listen. It was best not to surprise them by entering unannounced.

"... lucky we escaped at all. If I wasn't so good with my knives, they would have had us," Khita said.

"It sounds like you were more than lucky. Both of you should still be back there in that alley, as corpses. It's more than a little odd that their reinforcements didn't show up like that," Saeter replied. Blacknail easily recognized his voice.

"That's not important. I'll have their hides for this! I can't believe those bloody fools dare move so openly against me. This could mean war!" hissed the infuriated voice of Herad.

Blacknail winced and cringed at the anger in her tone. He'd been about to slip into the room and take credit for saving Khita—and that other guy—but now he hesitated. He didn't really want to approach Herad right now. He wasn't, technically, supposed to be in Daggerpoint after all. No one had actually forbidden him, but it didn't sound like Herad was in the mood to argue the point. There was no harm in waiting a bit...

"They must have something planned. This doesn't sound like a subordinate getting out of hand. They wouldn't risk this if they weren't sure of their victory," Saeter explained calmly as Blacknail resumed listening.

"It must be those fuckers Fang and Galive. The rumors that Zelena managed to buy them off must be true. That means Werrick's bitch has turned over half the larger bands against me. They're not afraid of a war because they think they'll win," Herad speculated darkly.

"That would be bad. We've recruited some more men, but not nearly enough to fight so many other bands. We also don't have much in the way of allies among the other chiefs. Several of them wouldn't turn against us, but they also wouldn't fight Werrick for us either," the old scout told her.

"Then I'll have to kill Fang and Galive. That will serve as a message to the others, plus it will be very satisfying. I always hated those pricks," Herad replied.

"Sounds like a great plan, but I don't see how it would ever get done. Both of them are veteran bandit chiefs, so they'll have measures in place against killers. Also, word on the street is the first thing Zelena did when she got here was buy the services of all the best assassins. With all the money she's been throwing around, I doubt you'll be able to turn any of them," Saeter commented.

"I could call them out and cut them down myself." Herad still sounded angry, but now her frustration was clearly perceptible as well.

"I doubt they'd go for that," Saeter remarked dryly. "We probably won't see heads or tails of them until they swarm over us like ants to carrion."

"You're not here to tell me what I can't do, Saeter! Come up with a solution. You must have contacts or something that will help. I brought you here for a reason, not so you could whine!" Herad hissed at him.

"I'll see what I can come up with," Saeter answered stiffly.

Blacknail heard the sound of footsteps as his master left the room. He was fairly confident that now would be a really bad time to approach Herad. He didn't want to wander the city forever though...

So he needed a way to get into her good graces, if they actually existed. There had to be something that would impress her enough she would welcome him and set aside the issue of whether he was really supposed to be in Daggerpoint or not. Only one thing came to mind. He would present her with the severed heads of her enemies. That meant he had to kill the men known as Fang and Galive, or at least one of them anyway. No one could possibly stay upset after receiving such a great present! Herad would love it.

The only problem was he had no idea where to find those men. If wandering the city for the past day had taught him anything, it was that Daggerpoint was a hard place to find specific humans. Threatening random people until they told him what he wanted to know would probably take too long. It would also attract attention, and thus be more than a little dangerous. How else could he find those men though?

Blacknail frowned as a troubling answer occurred to him. He had met one person who apparently knew if people were around. He didn't really want to go back there, but he didn't see any other option. He would have to very careful if he talked to her again.

The hobgoblin sighed and slipped away from his tribe's new home. It took him a while to travel stealthily through the back streets and arrive at his destination. As he stood outside the large building, he eyed the window he'd climbed through earlier warily. Should he just climb through again? Should he leave...?

The tiniest hint of the spicy perfume from his first visit tickled his nose, and his heart quickened. A desire to seek the source of the aroma began pulling him toward the building. Blacknail snorted violently and shook his head in an attempt to clear it. Fortified, he then crept back over to the window and carefully climbed up the face of the wall. Once again, he listened carefully for a minute before entering, but once that was done, he swung himself through the window and landed on the floor.

This time, he made absolutely sure he was alone and carefully scanned the entire room. However, there was no one hidden among the sheets or anywhere else, so he relaxed. The room being empty did present him with another problem though. What was he supposed to do now, wait for Luphera to come back? He had no idea how long that would take; none at all.

He stood in the center of the room for less than a minute before he gave up. If she wasn't going to come to him, then he would have to go find her. Blacknail tiptoed over to the entrance on the far wall of the room and placed his ear up against the door. It was a large building, and he could hear several people moving through it, but none of them seemed to be in the next room. Feeling reassured, he reached out and pulled the door open slightly. Or at least he tried, it didn't actually move.

With an annoyed grimace, the hobgoblin pulled on the doorknob slightly harder. The door still didn't budge. He hissed in annoyance and stared and the polished bronze handle. Was it locked? He gave it another tug before frustration overwhelmed him. He stepped back and growled at the offensive metal protrusion. The urge to smash his way through the door in front of him was getting harder and harder to ignore.

Then, he heard noise from the room on the other side. He froze, and his ears perked up as he listened. Someone was approaching. No, make that two people. He definitely heard two sets of footsteps. A panicky twitch went through him as he instinctively looked around for somewhere to hide. He shook the reaction off though and started planning. Hiding somewhere in the room would be stupid; he needed to talk to Luphera.

Just as he was thinking of her, Blacknail picked up the sound of her voice from the other side of the door. It sounded like she was the closer of the two people to the door. He grinned as he instantly decided on a course of action. With sudden calm, the hobgoblin strolled over to stand behind the door. He would wait to see what Luphera did.

He was momentarily distracted from his scheme as the doorknob turned, and the door opened. He stared at the bronze handle in surprise. So that was the secret to the humans' nefarious goblin-proof door...

"... I have a delightful red wine that I think—" Luphera faltered as the door she was pushing open hit Blacknail's boot and came to an unexpected stop.

She froze, and the hobgoblin could practically smell her hesitation hanging in the air. The woman's black hair cascaded over her face as she slowly peered around the door. Her eyes widened slightly when she saw Blacknail's cloaked form. The hobgoblin smirked beneath his hood and raised a hand to make a shushing gesture. Luphera gave him an annoyed glare then turned back around and addressed the person behind her.

"You know what? Why don't you stay here for a second while I attend to some brief chores. Just make yourself comfortable out here," she said before quickly stepping through the door and closing it shut behind her.

As she moved into the room, the hobgoblin noticed she was wearing clothes this time, although not a lot of them. She wore a flimsy-looking white gown that was almost transparent. It didn't seem very practical or warm, so he wasn't sure why she bothered.

Luphera scowled at Blacknail and then walked over to the bed while motioning for him to follow. Blacknail did as she asked and moved away from the door.

"I can't say I expected you back so soon. I'm honestly not sure if I'm pleased or annoyed. If you're here for more answers, you'll have to be quick and willing to pay my price. I'm currently in the middle of another piece of business, and he's rather handsome," she told Blacknail with a confident smirk, which went right over his head.

"Yes, I want answers to new questions," the hobgoblin replied.

"Oh, so you found Herad did you?" she asked.

"I did. Now I must find two men known as Fang and Galive," he told her.

Her eyes narrowed, and her head tilted in response to his words. She looked thoughtful. "I'm sensing a pattern here. What could you possibly want with the locations of three bandit chiefs? Before I answer your question, I'm afraid I'm going to have to ask you to answer mine."

It was Blacknail's turn to scowl now as he considered his options. Once again though, he didn't seem to have much of a choice. She clearly had the advantage when it came to this game of answers. Should he lie though? The problem with that was he didn't know what an effective lie would even be...

"Very well, I will-ss answer first. I wish to serve Mistress Herad, and so I seek-ss a gift for her. I will give her the men known as Fang and Galive," Blacknail replied.

If she didn't like his answer, he could always jump out the window... or kill her. Maybe it was the flowery scent in the air, but she was looking unusually tasty for a human. Luphera didn't overreact to his answer though; she looked thoughtful. She murmured something to herself before giving him an appraising look. Blacknail relaxed in response.

"You plan on killing two of the local bandit chiefs, by yourself? That won't be easy," she told him.

"They're only human," Blacknail replied with a shrug.

"True enough, I guess. I find it's a common flaw in most the people I meet. Anyway, my time's running short, so I'll answer your question for you. I've never been a fan of either of those butchers anyway. If you manage to kill them, and not before, feel free to return and we'll have another lovely chat," she told him dismissively.

Blacknail grinned at her choice of words. They were more than a little amusing, and he totally agreed. Saeter had told him to always say thanks when someone gave him something, including information, so he did.

"Thank-ss you," hereplied and fell deep into thought. He couldn't understand this woman at all. Usually, humans were very simple creatures. They liked coins, and they didn't like being stabbed. Luphera was more complicated than that though. Her lack of fear confused him. Blacknail also had the distinct impression she had been pleased by how the conversation had gone but was trying not to show it.

After Luphera quickly explained to the hobgoblin how to find both of the men's lairs, Blacknail took his leave. He hopped out the window and quickly climbed down the outside face of the building. This time, he was better able to ignore the draw of the floral scent. The hobgoblin couldn't wait to begin his new hunt. He was going after big game now.

# Chapter 11

Once he was back out on the street, the hobgoblin broke into a jog. He swiftly headed toward the first of the locations Luphera had told him about. The man named Fang apparently lived in the northern part of the city. His lair was atop a place where humans bought drinks. Blacknail had been told it would be easy to find, but full of guards. If they were anything like the other men that lived in the city, then Blacknail doubted they would be much of a problem.

The hobgoblin traveled through the back alleys most of the way to Fang's tavern. Only when he got close to his destination did he emerge from the shadows and walk out onto one of the more crowded main streets. He kept his hood up as he scanned all the nearby buildings. Almost immediately he found what he was looking for.

The left side of the street was dominated by a large building that towered over the rest. It was a huge sprawling structure with two wings that protruded from either side. The central part even had three floors and a wooden balcony. Most of the buildings in the city weren't nearly that tall.

Quite a few people were moving in and out of the front entrance, and a clamor of human voices could be heard from within. Humans apparently liked to yell a lot while they drank their foul poisons, or maybe it was only the louder and stupider humans that drank it? Blacknail had tried alcohol once before and hadn't like it much. It tasted terrible and made him sick.

There was a wooden sign hanging out in front of the building, so Blacknail knew he was in the right place. It had what looked like a long, bloody troll's tooth painted on it. Luphera had told him to look for that symbol. This wasn't a building he could just walk into though. Two of the largest humans he had ever seen stood outside the entrance. They were obviously guards of some sort, because everyone who entered had to stop and speak to them first. Every once in a while, the pair of giants would turn someone away and force them to leave. Blacknail didn't think he could bluff his way past them. There were also too many people around out front for him to try and sneak in. He even saw several humans at windows who were obviously sentries of some sort, and one man who was loitering across the road was already glaring at him suspiciously.

Undaunted, Blacknail started walking down the street until he was out of sight of anyone watching. He briefly scanned the crowd to make sure he wasn't being followed before slipping back into the maze of shadowy alleys that bordered the main streets. He then worked his way around to the rear of his target's base. It wasn't long before he began to notice small patrols of humans wandering around. He could hear their footsteps as they walked back and forth through the alleys. Fang must have sent them out to protect himself, but they were no threat to the hobgoblin. He easily avoided them or hid as they moved past.

There were also several men and women in the windows of the nearby buildings. The way they kept looking around at the streets below identified them as more than casual observers. These sentries were more trouble for Blacknail than the patrols were. The hobgoblin was sneaky, but he wasn't invisible. He marked their positions as he circled the compound and looked for a way in undetected. It took him a while to find one. Whoever had posted the sentries had known what they were doing, but Blacknail knew he could find a flaw in any defense if he looked hard enough. That was especially true for any defense made by mere humans. Blacknail grinned to himself as he watched one of the sentries from around a corner. Most humans weren't nearly as smart as they thought they were.

After a few minutes of searching, the hobgoblin managed to sneak right under the nose of the sentry. The woman was watching the street from a second-floor window, so Blacknail slipped through the front door of her house and then right out the back. His ears and nose had told him there'd only been the one person in the house.

Blacknail crept past the smaller buildings as he moved toward the largest structure. He'd been told Fang lived on the top floor of it. The hobgoblin moved slowly enough that he could hear anyone before they saw him. He had to be super sneaky now; there were a lot of men wandering around the area. It would be bad if he stumbled into them.

When he got to the central building, the first thing he did was find an empty second-floor window. Then he hid himself behind a row of barrels in the alley directly below it. Once he was out of sight, he closed his eyes and began to concentrate on listening. A multitude of voices echoed through the building, but almost all of them were in the large room on the first floor just past the front entrance. The second floor was much quieter, with only the occasional noise as someone spoke or boards creaked under people's feet as they moved. The third floor was utterly silent as far as Blacknail could tell. That was good. The hobgoblin felt a wave of hungry excitement surge from within. He couldn't have asked for a better setup.

He waited for several minutes before making his move. He had to be sure no one was looking his way or near a window before he started scaling the wall to get inside. He was aiming for a second-floor window because climbing all the way to the third floor would leave him exposed to watchers. None of the surrounding buildings were taller than two stories.

It was easy enough for him to quickly scramble up the side of the building and pull himself through the window and onto the second floor. Once he was inside the empty hallway on the other side of the window, he crouched down and listened again. He still didn't hear anyone nearby, so he got up and began to look for a way up to the third floor. He exited the hallway and walked into some sort of wide eating room full of tables, chairs, and other furniture. Most of the room was dark and smelled strongly of many different types of food. None of the scents were fresh though, and after a brief exploration, Blacknail didn't find anything worth eating. Reluctantly, the hobgoblin stopped looking for a snack and went back to work. He would have to get a bite to eat when he was done.

As he crossed the room, he heard the creaking of

floorboards, so he dashed off to one side and hid himself under a nearby table. Moments later, a smaller man walked briskly through the room and disappeared through the far door. When the man was gone, Blacknail crawled out from under the table and resumed his search for the way up. He found it several minutes later. Off to one side of the building, there was a staircase that led upward. Blacknail smirked eagerly as he carefully crept up the stairs and toward his target.

At the top of the stairs there was a door. Blacknail stopped and stared at it for a moment before tentatively reaching out and grasping the doorknob. First, he tried to push it. That didn't work, so next he gave the door a slight pull. When that didn't work either, his stomach turned nervously. He only had one more idea to try... Blacknail held his breath as he attempted to twist the handle. There was a muted click, and he almost jumped out of his skin in alarm as the door slid open slightly. He froze and listened, in case someone had heard something, before sliding through the doorway. He couldn't help chuckling quietly to himself as he moved. He'd successfully defeated the clever human lock! Had there ever been a smarter hobgoblin than him? He doubted it.

Expensive furniture lined the small room on the other side. It didn't seem as nice as the pieces in Luphera's chamber though, or as organized. Some of the furniture clearly didn't match, even if it all looked fancy. There certainly was a lot of it though. The walls were even covered in pictures drawn on rectangles of various sizes.

Blacknail walked up to one of the pictures and examined one. He had seen similar things before but never really had an opportunity to look at one closely. This one seemed to be of a man's face. It was really quite realistic. Blacknail had no idea how humans made things like this. Was it some sort of magic? The hobgoblin reached out and gently poked the portrait. He was somewhat relieved when his finger hit the flat canvas. For a second there, he'd almost been afraid there was a real person in there or something. That would have been awkward.

With his curiosity satisfied, Blacknail moved away and explored the room. There was only one other door in the chamber, and after failing to find anything worth collecting, he went over to examine it. He grinned confidently as he turned the door's handle, but nothing happened. The handle wouldn't turn. Blacknail hissed angrily as he clenched his teeth. Why wouldn't it turn? The stupid thing must be broken...

As he went to try and give the handle another twist, he noticed a tiny hole in the door above it. He stared at it for a second before realizing it reminded him of the locks he had seen on chests. The door required a key! No wonder he couldn't open it. Apparently, the stuff on the other side of this door was super important because it not only required one of the turning puzzle locks but a key as well. Blacknail thought that was overkill and more than a little unfair. He'd had a key once, but he'd given it to Saeter. How was he going to get past this door now? Fang's room undoubtedly lay on the other side of it.

He was about to try shoving random stuff into the keyhole when he heard the sound of footsteps on the stairs behind him. Blacknail stepped away from the door and frantically searched the room for someplace to hide.

Should he hide behind the chair? No, too visible. What about in the chest? No, too uncomfortable. The thud of footsteps grew closer until it reached the top of the stairs. Blacknail had no more time to waste, so he quickly threw himself behind a long, padded sofa. He really hoped whoever was coming up the stairs didn't look too closely in his direction. The sofa's cushions didn't go all the way down, so his feet were visible underneath it.

The wide-eyed hobgoblin peeked out from his hiding spot as the stairway door opened. An older-looking human woman in a long, plain dress and shirt stepped out with a pile of clothes in her hands. As Blacknail watched, she crossed the floor and reached the other door. She pulled a key out from her pocket, and there was a click as she unlocked the door. She pushed through and disappeared inside, but she left the door open behind her. Blacknail smirked excitedly as he rose from his hiding spot and crept over to the now open door. He looked through to make sure the woman was out of sight and then slipped through as well. Problem solved!

The room on the other side was pretty much the same as the last one. There was a lot of furniture and paintings. Blacknail didn't have a lot of time to look around though, as he soon heard the woman coming back. He hurried into a small, dark side room as she passed, and then he heard the door to the stairway shut behind her and the click of it being locked. It seemed like he wouldn't be leaving the same way he'd come in...

Blacknail didn't hear or smell anyone nearby, so he began to carefully explore the suite. He found a few trinkets and shinies someone had forgotten, so he picked them up so they wouldn't get lost. There were several more rooms as well, including a bedroom, but they didn't contain anything that was interesting or edible. They were also all empty; Fang wasn't here. That was a problem. This was supposed to be his lair, but that didn't mean he was always here. Obviously, he left it sometimes. Blacknail sighed; he really should have thought of that earlier...

Oh, well. There was no other option but to wait for the man to come back. What was he going to do in the meantime though? He should probably find somewhere to hide. There weren't a lot of comfortable places he could hide for a long period of time, so after a brief search, Blacknail chose to conceal himself under the bed. The sheets that fell over the sides of the frame would conceal him, and as a bonus, he could lie down on the floor. It was actually quite comfy. However, after a few minutes Blacknail began to grow bored. How long was this going to take? He gave a quiet yawn as he shifted around to get more comfortable. The entire bed had been placed over a rug, so the floor wasn't too hard. Blacknail closed his eyes as he let out a deep breath and relaxed. He probably shouldn't let himself fall asleep...

Blacknail was awakened by the sound of a door being slammed shut. As he blinked the sleep from his eyes, he heard a pair of loud voices.

"Make sure I know the instant Zelena's message arrives. When we move to take Herad out, I plan on being right out front. That crazy hag has been a pain in my side for too long. How arrogant do you have to be to just move south and claim the best territory around as your own exclusive little playground?" the first, deeper voice said.

"You'd have to have an ogre-sized ego to think it would work, boss. That's for sure," the other man replied.

"Well, the Black Snake is about to be cut down to size, because soon her ugly head is going to be decorating my mantle. Zelena's bought the cooperation, or at least the approval, of practically every chief in town. Only that pompous fool the governor objects, and he's just worried about not being able to play us off against each other anymore," the voice that Blacknail was sure belonged to Fang said.

The hobgoblin ground his teeth as he listened. How dare they insult the chief of his tribe! So what if Herad was ugly? All humans were, they were pink! What a stupid color for skin to be. Green was so much better. Blacknail also knew Herad wasn't crazy, she was one of the sanest people he'd had ever met. It was the rest of the humans who were weird...

"Very true, boss. There's no way she can stand against you and your allies." The other man sounded like a suck-up.

"She'll be outnumbered five to one, and she's the only Vessel in her pathetic little band. Including me and that assassin of Zelena's, we'll have at least five. Herad will be dead by the end of the week, and then all that nice territory she's claimed will be mine!" Fang exclaimed excitedly.

"As well as whatever treasures she's hoarded away at her base."

Under the bed, Blacknail went rigid with surprise. Fang was a Slosher! That complicated things. Vessels, or Sloshers, were stronger and faster than normal people due to the potions they drank. Blacknail didn't know much about them other than that magic was involved.

"True, although I don't imagine it's any great prize," Fang told the other man. "That's enough of this useless talk. Go downstairs and send one of the wenches up, make it the new blonde. I'm feeling like a good romp."

"Yes, sir. Sure thing," his subordinate replied before heading back down the stairs.

Blacknail's target was now alone on the third floor. The hobgoblin under the bed grinned with eager anticipation as he plotted the man's murder. This was going perfectly and would be so much fun! Since Fang was a Slosher, the safest plan was probably to wait until he fell asleep and slit his throat. However, that would involve a lot of waiting, and Blacknail had already had a nice long nap. He really didn't want to fight a Slosher though. If he was anywhere near as dangerous as Herad, he would be very unlikely to win.

So Blacknail waited and listened as the man named Fang wandered around the apartment. After a few minutes, he walked over to the bed and sat down. His feet dangled and swayed right in front of Blacknail's face. Then, a shirt hit the floor as the man started getting undressed. The shirt was soon followed by a pair of pants. As the trousers landed, there was a whirring noise and several golden coins rolled out. Blacknail's eyes watched them intently as they rolled. They were so shiny...

He wanted to grab one, or more than one, but he knew it would be a dumb thing to do. Fang might be looking. As the hobgoblin watched, one of the coins rolled under the bed before falling over. Excitedly, Blacknail reached out and grabbed it. He smiled happily as he stared at its gleaming golden sides.

"Damn, bloody things," Fang suddenly swore. The bed then creaked as the man leaned over and began picking the coins up. Blacknail held his breath and started fervently hoping the man couldn't count.

The hobgoblin had no such luck. After he was done picking up the other coins, Fang got off the bed and dropped to his knees. He reached over and lifted the edge of the sheets up so he could look under the bed. The hobgoblin and the man stared at each other for a second. Neither of them said anything. Blacknail's hood wasn't up, so Fang got a good look at the hobgoblin's green, angular, and very inhuman face.

# *Chapter 12*

"Gods! What in all the hells..." the man whispered as his eyes went wide with shock.

Blacknail flashed the man a toothy smile and then stabbed him in the face with his knife. Surprise was still on his side! Fang screamed as the blade sliced into his cheek. He clutched his face and tried to back away from the bed. Blacknail didn't let him; he grabbed the man's hair and pulled him back down.

Blacknail had forgotten Fang was a Slosher though, and very strong. The entire bed flipped as the man pulled the hobgoblin out from under it and into the air. The violent motion wrenched Blacknail's arm, and he hissed in pain as his shoulder made an unpleasant grinding noise. This wasn't going the way he'd planned.

The hobgoblin swung through the air as Fang roared in pain. Blacknail tried to right himself using his feet but just ended up kicking Fang in the face several times. The large man snarled viciously and tried to reach over and grab Blacknail's neck with one hand. The hobgoblin let him, and then he stabbed the man again. Stabbing things seemed to solve most of his problems.

His knife gouged into Fang's shoulder and nicked his neck. The bandit chief roared in pain again and threw Blacknail across the room. Blood from Fang's wounds flew through the air as the hobgoblin smashed into a wall and slid to the floor. Ow, why did humans have to be so big and strong?

"Gods! What the fuck are you, a demon? Have the hells opened up for me?" Fang cursed as he staggered and tried to stand straight.

Blood poured from the cut on his neck. He was clutching it tightly with his hands, but that barely slowed the crimson flow. That was bad for him but good for Blacknail. The hobgoblin didn't feel much better though. Every bone in his body hurt, and the impact with the wall had knocked the air from him, explosively. However, the first rule of a challenge was not to show weakness.

"Yes, I'm a demon! Tonight-ss you die," Blacknail hissed dramatically in his scariest voice, which was actually just his normal voice.

The hobgoblin pulled himself off the ground. He was unsteady on his feet and wobbled a little, but he managed to start walking over to his target.

"Fuck you!"

Fang was injured and in his underwear, but he was still a Slosher. He looked around the room for something to use as a weapon. There was a vase on a nearby stand, so the man grabbed it and threw it at his attacker. Blacknail slid out of the way of the porcelain projectile and continued to close the distance. Fang picked up the wooden stand itself and hurled that. This time, one of its legs nicked Blacknail's shoulder. He stumbled slightly and winced. There was no real damage though, beyond another bruise.

Fang took this time to reach down with his one free hand and grab his pants from off the floor. Blacknail grinned with savage amusement. What was he planning to do with those? His smile slipped though when the man managed to fumble through the trousers and pull out a small dagger. Blacknail would have been more concerned, but Fang's eyes were starting to look unfocused, and he'd grown very pale. Still, it was better not to take any risks. Blacknail tucked his own knife away and drew his sword instead.

Fang grimaced in anger and frustration as the hobgoblin approached. Blacknail raised his sword and slashed down at the man. Fang raised an arm defensively and tried to block with his dagger, but Blacknail was too fast for him. The sword cut into the man's arm, and then Blackanil kicked him in the knee. There was a crunching noise as Fang collapsed onto his side. He shrieked in pain, and blood sprayed from his arm. The hobgoblin didn't give him time to recover. He mercilessly began hacking and slashing at the fallen man until Fang's struggling ceased and he went limp.

Blacknail only stopped when the gory mess at his feet was clearly a corpse. Then he lined the blade up just right… and cut the man's head off. Then he tried again because it hadn't quite come off right the first time.

When the head was completely severed, Blacknail gave it a brief shake to get some of the blood out and wrapped it in a sheet from the bed. He was interrupted from his work by the rather loud sound of the door at the top of the stairs exploding inward. Almost immediately after that, he heard the sound of hurried footsteps.

"Horse reek," Blacknail swore and stuffed his grisly trophy into his backpack.

The hobgoblin pulled his hood up and sheathed his sword. He knew he only had seconds before he would be mobbed by a horde of very large and very angry humans, so he dashed toward the nearest window. He had no idea what was outside of it, but it had to be better for his health than staying here would be.

It had gotten dark out while Blacknail had been napping. The hobgoblin grabbed the window frame and used it to swing around. Luckily for him, the exterior wall had a ridge he could grab. He used that to pull himself out of sight of anyone inside, and he began scrambling down the side of the building. Below him was one of the grimy alleys that lay beside the tavern. There didn't seem to be anyone there at the moment, but Blacknail could hear swearing and yelling from the room he had left. He was willing to bet people would soon pour out of Fang's lair and flood the streets.

The climb down wasn't easy or fast, even for the hobgoblin. He couldn't go straight down because parts of the wall were too smooth to grip. Instead, he had to carefully feel his way around and scramble sideways to find footholds as he descended feet first. He disliked how long this was taking; he didn't have a lot of time to spare.

The first story of the building was smaller than the others and recessed, so Blacknail had to jump down. His injured shoulder flared with pain as he landed on the ground. The hobgoblin grunted and began running away as fast as he could. He could hear humans all around him, several of which seemed dangerously close by, so he dashed into a nearby alley that sounded empty. Behind him, all the windows of Fang's lair started glowing brightly one by one as his men woke up and tried to respond to the turmoil around them. Angry shouts and cries of alarm began to fill the air.

As Blacknail desperately tried to flee through the now dark city streets, he hissed in pain. His pace slowed as his ankle began to hurt. He tried to fight past the pain, but his foot also felt weaker and unsteady when he put weight on it. He lurched sideways and limped into a small alley as he heard a group of humans approach from ahead. The tight pathway was free of debris and clutter. This made traversing it easier, but it also meant there was nothing to hide behind, and that mattered. The sound of footsteps echoed behind Blacknail as a mob of humans hurried his way.

There was no way the hobgoblin could outrun them, so he looked around for anything that would help him escape or hide. There was nothing on the ground, so he looked higher up. He hissed in annoyance as he noticed the large overhangs on the low roofs that bordered the alley. There was no way he could quickly get over them and onto the rooftops.

The sound of pursuit grew closer, and as Blacknail began to panic, an idea suddenly occurred to him. He sprinted toward the nearest wall and ran up it. His ankle flared with pain, but he disregarded it; he wanted to live. Using his momentum, he jumped up off the wall and grabbed the overhanging roof. Grunting with effort, Blacknail pulled himself up under the roof and against the wall. There were wooden supports along the wall he could hold on to.

He hung there as a dozen thugs suddenly burst into the alley. They had torches that burned away at the shadows that encircled them. Together, the mob of humans hurried down the alley. Thankfully, since the path was straight and empty, they didn't seem to be looking around too much, and the light from the torches didn't reach into the dark recesses of the overhanging roof. Blacknail was tucked away in those shadows as he watched the men pass below him. If anyone looked his way, they would have seen his eyes reflecting the light. No one looked though.

The wounded hobgoblin let out a deep breath of relief as his pursuers turned the corner and disappeared out of sight. That had been close; if humans weren't so blind and stupid, he might have been caught there. There was no way a hobgoblin, or any animal really, would have missed the smell of blood in the air.

He didn't hear anyone else close by, so Blacknail let himself drop back down to the ground. He then hurried back onto the street and away. Several times he was almost caught by groups of searching thugs, but he always managed to slip away at the last minute. There didn't seem to be any pattern or cooperation among the human search parties. They all appeared be running around randomly.

Eventually, Blacknail got far enough away that he left the search parties behind, and the city grew quiet. Once free of pursuit, he slowed down and began hobbling through the dark city toward Herad's residence. He would be safe when he got there and could lie down for a while...

He definitely wasn't going after the other bandit chief anytime soon. This hadn't been an experience he wanted to repeat. If only that ugly human bastard hadn't dropped those coins! It seemed unfair that Blacknail's perfect plan could be ruined by something so random. Herad would just have to be happy knowing Fang was dead and having his bloody head as proof. Two heads probably wouldn't fit in Blacknail's bag anyway.

The hobgoblin trudged through the dark and empty city streets for several minutes before he got to his destination. As he approached the front of Herad's lair, Blacknail saw two men standing guard outside. Light shone from a window beside them and illuminated the lair's yard. The bored-looking lookout glanced his way as the cloaked hobgoblin drew nearer. Blacknail caught a whiff of their scent and was very relieved that one of them smelled familiar. He was far too exhausted to try and sneak in right now.

"Halt, who goes there?" the first man asked as he placed a hand on the sword at his side.

"Me," Blacknail replied unhelpfully. He was too tired to say more, not to mention he was feeling rather cranky.

"Who?" the man asked suspiciously.

"I'm Blacknail."

"What the hells? The hobgoblin? I'll believe that when the gods reveal it. Ha, there's no way a hobgoblin could be wandering around the city!" the first man replied.

"I can if I want to," the hobgoblin replied as he pulled his hood down and glared at the man.

His eyes shone with barely suppressed anger and frustration. Both men took a surprised step away from him. The second man went pale as the moon and threw his partner a questioning look. After Blacknail was finished talking to Herad, he was going to smack these idiots. He began walking past the guards and up to the door of the building.

"Hey, you can't just go in there!"

"I can if I want to. I'm here to see mistress Herad. Get in my way, and I'll gut you like a rabbit," the hobgoblin hissed and marched past the guards.

They didn't try to stop him; they just stood aside and watched without moving. The dried splatters of blood all across his face might have had something to do with it. When Blacknail was safely past, the unfamiliar-smelling one turned to the other.

"That's not a real hobgoblin, is it? I mean, I heard some of the other guys talking, but I thought they were joking!" he said nervously.

"He was green, you idiot. Of course he's a hobgoblin; no human has ever had chompers like those, that's for damn sure!" the other man replied.

Blacknail flipped his hood back up and made his way inside. The room there was plain, and several people were sitting at a table playing cards. Their reactions to Blacknail's sudden presence varied, but every one of them looked surprised. That was amusing, but none of them were Saeter or Herad, so the hobgoblin kept moving. Behind him, several men pushed their chairs back and got to their feet as an anxious-sounding conversation broke out.

Blacknail could hear Herad's voice from deeper within the building. He followed it through the bare corridors. As he walked, everyone he saw moved out of his way without a word. Moments later, he stood outside a closed door. One of Herad's personal guards stood beside it. The sound of conversation between the bandit chief and several of her minions could clearly be heard from within.

"... It's suicide to try and fight them all. My men and I joined your band because it sounded like you had a sweet setup down south. We didn't agree to fight all of Daggerpoint for you!" a deep-voiced man was yelling.

"You swore to follow me, so you don't have a choice," Herad replied with frosty calm.

Herad still sounded more than a little angry, but Blacknail was too tired and sore to care. He was also willing to bet his present would cheer her up.

"Open the door," the hobgoblin hissed to the guard. The man flinched as Blacknail's voice issued forth from under his hood. He looked startled for a second, but then relaxed as a look of comprehension came over his face.

"Saeter's hobgoblin? What the hells are you doing here?" he asked.

Blacknail sighed in frustration. Why were most humans all so stupid? His reason for being here was really obvious. "Open the door-ss. I'm here to see Herad."

"She doesn't want to be disturbed. She told me not to open the door for anything short of an attack," the guard replied.

"I understand-ss. I could stab you a few times if you want-ss," Blacknail offered helpfully.

"Ha, no thanks. You don't scare me, you runt. I'll let you in though. If you piss the boss off, it will be on your head, not mine," he replied with a confident smile and stepped aside.

The hobgoblin gave him an annoyed look, but said nothing as he moved forward and politely knocked on the door. The argument going on inside subsided.

"Come in," Herad called out from within.

Blacknail took a second to remove the severed head from his backpack. It was still wrapped up, but the cloth was now completely soaked through with blood. The man standing beside Blacknail stared in revulsion at the object in the hobgoblin's hands.

The door swung open as Blacknail pushed it open and stepped through it. There was a soft thud when the doors hit the walls behind them. The spacious room on the other side had only one small window and was thus mostly illuminated by a black iron chandelier that held a dozen bright white candles. A large, square wooden table stood beneath the chandelier in the center of the room. The light from the candles revealed several people sitting around the table but left the rest of the room in shadow.

Herad, of course, was seated at the far end of the table in the largest chair. Saeter was sitting to her right. Blacknail threw them both confident looks as he walked in. Muted whispering broke out as the people around the table took in his cloaked form. Saeter, of course, recognized him immediately and frowned in concern. Herad raised an eyebrow in surprise as she gazed at him and noticed the bloody object in his hands.

"You're dripping on my floor, Blacknail," she told him with apparent calm.

"Sorry, mistress," he replied as he walked past the table and approached her.

Blacknail wasn't fooled by her voice. He knew she was angry at him, and getting angrier. A subtle clue was how she was stroking her sword hilt. He had best get right to the point. As the hobgoblin came to a halt in front of her, Herad leaned forward and addressed him.

"What are you doing here? I don't remember giving you permission to do that, hobgoblin. I also seriously doubt Red Dog sent you; that wouldn't be much like him," she whispered as she glared at Blacknail with her icy blue eyes.

"I wanted to serve, mistress. I heard there was something you wanted, so I went to get it for you. It's a present," Blacknail quickly explained. The corner of Herad's mouth twitched as the hobgoblin finished speaking. She turned and looked at the bloody object that dangled from his hand.

"That's your present? This had better be good, hobgoblin. Otherwise, you'll regret coming here, briefly," Herad told him.

Blacknail hurriedly pulled the cloth off and held up the severed head within by its hair. There were gasps around the table as everyone took in the sight. Fang's face was splattered with blood and loose strands of hair were stuck to it. His skin had gone corpse white, and his jaw hung loosely, so his mouth gaped open. Most disturbingly, his dead eyes stared forward unblinkingly. The hobgoblin's mistress looked at it with disgust. Blacknail realized he had better explain. She probably didn't recognize the man.

"For you, mistress. I give you the head of the man named Fang," he hissed dramatically.

# *Chapter 13*

The entire room went silent. Herad's mouth went slightly slack, and her eyes widened the tiniest bit. She stared in surprise at the severed head for several seconds. Blacknail really hoped it was a good type of surprise. The suspense was actually painful.

"By all that is holy and all that is profane, it is him," she whispered.

Nope, that didn't help. The hobgoblin still couldn't tell if Herad was pleased or not. Maybe she needed a reminder of why she had wanted Fang dead in the first place. "I killed him; he was fat, and you didn't like him."

As the anxious hobgoblin watched, a savage grin suddenly sprung into existence on Herad's lips. Her eyes began to gleam with excitement. Blacknail let out a breath of relief. He couldn't keep a happy smile from appearing on his lips, and he felt like dancing with joy. The chief was pleased by his gift. Truly, he was a genius. His plan was working perfectly!

"Why don't any of you bring me gifts like this?" Herad said with a laugh and an amused glance towards Saeter and the others around the table.

From under his hood, the happy hobgoblin grinned smugly at all the seated people. He was the chief's favorite! Blacknail threw the cloth onto the table and then put his trophy down on top of it. He'd carried the thing far enough already, and it was Herad's now anyway. He hoped she was going to put it somewhere it would look nice.

In the light of the chandelier hanging overhead, Blacknail could clearly see the other people around the table throwing disbelieving looks at him and the severed head. A few of them had even gone pale, and one looked like he was about to be sick.

They began chatting and whispering amongst themselves again, and the sound of their hushed voices echoed around the dark corners of the room. Saeter stood up to address his boss.

"I should go have a talk with Blacknail and get a report from him somewhere more private," he told her.

A thoughtful look appeared on Herad's face, and she glanced at the other men at the table. She then took another look at Blacknail and nodded. "Agreed. Take him to see Mahedium. He looks more than a little worse for wear."

"As you wish," Saeter replied emotionlessly.

He wasted no time in grabbing the hobgoblin's shoulder, and immediately began dragging him from the room. Blacknail was surprised at his master's sudden action. He wanted to stay and gloat some more. Everyone had been so surprised when he'd unwrapped Herad's gift! No one was going to look down on him now, and he wanted to make sure all the new recruits at the table knew his new status. He was better than them!

The sound of Herad's raised voice could be heard from behind them as she resumed her previous conversation with the other people at the table. The voices were quieter though, and unlike when he'd first entered, Herad now seemed to have control of the conversation.

Once they were out of the room and down the hallway where there was no one else around, Saeter turned to Blacknail. The hobgoblin grinned at his master proudly, but Saeter scowled back at him.

"Fool," the old scout said as he smacked the hobgoblin across the side of his head.

"Ow!" Blacknail rubbed the sore spot and cringed.

"What do you think you're doing? Look at you, you're half dead! If you were just going to wander around and pick fights, then you should have stayed at the camp."

"I won!" Blacknail whined.

"This time! What about the next time though? I have no idea how, or why, you pulled this stupid trick off. You wouldn't have if you'd stopped to think for a second though! Now that you've acted as Herad's personal assassin once, she's going to expect you to do it again!" Saeter told Blacknail angrily.

"Oh, that's not-ss good," Blacknail remarked hesitantly as he thought it through.

"Of course it's not! I hope you had fun getting the crap kicked out of you, because Daggerpoint is stuffed full of killers and Sloshers who hate Herad. So congratulations, you've just volunteered to fight every single one of them," Saeter explained scornfully.

The hobgoblin licked his lips nervously. This sounded like it was going to be a serious problem. He'd definitely not enjoyed fighting the man named Fang. Well, actually he'd had lots of fun sneaking around and cutting Fang up, but that didn't make up for the beating the bandit chief had given him. He still hurt in places he hadn't even known existed before.

"I'm too injured?" Blacknail tentatively offered as an excuse.

"Ha, as if she'll care. Herad has her own problems to deal with, and now she has a solution in you. How much do you think she'll care about your injuries?"

"Not at all..." the hobgoblin said with a sigh.

"Exactly, you idiot. Let's hope we can get you patched up quickly, although judging by the way your limping, I doubt that will happen. Here, lean on me; you shouldn't be putting weight on that ankle," his master told Blacknail.

"I'm fine-ss; I can walk," Blacknail replied with a stubborn tone.

"Don't make me smack you again, boy," Saeter threatened as he raised a hand.

Blacknail winced and hissed in annoyance, but when his master extended an arm, he took it. As they continued walking down the hallway, Blacknail leaned on Saeter's shoulder. Soon, they arrived outside a heavy wooden door. Without bothering to knock, Saeter pushed the door open and strode inside. Immediately after entering, the hobgoblin knew he was in Mahedium's new workshop. Everything about this room strongly reminded Blacknail of the mage's room back at the camp. Glass beakers of colorful liquids were scattered around an otherwise sparse chamber. More than a few crystals could be seen as well. They were either floating in some of the glasses or placed on shelves beside piles of books and delicate-looking pieces of equipment.

Mahedium was seated at a desk across the room and

scribbling something on some papers. He looked up at them as they entered the chamber. A scowl appeared on his face when he saw Saeter, but it disappeared when he saw Blacknail. His eyes shone with interest as he looked the hobgoblin over.

"Blacknail? I didn't know you'd joined us," he remarked cheerfully.

"I got an injured hobgoblin here, mage. You think you can patch him up? He looks like someone thrashed him until he was black and blue... and green," Saeter asked the mage.

Mahedium got up from the desk and met them in the center of the room. He didn't even look at Saeter and instead focused completely on Blacknail. "I'll have to examine him first, and then hope hobgoblins react to drugs in a similar way to humans."

"You don't have healing magic?" Saeter asked.

"No, I don't; for a lot of reasons. I used to belong to the Fiery Eye. They are not a mage guild that worries about healing too much, and even if they were, there's no way I would have gotten my hands on any healing spells. Healers are highly trained specialists, and they're treated much better than combat mages," Mahedium replied with a frown as he leaned over and examined Blacknail's bruised neck.

"I should have figured," Saeter responded grumpily.

"Let's get him into the light where I can get a better look at him. Over there on that chair should serve our purpose," Mahedium remarked.

Saeter guided Blacknail toward the seat Mahedium had indicated and then placed him gently down, while Mahedium wandered the room and gathered a few things from the shelves. A few minutes later, the mage returned and stared thoughtfully at Blacknail. He touched a crystal on a nearby desk, and it flared to life. This new light made it much easier to see.

"Hmmm, how do you feel, Blacknail? You definitely looked unsteady earlier. Are you suffering from nausea or a headache as well?" he asked the hobgoblin.

"My head-ss hurts, but what's nausea?" Blacknail replied in confusion.

"Er, does your stomach hurt?" the mage clarified.

"My everything hurts," the hobgoblin whined in response.

"Fine... but does it feel like you're going to vomit?" Mahedium asked him.

Why couldn't the man have asked that in the first place? All these annoying questions were making Blacknail think, and thinking was making his headache worse.

"No, I'm hungry though," Blacknail remarked hopefully.

"You're always hungry. Sometimes I think you're half pig," Saeter told the hobgoblin with a smile.

"That's probably a good sign; an appetite is a sign of health," Mahedium mused aloud before turning to Saeter.

"Please hold his left and then right eye open for me while I check something," he asked the scout in a businesslike manner, as he reached into one of his pockets and withdrew something.

Blacknail tried to squirm away as his master grabbed his head and proceeded to pry one of his eyes open. He was still feeling weak though, so even raising his arms took an effort. Ouch, what the hells were they trying to do to him?

"Hold still, you silly runt, that's an order," Saeter barked as he tried to keep his hold on the hobgoblin.

Reluctantly, Blacknail relaxed and stopped struggling. It hadn't really been doing him much good anyway. Saeter was also unusually strong right now for some reason. He must have been eating well recently. Mahedium reached into his pocket and pulled out a tiny crystal that was barely bigger than his fingertip and held it up to Blacknail's face. The hobgoblin tried to blink but couldn't because Saeter was still holding his eyelid up.

"I thought you weren't going to use magic," Saeter remarked suspiciously.

"This is just a light crystal," the mage replied.

As Blacknail stared at the mana stone, it suddenly burst to life. He instinctively tried to flinch away, but Saeter was still gripping him tightly. He relaxed a second later when he realized the light wasn't really all that bright and didn't actually hurt his eyes.

In fact, the crystal was more than a little interesting to look at. He had never stared right at one while it was lit before. There was a tiny speck in the very middle that seemed brighter than the other parts.

"His reaction seems fine as well, so I don't think he's suffered a dangerous head injury," Mahedium observed aloud and pocketed the crystal again.

After seeing the mage was finished, Saeter let go of Blacknail. The hobgoblin shook himself and started blinking frantically to moisten his dry eyes. Meanwhile, the mage stood up and frowned at Blacknail with concern.

"What's the matter now?" Saeter grumbled impatiently.

"He's a hobgoblin," Mahedium answered as he looked off to the side in a distracted manner.

"I had noticed that, since a while back actually," the old scout replied scornfully.

"Hmm yes, most people would. He also has obvious external injuries, but trying to figure out which herbs to apply is... an interesting challenge. He might not react the same way a human would, so I've chosen one of my more innoxious mixtures," the mage explained carefully.

"So apply it. Standing around and scowling isn't going to change anything," Saeter replied.

Mahedium gave the older man an irritated look but then got to work. Together, he and Saeter stripped Blacknail of most of his clothes. They then examined his wounds. The hobgoblin had only a few shallow cuts, but several rather impressive purple bruises decorated his skin.

"Huh, some of these are obviously at least a few days old." Mahedium began applying a sweet-smelling paste to Blacknail's wounds, which numbed and cooled his skin. It was rather nice feeling, and soon the tension leaked from his body as he leaned back into the chair.

"What's in that stuff? It doesn't smell like anything I would use," Saeter remarked.

"It's White Duff, Clegorvein, and ground Scalewood bark," Mahedium responded.

"Why are you using that crap? None of that has any real strength to it," Saeter asked him.

"I've been a master apothecary for almost a decade. I think I know which compounds to use," the mage replied as he scowled with indignation.

"Apparently not, because I might not have a fancy title, but

I've been treating wounds since before you were born. So I know..." Saeter countered as the two men fell into an argument.

The argument went on for several minutes, and both of them grew louder and more belligerent as time went on. It continued even after they had finished bandaging his wounds. Blacknail wasn't paying attention though. Despite the increasing noise levels, he was starting to fall asleep.

Blacknail was still drifting back and forth across the black borders of consciousness when the argument ended. Thus, he barely noticed when Mahedium collected a small sample of his blood from one of his wounds. Saeter also noticed, and quickly turned toward the mage with an angry expression on his face.

"What do you think you're doing with that? What possible use could you have for his blood?" Saeter loudly demanded of the mage.

The harsh sound of his voice woke Blacknail. The hobgoblin opened his eyes to see his master and Mahedium glaring hostilely at each other. So nothing much had changed.

"I simply want to run some tests on it. Hopefully, I can use it to discover whether goblin blood will react differently than human blood to several chemicals. That way, I can be reasonably sure they'll be safe to use on Blacknail. Why do you care?" Mahedium answered confrontationally.

"Even a complete fool knows better than to let a mage take their blood! You could use it to place him under your power," Saeter responded.

"Then you definitely know as much as a complete fool. Even if those peasant superstitions are true, and I have no idea if they are, then do you really think that's the sort of thing the guilds would teach combat mages? No, of course it isn't! So why don't you just be quiet and let me work," Mahedium said with a glare at the old scout.

Saeter opened his mouth as if to respond but then stopped and seemed to think better of it. He appeared to think something over for a second before he spoke again. "Fine, do as you will. I'm watching you though."

Mahedium snorted dismissively and walked away to the other side of the room. Once there, he started going through his equipment and picking stuff out. Meanwhile, Saeter turned back to Blacknail.

"How are you feeling?" his master asked as he waved his hand in front of the hobgoblin's face.

"Sleepy. I want-ss to nap," Blacknail replied before yawning.

As he drowsily watched Saeter's hand move in front of his face, he felt a strange urge to snap at it. It kind of looked like a bird or something. He didn't actually try and bite it though; that would have involved getting up out of the chair.

"You can stay awake for a few minutes, you lazy runt. I have some questions that need answering. It's important."

Blacknail failed to respond, and his eyes slipped shut again. Saeter got his attention with a smack to the side of his head. The hobgoblin sprang awake as a new source of pain flared into existence above his ear.

"Ow! I'm injured," Blacknail whined.

"You're too tough for your own good, so you'll survive. Now are you going to answer my questions, or do you need another smack?" Saeter said.

"I'll answer." Blacknail rubbed the side of his head. What was the question again?

"Good, so I'm guessing you slipped away from camp and followed us here. What took you so long?" Saeter asked him.

The hobgoblin considered the question for a second; it was a long story. Where to even start? Also, how could he tell it so that it would make him look the best? An impatient look appeared on Saeter's face as Blacknail tried to figure out what to say.

"I got attacked by a hobgoblin and had to rest," he blurted out as Saeter raised a hand to hit him again.

"Explain," Saeter said as his eyes narrowed with interest.

"I was following-ss you when you went past the bushy place. A nasty, huge hobgoblin with impressive horns then jumped out and attacked me! He had lots and lots-ss of goblins with him, and they all tried to kill me. I kicked and bit them all though and managed to fight them off by myself. I then killed the hobgoblin and became the new chief. Since I was injured by the cheating, no-good hobgoblin's lucky hit, I decided to stay there awhile and rest," Blacknail explained.

"Sounds like quite the adventure... if any of it's true. How did you get to the city?" the old scout asked doubtfully.

His master didn't seem to believe Blacknail was telling the truth for some reason. It was kind of insulting. He was just leaving some stuff out... and maybe exaggerating a little.

"I asked for directions, twice." Blacknail shrugged. It hadn't been a big deal or anything.

"What, how? Nevermind, I'll probably sleep better at night if I don't know the details," Seater remarked. "How did you end up killing Fang though? He was a blowhard but still a Slosher. How did you even know he was Herad's enemy or where to find him?"

"I listened to Herad yell at some people, she was very loud," Blacknail explained.

"Ha, yes she is that. It probably wasn't all that hard to find us since all you had to do was follow the sound of her constant screaming," Saeter said with a chuckle.

Blacknail's eyelids were heavy, and he didn't feel up to correcting Saeter, so he gave his master a brief nod. He also didn't want any part of insulting Herad. It was probably a good idea to change the topic of their conversation. "I found Fang by playing a guessing game with a weird naked lady."

There was silence. The smile on Saeter's face grew strained, and one of his eyes twitched. Across the room, Mahedium broke out into a fit of coughing. Had Blacknail said something wrong?

"You didn't um... murder this woman, did you?" Saeter asked apprehensively.

"Nope, we just traded answers to questions. Do you usually kill people during guessing games?" Blacknail asked with interest.

"No, I don't usually play them. Just in general, it's a bad idea to kill people, okay?" Saeter replied.

"Why? You do it all the time, and so does Herad."

There was another amused snort from Mahedium. Saeter closed his eyes and massaged his forehead with his fingertips. Blacknail thought he looked a little upset.

"Ugh, I just realized Red Dog may have had a point after all. This is my fault as much as yours. I should have taught you about morals and civilized behavior. I guess I just never expected you to leave the woods," Saeter remarked.

"The round things you put stuff in?" Blacknail asked in

confusion.

“No, those are barrels. Morals are very different,” Saeter explained with a sigh.

The sound of steps echoed from the doorway, so Blacknail twisted around to see who was approaching. The doorway was soon darkened by the redheaded form of Khita. The hobgoblin groaned when he saw her. Why did it have to be her? She was incredibly annoying, and he was stuck in this chair, so he couldn’t even escape! He already regretted saving her.

“Blacknail, I heard that you’d shown up! Everyone was talking about the small, creepy cloaked guy who killed that bastard Fang and then presented his bloody head to Herad. How sharp is that! When they mentioned the assassin had disappeared with Saeter, I knew for sure it must have been you,” she exclaimed happily with a cheerful grin on her face.

“Blacknail is injured so don’t get too close, and you can’t stay long,” Saeter told the young woman. The hobgoblin threw his master a grateful look, and Saeter gave him a knowing smile. Mahedium also responded from across the room.

“Oh, quite right. Keep at least a few feet away please, and no touching the patient,” the mage told Khita distractedly. He seemed engrossed in studying something at his desk.

“Sure thing, I got stuff to do anyway. I’m super useful, so Herad keeps me pretty busy,” Khita responded with undaunted cheer.

“You deliver messages,” Saeter replied dryly.

“That’s important. What if someone tried to steal the message? I would have to fight them off. In fact, I got into a fight earlier today, so ha!” Khita stabbed the air with a make-believe knife.

“That had nothing to do with a message, they attacked you because... You know what? Nevermind,” Saeter said with obvious frustration.

“Anyway, I wanted to tell you that you killing Fang was the sharpest thing I’ve ever heard of by far. I mean come on, you brought his bleeding head to Herad in the middle of a meeting! How awesome is that!” she told the hobgoblin.

“Does she know what morals are?” Blacknail asked curiously while glancing at the still-smiling Khita.

"I seriously doubt it," Saeter responded as he grimaced.

"Who does then?" Blacknail inquired. Now he kind of wanted to know more.

Saeter sighed and rubbed his forehead again. He suddenly seemed more than a little tired, and his forehead had become creased by wrinkles. "You know what? Forget I said anything. Just try to kill as few people as possible, okay?"

"Advice to live by, unless you're an assassin, of course," Khita interjected.

"Sure," Blacknail replied to his master happily. He never killed anyone he didn't have to anyway. Why would he? That would be a lot of work, and more than a little silly.

# *Chapter 14*

All of a sudden, there was a gasp of surprise from where Mahedium was working, and then the mage began madly scribbling away and sorting through a pile of papers. Everyone looked over his way at the unexpected noise.

"Ha, I can't believe my luck," Mahedium exclaimed as he worked.

"Made a discovery, have you? Perhaps Highwart plant is a goblin love potion or something?" Saeter asked with a roll of his eyes.

The mage didn't bother answering or even appear to hear the other man. He just started chuckling to himself as he stared at Blacknail's blood sample. Saeter scowled and looked worried.

"I think our mage has lost it," the old scout remarked.

Even Blacknail found the mage's behavior more than a little odd. The hobgoblin got excited over blood sometimes, but only when it was fresher and there was a lot more of it.

"He needs to stop sniffing his own herbs, if you know what I mean," Khita said.

Blacknail had no idea what she meant. Saeter apparently did though, because the corner of his mouth curled up into something that sort of resembled a grin. Mahedium ignored Khita and turned to Saeter.

"I've made an incredibly exciting find. It has nothing to do with herbs though. After the surprise revelation that Varhs's pet goblin had the mage spark, I decided to run some tests on Blacknail's blood just in case, and I just found something," he announced with obvious excitement. The young mage was practically vibrating with enthusiasm. In one hand, he held up a small vial of purple liquid.

"Oh, is goblin blood like deadly poison or secretly magical?"

Khita remarked.

"No, that's idiotic. Stay silent while the grownups are talking, please," Mahedium replied irritably.

"What did you find?" Saeter asked curiously, as Khita glared at Mahedium.

"Before I say anything, I want to be absolutely sure I'm right, so I need to perform a few more quick tests." The mage gathered several things from his desk.

Once Mahedium had what he wanted, he hurried over to where Blacknail was sitting. The hobgoblin eyed him warily. He was fairly sure he didn't want the mage running any more tests or performing any weird magic on him. The eye test from earlier had been uncomfortable enough.

"Open your mouth, please. Normally, I'd just take a hair sample. Since you don't have much in the way of hair though, I'm going to have to take a look at your teeth," Mahedium told Blacknail.

The mage raised his hands in front of Blacknail's face and waited expectantly. The hobgoblin met the mage's gaze and gave him a dubious stare. The man couldn't seriously be planning on shoving his hands in between Blacknail's jaws, could he?

"I don't want your fatty human hands in my mouth. They'll taste bad." Blacknail stuck out his tongue in disgust.

"I keep my hands very clean, and I just washed them," Mahedium responded.

"You're still human and oily," the hobgoblin muttered.

"Just get it over with, Blacknail. I'll get you a treat right after," Saeter told him impatiently. The hobgoblin sighed but did as he was told. Maybe he could convince his master to get him one of those meat pies from earlier...

Mahedium raised his tiny light crystal up to Blacknail's mouth. As it flared to life, he raised a small knife and began to carefully poke and prod around the hobgoblin's teeth. It was more than a little annoying, and Blacknail gave Mahedium an irritated look. As he had suspected, the man's fingers tasted horrible, like old sweat.

"Huh, I expected them to be dirtier. You actually keep your teeth fairly clean," the mage commented as he worked.

Blacknail's eyes narrowed. Why wouldn't his mouth be clean? It was humans that were weird and smelly.

"I know it's tempting, but don't bite him," Saeter told Blacknail.

This comment flew over Mahedium's head, and a few seconds later, the mage withdrew his hand and smiled proudly to himself. Blacknail shut his mouth and rubbed his jaw. Holding it open like that had been kind of painful.

"I was right! An elemental test of his blood revealed traces of crystal integration, and just now I discovered his teeth show subtle signs of fairly recent crystallization," Mahedium announced.

"So he's a mage too, like that other goblin, Scamp?" Saeter replied warily.

He didn't seem too happy at the idea, which kind of hurt Blacknail's feelings. Hadn't he earned his master's trust yet? The hobgoblin wouldn't mind becoming a mage. There were so many things he wanted to blow up! It would be glorious.

"No, that's not indicative of the evidence I found. If he were a mage, he wouldn't show the secondary signs such as crystallization of the teeth. Not to mention, I tested him for that not too long ago and found nothing. He's also not a mutant, for obvious reasons. So by process of elimination, we can conclude that Blacknail is actually a dormant Vessel," Mahedium explained happily.

"Hey, that's what I said; his blood's magical," Khita muttered as she glared angrily at the mage. No one bothered to respond to her.

Blacknail sighed in disappointment. So he wasn't a mage, and he wouldn't get to start blowing things up with magic. At least he was a Vessel thingy though. That made him super strong or something, right?

"How's that possible? He's never shown any signs of that, and he's certainly never taken any Elixir," Saeter asked with a voice full of doubt as he crossed his arms in front of himself.

"I don't know how he was initially exposed to some form of Elixir, but at some point he undoubtedly was. As to him not showing any signs of being a Vessel, well the answer to that is obvious. He hasn't had any Elixir to fuel himself, so the ability is now completely dormant," the mage replied.

"So it's utterly useless, since we have no way of getting him Elixir or even knowing what the right type is," Saeter pointed out with more than a little evident relief.

"Maybe... I'd like to run a few more tests, and there's someone in town that I may be able to consult with. It might be technically possible to find the correct formula," Mahedium replied thoughtfully.

"Well, good luck with that. Just don't be expecting to draw too much more of Blacknail's blood. With the way things are going, he's going to need it right where it is. If you want to play around with a Vessel's blood, feel free to ask Herad though," Saeter told the mage.

"I have as of yet not decided on the proper time or method of asking Herad for a blood sample..."

"And that's why you're still alive," Saeter told him. His remark caused Khita to chuckle, which earned her a glare from Mahedium. Blacknail wasn't quite sure what was going on, so he decided to ask.

"What does me being a Vessel mean?" he asked the others.

"Nothing really, don't worry about it," Saeter replied.

"It means if you find this one type of magic potion then it will give you magical powers, and you won't die, or explode, or anything," Khita added

"Good, that's good," Blacknail mused aloud. He really wanted magic of his own, and he definitely didn't want to explode. It sounded like he needed to find this Elixir stuff.

"There's absolutely no way to find the right Elixir though. That'd be like finding a diamond in the sea," Saeter told the hobgoblin.

"That's not completely true. I just finished telling you that I may know of someone who could help," Mahedium argued.

"Fine, you do what you want. If you manage to find anything then tell us, but don't expect any help looking. Also, if you tell Herad about any of this nonsense, then I'll make sure you regret it for the rest of your life," Saeter warned the mage. "Thanks to Blacknail's recent idiocy, she already has enough weird notions in her head about using him. If you tell her about this—"

Blacknail poked him urgently on the shoulder, and he threw

the hobgoblin a confused glance. Blacknail's eyes were wide with concern. He hadn't noticed it at first because he'd been distracted by the conversation, but now he definitely heard the sound of familiar footsteps approaching.

"Ah, Saeter, you're so predictable sometimes. I knew you'd try to keep the hobgoblin away from me," Herad said as she walked through the doorway and into the room. "I'm sorry if I'm intruding, but the things you were just saying sound so intriguing. I'm having weird notions, am I? We'll have to talk about that later. Right now though, I want my mage to tell me more about the rather interesting conversation you were all having."

There was a rather nasty-looking grin on her face that was directed Saeter's way, and from under her dark bangs, her eyes gleamed with furious excitement. Blacknail winced in apprehension and took a step away from Saeter. His master should have kept his big mouth shut.

"Fuck." Saeter grunted quietly before turning around and facing his boss.

"Explain, now," Herad commanded Mahedium.

"Right, of course," the mage stuttered in reply. "As you undoubtedly heard just now, after running some tests on Blacknail's blood, I discovered that some time ago he must have ingested a sample of Elixir. Obviously, he managed to survive the transformation into a Vessel, but he hasn't been showing any signs..."

Herad cut him off with an annoyed glare and wave of her hand. "I heard that part, and I don't much care. I don't need another Vessel, I need access to Elixir for myself. Get to the part where you mentioned knowing someone that might be able to supply you with some," she told him with a disdainful sneer.

Mahedium opened his mouth as if to talk but then closed it again. His forehead grew creased and he seemed reluctant to speak. Herad made an irritated growling noise, and he flinched before finally answering. "Since my arrival in Daggerpoint, I've been making inquiries about any other rogue mages that might be in the city. Most of the leads I've found were... dead ends, unfortunately. None of the mages in this city are very knowledgeable about the magic they flaunt. They're the lowest sort of combat mage with not a true scholar among them."

As the mage talked, Saeter's eyes flickered toward the exit. He looked to be considering trying to slip away while Herad was distracted. Blacknail didn't blame him.

"Even the market for spell stones and Elixirs is very limited and expensive. It contains nothing but the occasional piece of loot taken off a corpse. I highly suspect most of the crystals get purchased and then returned unused to the market when their owner is murdered," Mahedium continued.

"But you said you found someone," Herad pointed out impatiently.

"Yes, there was one merchant who seems to have a steady source of several Elixers, including Braxwells and Whitestrom. He refused to even discuss where he got it at first, but I was... persistent. Eventually, I managed to get him to deliver a message to his supplier. I only got a short reply back, but it was enough to confirm my suspicions that someone in town is creating the Elixir. They've agreed to meet with me in order to facilitate an exchange of knowledge," the mage concluded.

"Tricky..." Saeter remarked softly.

"Yet more than worth a little risk. A reliable source of Elixir could change the odds against us completely," Herad added with a hostile glare at Saeter.

Blacknail blinked in surprise at Herad's reaction to Saeter. The hobgoblin was more than a little surprised she hadn't sheathed a few of her knives into his master's chest already. She seemed really focused on getting her hands on this Elixir stuff. He almost thought he detected the tiniest bit of sour-smelling desperation from her...

"True, but that doesn't mean we should run right into this. Anyone with a monopoly on such a lucrative trade isn't going to just give it up and is more than likely working with one of the other chiefs. It's probably a trap," Saeter replied as he frowned in concern.

"Obviously, it could be a trap. I don't need you to tell me that, Saeter. We'll just have to take precautions and turn it back on them if they're stupid enough to try something," Herad told him scornfully.

Blacknail smiled as he listened. He thought that sounded

fun. The idea of the hunter becoming the hunted amused him.

"When and where's this meeting supposed to take place," Saeter asked Mahedium.

"Two days from now at a residence in the Central District of the city. I'm allowed to come armed and bring one companion."

"You agreed to enter a location of their choosing with only one man for backup? I honestly thought you were smarter than that, Mahedium! This magic stuff sure makes idiots out of people," Saeter told him.

"I'm not stupid, Saeter. They're allowing me to bring my gear, and I'm a combat mage. I'll have someone with me to watch my back and enough magic at my disposal to level a small building. Besides, meeting in a public place wouldn't do me any good. I'll be visiting their lab. We'll need equipment and resources in order to accomplish anything."

"What if they take you by surprise?" Saeter asked.

"I'll just have to make sure that doesn't happen. You're worrying too much anyway. I'll be going to the Inner City which is neutral territory. If they cause a disturbance there, it will draw the attention of the governor," Mahedium responded.

"Ha, I have way more experience with this city than you, boy. The governor and his men may enforce peace within the center of this snake pit, but they're powerless outside of it without the backing of the band leaders. They also don't care about murder, just that it doesn't happen on the streets," Blacknail's master countered scornfully.

"It's worth the risk, Saeter. You've said enough, don't you think? So shut your toothy trap," Herad ordered the old scout before turning to the mage. "Who were you planning on taking with you, Mahedium?"

"Yesterday I couldn't have told you, but just now I decided on taking Blacknail," Mahedium replied.

"Absolutely not!" Saeter barked immediately. Herad threw him a dark look, and the old scout took a step back. He looked like he really regretted speaking.

"It's not up to you, so be quiet. Blacknail is no longer your servant," Herad told him coldly before turning to Blacknail. "It's up the hobgoblin himself, and me. You're both my minions."

Blacknail froze as everyone looked his way. Uh oh, this

wasn't good. He really didn't like being in the middle of a fight between Herad and Saeter. No matter which side he chose, it wouldn't be good for him. Why couldn't everyone get along?

"I had intended his presence to serve several purposes. You mentioned that I should be concerned about being taken by surprise. I think we can agree that's unlikely to happen if Blacknail is with me. They will be unprepared for the superior senses of a hobgoblin," Mahedium reasoned.

Saeter scowled and grunted vaguely in response. Blacknail, however, grinned happily to himself. Mahedium was right; hobgoblins were both superior and more sensible than humans.

"If they have good intentions, and we can come to a deal, then Blacknail will also serve as a test of their skill. If they can make an Elixir for him, they can undoubtedly make one for Herad as well," Mahedium explained to Saeter.

"You could just take a blood sample with you," Saeter told him.

"I thought you didn't want me taking any more samples from Blacknail," Mahedium replied scornfully.

"Blacknail will go with Mahedium, and he'll even get a pay raise for volunteering... to reflect his increased usefulness," Herad said with a meaningful look at Blacknail.

The hobgoblin gave her a confused look before realizing what she wanted a second later. Oh well, surely Saeter wouldn't blame him since Herad was giving him an order, sort of. He kind of wanted to go anyway. From what he had heard, this might be his best shot of getting some magic of his own. That would be so useful...

"I'll go with Mahedium-ss. I'll fill these men with fear and stab the people who try to hurt him," Blacknail told Herad with an enthusiastic nod of his head.

Saeter scowled grumpily at the hobgoblin's reply, but he didn't say anything. Herad threw a smug grin his way. She seemed to take a lot of pleasure from gloating over Saeter.

"I'll go too. I'm also great at stabbing people," Khita added from where she was standing off to one side.

"You'll be staying here, safely out of the way," Herad told the younger woman without even looking at her.

"But—"

Blacknail kicked Khita in the back of the knee. She stumbled and glared with narrowed eyes at the hobgoblin, but he didn't care. She seriously didn't know when to stop talking. You didn't argue with Herad; you shut up and did as she told you. She was the chief.

"It's settled then. Mahedium will take Blacknail, and together they'll enter this rogue mage's laboratory. I'll prepare a squad of men that will wait nearby. If there's trouble, then Mahedium will signal us using magic," Herad told everyone.

"Thank you for your support in this, Mistress Herad," the mage remarked with subtle bow. "I predict this endeavor will benefit us both greatly. As for a signal, I could always aim a force blast upward. That should make a lot of noise and throw quite a bit of debris into the air. It would be hard to miss."

"What could go wrong?" Saeter muttered grouchily as he glanced at Herad's turned back.

# *Chapter 15*

The din of human masses going about their daily business filled Blacknail's ears. The sky was cloudy overhead as he and Mahedium made their way down one of the city's main streets. Several days had passed since the hobgoblin had rejoined Herad's band. He'd spent most of that time lying around, healing, and stuffing his face full of delicious new foods. Eventually though, he'd been ordered to accompany Mahedium on this outing.

Crowds of bustling people were everywhere, so Blacknail wore his long, dark brown cloak. With the hood up, it completely concealed his form and prevented him from drawing unwanted attention. Mahedium was dressed up to impress. He wore a set of fine clothes, including a red shirt with long, loose sleeves. He had also shaved and gotten a haircut, which made him look much different than the disheveled and distracted man he usually seemed to be. Most importantly, he wore several pouches around his waist and was carrying his staff. Even though everyone on the street was armed, and half of them were thieves and killers, no one bothered the pair. Mahedium was obviously a mage, and thus the local thugs and pickpockets were unwilling to tangle with him.

The crowds grew thinner as they neared the Central Quarter of the city. The border was obvious in the daytime, but Blacknail had only ever been here at night before. Not only were the houses larger and better maintained, but there were far less people on the streets.

There were also guards. Several men with helmets and steel breastplates watched everyone who passed. Their choice of equipment made them stand out. Heavy metal armor wasn't popular with most of the other humans in the city, probably because it made it harder to run away. The guards weren't stopping anyone from passing into the Central Quarter, but only a few people were even trying. Blacknail noticed that the shiny men got a lot of hostile looks from other people on the street. However, even though they were badly outnumbered by the nearby crowds, no one tried to start anything with them. Obviously, the guards weren't very popular, but they were respected warriors nonetheless.

"Those are the governor's men, and we're entering his territory. He allows anyone entry, but they have to obey his rules. Mostly, they involve keeping the streets orderly and clear. Stick by me, and don't draw attention to us," the mage told the hobgoblin as he pointed toward the guards.

Blacknail gave the mage an annoyed glare. That had been his plan anyway. He had obviously been behaving himself the entire way here, so why did Mahedium feel the need to mention it? Humans, other than his master, just really liked to hear themselves talk.

As they crossed the border, Mahedium started to look nervous. He was very obviously staring at the guards out of the corner of his eye, and he'd grown twitchy. Blacknail, on the other hand, strolled casually by; he didn't see a reason to be nervous. There were already plenty of humans around, and these were just a few more. He was right; nothing happened. The mage and the hobgoblin made it past the governor's men unimpeded.

As they headed deeper into the inner part of the city, the houses and buildings began to get larger and fancier. There were noticeably less people out and about as well. The humans here were better dressed, but the occasional group of thugs and miscreants still could be seen wandering around. The crowds were also quieter. There was a lot less shouting and yelling. As Blacknail observed the surroundings, a patrol of half a dozen guards came down the street. These ones had spears, but that was the only real difference.

"We should be near the right place. Keep a lookout for any signs that mention our destination," Mahedium told the hobgoblin as they walked.

"I can't do the reading thing," Blacknail pointed out.

"Ah, of course you can't. I should have realized that; you've obviously never had a chance to learn. Maybe I'll teach you the basics sometime," Mahedium replied as he looked around.

Blacknail snorted. Why would he want to learn to read anyway? All his time was spent doing chores and learning useful things, like cooking and sword fighting. There were so many things he had to practice already. Reading seemed useless to him anyway; he would be better off burning books for warmth or clubbing people over the head with them.

"Ah, there it is." Mahedium pointed to a building up ahead of them. It was a large mansion surrounded by a wrought iron fence. The inner section of the city was where all the larger and better maintained homes were located, which in Daggerpoint simply meant they were more than one story and weren't in immediate danger of falling down.

This home, however, looked to be in good repair. There wasn't a single shingle missing from the roof. The only obvious flaw was that the grounds were overgrown, but the fact it had grounds at all was impressive. Most the other buildings had a large patch of mud out front. The yard behind the iron fence had several large trees scattered across it. A long, wild-looking row of hedges ran along the path that led from the gate to the front door of the residence. There were also a few overgrown flower beds full of weeds. All the unkempt greenery cast a lot of shadows in the afternoon sun and gave the building a sinister air.

Blacknail barely gave the house and yard a second glance though; his attention was focused on the large, rough-looking man standing on the other side of the gate. He had a sword at his hip and a mean look in his eyes that reminded Blacknail of the more dangerous bandits from Herad's band. The man was without a doubt an experienced killer, and not one of the governor's men. The hobgoblin eyed the man carefully as he and the mage approached, and he couldn't help but growl softly. The fact that such a human was being used as a guard made him more than a little uneasy. The owner of the house wasn't messing around when it came to security.

The guard wasn't looking their way, but Blacknail wasn't fooled. He could tell by the man's posture and movements that he'd noticed the two of them approaching. The man was good... not great, but still good. Mahedium didn't seem to notice Blacknail's concern because he walked right up to the man and announced himself.

"I'm Mahedium Loggart, and I have an appointment with your master. As per the agreement, I have come armed and with one escort," the mage declared confidently.

The guard gave Mahedium and Blacknail a brief look-over. His stare was intense but also indifferent at the same time. Blacknail had to stifle another growl; the man's condescending attitude raised his hackles. However, without a word, the guard unlocked the gate and threw it open.

"Enter," he told them emotionlessly.

Mahedium hesitated, and an uneasy look flashed across his face. He was clearly thrown a little off-balance by the guard's attitude. After a few seconds though, he unfroze and walked through the gate. The hobgoblin shadowed him closely while keeping careful watch on the guard. He already didn't like this place.

"He certainly wasn't a cheery fellow. The master of this abode should really consider getting some friendlier staff. There's something to be said for basic courtesy after all," the mage muttered as he walked up the path to the house. "Why would anyone want such inhuman thugs around?"

Blacknail met Mahedium's gaze.

The mage blinked and stared at the hobgoblin for a second before sighing. "Right, nevermind."

The hedge loomed to their right as they approached the end of the path. When they got to the entrance, Mahedium knocked politely on the massive wooden double doors. Almost immediately, they began to swing open. The mage looked nervously through the entranceway. Another guard, similar to the first one, stood on the other side and had opened the doors.

"Please take a seat," he told them before stepping aside.

The room on the other side was huge and dark. It was two stories tall and large enough to fit dozens of people. A pair of staircases ran up the walls on either side of the room and led to the second floor. The windows were few in number, however, and had curtains on them that blocked the light. As a result, the corners of the room were dim and shadowy.

Mahedium threw Blacknail a nervous glance, but the hobgoblin just shrugged. The mage had been the one that had wanted to come here, and hobgoblins could see in the dark. With another sigh, Mahedium stepped into the house.

"A flair for the dramatic is pretty common in mages, but this seems like overkill, even to me," he muttered to himself.

Plush red furniture lined the room, including several couches and chairs, so Mahedium headed for the nearest seat and sat down. Blacknail sat down beside him in a chair that was as comfy as it was ornate and red. As he was settling down, a casual breath brought an unexpected scent with it. The building smelled of human blood. Not just one person either but many different humans.

Blacknail was unsure of what to make of it, so he decided to ask. The hobgoblin casually leaned over toward his companion and whispered in his ear. "It smells of human-ss blood here. Many different people-ss."

Mahedium looked rather uncomfortable and wary of having Blacknail so close, but after the hobgoblin finished speaking, his eyes narrowed and he frowned uneasily. He appeared to be thinking something over.

"It's probably nothing. Don't worry about it," the mage replied after a few seconds.

Blacknail shrugged and sat back down in his chair. He could tell the mage wasn't being entirely forthcoming and was concerned about something, but Blacknail didn't really care. It was probably some pointless human thing anyway.

After a few minutes of waiting for something to happen, Mahedium began to scowl impatiently, and Blacknail grew bored. The hobgoblin could only amuse himself by examining the contents of the room for so long. The guard by the door was particularly boring, as all he did was stare straight ahead. The hobgoblin was tempted to throw something at him just to see what would happen. He doubted Mahedium would approve though.

Blacknail shifted restlessly in his seat. At least the chair he was sitting in was very comfy. As he moved, the plush cushions made him spring up into the air slightly. He smiled at the unusual sensation, and did it again on purpose. Soon, the bored hobgoblin was bouncing up and down on the chair and snickering to himself in amusement. The chair was so soft and springy! He needed to find a chair like this to borrow when no one was using it. Blacknail's antics finally caused the man by the door to turn toward the visitors. He began scowling at the hobgoblin in annoyance and with more than a little disbelief. Mahedium noticed as well.

"Stop that, it's impolite. Just sit still," he whispered to Blacknail.

The hobgoblin sighed but did as he'd been told. It had been getting old anyway. Once Blacknail had settled down, they only had to wait a few more minutes for their host to arrive. A set of doors across the room were thrown open, and two men stepped out. The first was an older man, even older than Saeter. He wore immaculate black clothing with silver lining, was bald, and sported a neatly trimmed white beard. His face was wrinkled with age, but his eyes were sharp and his movements swift and full of purpose. Behind him came another man who looked to be another one of the house's guards. Like the others, he was a large man with a cold focused stare. He also wore the same black and gray uniform. Blacknail could tell by the warrior's body language that he was subordinate to the white-haired elder.

The pair quickly crossed the floor of the room and drew near their guests. Mahedium politely rose to meet them, and Blacknail followed suit, mostly because it made it easier for him to fight or flee. As Mahedium stepped forward, the hobgoblin fell in behind him in mimicry of the old man's guard. By doing so, he made his role obvious and was thus much more likely to be overlooked.

"Welcome, you must be Mahedium. Thank you for waiting. I simply had some other business I had to attend to. I'm known as Master Avorlus, and that is how you may address me," the older man told the mage. He reached out and extended a white gloved hand. After a second of hesitation, Mahedium extended his own arm and they shook hands.

"Ah, it's a pleasure to meet you, Master Avorlus. Pardon me, but you must be the mage I corresponded with then?"

Mahedium asked respectfully.

"Indeed, I am. I must say that I'm also glad to meet you. It's been a while since I've had an opportunity to converse with a colleague. Rogue mages with an interest in thaumaturgic research are very rare. The guilds are usually very successful in weeding us out, and of course, they're not the only ones who benefit from monopolizing magical knowledge," Avorlus said with a smile that didn't quite reach his eyes.

Mahedium's eyes narrowed slightly at the other man's words and tone. They were more than a little suspicious, and Blacknail was sure he detected a hint of threat in them.

"Yes, well, I'm a skilled combat mage with quite a few powerful crystals at my disposal. I could show them to you if you'd like. I was also very lucky in coming across Mistress Herad and in being allowed to join her band. In fact, she expressed interest in this visit herself and wanted me to tell her all about it as soon as I got back," Mahedium replied dryly.

"Well then, I'd better be on my best behavior. I'd hate for her to think badly of me," the older man said with a faint smile.

Blacknail didn't like the older man's grin. He looked like he knew some secret joke no one else was aware of. The hobgoblin hated not getting a joke. He also didn't like what the body language of the old man's guard was telling him. The huge thug's face was calm and unreadable, but his posture betrayed his contempt for his master's guests. Yet the bodyguard also looked ready to act at anytime, as if he expected a fight of some sort to break out.

"I feel like sitting," Avorlus suddenly remarked.

He snapped his fingers and pointed to a small nearby table. Instantly, the guard by the door hurried over and picked the table up. He rushed over and put it down in front of the older man. Avorlus then pointed to a nearby chair, and the guard brought that over as well.

Mahedium nodded and both mages sat down across from each other at the table. Avorlus's guard took up position standing behind his master's chair. Blacknail copied him again and stood behind Mahedium.

"Well then, now that we've been properly introduced, feel free to make yourself comfortable. We have much to discuss," the older mage told them.

"This is a rather nice home you have here, your business must be quite profitable," Mahedium politely commented.

"It certainly pays the bills and keeps me fed. There's always a demand for Elixir in Daggerpoint, and the city is short on suppliers. What about you, how are you finding the city?" Avorlus replied with a smug grin.

"Well enough. It's nice to be out from under the guilds and take destiny into my own hands. There are no lords or guild masters here to exploit me and tell me what I can and can't learn," the other mage answered.

"Very true. I myself found them quite stifling as well. Daggerpoint of course is not without its own dangers," Avorlus replied.

"Obviously, you've managed to prosper despite them," the younger mage remarked.

"You seem to know a fair bit about my own operations, but I know next to nothing about you. May I inquire as to your own knowledge and background? Your note was intriguing but severely lacking in detail," Avorlus asked.

Now it was Mahedium's turn to smile knowingly before replying. "I'm sure there's not much I could tell you that you don't already know. A man so obviously as intelligent and successful as yourself would have already looked into my history as soon as my note arrived. It's also not like my past is a secret. You, on the other hand, are quite the enigma."

"Straight down to business it is then," Avorlus remarked as he leaned back. "When you first contacted me, you suggested an exchange of knowledge would be to both our interests. That seems unlikely to me, but I'd like to know what you have to offer anyway. As you've already correctly determined, I'm a maker of Elixirs. That is my area of expertise."

"And you've amassed yourself a fortune by secretly selling them to bandit chieftains using intermediaries."

Avorlus nodded in response, so Mahedium continued speaking and reached into his coat. "My own area of expertise lies in a different area of research. I specialize in creating spell crystals. I have the skills and knowledge to grow them from scratch."

The old mage's guard tensed at Mahedium's movement but didn't act further. Master Avorlus barely reacted. His fake-looking smile didn't falter at all as the younger mage pulled out a small pouch and emptied it onto the table. Half a dozen transparent crystals rolled across it. Avorlus's white eyebrows rose slightly in surprise.

"They are a gift, from me to you. A token of my respect and an offer of friendship," the younger mage explained.

# *Chapter 16*

Master Avorlus reached down and picked the largest stone up with two fingers. It was slightly smaller than his closed fist. He stared at it for a second, and it pulsed with light. "These are all light crystals."

"Yes, well, since I see that you're using candles to light your home, I think these will be quite useful to you," Mahedium replied.

The older man grunted and eyed Mahedium with new interest. "Yes, these would be quite useful, but worth Elixirs? I don't believe so. You can't compare the ability to uplift mere men into Vessels to something that's a small improvement over a candle."

"Perhaps, but light crystals don't kill most the people who try and use them either, and I have other stones," Mahedium countered.

"So what if you do? I make more than enough money to buy as many crystals as I want by selling Elixirs. Why do I need you?" the older mage replied.

Mahedium didn't seem concerned by Avorlus's argument. He leaned back in his chair and appeared to relax. "You can't use your potions yourself though. You're a mage not a Vessel. Are you really satisfied with granting other people power and not finding ways to make and use magic for yourself?"

"You're assuming I don't know how to make my own spell stones," Avorlus responded coldly.

Blacknail wasn't fooled though. The older man was looking less composed and sure of himself now. Mahedium leaned forward and stared hard into the other mage's eyes.

"I know you can't, for the same reasons I know you can't actually buy all the crystals you want. This home is lit by candles instead of magic. Where are all the crystals you're supposedly buying? I'll tell you where. They're tucked away somewhere safe or hidden about your person in case of an emergency. You're never going to use them though; they'll lay there forever. You won't risk wasting them when you can never be sure you'll be able to replace them, and thus, you'll never be truly free to use the power that is yours by right," Mahedium explained with calm intensity.

The younger mage kept eye contact with the older mage as he reached down and picked up one of the spell stones on the table. He concealed it in his closed fist before it burst to life. The light from the crystal was so strong, the shadows of the bones in his hand were visible as light blazed out from between his fingers. Then the light died, and Mahedium dropped the used spell stone onto the table.

"Power that can't be used as one wishes, is not truly power at all," he commented dryly.

Avorlus looked away. His teeth were clenched hard together, and he looked unsettled now.

"Very well, I'm listening. What do you propose?" he replied a few seconds later in a defeated tone.

"Let us start by being forthright with each other. We could sit here all day making cryptic comments and never accomplish anything. Instead though, let's put our cards on the table and see what we have to trade," Mahedium suggested.

Avorlus coolly eyed the younger mage for a few seconds but then nodded.

Seeing this, Mahedium continued talking. "I have next to no information on the process of creating Elixirs, and you do. I can show you the basic techniques for creating spell stones, however. What would you be willing to trade for it?"

"Trade? You're here in my home begging favors from me. I'm an experienced mage, and you're nothing but a young upstart. I might teach you something in exchange for the scraps of knowledge you possess, but that doesn't make us equals," Avorlus responded coldly.

The old, bald, bearded mage raised a gloved hand to reveal he held a crystal against his palm. Black smoke began to curl and rise menacingly upward from the spell stone. Blacknail really didn't like the look of that, or the smell. It reminded him of rotten eggs. Mahedium tensed at the other mage's actions. His own hand inched toward one of the spell stones concealed up his sleeve.

"I should warn you that I have a rather large force stone tucked up against my skin right now. If you do anything too sudden, I might ignite it and reduce everything in this room to smithereens." Mahedium reached up his sleeve and pulled out a small wand. The end of the rod held a small crystal, and it began to thrum and vibrate.

He didn't point it at anyone, but he didn't have to, the message was clear. He wasn't intimidated by the other mage's display. Blacknail got ready to draw his own weapon and fight as well. He would have preferred to flee, but the door was guarded, and all the windows were too small to squeeze through.

The two mages' eyes met, and they stared defiantly at each other. Then Avorlus chuckled and smiled humorlessly. "You're very determined I see. Good, maybe you're worth dealing with after all."

Mahedium's posture relaxed at the other man's words, but he didn't put his wand back away. Blacknail continued to stare at the mage's bodyguard, who was staring right back at him. The hobgoblin wasn't exactly sure what he was going to do if he actually had to fight this massive human, but that didn't stop him from glaring menacingly.

Avorlus noticed his guest's hostility and sighed dramatically. He then carefully placed his spell stone on the table in front of him.

"Your turn," he remarked confidently. Mahedium gave the older mage a hard stare but relented a second later. He tucked his wand back into his sleeve and out of sight.

"I think you'll find that I'm willing to do practically anything to increase my knowledge of magic. Now, what are you willing to trade for the basic techniques for creating spell stones," Mahedium asked the other mage.

"As am I, young mage. Over the years, I have collected quite a bit of information on the crystal growing process. I've never had any luck making it work though; the information is incomplete. There are, however, a few formulas for spells in there that I'm sure would be of great value to you. I will exchange this knowledge for the basic techniques you've acquired," Avorlus offered carefully.

"I would have to look it over before agreeing to anything."

"I will allow you to read a sample of the writings beforehand."

"Acceptable, but there are other areas I'm interested in as well," the younger mage replied.

Avorlus tensed slightly and leaned backward. The hostile look from earlier returned to his eyes. Mahedium didn't seem surprised or concerned though.

"You have nothing valuable enough to trade for my knowledge of Elixirs," the older man replied coldly.

"So I understand, but I'm not asking for anything like all your knowledge. I simply need to be able to create one specific formula, that which my leader Herad uses. She requires a new source of the Ressertein Elixir and has tasked me with procuring it for her. Your business would remain undisturbed," Mahedium explained.

"Do you have anything to offer me for this? If not, then she'll just have to purchase it from me like everyone else. I'm not afraid of the bandit chiefs," Avorlus told him coldly.

Mahedium rubbed his chin thoughtfully and looked off to one side for a second. "I have some unique Vessel samples you might be interested in. They come from a rather interesting source."

"They would have to be very interesting indeed," Avorlus remarked doubtfully.

"Oh, they are. Blacknail would you please remove your hood?" Mahedium asked.

From where he was standing behind his chair, the hobgoblin gave Mahedium a curious look. He didn't really want to reveal himself in such a plain manner. It wasn't... fun enough. Everyone was now looking his way, and Avorlus looked caught between curiosity and confusion.

"Now, please," Mahedium requested impatiently but with a trace of humor.

Blacknail sighed but did as he was told. He flipped his hood down, and gave the guard across from him a broad, toothy smile. The reaction was immediate. Avorlus flinched away from him, and his guard went for his sword.

"Bloody burning hells," the guard cursed. This caused Blacknail's smile to widen. He had won the game and made the stupid human say something aloud! Mahedium was less sanguine. He slowly reached into his sleeve and withdrew the small wand again, which he pointed at the guard.

"There's no need for violence; he's friendly as long as you are. However, if you attempt to raise your blade against him then he'll be the least of your worries, because I'll blast you across the room so fast you won't know what hit you," Mahedium told them.

"What is this thing that you've brought into my home?" Avorlus asked in shock. His eyes were wide with alarm, and his wrinkled face had grown paler.

Blacknail hissed in annoyance at the man's tone and words. It was more than a little insulting. He wasn't a thing! The older mage's hand had also slipped into one of his pockets where it was likely clenching something. Blacknail was sure it was a weapon or spell stone of some sort.

"It's a hobgoblin and also a Vessel. He's the sample I was talking about before. Introduce yourself, Blacknail," Mahedium said.

"Hello. I promise not to kill you or do other bad things," Blacknail told them cheerfully. Avorlus continued to stare in shock at Blacknail; he didn't seem reassured.

"See? He's actually a rather nice fellow when you get to know him," Mahedium added with a smile of his own.

Avorlus turned his attention to the younger mage and then seemed to relax and regain his composure. He made a waving motion at the guard behind him, and the other man relaxed as well.

"It's a Vessel you say? Any idea which Elixir?" the older mage asked with obvious interest.

"I'm a he, not an it," Blacknail told the man with a forced smile.

"I have no idea, but the blood work I did was conclusive. I was hoping you could tell us more," Mahedium answered.

"I must admit to never seeing a non-human Vessel before. I've heard of them of course though. Some of the guilds create hunting dogs or warhorses, but they're the play toys of the high nobility. How did he become a Vessel, and why do you think I will be interested in studying him?" Avorlus asked.

"That's an interesting question. Blacknail was originally picked up by one of Herad's men when they liberated him from a caravan, which just happened to have been guarded by a mage."

"From which guild?" Avorlus asked curiously.

"I'm getting to that. It was before I joined, but Herad actually keeps records of everything she procures and sells. She also had some papers from the merchants themselves. From descriptions of the mage and the records, I was able to determine that he was attached to that caravan in order to guard a shipment of materials for his guild, the Purple Hearts," Mahedium explained.

"I see; the goblin was part of the cargo," Avorlus whispered to himself, and an excited grin broke out on his wrinkled face. Blacknail didn't understand. What were these mages talking about?

"Indeed, the Purple Heart guild is known for its work on non-human vessels," Mahedium remarked.

"Why would they experiment in order to create a goblin Vessel though?" Avorlus mused.

"Why do the guilds do anything? I've heard the Purple Hearts have an elixir for house cats! Goblin Vessels seem sane compared to that," Mahedium replied with a roll of his eyes.

"True, it was probably just some student's thesis project, which turned out to be an unexpected success. Was the goblin the only thing of interest from the caravan?"

"No, when she raided the caravan, Herad captured some other wares that I believe were also their work. She didn't think much of them and neither did any of her buyers, so they were still sitting around her base camp when I joined," Mahedium remarked.

"You have them, here?" the older gentleman asked with eyes that shone with hunger.

"Of course. Naturally, I collected everything that even hinted at magic when I joined. At the time though, I couldn't figure out what any of it was, so I dismissed it as useless. With your help though, and knowing that one of the samples is probably an Elixir for Blacknail..."

"Reverse engineering an Elixir is not an easy task. The Elixir itself is far more than the sum of its parts; once the mage blood is added, it becomes active and is completely transformed," Avorlus explained.

"In the same way a crystal is grown from a mineral base and mage's blood," Mahedium commented.

Blacknail frowned in frustration as he realized what the mages had said. You needed mage blood to make Elixirs. That ruined his plan to find out how to make it for himself and not be reliant on Mahedium for his magic.

"You're asking for time-tested knowledge in exchange for nothing but possibilities," their bearded host said.

"True, but I'm only asking for very basic knowledge that costs you nothing. If you're nearly as good an alchemist as you seem to be, then you should be able to reverse engineer the Purple Heart's work. Think about what you would get from that, cutting-edge guild research. A brand new, unknown Elixir," Mahedium countered.

Blacknail grinned as an idea occurred to him. Scamp was a mage, right? He could use his blood! The little troublemaker undoubtedly had more blood than he was using anyway.

"You're playing me like a flute," Avorlus told the other mage with a dramatic sigh.

"We're simply engaging in an exchange. You're losing nothing," the other mage replied with a smile.

"We'll see. I agree to both of the deals. I'd like to start as soon as possible. Come back tomorrow morning, and I'll have a lab set up," their host told Mahedium.

The other mage nodded, stood up, and then extended a hand. The two men shook, and after a few brief words, one of the guards escorted them out. They had no more trouble from their hosts on the way out. That was good because Avorlus's smoke crystal had apparently ended up in Blacknail's pocket. Blacknail wasn't sure how; it wasn't like he wanted the smelly thing.

Blacknail led the way off Avorlus's property and toward the house where Herad was waiting. In case things had gone badly, she had brought some men, and they were waiting nearby. As they moved onto a deserted street, the hobgoblin heard several people step out of an alley onto the road behind them. The noise was out of place and immediately drew his attention. He turned around to see what was up and saw a group of thugs. Such men weren't uncommon in Daggerpoint, but this was the Central District, and groups of a dozen men such as them were very rare here. Blacknail was too paranoid to think their presence was a coincidence.

Then one of the men raised a crossbow, and Blacknail's eyes went wide in alarm. He tackled Mahedium and threw both the mage and himself to the ground just as a crossbow bolt zoomed past them. They hit the cobblestones hard, and Mahedium grunted in surprise and pain.

"What's going on?" the mage wheezed.

"Enemies and a crossbow!" Blacknail hissed angrily as he scrambled back to his feet. He didn't like being ambushed. That was his thing; he did the ambushing, not the other way around!

The man with the crossbow began to load it again, and his companions drew their own weapons and rushed toward Blacknail and Mahedium. The hobgoblin immediately began looking for somewhere to run. There was no way he could fight so many humans. He would also probably have to leave Mahedium behind...

As Blacknail was planning his escape, Mahedium pushed himself up onto his knees. The mage leveled his staff at the armed thugs racing toward him. The crystal at the end glowed orange, and its power exploded out. The thugs between Mahedium and the crossbowman were knocked backward by the blast. A hot wind blew past Blacknail, and the stricken men suddenly caught fire. Several of the attackers died instantly, but they were the lucky ones. Screams of pain filled the air as some of the other flaming thugs began flailing around in pain and panic. The smell of roasting meat filled the corpse-littered street. The remaining attackers looked stunned before deciding to make a run for it. They all quickly dashed out of sight and into nearby alleys. As they fled, Mahedium looked at the destruction he had wrought with a satisfied look on his face.

"Now, the question is whether these were Werrick's men, or if Avorlus sent them," the mage mused aloud as he brushed himself off. There were no more functional enemies in sight.

"Think later! We need to go, now!" Blacknail hissed. He heard yelling off in the distance. He was pretty sure it was the governor's men coming to investigate the disturbance. Quickly, the hobgoblin grabbed Mahedium and began dragging the mage toward Herad and the rest of the band.

Mahedium had surprised him. He was far more clever and dangerous than he usually pretended to be. He acted so clueless sometimes, it was easy to forget all the power he had at his fingertips. Blacknail wondered if the man was hiding his real self, or if he had simply risen to the occasion. Regardless, the hobgoblin planned to keep an eye on him in the future—if only to make sure they never became enemies and so he could find the man's weaknesses if they ever did.

# *Part Three:*
# *A Tradesman's Tools*

# *Chapter 17*

Blacknail yawned luxuriously as he slowly stretched out his long, slender body. His movements caused the sheets beneath him to rub pleasantly against his skin. He then smiled contentedly as he sank into the soft fluffy mattress. He was really enjoying having a bed of his own. He'd never had one before, only a blanket to curl up onto. This was much nicer and bouncier.

As he lay there, his stomach grumbled slightly. This raised a dilemma. Should he get up and grab some food or try and get back to sleep? On one hand, the food here was very tasty, but on the other hand, the bed was amazingly soft. It was thus a difficult choice to make. Sloth eventually overcame gluttony, and the decision was made for Blacknail. The hobgoblin fell back to sleep before he could make up his mind.

When he next awoke, red-tinted sunlight was leaking into the room from behind the curtains that blocked the window. Blacknail gazed lazily at it and yawned deeply again before grinning happily to himself. It wasn't only the bed that was his, the entire room was! Herad had given it to him, and it was just down the hall from hers. Most the other bandits had roommates, but he had his room all to himself. Blacknail had been told this was because he was special, which probably meant he was Herad's favorite.

Having his own space was definitely a good thing; humans tended to smell funny, so he didn't want to share a room with one. Unlike his master, most of them didn't even try to hide their weird human scent. Saeter usually smelled strongly of herbs, soil, and the forest.

Judging by the amount of light coming in through the curtains, it was around noon now. Blacknail rarely got out of bed this early in the morning anymore. Mostly, he lounged around inside until he got hungry or it got dark, or both. He still did a lot of training; he just did it in the afternoon, when it was harder for people see. Herad wanted to keep Blacknail's presence a secret, or at least make sure he remained mysterious. Blacknail understood her reasons and even approved of them. The less people knew about him, the more they would fear him. It was a very hobgoblin way of thinking, and Blacknail liked being feared.

For a while, Saeter had tried to find chores for the hobgoblin to do, but he had given up eventually when he hadn't found anything appropriate. The city was a much easier place to live than the forest, and Blacknail liked it that way. He didn't have to make things himself. Everything he needed was lying around or in some oblivious human's pocket. Blacknail wasn't a thief—thieving was wrong—but he strongly believed that if no one complained about you taking something, it was because they didn't really want or deserve it.

After his daily training, Blacknail's master had to go do his own jobs. This left Blacknail free to slip away and out into the city. He hadn't been told he wasn't supposed to go out, and he liked it that way, so he wasn't about to ruin anything by asking for permission. Sleeping in his room was great but so was the city. There were so many tasty treats out there for him to eat! It seemed like Daggerpoint contained endless different types of food for him to try.

As the hobgoblin was contemplating the contents of his next meal, he heard the sound of footsteps approaching. He sighed in irritation when he realized they were headed his way. It was unlikely to be someone bringing him food.

A few seconds later, the door opened and Saeter stepped into the room. The hobgoblin gazed up at him curiously from his bed. What did his master want this early in the day? Saeter didn't immediately say anything. He just grunted and gave Blacknail an irritated scowl when he saw the hobgoblin was still in bed.

"Get up, you lazy green lump. You don't get to sleep in till sundown today," Saeter told the hobgoblin.

"Why?" muttered Blacknail in annoyance. He wanted to

sleep in until sundown. It sounded like fun.

"Herad wants to see you."

"Why?" The hobgoblin slowly picked himself off the bed. He shouldn't keep his chieftain waiting, it would be bad for his health. Knives were funny that way.

"It's a surprise," his master told him.

Saeter threw Blacknail his scabbard and belt. Blacknail caught them and started putting them on. If whatever Herad wanted required a sword, it would probably be interesting at least.

"Come on, we don't have all day," Saeter told the hobgoblin as soon as he was finished dressing.

Blacknail followed his master out into the hallway, down a flight of stairs, and out into the yard behind Herad's hideout. The enclosure was usually used for training, but this time as Blacknail walked outside, he immediately noticed Herad standing in the middle of the yard. The bandit chieftain was wearing her usual black leathers and carrying her usual plethora of blades. Her dark eyes stared out from under her short black hair as it waved in the wind. Mahedium was the only other person present and was standing off to one side. He was wearing a long gray coat today, probably because the air outside had a chilly edge to it. The sky overhead was full of gray clouds that hid the sun away.

Blacknail didn't see any sign of a single other person. Both Herad and the mage seemed excited. The hobgoblin was now very curious about what was going on and more than a little apprehensive as well.

"Finally, you sure like making me wait, Saeter. Or maybe you're just getting slower in your old age," Herad remarked as Saeter and the hobgoblin approached.

"I must be getting old then, how could I ever resist the attraction of your company?" Saeter replied without an ounce of humor or disrespect in his voice.

Herad eyed the gray-haired scout carefully, and her hand dropped toward one of her daggers. Blacknail held his breath, but after a few seconds she relaxed.

"Mahedium has something for you, Blacknail," she told the hobgoblin.

Now that it was safe, Blacknail shifted his gaze to the mage. Maybe Herad was giving him a gift in return for his earlier present! He hoped it was edible. He still hadn't had breakfast.

"Hmm, I do indeed," the mage remarked as he walked over to Blacknail. He then reached into one of his coat pockets and withdrew a small vial.

Blacknail stared at it for a second and frowned. The liquid inside was light blue, and he didn't think it looked very tasty.

"Finally, after several days of research and hard work, Avorlus and I managed to recreate your Elixir! We're almost completely sure it will work!" Mahedium grinned in excitement.

"Oh, good..." Blacknail remarked skeptically. He was excited about getting his own magic, but he'd caught that "almost." Then there was that color... Elixirs were edible, or drinkable at least. What did Elixir taste like anyway? He hoped the color meant it would taste like blueberries. Wait, what had he been worrying about?

Mahedium handed Blacknail the vial and gave him an expectant look. "Just pop it open and drink the contents. You should be able to feel a difference right away since you're already a Vessel."

"Thank you," the hobgoblin politely and happily replied. He couldn't wait! Blacknail grasped the vial and quickly twisted the top off. Soon, he would have magic of his own; he'd be a magic hobgoblin! Nothing could stop him from drinking this. The world needed a magic hobgoblin!

"Oh, and if you suddenly develop a headache, nausea, diarrhea, break out into a rash, or start losing your hair, tell me," the mage added as a side thought.

Blacknail froze and gave Mahedium a startled look. Suddenly drinking the vial didn't seem like such a great idea to him, magic or not. "It's poison?" he asked in concern as he held the vial above his lips.

"No, all those symptoms are very unlikely. I'll be right here if anything happens, anyway," the mage replied.

"And you have a cure?" the hobgoblin asked hopefully.

"Um, no... I have some basic soothing herbs and water here though, and I'm told that sometimes helps," Mahedium explained.

What? That didn't really seem all that helpful to Blacknail. He looked over toward his master, but Saeter had a carefully neutral expression on his face. The hobgoblin still didn't feel like taking the Elixir...

"Stop wasting my time, goblin. Drink the damned potion! Don't make me come over there and shove it down your throat," Herad suddenly ordered him with a snarl.

Blacknail looked over to see her staring at him coldly. He raised the vial again. It didn't seem like he had any choice but to drink the stuff. Quickly, he gulped the liquid within down. It tasted nothing like blueberries. In fact, it tasted more like salty dirt. Yuck.

No one said anything as they all waited for something to happen, especially Blacknail. The hobgoblin was holding his breath while he stared at his arms and searched for any sign of a developing rash. He had little in the way of hair to lose.

"Try moving around," Saeter suggested after a few moments.

Tentatively, Blacknail began walking around. Then he jumped on the spot a few times. It didn't feel like he was about to become sick or explode...

"Ah, good. It would appear we found the right mixture. He's not showing any signs of rejection. Master Avorlus will be very pleased," Mahedium commented proudly.

"Just as long as he keeps supplying me with Elixir. Now run around the yard a few times, Blacknail," Herad commanded him.

The hobgoblin immediately began jogging around.

"Faster, you lazy green runt, or I'll have you dodging arrows," she yelled a few seconds later.

Blacknail broke out into a sprint. He wasn't sure what this was supposed to accomplish, but he wasn't going to argue with his boss.

"Do we have any idea what type of Elixir he's using or if it has secondary effects?" Herad asked the mage as she watched Blacknail run.

"Um, no. We don't. It's impossible to say just from the recipe, not to mention it seems to be a completely new experimental mixture," Mahedium replied.

Blacknail was listening carefully. Elixirs could have

secondary effects? None of the Vessels he'd seen had done anything special. As he ran, he began to feel an odd, familiar burning sensation in his legs. The hobgoblin ignored it though and continued to listen in on the others.

Herad frowned as she considered the mage's words. "So we won't know what, if anything, it does until he starts breathing fire or jumping ten feet up into the air?"

"Pretty much, although most Elixirs don't apparently have much in the way of secondary effects. Like your own Ressertein recipe, they mostly just grant increased physical vigor, or so Avorlus has told me."

"Blacknail's pretty fast, but I think he's doing a fair bit better than usual," Saeter suddenly interjected.

Herad and the mage looked at the hobgoblin that was running around the yard. There was a small dust trail rising behind him as he moved.

"Huh, ya. He's definitely a fast little beast. It's hard to tell if that's from the Elixir though. Let's test his strength," Herad said.

"You can stop now, Blacknail. Come over here," Saeter yelled out to the hobgoblin.

Blacknail immediately stopped and made his way back to the others. His chest rose and fell as he breathed heavily, but he wasn't feeling all that tired.

"Blacknail come over here and take my hand," Herad said, as she raised one arm in his direction. Blacknail had never actually touched the chief before, and the idea made him more than a little uncomfortable. Hopefully it was a sign of her favor and she wasn't about to hurt him.

When the hobgoblin hesitated to approach, Herad gave him an impatient glare. Blacknail quickly reached out and took her hand. Immediately, Herad's fingers closed tightly around his wrist and held him in place. This didn't seem promising...

"Now, goblin, you have to try and pull your hand away from mine. If you can't, then I'm going to punch you in the face a few times," she told him dispassionately.

Blacknail's eyes went wide. This was definitely not good. The hobgoblin grabbed his own arm and lowered his stance as he began frantically trying to pull his hand free. His heels dug into the earth as he squirmed and fought to free himself. However, Herad's fingers seemed as strong as iron, and he couldn't get his arm loose. She scowled in annoyance at Blacknail's futile struggling. Slowly, she raised a clenched fist. The hobgoblin redoubled his efforts, and all of a sudden, the burning sensation from before washed through his entire body. Fear spurred him on as he pulled desperately on his arm, and Herad moved. She kept her grip on him, but her body twisted as she kept her balance, and her feet slid forward slightly. Before he could react, Herad grinned and released him. Off-balance and in the middle of pulling, the hobgoblin was sent sprawling over backward.

"Ouch, cheese rot," Blacknail hissed when he landed painfully on his ass.

"Hmm, that last pull was definitely above normal human, or hobgoblin, strength. It seems to have worked," Herad remarked.

A grinning Blacknail picked himself off the ground and jumped into the air experimentally a few times. He had super strength! He thought he was jumping a little higher than before, but nothing like ten feet. He began breathing out as hard as he could.

"Do you have something in your throat?" Saeter asked him.

"Uh, no-ss, it's nothing." The embarrassed hobgoblin turned away to hide his face. He apparently didn't breathe fire either... which was too bad, that would have been amazing!

"So now I've got both a Vessel hobgoblin and a reliable source of Elixir for both of us. Good work, Mahedium. It's nice to know that not all my subordinates are completely useless," she told the mage as he nodded respectfully back.

An eager smile spread across Herad's lips, and she turned to look toward the rest of the city. There was a building blocking her view, but she didn't seem to care. Blacknail recognized that bloodthirsty smile. He shivered in excitement. That look meant Herad was about to start a fight and Blacknail was about to have a lot of fun! Not only had he finally gotten some magic of his own, but it looked like his tribe was about to go to war. This was the best day ever!

"This shifts the odds our way by a fair bit, and if I leverage this right, I ought to be able to mess up Werrick's plans. I'm done playing defense. Now it's time to go for their throats. I'll isolate them and take my enemies out one by one. Then the chiefs that are left won't dare raise a hand against me, no matter what Werrick offers them," Herad bragged. She then turned to Blacknail.

"You've already proved that you're a half-decent assassin, so I'm going to unleash you. With Fang dead, my biggest enemy is Galive, so I'll be sending you after him. I want Zelena dead as well, but word is she's surrounded herself with over half the bodyguards and assassins in the city," Herad told the hobgoblin.

Blacknail smiled in anticipation. Now that he was a Vessel, he was sure it would be much easier to take out Herad's enemies. If nothing else, he was now an even faster runner. There was no way he'd get himself into trouble like the last time.

"Blacknail needs training before you throw him out there, or he'll get himself killed," Saeter interjected. There was a hint of concern in his voice.

"True, but that's easily fixed. You've already been teaching him how to fight. I'll just have to beat all the bad habits you've taught Blacknail out of him," Herad remarked. Blacknail felt a sinking sensation in his stomach. This didn't sound good.

"He'll need more than just the ability to fight. He's a natural stalker and hunter but totally ignorant of a lot of things. He's going to need some new equipment, and training in things like lock picking as well," Saeter countered.

"I'll let you handle that stuff; I don't have time for it. I will, however, show him how a true Vessel fights. It's time that Blacknail and I had that spar," Herad told Saeter.

The hobgoblin's eyes went wide in alarm. This couldn't be happening! There was no way he could fight Herad; she'd cut him into tiny little pieces. He turned to Saeter and threw him a desperate, pleading look. Blacknail's master was frowning, but when he noticed the hobgoblin's attention, he just shrugged helplessly. Blacknail grimaced in dismay. He'd really been hoping Saeter would save him! Herad was going to kill him...

Behind Blacknail, there was the sound of a blade being

slowly drawn from its sheath. He shuddered in dread as he turned around to see Herad pointing her naked blade toward his throat.

"Draw your sword, hobgoblin. It's time to test your mettle," she told him.

Blacknail peed himself a little. He was too young and smart to die!

Herad didn't wait for him to respond; her blade sliced toward his head. The hobgoblin yelped as he ducked under the attack. He then scrambled backward.

"You can't run, hobgoblin. Draw your sword or I'll skin you alive, you little green coward," Herad growled viciously.

Blacknail considered his options. Herad was way too into this, but she probably wouldn't actually kill him if he did as he was told. If he tried to run away though...

Blacknail thus reluctantly unsheathed his own blade and faced Herad. He even managed to keep his trembling to a minimum. The bandit chieftain immediately reacted and attacked again. The hobgoblin raised his blade to intercept it, but Herad's blade disappeared from his sight. He then reeled in shock as something smacked into the side of his head and knocked him sideways.

From where he was lying on the ground, Blacknail looked up with cloudy eyes to see Herad sneering down at him. She'd hit him with the flat of her blade. Out of the corner of his eye, the hobgoblin saw his master wince.

"Pathetic. We're going to keep doing this until you can burn your Elixir at will and you know one end of a blade from another. Now get up, or I'll smack you again," Herad told him condescendingly.

Blacknail whimpered in self pity. This was the worst day ever! Herad evidently heard him, because she gave him adisproving look and attacked again. Blacknail's eyes widened fearfully as her blade sliced toward his face. She hadn't even given him time to raise his ownsword. This was going to be a horribly painful training session.

# *Chapter 18*

"Blacknail, you need to come out from under there," Saeter said with obvious frustration before continuing to grind his teeth.

"No, I don't want to," Blacknail whined.

"Seriously, don't make me get down there and drag you out."

The hobgoblin sniffled miserably and groaned in pain and humiliation. Herad's lessons had gone on for hours! She'd beat him black and blue, and then purple and green. It had been so much worse than even his first lesson with Saeter.

"I can't believe I'm doing this," Saeter mumbled to himself. The old scout crossed his arms and scowled in annoyance as he glanced around the room. There was no one around to see his expression though, so a few seconds later, he sighed in defeat and turned back to where the hobgoblin was hiding.

"What are you doing? You can't be all that scared of Herad," Saeter asked.

Blacknail stifled another whimper. Getting beaten up by the chief had crushed his ego into pulp. Why did she hate him so much? He'd thought he was the chief's favorite. He'd killed her enemies for her and everything! There was no way he was ever going to show his face in public ever again. He'd just never leave this hiding spot and slowly fade away.

"The chief hates me and made me look bad in front of you," Blacknail whined in response.

"She doesn't hate you, Blacknail. That's just how Herad is. No matter how much she acts like it sometimes, she isn't a hobgoblin. She wasn't punishing you. In fact, in her own weird way, she was actually helping you out," Saeter explained while managing to keep a straight face.

"Really?" Blacknail asked hopefully.

"Yep, do you know how many men, er, people she's ever agreed to train personally?" Saeter asked.

"No."

"None, which means you really are her favorite. Now come out from under there, and I'll buy you all the meat pies you can eat."

Blacknail's ears perked up. Now that his master had mentioned food, the hobgoblin realized he was hungry. He still hadn't had breakfast yet, and meat pies sounded like just the thing. Blacknail reluctantly got up and crawled out from under his bed. It had been getting kind of stuffy under there anyway. "Fine, let's go eat. I want some cheese."

"I offered meat pies, so if you want cheese, you'll have to get it yourself," Saeter replied.

"Fine-ss, I know a place I can take some from anyway," Blacknail muttered.

"You know you have money, right? You could just buy some bloody cheese; you don't have to steal it," his master pointed out. The hobgoblin gave Saeter an uncomprehending look. What was this now?

"Buying means taking, doesn't it?" he asked in confusion.

"No, it doesn't. Buying means trading. Humans trade money for other things they want. It's why we get paid and want coins in the first place," Saeter explained. That was stupid! Why would Blacknail give his shiny coins away when everything he wanted was lying around?

"Why not just pick up the things you want-ss?" he asked his master. Saeter gave the hobgoblin a questioning look. Blacknail returned it.

"Because you can't steal everything you want, and it's often a lot more work than just buying stuff," Saeter answered gruffly. Who said anything about stealing? Blacknail wasn't a thief. His master sure got confused sometimes. Good thing he had Blacknail around to help him out!

"But I like my coins. I want-ss to keep them," the hobgoblin explained.

"Ha, you don't even use them for anything! In fact, you lose half of them," Saeter replied.

Blacknail hissed in annoyance. That wasn't true at all; he

didn't lose them. He just put them somewhere safe and hidden, and then forgot about them... Okay, he kind of lost them.

"When we get to the market, I'll show you how to buy stuff. In fact, we won't be coming back until you purchase some stuff for yourself. Think of it as a skill I'm teaching you," Saeter told him.

Together, the two of them headed out of Herad's compound and toward the market. As usual, the city was bustling with life, and the streets were full of people. Merchants were calling out to customers from their colorful stalls, and their wares were piled up in front of them. Saeter went over to one, and after a brief exchange with its owner, he walked away with several delicious-smelling meat pies. He handed them to Blacknail and then grimaced in disgust as the hobgoblin inhaled them down within seconds.

"Thanks, master," Blacknail told him right before burping.

"Slow down, you don't need to eat so quickly, or while I'm looking. Anyway, now it's time for you to buy some stuff, so we're going to wander around until you find something you like," the old scout replied.

Blacknail sighed and tried to think up some excuse to keep his coins. He couldn't think of anything though, so he reluctantly nodded his assent. He still thought it would be much smarter to just take something no one else was using...

"Where's the cheese?" he asked Saeter.

Several minutes later, after some bargaining with a confused and more-than-slightly-frightened shopkeeper, the two of them headed back to base. As he walked, Blacknail was twitching with anticipation and hugging a huge wheel of stinking cheese to his chest while trying to resist the powerful urge to immediately bite into it. He wanted to taste it so bad!

"You're so tasty and delicious. I will hide you away in my room and eat you for days," Blacknail told the cheese. This caused Saeter to give him a concerned look.

"You're not taking that back to your room. It would stink up the entire floor," Saeter told him.

Blacknail wasn't sure why that was something people would complain about. The cheese smelled great to him, almost like meat that had spoiled only the tiniest bit. The hobgoblin licked his lips in anticipation, but he had to tear his gaze away from the tasty treat he was holding in order to see where he was going. As he was looking around, his eyes wandered across a nearby stall and the false faces it was selling.

The merchant that was running the small shop didn't seem to be doing a lot of business, but the occasional person stopped to take a look at his wares. His booth was covered in wooden carvings, including several of the masks that had caught the hobgoblin's attention. Most intriguingly, like Blacknail did, the shopkeeper wore a long, hooded cloak that concealed his features. The merchant wasn't a hobgoblin though, because he was large, even for a human. Blacknail also would have noticed the smell of another hobgoblin immediately if there was one so close by, and the idea of a hobgoblin selling wooden carvings was silly.

However, Blacknail really liked the look of some of the work, so he wandered over. Most the little statues were of animals, but a few were of people going about their everyday business. Blacknail didn't see one of someone being mugged though, which was a pretty common part of life in Daggerpoint.

The cloaked man looked up as Blacknail approached yet remained silent as the hobgoblin examined his wares. Blacknail was most interested in the masks; he liked how fierce they looked. One was of a snarling wolf, and another beaked mask bore the image of a tyrant turtle. The turtle one was so lifelike, Blacknail hesitated to pick it up; he was afraid it would bite him. Saeter walked up beside him and examined one of the small figures. It was a perfectly crafted statue of a harpy in flight. He stared at it for a few seconds before saying anything.

"This doesn't look like normal wood to me," he whispered as he turned to look at the seller.

"You are a craftsman yourself, then?" the other man asked.

The merchant's voice was smooth and clear, so much so that its uniqueness drew Blacknail's attention. He couldn't make out any of the man's features though. His clothing concealed everything. Blacknail tried sniffing the air for his scent, but could only smell the wooden figurines. They reminded him of something...

"I dabble in wood carving sometimes, yes. Nothing like this

though," Saeter told the man respectfully.

Blacknail's master was gazing at the merchant inquisitively and seemed off guard. His posture was tight and his eyes were slightly wide, as if something had startled him.

"Indeed, you obviously know something of my work. I hadn't expected to find anyone here with such knowledge," the cloaked man replied slowly.

Blacknail shuffled over a bit and bent down to examine another figurine. Then, when he thought no one was looking, he tried to look up into the man's hood. He ended up disappointed though, because all he managed to glimpse were the edges of a wooden mask, like the ones on sale.

The merchant turned to Blacknail, and the hobgoblin quickly looked away. If the man was going to conceal his face, Blacknail sure wasn't going to let him see his! Wearing clothing like that was kind of rude.

"And you travel in very interesting company, forest walker," the large, robed shopkeeper observed aloud. Saeter stiffened but nodded reluctantly.

"I want a mask too. I like the turtle." Blacknail waved a hand in front of the merchant's face. This man sure was slow. The other shopkeeper had practically shoved his goods into Blacknail's hands.

Saeter winced at the hobgoblin's behavior and reached over to grab his shoulder. He was interrupted when the shopkeeper stood up.

"Then you shall have one, but not of a turtle. I have something more fitting for you," he replied and reached under his stall.

A second later, the shopkeeper pulled out several items. First, he handed Blacknail a new mask that was different from the ones on display and then he set two long poles on the stand in front of him. Blacknail stared at the mask for a second. He wasn't sure what it was supposed to be. It most resembled a smiling human, but the proportions were all wrong. He liked it though. It was intimidating in its own way, and the mask looked like it was having fun.

"What's it supposed to be?" he asked.

"The spirit of hunger." The man turned to Saeter and

handed him the two poles. Saeter's eyes widened in surprise when he got a good look at them.

"These are bowstaves. I didn't think you made those," he replied in shock.

"Ignorance is the root of knowledge. Everything grows, or it dies. Remember that," the cloaked merchant replied.

Saeter nodded and reached into his money pouch to withdraw a gold coin, which he handed to the man. The man took it and nodded in thanks before sitting back down and turning away from both his customers to watch his surroundings. It was clearly a dismissal, and Blacknail found it more than a little rude. No wonder the man had so few customers; he was kind of a jerk.

Blacknail wasn't sure if he wanted this mask; he liked it, but the turtle was also pretty frightening. He reached over to pick the turtle mask up again, but Saeter grabbed his arm and pulled him away.

"Hey, I'm not done buying stuff!" Blacknail exclaimed.

"You're done now; we need to get back," Saeter told him and dragged the hobgoblin down the street.

Blacknail frowned in annoyance, but he followed his master. It didn't take them long to get back to Herad's base. Blacknail got more than a few stares from the other bandits as he carried his massive wheel of cheese inside.

"Just put the cheese in that cupboard," Saeter told the hobgoblin as they entered the main building.

"What if someone steals it? I need to hide-ss it somewhere close where no one will look. I need to watch-ss over it always, it's mine!" Blacknail argued in concern as he hugged it close.

"No one is going to steal it. It's a huge lump of foul-smelling cheese!"

"Exactly!" Blacknail exclaimed as he gave one of the bandits walking past them a suspicious glare. There was no way he was going to leave his precious treat where other people could steal it. Humans were all thieves...

Just then, Khita appeared from around the corner and saw them. "Herad's looking for you two, and I wouldn't keep her waiting."

"Oh, why?" Saeter asked curiously, while Blacknail tried to

hide behind the huge snack he was carrying.

The hobgoblin wanted to meet with Herad right now about as much as he wanted to try and swallow his sword. He shivered shamefully at the very thought of talking to her again. He still hadn't completely gotten over the humiliation of their last meeting.

"I think she wants to train with Blacknail again. I can't believe he's being taught by Herad personally. I'm just so jealous of him! I bet she's a much better teacher than Vorscha. All she does is tell me to do drills," Khita complained bitterly.

Blacknail glared maliciously at Khita. She was such a foolish human. Blacknail would gladly let her take his place. There was no way he could face Herad right now. The very thought made him queasy and gassy.

"Well—"

Saeter was interrupted by a wet thud as a large wheel of cheese hit the floor. He whirled around just in time to catch Blacknail before the hobgoblin could make a run for it.

"You'll be fine, except for all the bruises," he told Blacknail reassuringly.

The hobgoblin didn't believe him. He whined as he tried to pull away, but Saeter kept a solid grip on him. Briefly, Blacknail considered cutting his own arm off so he could escape.

"The boss is up in her room," Khita told them as she stared in confusion at Blacknail's response.

"Right." Saeter grunted. He then dragged the whimpering hobgoblin up the stairs and to Herad's chamber.

"Now, don't be a bloody coward!" Saeter hissed as he shoved Blacknail through her door.

Herad looked up from her desk as the two of them entered. Blacknail smiled nervously as he fought down his panic, and Saeter gave her a respectful nod.

"Ah, I was just looking for you two," she said as she looked back down and scribbled something across a piece of paper in front of her.

"Well, here we are. What do you need?" Saeter responded.

"Galive has become a thorn in my side. He's taken over a lot of Fang's gang and is obviously under Zelena's thumb. All those men make him the biggest threat to me right now, and I would prefer not to have to fight him directly," Herad explained.

"What would you like us to do about it?" Saeter asked.

"I need him dead," Herad said before dropping her pen and looking up at them.

"Sure." Blacknail grinned happily at Herad, and his earlier queasiness disappeared. This was much better than another round of training. He'd rather fight the entire city than go through that again.

"He's not ready," Saeter responded sternly.

"Oh relax, Saeter. You're like an old mother hen fussing over its big ugly green chick. The hobgoblin can take care of himself. It's not like I'm throwing him away without preparation. I wouldn't risk such a useful asset if I didn't think he could succeed," Herad said as she threw him a dangerous grin.

"You're asking him to try and fight a Vessel with a small army of killers at his disposal," Saeter told her.

"No, I'm not asking. Now let's go over the details."

Blacknail sighed and took a step away from Saeter. His master really needed to stop trying to argue with the chieftain. That never worked.

"Now, I can't have my favorite assassin going out unprepared or anyone learning his true identity. So I had some gear prepared for you," Herad explained as she gave the hobgoblin a comradely smile.

Blacknail straightened up proudly at Herad's words. So he was her favorite after all! He felt all giddy inside. He'd show her that he deserved such an honor.

Herad picked up a small sack from her desk and handed it to Saeter. The old scout reached inside and withdrew a glass vial of Elixir, which he then passed to the hobgoblin. Next, he pulled out a large roll of bandages.

"To hide his skin, it's rather distinctive. His cloak has worked so far but there is no point in taking a risk," Herad explained as Saeter gave it a dubious look.

"If you're worried about people figuring out he's a hobgoblin, then I guess he could use the mask he just got as well," Saeter remarked.

Blacknail thought that was a great idea. He reached into his cloak and held the wooden mask up in front of his face. Herad stared at its stretchedfeatures and the intricate patterns of lines that decorated it.

"That's an interesting mask. Where did you get it?" sheasked curiously.

"I bought-ss it, with money," Blacknail replied cheerfully.

Saeter hesitated before responding. He looked like he couldn't decide what to say. "From a stall at the market."

Herad eyed him doubtfully. She obviously sensed his reluctance but chose not to pry, so she turned away from the old scout and looked at Blacknail instead. "Now he looks like a real assassin, and one worthy of being in my service," Herad observed aloud with a vicious grin.

"He's still not ready," Saeter muttered.

"Well, one of you is going to do it. So decide amongst yourselves, because I don't really care. Now get out of here, and I don't want to see either of you until the job is done," Herad told them with an annoyed scowl.

Saeter immediately marched out of the room. Blacknail followed him.

"I want to do it, you can stay-ss here," Blacknail told his master as they walked through the hallway.

"We're both going to do it. I'm not letting you mess this up!" Saeter ground his teeth in frustration.

That sounded like even more fun than going alone! With both of them working together, and his new but foul-tasting Elixir, this job was going to be too easy! Blacknail grinned in anticipation, and his smile matched that of the mask exactly.

# *Chapter 19*

Blacknail and Saeter stood across the street from their target and observed the people coming and going. Both of them had their hoods up and were taking shelter from the afternoon sun within the shadows of a nearby building. A huge, rectangular stone building stood before them. Its walls were straight and decorated with intricate carvings of people and animals. Stone pillars several times taller than a man lined the front of the building. They supported a wide, peaked roof, which extended past the walls. At one point, it looked like there had been statues between the pillars as well, but all that remained of them now were ruins and rubble.

Saeter's arms were crossed in front of him, and he scowled in disgust as he looked it over. "A few years ago, Galive appointed himself a priest of Cor-Dius. I've met few people in my life less priest-like than him, even by the shadow god's lax standards. It's hard to argue against a man with a small army though. Anyway, every priest needs a temple, so Galive commandeered this one. He'll be in there somewhere, all we have to do is find him."

Blacknail nodded sagely as he considered Saeter's words. Before leaving Herad's lair, the hobgoblin had donned his new and improved disguise. Under his usual hood, his face was covered by the wooden mask and his skin was wrapped in bandages that concealed its color.

"What's a priest?" he asked a few seconds later with obvious confusion. Whenever the hobgoblin thought he'd learned all the humans' words, they came up with new ones. Saeter let out a frustrated sigh before responding.

"Someone who thinks they can talk to the gods," Saeter explained

“Everyone can talk to spirits. You do all the time, like after you had that fight with Red Dog, and you asked them to make a spine toad crawl up his butt,” Blacknail pointed out.

“Um, sort of. The thing is, priests think the spirits talk back to them,” Saeter replied with a smile.

“Do they?”

“No, I’ve yet to meet anyone who has heard the voice of a god. If the gods communicate with us, then it’s through the world around us. Perhaps the rustling of leaves in the wind are their whispers,” Saeter replied seriously and looked up at the clear blue sky.

“So, that means you do think the gods talk to people?” Blacknail asked uncertainly. Saeter turned toward him and gave him an annoyed glare.

“Shut up, you’re just a hobgoblin. What do you know?” the old scout growled irritably as he absentmindedly tried to swat Blacknail across the side of his head. The hobgoblin saw it coming and easily ducked out of the way. What had he said to annoy his master? Humans could be so confusing sometimes.

“I’m morbidly curious about what your plan for getting to Galive is,” Saeter asked a few seconds later.

“I have a great plan, and it’s a very nice and tricky one! I’m going to sneak inside his home, wait until no one else is around, and then stab him-ss a whole bunch of times. Maybe I’ll wait-ss until he’s asleep. Humans are stupid and like to sleep in the same place at the same time every day.”

“That’s pretty much what I thought.” Saeter grunted disdainfully.

“It’s a perfect plan!” Blacknail responded. What was wrong with his plan?

“Sure, it is, let’s just work on the details a little,” Saeter told him sarcastically. “For instance, how do you plan to get in? Also, do you even know what Galive looks like?”

Blacknail looked back across the street at the bandit’s lair. It was a large, sprawling structure with plenty of places to hide. A small stone wall circled around what had once been the temple’s grounds. Blacknail wouldn’t have any problem scaling it, but doing so would make him very visible to any watchers. The center portion that used to be a temple was stone, but a large wooden addition had been constructed beside it. Only a few parts of it had a second floor, and as a result, most the windows were small and barred.

It certainly looked to be a larger challenge than Fang's lair had been, and then he'd known where to go.Blacknail had sort of assumed it would be obvious which human was Galive and which room belonged to him. It usually wasn't that hard to figure out. Couldn't he just go after the loudest person with the fanciest room?

"I'll go-ss in a window," Blacknail told Saeter hesitantly.

Saeter snorted in disbelief and eyed the hobgoblin critically. "Even if you managed that, how would you find Galive? You have no idea where his room is."

"It worked last time," Blacknail whined.

"It almost didn't, and you got lucky!" Saeter sternly pointed out. Blacknail scrunched up his face as he scowled in irritation. He had so not gotten lucky; it had been all skill!

"Do you know a better way?" he asked grumpily.

"I think I just might. It's like hunting; you have to know your prey," Saeter remarked with a knowing glance.

Several hours later, after the sky overhead had grown darker and evening had set in, Blacknail found himself following Saeter through Galive's front door. They weren't alone; dozens of other men and women were all around them. The rhythm and roil of many different conversations surrounded them as they walked calmly into their enemy's stronghold. A dozen men wearing long black cloaks stood guard around the building, one of which looked directly at the pair for a second before turning away. Saeter and Blacknail apparently didn't stand out.

"Look at those idiots. Thank the gods Herad doesn't make us wear a uniform," Saeter commented as he rolled his eyes at one of the cloaked guards.

Torches had been placed around the yard and up the walkway that led into the old temple, and their wavering orange light threw back the darkness of the night. Blacknail didn't like it; he preferred the dark. With all the stone pillars around, the torches cast a host of shifting shadows that was actually harder to see through.

"Why is our prey letting us, and all-ss these other people,

just walk-ss into his home? It's so stupid!" Blacknail asked his master uncertainly. The hobgoblin was very confused. Was this bandit chieftain suicidal, or was this a trap? It sort of seemed like a trap to him.

"Like I said, Galive thinks he's a priest. And what's a priest without a congregation?"

"I dunno, what's a congregation?" Blacknail whispered back nervously. Saeter snorted in amusement before responding.

"In this case, it's a big party. Galive throws a feast every week. Supposedly it's in Cor-Dius's honor, but really, it's just so he can show off," Saeter told the hobgoblin with obvious disapproval.

"Oh!" Blacknail replied excitedly. A feast meant there would be food!

The pair made their way through the crowd that was entering the building and down a wide, stone hallway. Blacknail froze as the guards gave them a brief look-over, but after seeing the pair had no obvious weapons, they waved them through. A few seconds later, Saeter and Blacknail walked into a huge, round chamber. Crude wooden tables and benches filled the center of the floor, and a long counter ran along the far wall. A lot of humans were sitting down or moving about the room. Quite a few of them were also crowded around the counter to get drinks.

Long, simple black tapestries and quite a few lamps hung from the walls, and a raised platform ran along another of the walls. More black tapestries hung around the stage, and a large bronze statue stood at the back of it. The statue was of a man in a hood, and he was holding a dagger in one hand and a flaming brazier in the other.

Blacknail's eyes were wide open in surprise as he looked around. The room was actually quite impressive. It didn't even seem like the inside of a building to him but more like a massive cave. He wanted one of his own just like it, except he'd replace the statue with an even bigger one of himself! If he killed Galive, would Herad let him keep this one? Would the statue look better with him holding a sword or Galive's severed head? Saeter must have seen Blacknail staring off into the distance and whacked him across the back of the head to get his attention.

"Just stay close to me and don't make a scene. For now, we have to wait," Saeter told Blacknail as they pushed their way toward a relatively empty corner of the room.

Up against the wall was an unused wooden bench. Saeter took a seat along its length, as far from anyone else as possible, and Blacknail sat down beside him. The old scout then leaned forward and scanned the throng of people around them.

"We'll just stay here until Galive shows himself..." Saeter told Blacknail, and he would have continued if the hobgoblin had still been there. Blacknail had smelled something delicious and wandered off to find it.

"Bloody damnation," the hobgoblin heard Saeter swear as he slipped through the crowds and out of sight of his master.

Blacknail's stomach was grumbling, and there was no way he was going to pass up an opportunity to fill it. Besides, there was really no reason for him to stay there. He'd get back to his master in a few minutes.

As he weaved through the crowds, the hobgoblin observed the people around him. He made sure to avoid walking into the direct line of sight of anyone who looked threatening, and he also kept an eye out for conveniently unattended food. Almost all the humans had drinks, but most of the ones with food were sitting down. Blacknail wanted nothing to do with the crazy human liquid that made them even crazier, but he definitely wanted something to eat. It would be hard to sneak food from the people sitting down though. They were kind of eating it...

He also couldn't take food from the people walking around with it. It was busy enough in the hall that people were watching where they were going and making sure they didn't drop their food if they bumped into someone. So Blacknail decided to head toward the smell of cooking meat; that was where the freshest morsels would be anyway. After sniffing and looking around for a few seconds, he noticed most the humans were getting their food from a man behind a counter. Blacknail headed that way. How would he get the food though? It seemed to be kept out of sight until someone arrived to take it. The other men behind the counter were probably making it...

After giving it some thought, Blacknail decided to simply

wander over to the counter and loiter around until an opportunity presented itself. The drooling hobgoblin thus casually walked over to it and leaned against it in a totally unremarkable manner. Now he just had to wait, and the tasty-smelling meat would be his. Yep, he was just another human doing stupid human things. There was absolutely no reason to look his way!

Much to the hobgoblin's alarm, his plan almost immediately went wrong. The man behind the counter noticed his approach and turned his way. He gave Blacknail a frown as he looked him over.

"Well?" The man grunted. Blacknail flinched and panicked at the unexpected question. What had he done wrong, and what did the human want? He didn't understand!

"I'm human," he blurted out before cringing at his own stupidity.

"What? It's three copper for chicken and bread, and it's four for pork. Ale is extra. What do you want?" the bearded man asked Blacknail. The hobgoblin stared blankly at the speaker in surprise. Right... he could just buy the food. That made things simpler.

"Chicken," Blacknail responded as he leaned back and attempted to look calm and collected. He liked chicken.

A few seconds later, a plate of food was placed in front of him, and Blacknail gave the nice man three copper. It wasn't his money though; he'd somehow acquired it from someone's pocket on the way over.

The roasted chicken smelled so nice, and its flesh looked soft and juicy. Blacknail wanted to start eating it right away, but he couldn't until he took off his mask. With a frustrated sigh, he wandered back over to where Saeter was sitting.

"Where in all the hells have you been, and where'd you get the grub?" Saeter asked angrily as the hobgoblin approached.

"I bought some food. I was hungry, and I stayed out of trouble," Blacknail replied smugly. He took off his mask and chewed a bird leg. Saeter stared at him for a few seconds; he didn't seem to know what to say.

"Bah, whatever. Just don't wander off again. We have a mission."

"I have food now-ss anyway," Blacknail replied without concern.

"You sure have been getting uppity lately. Remind me to schedule you more sword practice."

Blacknail opened his mouth to reply, but froze when the atmosphere around him suddenly changed. The formerly loud and wild-sounding room had grown completely quiet. The unnatural suddenness of it unnerved him, and he hissed in alarm as he looked up.

"And here's the man himself. That's Galive," Saeter remarked calmly. The steady and sure sound of his master's voice reassured Blacknail somewhat.

The hobgoblin swiftly found the source of the disturbance as he looked around the temple antechamber. Everyone was now facing the same direction and focused on the same thing. A man had walked out onto the raised stage across the room, and he was the center of attention. This new arrival was alone on the platform, but quite a few of the black-cloaked men stood in a ring along the stage and kept people away from him.

Blacknail instantly knew that this had to be Galive. Not only did he have an air of authority, but the warriors were clearly protecting him. Herad's enemy was tall and muscled. Long black hair fell down his back, and he was dressed in dark expensive-looking clothes. Like the guards below him, he also wore a long black cloak, but his was lined with silver. He was rather similar to Herad actually, except for the friendly smile on his face.

"Welcome, my fellow bandits and dwellers in darkness to this blessed festival. Tonight, we gather together to worship our divine patron Cor-Dius, he who keeps watch over those who move in secret. So feast, rejoice, and drink to your heart's content, for how better to show our appreciation than in revelry!" Galive announced enthusiastically as he raised his hands dramatically above his head.

His voice was loud and clear as it echoed throughout the stone chamber. As soon as he was done speaking, the crowd burst into cheers and joyous laughter. Ale splashed into the air as it escaped from people's raised mugs. Blacknail grimaced in distaste at what he saw; the humans were getting that stuff everywhere...

Galive was basking in the crowd's adoration, but after a few minutes, he stepped down from the stage. As the guards moved to protect him, he walked over toward an empty table that had been set aside and took a seat. Immediately, a few other figures detached themselves from the crowd and moved toward the bandit chief. Most of these people were turned away by the black-cloaked guards, but a few were let through. Among these was a group of three women, wearing next to no clothing, and several tough-looking men. Galive smiled and invited the women to sit next to him, and they were soon draped around him. The men took seats across the table from Galive and started talking amongst themselves.

"What now, master?" Blacknail asked as he watched. He didn't think it would be a good idea to go after the man now. He had a lot of guards around to protect him.

"Take a second to memorize his face. When they retire for the night, you can go over there and catch his scent and then you can track him to his room when things quiet down," Saeter explained.

Blacknail sighed; he didn't feel much like waiting around. Normally, he would enjoy lying in wait for the perfect time to strike, but all the movement and noise in the room had him at the edge of his seat and bursting with energy. He wanted to do something now!

"I could-ss go over there and listen in. They wouldn't suspect it, since humans are-ss terrible listeners with tiny little ears," Blacknail remarked.

"That's pointless. They won't be saying anything important, and you'd only be drawing attention to yourself," Saeter replied. Blacknail groaned and leaned back against the wall. His master sure knew how to take all the fun out of assassination...

The hobgoblin impatiently started looking around for something interesting to watch. Mostly, all he saw was humans staggering around, shouting, and making fools of themselves. It would be so easy to stab some of them... The minutes passed, and Blacknail grew more and more frustrated. Eventually, with an annoyed hiss, he sprung to his feet and tried to find something to do. This time though, Saeter reached out and grabbed his shoulder before he could get away.

"Sit back down and wait." The old scout pulled the hobgoblin back onto the bench. Blacknail grunted when he sat back down. He was so bored! Why couldn't he wander around a bit?

Several hours passed, and they seemed like an eternity. Saeter only allowed Blacknail up to purchase more food and drinks, and even then he accompanied the hobgoblin to the counter. Eventually, the celebration started to die down. Some of the noisy human revelers began to leave and others simply collapsed onto tables, chairs, and even the floor.

As Blacknail was throwing another bored look around the room, he noticed movement from his prey. The hobgoblin immediately sat up and focused completely on Galive; his eyes narrowed behind his mask and his ears perked up as he stared. The man had gotten up and was headed for a doorway that led further into the building. He had two of the women from earlier on each of his arms, and his guards were following him as well. Saeter had noticed this as well.

"Let's go." He grunted to the hobgoblin and stood up.

Finally! Blacknail smiled as he and his master walked across the room toward the now deserted table. They made their way past drunken humans and the garbage they had left behind. Bodies and empty tankards littered the floor.

When they reached the table, Blacknail immediately started sniffing around. He could detect the scent of several distinct humans. So he quickly leaned down over where Galive had been sitting and started smelling it. He was so engrossed in this, he didn't notice the man approach him from behind.

"What in all the hells do you two think you're doing?" one of Galive's guards asked them.

A huge, muscled thug had drawn his sword and was standing behind Blacknail while glaring suspiciously at the masked hobgoblin and his master. Blacknail stiffened in alarm, and his hand crept toward one of his daggers. Out of the corner of his eye, he quickly glanced around the room and noticed several other guards looking their way as well. That wasn't good; if it came down to a fight, then things were going to get messy quickly.

# *Chapter 20*

Before the hobgoblin could act and draw his weapon, Saeter quickly spoke up. A huge content smile appeared on his face as he turned toward the thug, and it kind of freaked Blacknail out. His master's face didn't look right unless he was glaring or scowling.

"We were just checking to see if any of the bigwigs dropped any coins. We already spent all of ours, but we still need some more drinks," Saeter muttered brokenly as if he'd been hit over the head a few times. The old scout swayed slightly as he waited for Galive's minion to respond. The guard eyed them critically for a second but then snorted in disgust.

"If you don't have any more money, then get out of here. A man of your age should bloody well know better than this," the cloaked thug told Saeter before turning around and walking away. When the other man was gone, the smile immediately dropped from Saeter's face, and a familiar scowl reappeared.

"Ya, fuck you too," he muttered and turned back to Blacknail. "Did you get it? We need to move."

"I got it; the human Galive can't hide from me!" Blacknail whispered excitedly.

"He doesn't need to hide, he's a bloody Vessel and an experienced fighter. In anything like a fair fight, he'll rip your scrawny green ass apart," Saeter growled back.

"I'll be very sneaky." Blacknail wasn't too worried about it. Galive wouldn't be the first Vessel he'd faced, and fair fights were for idiots and humans anyway.

"You'd better. Don't take any foolish risks. We can always try again another night," Saeter explained.

"Yes, master. What-ss now?"

"Now you're on your own. I'm not much good at sneaking around a building like this. Find Galive and kill him. Just don't let anyone see you, especially not Galive," Saeter ordered him sternly.

"Yes, master," Blacknail whispered back gleefully.

It was time for the hunt to begin, the oh-so-delicious hunt. Blacknail licked his lips and started salivating just thinking about it.

"I'll be outside across the street and a bit down the escape path we planned out," Saeter said. The old scout gave Blacknail a farewell nod and started walking toward the front entrance. Blacknail watched him go for a second before turning around and smirking at the door Galive had gone through.

At last, it was time to have some fun! Galive was going to regret making him sit still so long! He would also regret making Herad angry too, of course. Either one was really a bad idea.

Now, what was the best way of tracking down his prey? Blacknail slowly turned and regarded the room around him. There were still a lot of random residents of Daggerpoint around, but none of them were looking his way. The only problem was the cloaked guards standing around the perimeter of the room. Two stood by the bar, two more were by the main entrance, and one was stationed by the door Galive had gone through. As Blacknail watched, the last guard glanced his way. Blacknail knew he was acting somewhat suspicious, so he casually turned around and mingled with the remains of the earlier crowds. He then looked around the room. There was no easy way into any of the doors that led inside; they were all guarded. He'd have to make his own way in, and that meant he needed a distraction. What would work?

After a few more seconds of thought, Blacknail headed over to the table closest to the door Galive had gone through. There were two men and one woman sitting at it, and they all seemed quite drunk. The woman seemed unsteady and was leaning onto the larger of the two men. Blacknail grinned as he walked past them. They would work perfectly.

For his plan to work, he still needed another human, and none happened to be nearby. That was easily solved though. All he had to do was use a human trap. Blacknail nonchalantly strolled up behind the people seated at the table and placed several coins on the ground behind them. He then took a seat at a nearby table and waited. Within a few minutes, a human took his bait. A man from across the room noticed them and walked over to pick them up. As he passed Blacknail, the hobgoblin got up and quietly shadowed him. Just as the man was about to reach down and pick up the coins, Blacknail tripped him. The man grunted in surprise as he fell over and hit the woman at the table, and she screeched in alarm. Immediately, her large companion got up and pushed the other man away.

"You little bastard, what do you think you're doing?" the larger man roared angrily.

"Shit, it was an accident," swore the other man. He tried to pick himself off the ground. Blacknail rushed over to assist him. He extended an arm and helped the man get up.

"Thanks," the confused man told him as he stood.

"You dropped this," Blacknail told him as he pressed an item into the man's outstretched hand.

"So it's a fight you want," roared the bigger man while he drew a knife.

"Um, what..." the smaller one replied as he twitched in nervous surprise. He then looked down and noticed what he was brandishing in his hand. He was holding up a dagger of his own, the one Blacknail had put there. He paled slightly and opened his mouth.

"No, I—"

His opponent lunged toward him, and the smaller man had to defend himself. Laughter and shouts of excitement soon filled the air as everyone else began to notice a fight had started. A crowd formed.

By this time, Blacknail had already slipped away and mingled into the crowd that had rapidly formed to watch the fight. The noise and mob quickly grew large enough to attract the attention of the guards, and several rushed over, including the one that had been guarding the door. With a smug smile, Blacknail broke away from the others and walked through the now unguarded entrance while everyone was distracted. He giggled merrily to himself as he moved. It was so easy to fool humans sometimes! Why did they even bother placing sentries?

The hallway on the other side was dark, and Blacknail happily scurried into the shadows. He stopped for a second to listen for signs of movement. A second later, when he was sure there was no one nearby, he began to follow Galive's trail.

After a few seconds, he heard someone approaching, so he slipped into a side room until they had passed by. Blacknail was finding it very easy to stay out of sight. The temple had a lot of dark, unused rooms in it for him to hide in. It was hard to follow Galive's scent though. The bandit's trail was mixed up with that of many other humans, and it had been muddled up by how many times Galive had walked these halls. It was hard to figure out which trail was the freshest.

Thankfully, Blacknail didn't really need to use his nose. As he moved out of the dark hallway and into better lit areas of the temple, he heard talking up ahead, and thanks to Galive's rather boring speech from earlier, he knew exactly what the man sounded like. Blacknail couldn't make out what was being said, but he definitely knew which direction the man lay in. It was only a matter of time until he found his prey. The hobgoblin stalked forward eagerly but soon ran into a rather annoying obstacle. The room up ahead of him was brightly lit, and four of Galive's cloaked henchmen were playing cards in the middle of it.

Blacknail couldn't think of any way to sneak past them or any way to take them all out silently. He hissed in frustration and tried to think of a solution. A few moments later, he heard someone coming from behind him, so he quickly slipped into another side room and out of sight. He waited for several moments until the person had walked past, then Blacknail peeked out from around the door frame. As the hobgoblin took in the sight of another dark cloak, a great idea occurred to him.

Blacknail quickly took out his coin purse and lunged forward. Before the man could react, the hobgoblin had swung his makeshift weapon and smashed him across the back of the head. The man immediately slumped and started to collapse. Humans were apparently weak to coins in more than one way. Before the thug could hit the floor, Blacknail caught him and dragged him into the side room and then behind a pile of crates. The hobgoblin claimed the defeated warrior's cloak for his own. It was rather nice looking and much smoother feeling on his skin than his own.

The grinning hobgoblin pulled the cloak on and walked back out into the hall. When he reached the occupied room up ahead, he simply flipped the hood up and kept walking. None of the men playing the game did more than casually glance his way. Blacknail fingered the dagger and sling he had up his sleeves and ready to go just in case, but he didn't need them. The humans were engrossed in their game, and Blacknail was soon through the far door and out of their view.

The hobgoblin stopped to listen again. A few seconds later, he swerved left and headed toward a staircase. The voices sounded like they were coming from above. Once up there, he stepped out into another hallway and quickly darted into an empty-looking room before anyone came. The room was rather large, but it only contained a few chairs and crates. Blacknail had to stifle a sneeze from all the dust in it as well.

The hobgoblin could feel the floorboards tremor slightly as a group of people approached, so he moved out of sight. He hid up against the wall, behind a table that had been flipped on its side. The pack of humans quickly passed, but Blacknail didn't move. He was now close enough to Galive that he could make out the chieftain's words. In fact, the man sounded like he was in the very next room.

"Listen, I appreciate the sentiment, but you can't stay in here," Galive told someone with obvious frustration.

"Zelena sent me to protect you, and that's what I plan on doing. Need I remind you what happened to Fang? He also thought he was safe in his hideout, but Herad's assassin got to him," the other voice explained.

"I've done everything else you asked; I switched rooms, I doubled the guards, and I've let you tag along, but this is my home and you're staying out of my bedroom! This is not a debate," Galive responded.

"You're putting yourself at risk," the other man told him.

"Maybe, but how would anyone even get in here? This is the second floor, there are guards outside, and the window is too small for a man to slip through. I'm far from helpless as well; I'm a Vessel you know," Galive told him.

"A good assassin can get into anywhere."

"I guess you would know. You're the most expensive

knifeman in Daggerpoint after all, Malthus," Galive said.

"I am the best, and that's why you should listen to me," Malthus replied.

The bandit chieftain grunted disdainfully before responding. "I thought Zelena had bought out the entire assassin's guild anyway. If that's true, where did Herad's knifeman come from?"

"Zelena has entered into such an agreement with us, but we only have a monopoly on knifemen in Daggerpoint. Herad seems to have picked her killer up from outside," the assassin explained.

"Huh, I heard she's been wandering around the countryside down south. What, did she randomly come across him in the middle of the forest?" Galive laughed.

"I don't know. I've tried to find out, but I haven't had much luck. Herad is keeping him hidden, even from most of her own men. Normally that wouldn't stop me, but I suspect someone else is covering for him as well. Some of the guild informants have gone silent recently," Malthus admitted with obvious frustration.

"Seems like Zelena is paying you guys way too much then," Galive pointed out.

"That's not your concern. You just need to worry about yourself. This mysterious assassin doesn't even need to enter your room to kill you; he could poison your food or drink," the assassin-turned-bodyguard explained.

While crouched in his hiding spot, Blacknail smiled to himself. That was a great idea. He wondered if he could do that right now...

"All my food is checked anyway. Herad is far from my only enemy. You're welcome to test it yourself though," the chieftain replied.

The hobgoblin hissed in annoyance. Apparently, he couldn't poison the man after all. Oh well, he would remember the idea for later. He was sure it would come in handy eventually.

"He could also use some sort of magical device or throw a firebomb into the room," Maltheus added. Blacknail didn't have either of those, but they sure sounded cool! He was definitely going to ask for some of those when he got back.

"That's enough of this, I gave you an order. You can stay

here or guard the window from outside, it's up to you. Now, I'm going to go tell the girls to join me and you won't be there to watch, got it?" Galive commanded the assassin sternly.

"As you wish, I'll stay here and guard the door."

Galive then huffed, and Blacknail heard him walk away. Blacknail didn't worry though, he knew his target would be back. The hobgoblin made himself comfortable and prepared himself to wait for the right moment to strike.

A few minutes later, he heard the sound of Galive returning, and he wasn't alone.

"I'm going to show you ladies a great time," the chieftain bragged as he approached his room. This was quickly followed by quiet chuckling and excited murmurs from the females accompanying him.

"So, you think you're a great lover, eh?" one of them asked.

"Of course I am. Cor-Dius is the god of things done in darkness, so as his head priest, I'm obviously the greatest lover in the city, if not the world," Galive bragged as the door opened.

There was more murmuring before the door shut and blocked the noise. The assassin snorted in disgust as soon as Galive was safely out of earshot. He apparently didn't agree with the chieftain's high opinion of himself.

Just as Blacknail was settling back down to wait, noises began to erupt from the other side of the wall he was leaning on. He heard the creaking of a bed, followed by high-pitched human squeals, and the sound of flesh slapping against flesh. The hobgoblin groaned quietly to himself. He really didn't want to sit there and listen to humans mating. Hopefully it would be over soon. However, the noises actually soon grew louder, and groans of pleasure were added to the mix. Blacknail stuck his tongue out in disgust as he plugged his fingers into his ears. The noises were giving him a huge headache.

"Stupid pink-ss humans," he quietly hissed as his imagination started supplying images to go along with the noises. The hobgoblin now had another reason to kill Galive.

After what seemed like hours, but was probably actually much less time, the noises finally stopped and the room grew quiet. Blacknail heard a groan of relief from the man guarding Galive's door and nodded in agreement. He was also glad they had finally stopped. When enough time had passed that the hobgoblin was sure his target and his company were asleep, he put his plan into motion. On the outside wall of the room, there was a small cross-shaped window. Blacknail was pretty sure it was exactly the same as the one in his target's room. It was too small for all but the smallest humans to fit through, but Blacknail thought he could slip through. Hobgoblins were very skinny, that was part of the reason they were so attractive.

Silently, he crept over to the window and looked outside. There was a guard holding a lantern down in the yard below. The man seemed to be patrolling the perimeter of the temple. He was doing a terrible job of it though, which was typical for a human. Blacknail took a second to take off his new cloak and put it away. It was comfy, and he'd decided to keep it. He then looked out the window and observed the below guard's routine for a few minutes. When the hobgoblin was satisfied that the man was unlikely to look up and spot him, he squeezed through the outside window. It was a tight squeeze, and getting his head through was uncomfortable—because his brain was so big—but Blacknail managed it. There was a small ridge on the wall outside, so the hobgoblin grabbed it and began to shimmy carefully along it toward the window to the next room. His claws dug into the wood and gave him nice firm handholds.

After a few minutes of climbing and clambering along the wall,Blacknail managed to make itacross the outside wallwithout alerting the guard below. The hobgoblin let out a small sigh of relief when he reached his destination and saw it was indeed the same type of window he had just come through. It would have been really awkward if it hadn't been. Blacknail carefully reached up to get a solid hold on the windowsill and hauled himself over to it. As he hung there, and the light of the guard's lamp passed below him, he carefully pulled himself up to the window opening. There was a heavy blue curtain in the way, so he gently pushed it aside.

The hobgoblin grinned wickedly and shivered with anticipation. His prey was right there and sleeping defenselessly. Soon the hunt would be complete, and the sweet taste of victory would be his! The clouds above shifted, and for a second, the moon shone brightly in the sky. Blacknail's thin, clawed shadow stretched out and into the room.Seeing this, the hobgoblin giggled and moved eagerly in for the kill.

# *Chapter 21*

There was a lamp on a dresser against one of the walls, and it lit the room that lay on the other side of the window. From where he was hanging outside, Blacknail could see the room's occupants just fine. All five of the humans within were lying next to each other on the big bed that dominated the room. The sleepers' relaxed breathing made soft sighing sounds as they slept. The hobgoblin's skin tingled in anticipation as he gazed upon his helpless prey. Excitedly, he started to slip through the window.

Unfortunately, he'd misjudged the size of the opening slightly, and his head got momentarily stuck. After a second or two of trying to painfully squeeze his skull through the tight frame, he succeeded and popped through. A soft thud echoed forth as Blacknail lost his balance and landed on the floor at the base of the window. He froze for a moment to make sure he hadn't spooked anyone, but the only sound he heard was the gentle breathing of slumbering humans. With renewed confidence, the hobgoblin got up and crept up to the bed. It wasn't that fancy of a bed, but it certainly was huge. Blacknail thought it could easily fit a dozen humans lying side by side. Why did this man need such a huge bed? Maybe it was some sort of human status symbol?

Blacknail loomed over Galive's slumbering face and smiled smugly. The bandit chieftain didn't seem so tough now! He was just prey. In fact, it would be so easy to toy with him a little before finishing him off... The hobgoblin reached over until his hand hung over the sleeping man's face. His claws were a hair's breadth from the man's eyes when he froze. No, fooling around now would be a bad idea. It would be really messy and would probably make a lot of noise. Blacknail frowned in regret and pulled his hand back and drew his dagger. It was best to do this quickly.

Suddenly, Galive stirred slightly and started murmuring something. Blacknail panicked for a second and jumped slightly in surprise before he realized the man was still unconscious. He was talking in his sleep. Feeling curious, the hobgoblin leaned over to listen.

"Oh ya, that's the way. Spread that honey around," Galive whispered.

Blacknail blinked in confusion. What was this now? What could this weird human possibly be talking about? Well, whatever. He was here to kill Galive, not try to understand him.

Blacknail stopped wasting time. He quickly grabbed Galive's long dark hair and pulled it down as he dragged his dagger against the man's exposed throat. Blood poured from the long, jagged wound and onto the sheets as the knife bit deep into Galive's flesh.

Galive's dark eyes shot open and fluttered briefly before going dead. Blacknail smirked as he stared intently into their confused depths. When he was sure the man was dead, he stepped quietly away. That was one less bandit chief that would be trying to take his and Herad's territory, and it hadn't even been hard to get rid of him.

Blacknail was about to make his exit, when the woman to the right of Galive's bloody corpse stirred in her sleep. The movement caused Blacknail to instantly focus on her. Some of Galive's blood was pooling beneath the woman's bare shoulders and was staining her long blonde hair. It was also clearly disturbing her slumber. She stirred again, and Blacknail realized he had to do something before she woke up and raised the alarm. He stalked back over to her, trying to come up with a solution. He couldn't remove the blood; there was too much of it, and he wasn't that thirsty. He also couldn't move woman without waking her... With an annoyed sigh, Blacknail leaned over her and cut her throat too. When he was sure she was dead, and no one else was about to wake up, he tiptoed over to the window and made his exit. He managed to make it through without getting his head stuck this time.

As Blacknail crouched on the windowsill, he observed the

yard below him. The guard from earlier was still out there, but he was walking away from the hobgoblin. The man was about to turn the corner of the building and disappear out of sight.

With his mission accomplished, Blacknail was beginning to feel impatient, so he climbed down the exterior wall as far as he could and then simply dropped the rest of the way. He landed unharmed on all four limbs and dashed for the stone fence that encircled the temple. He hit it at full speed and vaulted over it onto the street on the other side. With that done, he'd successfully escaped from Galive's lair unharmed.

As he raced through the dark and dirty streets of Daggerpoint, toward safety and his rendezvous with Saeter, the hobgoblin giggled happily to himself. That had been too easy. The bandit chieftain had been supposed to be so tough, but he hadn't been a problem for Blacknail! That other assassin guy, Malthus, had been useless and impotent. Blacknail giggled again as he turned into an alley. The fool had just stood outside the door as Blacknail slit the throat of the man he was supposed to be protecting! It was hilarious how bad the man was at his job, or maybe Blacknail was just that good. Obviously, Blacknail was an amazing assassin, probably the best ever! He was like Herad's fearsome, unstoppable shadow-killer guy! When he returned with news of Galive's death, there was no way Herad would beat him up ever again. In fact, she would probably tell everyone how amazing he was and then give him some pie.

Blacknail reached the corner right before his destination, so he slowed down and looked for any sign of Saeter. A brief inspection didn't reveal any traces of him, and the hobgoblin grew slightly concerned. Had something happened to him?

"Where are you, master?" he muttered to himself.

Blacknail began to creep around stealthily as he searched. He moved from shadow to shadow as he wandered around the area near the meeting place. He didn't find anything until he stumbled upon a faint scent trail. It led into a nearby building, so Blacknail followed it in. All the structures in this part of the city were small and tightly packed, and this one didn't stand out. It did appear to be abandoned though; the missing front door was a subtle clue.

Blacknail walked into the pitch-black interior and headed up the stairs to the room on the second floor. He was careful not to make any noise, because he didn't know what to expect. Also, creeping around all sneaky-like was more fun.

When the hobgoblin got to the top of stairs, he saw a dark figure looking out a window through a doorway. He froze for a second but soon realized it was Saeter. Before he started moving again, an idea occurred to him. His master didn't appear to know that Blacknail was here... so wouldn't it be fun to surprise him! Blacknail grinned gleefully to himself. This was going to be so much fun! As he stepped through the doorway, he felt something tug gently on his ankle and then heard a faint clattering noise. He looked down to see what it was and realized he'd stumbled over a piece of string that had been tied to a pile of sticks.

How had that gotten there? Well, hopefully it hadn't ruined his surprise. Blacknail looked back up to see something shiny. It was Saeter's unsheathed sword point, and it was less than an inch from his face. The surprised hobgoblin went very still as his eyes widened in alarm. Yep, the surprise was ruined, and this had definitely been a bad idea.

"The Deep Green has yet to spit out a beast that can sneak up on me, hobgoblin, and that includes the likes of you," Saeter whispered threateningly before relaxing and dropping his blade.

"I was just having fun. I wasn't going to do anything bad," Blacknail whined.

"If I thought you were, I'd have already skewered you. Missions aren't the time to be having fun. That's how people get hurt," Saeter replied gruffly.

Blacknail nodded enthusiastically in agreement. He'd certainly almost been hurt. His master grunted, and his hard expression softened. The hobgoblin thought he detected a slight smile on the man's lips.

"How'd the mission go; did you get Galive?" Saeter asked.

"Of course. I started a fight, crept through the shadows, went in and out some windows, and murdered the sleeping human. There was nothing to eat," Blacknail explained cheerfully.

The old scout rolled his eyes in an exasperated manner after the hobgoblin finished speaking. Blacknail frowned at his master's response. What was wrong with his answer? It covered all the important bits.

"You can tell Herad the details. Did that Elixir of Mahedium's come in handy?" Saeter inquired.

Blacknail mouth fell open slightly as the question caught him off guard. He had kind of forgotten he'd had it. There were definitely a few times a boost of speed and strength would have been useful though...

"It was too easy. I didn't need it," Blacknail bragged. Saeter gave him a suspicious glance but didn't bother to question the hobgoblin.

"Come on, let's get back to base. Winter's approaching, and it's getting bloody cold out." Saeter walked past him and headed downstairs.

The hobgoblin sighed regretfully as he followed the old scout. His master probably shouldn't have waited out in the cold for him; he was going to catch the sniffles. Obviously, he'd been worried Blacknail was going to mess things up, so he'd stuck around. Why couldn't his master have just trusted him? He was very trustworthy!

After several minutes of walking through the nearly pitch-black street, Blacknail was starting to wonder where they were going. They weren't headed anywhere near Herad's base. Saeter soon turned around and scowled at Blacknail.

"Why don't you lead the way? Waiting around for you so long has left my legs sore," he told the hobgoblin. Blacknail wasn't sure why that mattered. Wouldn't he have to walk the same distance anyway? Well, whatever...

"We're going back to the lair?" he asked, just to make sure.

"Of course we bloody are. Where else would we be headed?" Saeter huffed indignantly.

"Nowhere-ss, sorry," the hobgoblin replied and quickly took the lead.

He took a second to decide on the fastest route, and within minutes they were approaching Herad's stronghold. The guards out front simply nodded in greeting when they recognized Saeter, and Blacknail gave them a friendly nod back. The pair then walked through the front entrance and into the room on the other side. As usual, there were several bandits sitting around the table there playing a game of cards. This time, however, Khita was one of them. Judging by the pile of coins in front of her, and the dissatisfied looks on several of her opponents' faces, she appeared to be winning.

The young redhead glanced their way as Saeter and Blacknail entered and smiled cheerfully at them. She seemed to having fun. Blacknail didn't like that.

"You're back! How did your top secret mission for the boss go? I know she sent you out to do something, all hush-hush," she asked.

"If you know that, then you shouldn't be asking," interjected a large male bandit that was sitting across from her.

"Bah, you're just upset that you're losing," Khita responded as she beamed at Blacknail. The bandit scowled angrily at her, and one of his eyebrows started twitching.

"No, you're lucky the boss likes you so much," the man muttered angrily.

Blacknail agreed with him, but he found himself giving the man a steady disapproving glare. If anyone was going to kill Khita, it was going to be him! The bandit met his stare for a second but hurriedly looked away.

"Where's Herad?" Saeter asked Khita.

"She was in that big room down the hall to the left, the one with all the couches, the last time I checked," Khita replied.

Saeter grunted his acknowledgement and unceremoniously left the room. After one quick glance back at the man who had challenged him, Blacknail followed his master out. It only took a few seconds for them to reach the room Khita had mentioned, and Herad was indeed there. She was sprawled comfortably over the edge of one of the couches. A platter of food and drink had been set on a side table in front of her, and several of her usual guards were also there. Most of them were standing around the room, but two had seats of their own. Herad smiled eagerly when she saw Saeter and Blacknail and pulled herself up into more of a sitting position.

"Clear the room," she announced.

With a quick nod of acknowledgement, the guards got up and left the room. There was a quiet thud as they closed the doors behind them.

"Since you're both back, I take it that Galive is dead?" the chieftain asked them.

"So the hobgoblin tells me," Saeter replied.

"I totally killed him. I cut his neck deep as he slept, and he bled everywhere!" Blacknail answered cheerfully. Herad ignored Blacknail and raised an eyebrow dubiously at Saeter.

"You think he's lying?" she asked curiously.

"Ha, no. He went in, and he came out alive. That means Galive is dead," Saeter huffed.

"You never know. Maybe they found out about your hob's secret weakness for sweet cakes and bribed him," she replied with a chuckle and a grin.

Blacknail scowled in annoyance. That was just insulting. He would never betray his tribe for a sweet cake! There weren't enough cakes in the whole world for that. Of course, the world wasn't that big and mostly seemed to be made up of trees.

Herad saw the hobgoblin's look, but instead of growing angry, she smirked. She then reached out and grabbed one of the pastries from the platter and tossed it up into the air toward Blacknail. Instantly, the hobgoblin caught it and shoved it into his mouth.

"Thank-ss you so much, mistress," he told her happily as he chewed. All his previous feelings of irritation had been completely forgotten.

"If only all men were so easy to please," Herad remarked with a look toward Saeter.

"You mean control," Saeter replied dryly.

"That too," Herad added with another smug grin. "Saeter, I'll have you get a report from Blacknail and give it to me tomorrow. His full reports are... different."

"They certainly are," Saeter agreed.

Herad then turned to the hobgoblin. "For now, just tell me about anything important or unexpected that happened, and this time leave out any details about how things tasted or smelled. I don't need to know about that," Herad asked, as she grimaced in disgust.

Blackail sighed in disappointment. Those were usually the most interesting parts though! He took a moment to recall everything that had happened on his mission. He'd walked there with Saeter, there'd been some humans, he'd eaten the chicken, he'd tricked some more humans, bleh bleh, and then he'd killed Galive and ran away. Oh wait, there had been one thing.

"There was a man, an assassin. He was there to protect Galive, but he sucked at it," Blacknail told his chieftain.

"That's interesting. You overheard them talking?" Herad asked.

"Yes, he was sent by a Zelena human."

"See, Saeter? I knew they were working together. Galive swore he was a neutral party, but I wasn't fooled! That bastard lied like a village peddler; for all that, he was supposed to be a priest," Herad exclaimed excitedly.

"I didn't disagree with you about that," Saeter pointed out.

"I guess you didn't, for once," Herad commented with a roll of her eyes.

"If that's everything, then I'd like to get some sleep. I also wouldn't mind a hot cup of tea," Saeter told her.

"Fine, I'd hate to keep you up past your bedtime. You two can go rest," Herad answered dismissively.

"It's not my bedtime. I'm going to go out and find some food," Blacknail interjected.

"You're coming with me. Now is not the time to be wandering around," Saeter replied as he gave the hobgoblin a stern glance.

"But I'm still hungry," Blacknail whined.

"Grab something from the kitchen," Saeter told him and gave him a light push toward the door.

"Fine, but I'm eating whatever I want," the hobgoblin replied as he opened the door.

"Go ahead, just keep out of trouble," his master said when they passed by the guards from earlier.

After almost an hour of ransacking the kitchen and terrorizing the chef, Blacknail had stuffed himself enough that he began to grow sleepy. Saeter had already left, so the hobgoblin yawned and headed for his room. Once there, he disrobed and began rearranging his blankets for maximum comfort. The hobgoblin then curled up on his bed and almost immediately went to sleep. He'd earned his rest.

It wasn't to be as long a rest as he'd hoped though. Several hours later, he twitched in his sleep as an unexpected rhythm penetrated his subconscious. When the quiet sound repeated itself, the hobgoblin stirred and frowned in annoyance. He opened one eye slightly and saw it was still dark outside. He didn't like being awakened like this, so hopefully whatever the annoying thing was, it would soon stop or die horribly. It sounded like footsteps. In fact, it sounded like several people were trying to move quietly, and it was coming from the roof...

The hobgoblin growled softly as he pulled himself completely awake.His tribe was under attack!

# *Chapter 22*

Blacknail immediately pulled himself up from the tangle of sheets around him and growled menacingly. The sound of his anger echoed throughout his small room as he shot to his feet. Someone was trying to be sneaky and invade his tribe's lair!

"Enemies," he hissed to himself. The hobgoblin felt his drowsiness burn away under the relentless waves of his rage. His lips rose to reveal his teeth as he snarled. Whoever these people were, they were about to get a very nasty surprise. He was going to stab them, a lot.

Blacknail didn't waste any time. He quickly began throwing on his clothes and arming himself as he carefully listened in on the enemies' progress. The footsteps were slowly but steadily crossing the roof. At first the hobgoblin assumed they were coming to attack him, but he realized that was unlikely. No one knew who he was or where he'd stashed his cheese.

That meant they must be after Herad! They were assassins and aiming to murder Blacknail's chieftain the same way the hobgoblin had killed the other chiefs. Well, it wouldn't work, because they were much worse at it than Blacknail. The hobgoblin had already discovered them, and not being detected before reaching the target was the most important bit.

Blacknail pulled on his mask, slipped quietly through his door, and stalked quickly forward down the hallway toward Herad's room. The hallway was dark except for a single candle set on a small table, and there was a sleepy-looking guard leaning against the wall beside it. Blacknail growled as he noticed the man's eyes were closed. What kind of pathetic warrior went to sleep in the middle of a job?

The man was apparently a light sleeper though, because the hobgoblin's outraged growl woke him. He blinked and turned to see what was going on and jumped in alarm when he saw the masked and cloaked hobgoblin descending upon him.

"Shh, quiet." Blacknail raised a finger to his mouth. "There are-ss people on the roof."

"What?" the man whispered in confusion. He began to recognize Blacknail and started calming down.

"Assassins on the roof!" Blacknail whispered back. Why did he always have to repeat himself? Human hearing wasn't that bad, even if they had tiny pink ears.

Herad's guard flinched as the hobgoblin's words finally sank in. He threw a quick glance upward, as if he expected to see something. Blacknail sighed in frustration; he wasn't impressed.

"We need to raise the alarm," the man said a few seconds later.

"No, then-ss they would run. Give me a door key and go raise the alarm silently. Herad would-ss want us to warn her and then trap them so they end up dead," Blacknail argued. There was no way Herad would want to pass up an opportunity to kill some of her enemies. She was pretty consistent that way.

The guard seemed to agree with Blacknail's judgment of Herad's character, because he nodded reluctantly in agreement and handed Blacknail the key.

"I'll be right back. You wake the boss then. Better you than me anyway; she's not a morning person," the man told the hobgoblin. He then quickly disappeared into a side room, and several seconds later, the hobgoblin could hear him begin whispering to someone else.

Blacknail was tense and nervous as he unlocked the door and walked through it. Not because of the assassins, but rather because he was pretty sure the guard was right about how Herad wouldn't like being disturbed. She would, however, like not being informed of the assassins even less, which meant there really weren't any good options.

The chieftain's room was dark, except for the slivers of moonlight that squeezed through the cracks of the one small, shuttered window and the light of the candle in the hallway that shone out from under the closed door behind Blacknail. It was more than enough light for the hobgoblin's sensitive eyes. He could make out most the details of the room, including the bed Herad was sleeping on. The bandit chieftain was curled up under her sheets, and her sleeping face was pointed his way.

As he approached Herad, Blacknail very carefully calculated a minimum safe distance that was out of reach of a sword. He didn't believe for a second she didn't have one shoved somewhere around the bed or that she wouldn't use it on him if he angered her.

Once he had gotten as close as he dared, Blacknail took a second to study Herad. She looked different somehow, but the hobgoblin couldn't immediately figure out why. Then he realized her eyes weren't as shadowed and menacing as usual. Did Herad wear makeup? No wait, that was silly. Of course it was actually war paint. That made much more sense.

The creaking of wooden supports from above brought Blacknail back to reality. He knew he needed to wake his chief up before the assassins arrived, but he couldn't figure out how to do it safely. Yelling was out of the question, and so was touching her. Maybe he could poke her with a long stick? Blacknail looked her over again. She actually didn't seem all that dangerous at the moment. In fact, she seemed kind of vulnerable, so he should probably just go shake her awake. That would be the quietest way to do it after all. He took a tentative step forward...

"I can think of three reasons a hobgoblin would be creeping around in my bedroom after dark, and you'll only survive one of them," Herad told him as she lay unmoving in bed with her eyes closed.

Blacknail instantly froze, and he felt a cold shiver work its way through him. His eyes widened as he realized he'd almost gotten himself killed. Good thing he was a coward.

"There are bad assassins on the roof! When I—your ever-loyal servant—heard them, I told your guards. Then I came in here to tell you," Blacknail whispered to her nervously. The bandit chieftain grunted and opened her eyes. Her cold gaze bore into him as she studied his face. She was still scary, even without war paint.

"Good, because you're not my type, and it'd be a shame to have to kill you for being too ambitious," she told him as she sat up. Her movement caused her blankets to shift and slip off her shoulders. Underneath that, she was wearing a loose, plain white shirt and long dark pants.

“How many?” she asked as she stood up and pulled on a leather jacket that had been lying beside her bed.

“Five or six,” Blacknail replied uncertainly. He was just grateful his answer had apparently been the right one. What had the other two been?

“They’re coming for me?” Herad pulled a sheathed sword and hilt out from under her pillow.

“Sounds like,” Blacknail whispered back.

There was suddenly a slight creaking noise from the roof above, and both of them looked up. Herad narrowed her eyes and turned to the window. It was the only way in other than the door. There was then a creaking noise from behind them as the door swung open slightly. Both Herad and Blacknail tensed and reached for their weapons. However, it was only several of Herad’s guards. When they saw their boss up and about, they stopped and waited for orders. Herad studied them for a second before motioning silently for them to back off. The man in front nodded, took a step back out of the room, and then carefully shut the door behind him. The bandit chieftain moved over to her bed and pulled several pillows out from underneath it. She stuffed them under her blanket, so it looked like someone was still sleeping there. With that done, she crouched down beside the bed out of sight of the window.

This answered a question Blacknail had been wondering about. So that was where all the spare pillows had gone. They’d disappeared suddenly right after that one time he’d piled them all on his bed to make himself more comfortable. The hobgoblin ignored that for now though and tried to find somewhere to hide. Another creak, this time from the roof right above the window, meant the hobgoblin had to move quickly.

He didn’t see anything large enough to hide behind, except for the bed, so he crept up to the window and pulled himself up over it and into the rafters above. Humans rarely ever looked up; it was a weakness of the species. Herad gave him a dubious look but just shook her head and crouched back down out of sight. Blacknail was fairly sure that meant she trusted his judgment, and why wouldn't she?

Almost immediately, the shutters below Blacknail shook ever so slightly. A slim, hooked blade poked out from between them and slid upward until it hit the latch. There was the faintest of clicking noises as the blade knocked the latch loose and unlocked the window.

As the hobgoblin watched from above, the shutters swung slowly open. A second later, a man wrapped in dark clothing crept through the window and into the room. He quickly glanced around the room and stared apprehensively at the dummy beneath Herad's sheets for a few seconds before tiptoeing off to the side. The assassin was wearing a black hood and had a dark gray scarf wrapped around the lower part of his face, but Blacknail recognized his scent. It was Malthus, the assassin who had failed so badly at being Galive's bodyguard.

As soon as Malthus was out of the way, his companions followed him in until all five of them were inside. Blacknail watched with interest as Malthus raised a hand and signaled to his men using some sort of sign language the hobgoblin didn't understand. Almost instantly, the assassins spread out and stalked stealthily towards Herad's bed. Blacknail waited expectantly for them to step completely into the trap, but halfway there, Malthus froze and hurriedly signaled his men. Instantly, the two men closest to the window turned and ran for it. The other three, including the leader, drew their swords and began backing up slowly. Up in the dark rafters, Blacknail pouted in disappointment. Somehow, they'd obviously noticed the trap. That was no fun.

Several things then happened all at once. Blacknail dropped down onto the back of one of the fleeing assassins and then lashed out and kicked the other one savagely in the head. Meanwhile, Herad rose from behind the bed with her blade drawn and launched herself at the other three assassins. The ringing of clashing blades drew the attention of several of Herad's guards who had been waiting in the hallway. They threw the door open and moved to join the fight.

As Blacknail grappled his opponent to the floor, Herad engaged two of the assassins in a swordfight. The third attacker stepped back and quickly reached into his robe before pulling out a beaker and throwing it violently toward her charging minions. The glass container hit the floor and spilled liquid everywhere as it shattered. Herad's thugs stepped onto the mess as they ran toward her and began tripping all over themselves as their feet slid out from under them.

The man wrestling Blacknail finally went limp as the hobgoblin withdrew his knife from under his ribs. The assassin Blacknail had kicked earlier had gotten to his feet and was crawling through the window, so the hobgoblin grabbed the booted foot closest to him and pulled him back into the room.

The assassin who had thrown the vial used the time he had bought himself and his companions to turn back toward Herad. He was, however, too late to prevent Herad from parrying one of his companion's blades and unleashing a lightning-quick slash that sent the assassin's severed hand falling to the floor.

"Plan Dawn," Malthus barked as he ducked under a slash from Herad.

Hearing this, the assassin who had thrown the beaker broke away from the fight and made a dash for the window. He ran right past Blacknail as he fled. The hobgoblin was now wrestling with his second assassin, and he wasn't doing nearly as well as he had against the first. The man had got in a lucky blow at the start and kicked Blacknail's knife away. The masked hobgoblin had more, but he was too busy trying not to get choked out by the larger and stronger human to draw them. He also wished he wasn't wearing the mask so he could bite the stupid man's fingers off, or that he hadn't forgotten to take his Elixir again.

Herad was now locked in a brutal sword fight with the assassin leader. Both of them launched attack after attack at each other with furious precision. Their blades flashed through the air so quickly, they were almost impossible to see. It was obvious both combatants were Vessels; no one else could move so swiftly. However, they weren't evenly matched. Herad was slowly forcing Malthus back. She smiled cruelly as she fought, and she seemed to be having quite a bit of fun. The assassin leader, on the other hand, looked nervous. He was obviously having trouble avoiding some of her attacks and already had a few superficial gashes in his clothing.

The man who was fighting Blacknail suddenly lurched

backward and surprised the hobgoblin by punching him heavily in the side of the head. Blacknail's mask absorbed most of the blow, but it also shifted slightly to the side and blinded him. The now blind hobgoblin could only flail about and try to grab his opponent's hands. This didn't work very well though, and a few seconds later, he lurched backwards as something slammed into his stomach.

By this time, the third assassin had reached the window, but instead of diving through it, he turned and pulled something out of his coat.

"Dawn," he yelled at the top of his lungs, which caused everyone to look his way. Blinding light then burst forth and enveloped the room. Swearing rang out as everyone tried to shield their eyes.

"Fucking mage," Herad hissed.

The leader of the assassins had been facing away from the light and prepared for it, so he wasn't blinded. He took the opportunity to slash at Herad's neck. The bandit chieftain must have sensed something though, because she threw herself out of the way of the attack. The assassin's sword ended up only grazing her shoulder. Malthus didn't try for a second attack. He turned and fled toward the window as Herad and her men tried to organize themselves and regain their footing.

The assassin that was grappling with Blacknail pushed him aside and tried to rise to his feet. As Blacknail lurched backward, he growled in frustration. Rage and confusion pulsed through him until he couldn't take it anymore, and he ripped his mask off. His opponent froze, and his eyes widened in terror as the hobgoblin's inhuman visage was revealed. Blacknail didn't waste the opportunity. He grabbed one of the man's wrists, and before the man could recover, he lunged down and savagely bit into it with his now exposed teeth.

Screams filled the room as the hobgoblin dug his teeth deeper into the human's flesh. The iron taste of blood filled his mouth and excited him. Filled with a sudden bout of hungry energy, the hobgoblin let go of his opponent's ruined arm, jumped up, and dug his fingers into the man's eyes. The hobgoblin's long, sharp nails cut through his gloves and deep into the man's sockets. More tortured screams rent the air.

As the man lay helpless and writhing beneath him, Blacknail took the time to look around the room. The other assassins had already fled. Only Herad, her minions, and several corpses remained. Herad blinked and dropped the hand that was massaging her eyes. She looked at Blacknail and ground her teeth together furiously.

"Leave the wounded one, you idiot. After them!" she yelled at him.

Blacknail immediately grabbed his fallen mask and jumped to obey. He leapt off his defeated prey and launched himself at the window. In midair, he grabbed the windowsill and swung himself around to the outside wall, where he sank his claws into the wood and began to climb after the assassins. He could hear them running across the roof and see the discarded picce of rope they had used to escape to the street below.

With inhuman agility, the hobgoblin pulled himself onto the roof and scrambled after the fleeing assassins. Instinctively, he knew the best way to catch them was to make sure they didn't know they were being followed. Also, Blacknail wasn't sure what to do with them when he caught them. They still outnumbered him, and Malthus was apparently a much better swordsman than he was a bodyguard. So the hobgoblin kept his head down and used the angle of the roof to hide himself from sight. When the remaining pair of assassins reached the end of the roof, they disappeared. Blacknail scurried over and saw them on the ground below him. He also saw the rope they had used to get there. As he watched, the assassins ran across the dark city street and into an alley.

Blacknail slid down the rope and hurried after them. He couldn't see them, but he could still hear their heavy footsteps and follow their scent. His quarry twisted and weaved their way through the city as they tried to lose any possible pursuit. Blacknail found it highly amusing. All their efforts were utterly pointless against him; he followed after them through the alleys and back ways of the city without any problem.

Soon, Blacknail arrived in a familiar part of town. The trail of the assassins who had tried to kill Herad led up to the front entrance of a large, colorful building that the hobgoblin didn't immediately recognize because he hadn't really looked at it from the front before. It was the place he'd met Luphera. A suspicious growl escaped from Blacknail's lips as he stood at the opening of a nearby alleyway. The darkness of night hid him as he glared at the building and considered this new development.

Was Luphera involved in the attack on Herad? It wasn't impossible, she had bragged about having minions and connections. The idea upset Blacknail for some reason. He wasn't sure why though; it wasn't like they were of the same tribe, and he didn't really even know much about her. In fact, she was very unsettling to be around.

What should he do now? Could he just return to Herad and tell her where the assassins had gone? Did she expect him to kill them before returning? He probably could head back now without being punished, but Blacknail realized he didn't want to. He wanted to know exactly what was going on and whether Luphera was involved. Yes, perhaps it was time to be a little more... aggressive with the woman. He had let her weird perfume and behavior put him off guard before, but now he was done being on the defensive. He would find her and get answers, but this time there would be no stupid games. He would simply take what he wanted, no matter who he had to kill.

# *Chapter 23*

Blacknail growled as he made his way around the building. He sounded like a beast from the deepest corner of the Green, because that was what he was. He was headed toward the building's back exit. The way was familiar, and he'd been here enough times now that he wasn't really paying attention, and thus he almost walked right into a pair of guards. He heard them coming only seconds before they turned the corner. Startled, Blacknail immediately ducked behind a large barrel of rainwater and out of sight. A man and a woman with sheathed swords and leather armor stepped into view and headed his way.

Blacknail's stomach twisted as he watched them from concealment. He wasn't in a very good hiding spot, and if the two thugs got too close or walked behind the barrel, they would see him. The hobgoblin cursed himself for not paying attention. He held his breath as the two humans walked right by him. One of the pair suddenly stopped walking and threw a look backward at the barrel. She stared at it for a few seconds and frowned when she didn't see anything out of the ordinary.

"What are you doing?" her partner asked.

"Nothing, I thought I heard something, but there's nothing there," she replied before turning back around and walking away.

"This is Daggerpoint. If you jump at every shadow, you'll be spending the entire day on your toes," the man remarked.

"Maybe, but that means it's also one of the places where you're most likely to get a knife in your back," she replied before they both turned the corner and disappeared again.

Blacknail sighed with relief as soon as they were gone. When the humans had passed him by and he'd become exposed, he'd instinctively crept around to the other side of the barrel and back out of sight. His instincts had served him well, but then again, they almost always did. They weren't terrible and useless like those of a human.

The hobgoblin stood back up and continued on his way. He still burned with anger, but now he was struggling to keep it contained. Nothing good ever came from letting his fury loose. He prowled through the alley and toward Luphera's window. When he got to the corner that overlooked the passage behind the building, he stopped and peered stealthily around it.

The sun was now starting to rise. The tips of its rays had just begun to shine over the grungy buildings of the city. This gave Blacknail a very good view of the two guards that were standing by the back entrance of his destination. Both of them were large, armed men with purple vests, and one of them had placed a lit lantern on top of a nearby crate. The windows of the building behind them also shed light out on the back street. None of the sources of illumination were that strong, so together they cast a confusing maze of shadows onto the dirty cobblestones and mud of the alley.

Blacknail studied the guards from the mouth of the alley. Why were there all these guards around suddenly? There had never been so many before. Were they expecting him? It didn't matter though. There was no way he was going to let a few stupid humans stop him. He would get the answers he wanted. He didn't know why he felt so driven to question Luphera, and he didn't really care. The hobgoblin glared at the guards furiously for several seconds, and then several more. Okay, he had no idea how he was going to actually get past them...

There were a lot of shadows to work with, but it would still be difficult to sneak past them up into a window. No, he'd have to get rid of them somehow. How would he do it though? He could sneak up to them and try to take them out quickly before they could raise the alarm, but that would be risky even with Elixir. A distraction might work, if he could come up with a good enough one. He didn't feel like sneaking around anymore though. He was angry and wanted to hurt someone, and these men were undoubtedly connected to the assassins that had awakened him in the middle of the night! He really liked sleeping on his bed. So he would use a distraction and then attack them! Why do one when you could do both? Even so early in the morning Daggerpoint was never a quiet city, so a little noise ought to be fine.

The hobgoblin waited until the men were looking the other way then made his move. He stalked silently out of the alley and through the shadows. He kept the cool stone wall at his back until he reached an empty wheelbarrow someone had left at the side of the street. He ducked behind it and carefully prepped his sling.

Blacknail took out his vial of Elixir, lifted his mask, and gulped it down. Ugh, it still tasted like dirt, but he was going to need every bit of speed he could muster. When he was sure no one was looking again, he gently lobbed a stone from his pouch down the street, so it clattered against a wall on the other side of the guards.

"What was that?" one of them asked as he took a step closer to the noise to get a better view.

"Probably a rat, they get pretty big here," the other man replied without concern.

That was when the second stone from Blacknail's sling took him in the back of the head. The thug immediately crumpled as a muffled cracking echoed through the alley. His companion jumped and began to turn back around, but Blacknail had already erupted from the shadows.

With savage ferocity, he descended upon the man, and Elixir burned through his flesh and bone as he leapt. With inhuman speed, the hobgoblin's blade slashed through the air and sliced into the man's unprotected neck. The guard barely had time to gasp before he was dead on his feet. Then he crumpled and hit the ground.

Blacknail froze and scanned the windows around him for any sign that he'd been seen or heard. When he didn't see anything, he switched to focusing on listening. A few streets away, a horse neighed, and the pounding of footsteps and creaking of wheels came from everywhere. None of that was unusual though, so it didn't sound like he'd alerted anyone. The hobgoblin then crouched over the body of the man he'd hit with his sling and listened for any signs of breathing. Nope, nothing;

the human was dead. Blacknail grabbed the corpse's feet and dragged it out of sight behind a pile of wood. He was breathing slightly harder when he went to get the other body.

"Stupid fat city humans, they should-ss get outside more," Blacknail muttered as he strained to move the second corpse. The people of Daggerpoint were even more bloated than normal humans.

When that was done, he scowled at the blood trail he'd left in the dirt. A few seconds later, he shrugged and turned to look up at Luphera's window. It probably wouldn't matter; most humans were blind and couldn't smell at all anyway. Why did they even have noses?

Blacknail quickly began climbing up the stonework and wooden struts until he reached the opening on the second floor. He didn't have a lot of time. He wasn't stupid enough to believe that even humans wouldn't eventually find the bodies; soon the guards he'd taken out would be missed. Blacknail reached the window and peeked over the windowsill. He didn't see anyone there, so he pulled himself up and crawled inside. The bedroom was basically the same as before. The furniture was still lavish and comfortable looking, but only the faintest hint of the incense remained in the air.

Blacknail remembered his first visit here, so the first thing he did was double check the bed to make sure no one was hidden among the sheets, and just to be sure, he looked under the bed as well. There was no one in either of those spots, so Blacknail relaxed. After taking a second to scratch an itch, he then turned toward the room's only door and headed carefully over to it. As he approached, someone on the other side spoke up.

"Are you sure you don't want anything to drink? I have both wine and tea?" Luphera asked an unseen person.

Blacknail's ears perked up as he recognized her voice, and his heart beat a little faster. His prey was close. The only reply to Luphera's question, however, was a disdainful grunt from someone with a deep masculine voice.

"What, do you think I've poisoned it or something?" she chuckled at the unseen man.

"I'm not one of your clients, Luphera. I'm here to keep a

watch on you until all this is over with, not fraternize," the unseen man responded in a rather unfriendly tone.

Blacknail stalked silently over to the door and very carefully pulled it open ever so slightly. He then peered through the tiny crack into the room on the other side. Luphera was seated on a lavish purple couch and wore a delicate white dress. She had a bored look on her face as she regarded the only other person in the room. A large man stood by the far door with his arms crossed in front of him. Blacknail instantly pegged him as a companion to the men he'd followed here. He was dressed the same but looked a bit different than any of the attackers. His eyes were narrowed as he glared hostilely at Luphera.

"Is that what I do, fraternize?" Luphera asked with obvious amusement.

"No, what you are is a whore and a gossip monger."

"And you're an easily replaced murderer, so I wouldn't be so quick to judge another's profession," she replied coolly.

Blacknail eyed the two humans as they glared at each other. He was fairly sure these two weren't friends. He wasn't the best reader of human tone and body language, but he was fairly confident about this. Of course, that didn't mean Luphera wasn't involved in the attack.

"What I am is loyal, unlike you, and our master knows it," the man countered.

"I'm not loyal? You'd think that after all these years of service, Najget would trust me more. He certainly values my services." Luphera turned away from the man for a second and looked around the room. To Blacknail, it almost seemed like her gaze stopped on him as it passed by the door, but that was impossible. He was much too sneaky to be discovered.

"Silence, whore. You're not supposed to use the guild master's name, ever," the assassin growled angrily.

"You and the master are far too fond of your little drama. As if there's anyone around to hear it but us," she replied condescendingly as she turned back toward him and rolled her eyes.

Blacknail heard it. He grinned happily from behind the door. He'd discovered a secret! He had no idea what a guild master was, but he was sure it was important. A secret name sounded very... sharp. Maybe he should make one up for himself, like Sneaky Death Killer!

"Shut your mouth. I'm through getting lip from you. If you speak to me again then you'll regret it, no matter how useful you are to the master," the man snarled furiously.

"You would very much regret raising your hand against me," Luphera replied coldly with more than a hint of condescension.

"I guess we're going to find out." The assassin raised a fist and stepped toward her.

Blacknail wasn't sure what was going on here, so he considered his options. He had a limited amount of time, so he should use any opportunities that came up. He also had to make sure he could act without raising an alarm though.

He tried to remain detached, but his snarl grew tighter as he watched the man march across the room toward the woman. For some reason, he felt protective of Luphera, and he didn't know why. It wasn't like they were of the same tribe. He supposed he just liked talking to her, or maybe her perfume was rotting his brain. It wasn't because he... liked her though. Blacknail shuddered. She was just another fat pink human woman.

"What, you're going to hit a defenseless woman, Farghus?" Luphera sneered.

"And I'm going to enjoy it." The big brute loomed over the woman as he approached her. Luphera didn't react to him st first, except to deepen her scornful scowl. She did, however, flinch and shield her face when he swung his heavy fist down at her.

There was a cracking noise and a crash as Luphera was sent sprawling onto the floor. However, she didn't scream or even moan in pain. She pushed herself up and stared back up at the man with eyes that burned with dark fury. Her dress had slipped off her left shoulder as she'd fallen, and it also slid up to reveal her long slender legs. Blacknail found himself staring at them and quickly looked up. This meant he met her eyes though, and the controlled fury within them tugged at something primal inside him.

"That was stupid," Luphera spat angrily as she cradled her sore arm.

The man laughed. "Why, you going to do something about it?"

"No, I'm not going to do anything about it. I don't need to," Luphera replied icily and louder than she had to.

Rage and the dark instincts of a predator guided Blacknail's silent steps as he stalked forward with murderous intent. Luphera's assailant never knew what hit him. One second he was sneering down at Luphera, the next, Blacknail's hand was wrapped around the man's mouth and chin as the hobgoblin's other hand pushed a dagger up under his ribs where it tore his insides apart. Then Blacknail started twisting the knife, because he enjoyed the feeling of it.

The man choked, and blood bubbled out of his mouth as his body's strength drained away. He couldn't say anything or scream for help though, because Blacknail held his mouth closed. He tried to reach up and free himself from the hobgoblin's grip, but he was already too weak to do anything but struggle futilely.

"Shhhh, no talking please. I'm trying to be quiet," Blacknail whispered into his ear.

Blood poured from the gash in the man's side, and seconds later, he collapsed. There was already enough blood on the floor that there was a wet smacking noise as he hit the carpet beneath him.

Calmly, Luphera got to her feet and gave Blacknail a polite nod of greeting.

"You've completely ruined that rug," she told Blacknail as she fixed her dress.

Blacknail just stared silently at her with as much menace as he could muster... because he had no idea how to respond to that.

"Well, I guess I shouldn't complain. I was hoping you'd drop by tonight after all. That's a lovely new mask by the way," she told him.

"Thank you," Blacknail replied stiffly. He had no idea what was going on here. Was Luphera friend or foe? He hadn't really attacked the man to save her, but rather because he'd sensed weakness and an opportunity. He decided just to ask her, since he was here to get answers from her after all.

“Who was he, what’s going-ss on here? Also, what do you know about the men who attacked Mistress Herad?” the hobgoblin hissed at her. Luphera didn’t seem scared though. One of her eyebrows rose as she considered him for a second.

“That was one of Najget’s hired assassins. Najget is the owner of this establishment and several others like it. He’s also the one who sent those men after Herad. He uses this place to collect information, and I’m one of the best brokers in the city. I despise the man though and will gladly help you kill him,” Luphera explained.

Blacknail stared at her blankly for several seconds. That had been really frank... He had kind of been expecting to have to play some sort of game, or trick the information out of her. “Why would he challenge Herad?”

He’d never heard of the man before, and Herad was rather vocal about her enemies and what she wanted to do about them. So why would he try and pick a fight with her? That sounded like a great way to get killed. There was also something about Luphera's posture and tone that bugged him. He thought he detected some hostility from her, which didn't make sense. Why would she be angry at Blacknail? Hadn't he just saved her?

“He wasn’t challenging her, and the attack wasn’t entirely his idea. Lately, he’s become a little paranoid about the loyalty of some of the employees, so he’s been hiring men from the Dark Guild. They pretty much own him now, and since Zelena bought them out, that means she controls him,” Luphera explained.

Blacknail had definitely heard of Zelena. Herad had made her opinion on the other woman really obvious quite a few times. Blacknail didn’t know where she would get that many burning needles though...

The hobgoblin shook his head to clear it and looked back up at Luphera. He wasn’t quite sure what was going on here, but it seemed like this Najget worked for Zelena. That meant he was an enemy, and thus Blacknail should probably kill him. It's what his mistress would want him to do. “I see, so—”

“So you need to go downstairs and kill Najget. He usually stays hidden in various hideouts across the city that even I don’t know about, but right now, he’s here and vulnerable,” Luphera told him.

Blacknail was caught off guard again. He didn't like being told what to do, but that did sound about right...

"This may be your only chance to get him. He has a few guards, but I'm sure Herad's faceless assassin won't have a problem getting past them. You have quite the reputation after all," she told him appreciatively as she met the masked hobgoblin's eyes and smiled charmingly.

Blacknail found himself standing a little taller and grinning happily. Obviously, he'd been imagining any hostility from her. He was a great killer, and this was probably the right thing to do...

# *Chapter 24*

Luphera fluttered her eyelashes as Blacknail considered his options. He did really feel like killing someone. He was also very good at it, so he could probably murder Najget without any real difficulty. The feat would also certainly impress Luphera... Wait, what was he thinking? Why would he want to impress her anyway? She was just a human woman, not a prospective mate, and she wasn't even of his tribe! Not that he trusted everyone in Herad's tribe. Some of them weren't nearly as dependable as him.

The hobgoblin's confident look turned to one of suspicion as he met Luphera's gaze. He didn't even know if Najget was a real person. "How do I know you're telling the truth?"

"Well, I haven't raised the alarm," she pointed out with a friendly smile.

It was a nice smile... No, he had to concentrate. There might not be a lot of the perfume from before in the air, but there was still a lingering trace of it, and that was apparently enough to mess with his head.

"Yes, but if you were noisy, I would have stabbed you," Blacknail countered.

"Oh, stop being so paranoid, Blacknail. Haven't I always helped you out? Now, I just need you to do one small thing for me, kill Najget. It's what you should be doing anyway!" she exclaimed assertively.

"Maybe," Blacknail mused. It did sound like fun, but Saeter had once told Blacknail that paranoia was the only thing that kept you alive. His master was also really old, so he probably knew what he was talking about. Even if Luphera wasn't outright lying, she still might be playing down the danger involved. There were an awful lot of guards around, and

Blacknail didn't even know where Najget was or what he smelled like.

Luphera moved closer and leaned against his shoulder. Her body was surprisingly soft. As the hobgoblin watched her warily, she gave him a pleading look.

"I would be ever so grateful for your help, and I'm sure we can work out some sort of reward. I've heard some very interesting rumors about what's under that mask and look forward to finding out if they're right. I hope they are; it would be a novel experience, even for me," Luphera told him seductively as she gently dragged one of her fingers down his arm.

Blacknail immediately took a step back away from her. He didn't like the hungry look in her eyes; he wasn't used to being on the receiving end of an expression like that. The sudden mad beating of his heart also unnerved him, it hadn't been caused by fear.

"You're so shy. Not at all what one would expect from your reputation," Luphera purred as she took another step after him.

"I still don't trust you," Blacknail replied as he hastily backed away again.

Instinctively, the hobgoblin glanced around the room for something to hide behind, even though he knew it would be pointless and stupid. Luphera's attention was becoming more than a little uncomfortable. He didn't know what to say to her or even what to think. He just knew he wanted out of the room. He had no reason to put himself at risk to kill someone right now.

"Maybe later, I have-ss to get back," he muttered as he turned away from Luphera and her unsettling eyes.

"Please, Blacknail, I need your help," the woman pleaded.

Blacknail ignored her and immediately fled toward the window he'd used to enter the building. Once outside, the fresh air would clear his head. Before he could get more than a few feet though, he heard a commotion from outside the window. The sudden sound of several people shouting filled the air. Someone was raising the alarm! They must have discovered the bodies.

"Shit," Blacknail hissed. Almost immediately, he heard

heavy footsteps from below as people from the building flooded out into the street. There was at least a dozen of them, and there was no way Blacknail could escape that way anymore. He'd let himself grow distracted and had talked to Luphera for far too long!

"You were followed!" someone shouted angrily from outside.

"Impossible, I took precautions. No one could have followed us back here," a familiar voice replied. It belonged to one of the assassins Blacknail had followed here.

"So I suppose these two corpses by the door are just a coincidence?" the other person replied sarcastically.

"That doesn't matter now. Someone's here, but he won't be leaving in one piece. I want people watching every possible exit until we catch him," a third man added as Luphera walked up beside the frozen hobgoblin.

"It seems like you left a mess out there when you came in, and now you'll have to find a different way out if you want to leave," she told him.

"Yes." Blacknail grunted unhappily. He was fairly sure he detected a hint of smugness in her voice.

"I suggest heading out into the hall and taking a left. There's a window in that room you might be able to escape out of. I wouldn't say it's very likely though," she told him. Blacknail knew that tone of voice. It was one humans used when they thought they were so smart, but they rarely were.

"What's your plan?" he asked her sullenly. It was probably going to be terrible.

"Well, if Najget were to suddenly die, then I'm sure I could take control of the situation. Then you could just hide somewhere while I have the house guards kindly ask the assassins to leave," Luphera suggested.

The hobgoblin thought it over. Apparently Luphera was actually that smart, because her plan might actually work. Most of the humans inside the building seemed to be heading outside and forming a perimeter to stop him from leaving, which also meant picking a window and trying to make a run for it was probably a bad idea.

"Fine, I'll kill the man for you," Blacknail sighed reluctantly.

"You might want to get going then, time isn't on your side."

Blacknail nodded and quickly headed for the door that led deeper into the structure. He was more than happy to get away from Luphera for now.

"Najget is the old man in purple with the moustache, and try not to kill anyone but him and the assassins," Luphera called after him.

Blacknail grunted vaguely in reply. He didn't think he was going to have much choice but to kill anyone that got in his way, if he wanted to survive this mess. The hobgoblin quickly shut the door behind him as he stepped into the empty hallway on the other side. Once out there, he took a second to listen to the surroundings. He heard floorboards creek as people moved all around him. To his left was a door and a heavier human who—with a sword hilt slapping against his thigh as he walked—was about to step through it.

The hobgoblin didn't have the time or the patience to do this quietly. He was going to have to do this fast and brutal, so he swiftly pulled out the vial of Elixir and gulped the rest of it down. Then he stepped to the side of the door and drew his blade. When the door swung open and another assassin walked out, Blacknail was out of his line of sight. Before the man even noticed the hobgoblin's presence, Blacknail stepped into view and slashed savagely down at the man's head. The surprised assassin's eyes widened in the split second he had before Blacknail's sword smashed into the side of his head. There was a wet crunch, and the man collapsed into a bloody heap on the floor. Blacknail pulled his blade out of the man's skull, stepped over the corpse, and continued on his way. This wouldn't be the last human he killed before the night was over, and he couldn't afford to waste any time.

As he passed by the open doorway, Blacknail saw the window that Luphera had mentioned as a possible escape route. He briefly considered abandoning the plan and jumping out of it, but then he sighed and quickly reconsidered. There would be people watching all the exits, including that window. So Blacknail reluctantly kept going and picked up speed as he dashed toward the stairs at the end of the hallway. Now was not the time for stealth. The sound of people getting up and moving toward him could be heard from many of the adjacent rooms, and he planned to be long gone before they showed up.

Just before he reached the stairs, something creaked slightly from below, like there was someone climbing the stairs. Blacknail smiled, and instead of slowing, he sped up. As he turned the corner and began to rapidly descend the stairs, he caught sight of a purple-vested guard with a drawn club. Blacknail's downward charge surprised the guard and he flinched. That was all the time Blacknail needed. Instead of drawing his weapon or slowing down, the hobgoblin simply leaped toward the man and kneed him in the face.

There was a muted crack as the two individuals collided. The purple-vested guard's head snapped back, and he began to tip over backward. Blacknail didn't really feel like trying to roll down the rest of the stairs, that sounded very painful, so he grabbed the man's shirt and fell on top of him. The guard's back hit the stairs, and then repeated thuds were heard as he started to slide down the steps. Blacknail still had a tight grip on the guard's shirt and was perched on his chest. It was bumpy-going, but he managed to ride his opponent safely down until they hit the wall at the bottom and stopped.

Blacknail hurriedly got to his feet. His opponent seemed to be unconscious or dead. Sometimes it was hard to tell. The hobgoblin had effectively taken him out and done it quickly, but unfortunately it had been far from sneaky. He had attracted a lot of attention. Blacknail could already hear people heading toward him. He looked up from the unconscious man to see they'd landed in another hallway. It was empty except for one shocked-looking woman standing at a doorway. A second later, the woman gasped in shock, threw herself out of the hallway, and slammed the door behind her. Blacknail was more than happy to let her go. He had enough problems with human women right now. He just wished he knew what Najget's voice sounded like, so he could track him that way. All he could do now was head toward anyone that sounded like an old human male, and Blacknail thought there was a good chance of there being more than one of those here.

Quickly, the hobgoblin got up and dashed down the hallway. Where had Luphera said to go? Oh, right, Najget was supposed to be past the last door to the left. As the hobgoblin raced down the hallway, one of the doors in front of him swung open. A moment later, another of the purple-vested guards stepped out and turned to face Blacknail. He was right in the hobgoblin's way.

This guard also had a club, and he wasted no time in swinging it at the hobgoblin. Blacknail ducked under the weapon and shoved his attacker aside as he raced past. There was no point in sticking around to fight. Before the guard could pick himself up, the hobgoblin had reached the door and thrown it open. Blacknail then stepped through into a large sitting room lit by several brass lanterns that hung from the ceiling. Heavy bookshelves lined the walls, except for where two large windows and another door were set on the opposite side of the room. Tasteful chairs had been placed around several large, round tables, and there were several comfortable-looking couches as well. Fancy red curtains framed the windows, and there were a few scattered books lying out on the tables.

There was, however, no one that looked even remotely like a Najget. The room wasn't empty though, there were two assassins in it, and one of them looked really familiar. Blacknail groaned in frustration. He didn't like this turn of events at all, but at least there were windows he could jump out of.

"At last we meet, Faceless One! I've been looking forward to this for a while now. You've been making me look bad, but that ends today... because I'm going to kill you," Malthus shouted triumphantly from the center of the room.

Blacknail rolled his eyes. Here was another stupid human that liked to say the obvious. The hobgoblin just wished the man wasn't also a much better swordsman than him.

Malthus and his companion drew their blades and headed for Blacknail. Both of them were still dressed in their dark leather armor and cloaks, but they had removed their face masks and dropped their hoods. This was actually the first time Blacknail had gotten a good look at Malthus. The other times they'd been close, the assassin had been cloaked and hooded or out of sight. He was slightly taller than an average man with a thin face and brown hair that was almost long enough to reach his eyes.

The hobgoblin watched the assassins approach and tried to

come up with a new plan, one that didn't involve getting sliced into tiny green bits. Fighting Malthus would be a really stupid thing to do, so Blacknail needed to get out of here. He couldn't go back the way he'd come though, and Malthus was blocking the way forward. So some trickery seemed to be called for.

"We have met though, Malthus. I've seen-ss you around many times, you just haven't seen me," Blacknail shouted contemptuously.

Malthus's face grew slightly more lined as he frowned at the hobgoblin, but he also slowed his advance. He appeared to be trying to come up with a good comeback. Blacknail grinned beneath his mask. It had worked; the man really liked to talk.

"Yes, well, now you're going to pay for being so arrogant as to think you could get past me twice. You were simply lucky the first time that Galive wouldn't let me do my job properly," the assassin replied.

"I wasn't lucky, you're deaf-ss and stupid. While you stood there by the door like a frog on a log, I was cutting Galive's throat open and laughing-ss at you. Good thing Galive wasn't paying you anything," Blacknail countered viciously.

The hobgoblin and Malthus were slowly and cautiously approaching each other, but there were still several tables and couches between them. Blacknail began to circle a bit off to the side while trying to look like he was seeking a better position.

"I'll restore my title as the city's best knifeman when I string your corpse from the city gate. That's what usually happens to assassins who operate in Daggerpoint without the Dark Guild's permission," Malthus shot back.

"No you won't. I'm a far better hunter and killer than you'll-ss ever be. You're just a soft and weak city man, but I come from the Deep Green, and I'm Herad's chosen killer!"

The two assassins were fairly close now. Malthus scowled as he stepped around a couch. He seemed both annoyed and more than a bit confused by the hobgoblin's words. Maybe Blacknail needed to talk slower so the human could understand. A second later, the assassin's gaze focused on the hobgoblin's mask.

"Let's fight properly; face to face. Why hide behind a mask now? Let me see the visage of the man I'm about to kill. Only one of us is going to leave this room alive anyway," the man proposed. Blacknail snorted in amusement. That sounded so dumb. Weren't assassins supposed to be sneaky?

"No, besides you've a got a friend there." Blacknail pointed to the man beside Malthus.

The hobgoblin wasn't in the habit of doing what his enemies told him. If Malthus wanted him to remove his mask, then Blacknail intended to keep it on. The hobgoblin snuck a glance at the far door. Thanks to his maneuvering, Malthus and the other assassin were no longer directly between him and it.

"Don't worry, he won't interfere in our fight. He'll just make sure you don't attempt to run. I want to take care of you myself. My pride demands it," Malthus replied.

Blacknail's pride demanded he never act as stupid as Malthus. The more the assassin talked, the more convinced Blacknail became that he was an idiot.

"No, he can fight too. I brought friends of my own," Blacknail said smugly as he pointed at the window behind the assassins. The pair looked startled for a second and quickly glanced toward the window and the new threat, but there was nothing there. Blacknail had been lying through his teeth.

While the two assassins were looking at the window, Blacknail quickly drew the sling and stone he'd been stealthily preparing as he talked to them. With lightning-fast speed, he whirled the stone and sent it flying toward Malthus's companion. Blacknail was fast, but the sound of the stone spinning through the air alerted the assassin. It smashed into his arm as he raised it to protect himself. Blacknail grunted in disappointment. He'd been hoping to do damage to somewhere more vital or for a fatal strike.

"Fuck," the assassin roared as his blade dropped to the floor. He cradled his arm against his chest and hissed in pain.

"You vile bastard!" Malthus cursed when he realized his companion was now out of the fight.

"I didn't trust you. Now it really will be just you and me," Blacknail said with a shrug.

The assassin's face grew red with fury, and his grip on his sword tightened until his knuckles went white. "You have a bloody sling? What kind of weapon is that for an assassin?"

"It works, so it's a great one," Blacknail replied with an

amused chuckle.

Malthus's companion was still hopping around in pain and clutching his arm. He'd made no move to retrieve his sword.

"Fuck, this hurts! I think the bastard cracked my arm," he told Malthus.

"Fine, go get medical attention. I don't need you for this."

"You sure?" the injured man asked.

"You can't fight, so go!" Malthus hissed back angrily.

The injured assassin nodded and began stumbling away toward the far door. The hobgoblin and the remaining human were now only a dozen feet apart.

"I'm going to kill you for that!" Malthus told Blacknail as he turned back to face him.

The assassin's black cloak fluttered behind him as he kicked the last chair between them out of his way. The enraged Vessel's eyes gleamed with hatred, and the light from the bronze lanterns overhead reflected off the edge of his blade as he charged the hobgoblin.

# Chapter 25

The hobgoblin quickly drew his sword. There were no more obstacles and only a small section of floor between him and the skilled assassin he'd pissed off. Blacknail really wished he'd had time to dig a pit or set up a snare trap. That would have made his survival much more likely.

All of a sudden, Malthus lunged across the distance separating them and stabbed toward the hobgoblin's chest. Blacknail sidestepped the attack and countered with a quick downward slash of his own. The assassin easily knocked the hobgoblin's attack aside and launched a flurry of attacks at Blacknail. The hobgoblin hissed in frustration as he blocked and weaved his way around the strikes. Blades flashed and cloaks swirled as the two combatants fought.

Blacknail knew he was in trouble. He was already having a hard time defending himself, and Malthus was obviously just testing Blacknail. He'd seen the assassin move much faster and more skillfully when he'd fought Herad. The difference in ability and experience between them was too great. Blacknail jumped backward to avoid a lightning-fast slash aimed at his chest and quickly readied himself for the next blow. It never came though; his opponent relaxed his guard instead of following after him. Malthus grinned at the hobgoblin while Blacknail watched him warily.

"Good, you're only a passable swordsman, but at least you're a Vessel. There's no other way you could have kept up with me just now. I was worried this was going to be too easy, but you might be somewhat entertaining after all," Malthus arrogantly remarked as he showed off by flourishing his sword through the air.

Blacknail rolled his eyes in exasperation. Who was the

human trying to impress?

"If you want-ss a hard fight, why don't you go fight Herad? Oh wait, you did! You fought-ss my mistress, and then you ran away like a rat from a cat." Blacknail laughed viciously.

"I'm going to kill you," Malthus hissed angrily in reply.

"You already said that, idiot," Blacknail pointed out while he circled around to place a table between them. Seriously, what was with humans and repeating themselves? It was annoying.

"Enough games," the assassin roared as he lost his temper and charged. Blacknail jumped aside, so the large wooden table was between them. Malthus didn't slow down though. The assassin jumped right onto the table and lunged across it as he tried to catch the hobgoblin.

The man was fast; Blacknail had to give him that. Of course, he was a Vessel, so he was cheating more than a little. Fortunately, the hobgoblin had taken some Elixir as well. As the assassin was sailing over the table toward him, Blacknail dove under it and rolled safely away. If there was one thing being beaten up by Herad had taught him, it was how to burn the Elixir within himself to avoid attacks by really fast humans.

"But I like-ss games." The hobgoblin laughed as he rolled to his feet on the other side of the table. He could feel the Elixir flowing through his body and energizing his muscles. It tickled the inside of his skin.

The assassin's face was twisted into a snarl as he stared across the table at Blacknail. He started walking around it toward the hobgoblin, but Blacknail started moving as well. After several seconds of following him around the table, Malthus tried switching directions, but Blacknail instantly switched too. Malthus grabbed the table and flipped it on its side then snarled in rage as he charged again. Blacknail ducked into the blind spot created by the table's top and dashed away. When Malthus cleared the obstacle, the hobgoblin was gone and standing several feet away on the other end of another table. Malthus ground his teeth together, and his face went scarlet red. The tip of the sword he was holding shivered as he shook with rage.

"Fight me fair, you coward!" the assassin yelled at Blacknail.

"No," Blacknail hissed back.

"You are not amusing!" Malthus growled as he walked over to the table and stared hard at the hobgoblin from directly across it.

"Yes, I am." Blacknail pushed the table forward and slammed it into Malthus's gut.

"Ugh, hells and damnations." The assassin wheezed painfully before wincing and taking a step back to steady himself. Blacknail couldn't help himself, he began to chuckle. That had looked like it had hurt.

"Bloody bastard, you're going to pay for that," Malthus growled as he straightened back up.

The assassin quickly reached into a coat pocket with one hand and pulled out a vial. He pulled the cork out with his teeth and drained the contents. He didn't lower his guard though, because his other hand kept his short sword pointed at the hobgoblin. Blacknail felt his earlier levity drain away. There was no mistaking the contents of the vial; it was Elixir.

Malthus hurled the glass container aside and wiped his mouth with the sleeve of his free hand. The assassin glared at the hobgoblin as he gripped his sword with both hands and raised it over his head. Then he kicked the table forward. The move caught Blacknail by surprise, but he managed to push off of the edge of the tabletop with one hand and slide backward without being hit. Unfortunately, that was when the surface he was leaning on exploded; Malthus had brought his sword down and cleaved right through the table with all his strength.

Blacknail's support was pulled out from under him as the wooden surface collapsed. He stumbled unsteadily for a second, and that was all Malthus needed. He charged through the wooden wreckage and backhanded Blacknail across the face. The hobgoblin's mask absorbed some of the blow but not all of it. He grunted as pain shot through his jaw and up into his teeth. He tasted blood as he staggered sideways. There was a second of blackness, and the next thing Blacknail knew, he was lying down and the hard floor was pressed against his back.

He groaned in pain as he tried to clear his head. Where was he again, and why did he have such a terrible headache? He hadn't drunk any of that human poison they called ale, had he? Blacknail was gripping something tightly with one hand. It felt like a sword hilt. Why was he holding a sword as he slept? That seemed kind of silly. The sound of footsteps approaching penetrated his agony, and Blacknail swiftly looked over toward the source of the noise. It was a pair of black boots, and they looked really fancy and tight...

What kind of moron wore boots like that? Wait a second... it was Malthus! This wasn't good. Blacknail rolled aside just in time. There was a heavy thud as a blade bit into the wooden floorboards that had been under his head a second ago. Blacknail jumped back onto his feet as Malthus raised his sword again and descended upon him. The assassin's blade sliced toward Blacknail's head, but the hobgoblin stepped out of the way. Their eyes met, and they exchanged hateful glares for a second.

"That was very satisfying," Malthus said with a vicious grin.

"I'm still alive," Blacknail replied.

"Not for long. You can't run from me," the assassin remarked grimly.

Blacknail begged to differ; Malthus's anger and confidence were making his attacks easy to predict. This wasn't actually going so badly, other than that blow to the head he'd just taken. That had hurt a lot. All Blacknail had to do was keep dodging, and Malthus would eventually make a mistake. Then the hobgoblin could make a run for it.

"You can't catch me," Blacknail respond confidently.

"I don't have to, you little bastard. You're stuck here, and I'll soon have reinforcements."

Oh, right. Blacknail scowled behind his mask as he realized the man had a very good point. Should he just attack the assassin while he was off guard? He didn't seem to have any other choice.

"Fine, it's a challenge," Blacknail replied coldly before raising his blade and stepping forward.

Malthus smiled eagerly and raised his own blade. Their gazes met, and the two swordsmen locked eyes as they closed in on each other. That was when the hobgoblin grabbed a nearby chair and whipped it at his opponent. There was no bloody way he was going to fight Malthus fair. Blacknail still remembered seeing the assassin fight Herad, and he knew he was outmatched.

There was a grunt of effort from Malthus as he knocked the chair out of the air. Blacknail threw himself forward and tried to skewer the human while his sword was out of position. Blacknail was focused on Malthus's eyes, and that gave him a hint of a warning. Something was wrong; the assassin's eyes gleamed with confidence. Why would they do that? The hobgoblin hesitated in his attack right before he committed himself. While the chair still partly blocked Blacknail's view, Malthus's left hand blurred and something shot toward the hobgoblin. Blacknail instinctively ducked, and a throwing dagger ripped through the air where his head had been less than a second ago.

Blacknail jumped back and raised his sword up into a guard. He stared grimly at his opponent as he reevaluated him. Malthus was much sneakier than he pretended to be. Blacknail was almost impressed. As the hobgoblin watched, the angry expression slid off the assassin's face. Malthus grinned cheerfully and gave Blacknail a respectful nod.

"You missed," the hobgoblin told him.

"Yes, I did. I honestly thought I had you there though. I spent a fair bit of time and effort setting that trick up, so what gave me away?" Malthus asked Blacknail.

Blacknail ignored his question and stared at his transformed opponent. The man didn't seem angry at all anymore. Had he been acting? Why?

"You like games too," Blacknail replied accusingly.

"Ha, yes. You've got me here. I'm a knifeman not a paladin. Did you really think a man with a reputation such as mine could be such a straightforward fool?"

The answer to that had been yes.

"Why-ss the act?" Blacknail asked suspiciously. He really didn't like this turn of events.

The black-cloaked assassin grinned and shrugged. "It was fun. There's nothing I like more than a battle of wits. Locking blades pales in comparison to matching minds. We're assassins, so a duel between us should be about trickery and wits, not straightforward swordplay. Where would the fun be in just cutting you down without first proving myself superior?"

"You didn't look like you were having fun."

"Oh, but I was. It was a very interesting fight, and besides, I wanted to figure you out before I killed you. However, I must admit I still have no idea who you are. You're a very... odd man." The assassin titled his head to the side and gave Blacknail an inquisitive look.

The hobgoblin chuckled in response. Apparently, Malthus wasn't the only good actor here. In fact, Blacknail was obviously by far the better actor; he was pretending to be a completely different species.

"Wrong, you're very wrong," he replied cheerfully.

The assassin frowned when Blacknail spoke, and he looked him over again. "I don't care what you say, you're not a woman."

Blacknail laughed again. If it was the assassin's curiosity that was keeping him from attacking, then Blacknail was going to give him a mystery. Malthus had been a dangerous opponent even when he'd been acting like an idiot.

"No, not a woman, not a man, nor a child pink of flesh," the hobgoblin sang out tauntingly.

"But you can't deny being weird," Malthus replied as his eyes narrowed and he continued to look Blacknail over. He appeared to be deep in thought for a few seconds. "Fine, you win. I have no idea what you're talking about, but I should probably stop letting you stall. I can always figure it out after I've killed you and stripped that mask off your face." He brought his blade back up and stepped toward Blacknail.

The hobgoblin had much preferred it when the man had acted like an idiot. He needed a new plan, and he was running out of time. He had to somehow escape and do it without getting a knife in his back. Just then, there was a creaking noise as the door behind Malthus opened. Both the combatants slowed as they waited to see who was about to enter the room.

"Horse stink," Blacknail cursed when three more assassins entered the room.

The black-cloaked figures swiftly started fanning out in an attempt to surround him. It wouldn't take them very long to navigate through the furniture that filled the library.

"This is still a one-on-one fight," the hobgoblin remarked.

"And it will still be one, as long as you don't try to run," Malthus replied.

Yep, that was what Blacknail had expected. It was time to leave. He didn't really have anywhere to go, but he couldn't stay here. He had a plan, but it was terrible and was most likely going to get him killed. If he stayed here though, he was definitely going to die. Life was full of crap choices.

"Surround the intruder but don't interfere," Malthus yelled at his newly arrived companions.

Blacknail used this brief distraction to quickly grab another chair and throw it at Malthus. Before the assassin could finish throwing another knife, Blacknail hurled a stone from his pouch at him. Instinctively, the assassin dodged it, which ruined his throw. The knife sailed harmlessly across the room and nowhere near Blacknail. The hobgoblin wasted no time in making a mad dash for the nearest window. He sheathed his blade so he could concentrate on running.

Normally, Blacknail would have made a run for the windows earlier, but these ones were barred. Apparently, this Najget man didn't want anyone accidentally walking off with any of his books through a window.

The assassins behind Blacknail started shouting and chasing Blacknail as he raced toward the window, but there was no way a bunch of humans were going to catch up to him now that he had a head start. Blacknail just really hoped he was going to fit through those bars. If he didn't, the last few moments of his life were going to be very embarrassing. The hobgoblin suddenly ducked as something whizzed by his head, and then a knife ricocheted off the wall in front of him.

"Damn," Malthus cursed from behind Blacknail. "I want you all to spread out and make sure he can't double back. Those windows are barred, so he can't go out that way, but he might have a trick up his sleeve. He's a cunning bastard."

Good, the humans didn't think he would be able to escape through the window, so they weren't chasing him too quickly. He hoped they were wrong.

Blacknail was now only a few feet from the bars, and his feet were carrying him rapidly closer. He really didn't like how close together they looked; it was going to be a tight fit. Swiftly, the hobgoblin took off his mask and rearranged his pouches.

Before he hit the bars headfirst, Blacknail grabbed them and pulled himself up. He then swung his legs and feet forward. Momentum pushed them through without a problem, but next came his chest. Blacknail's ribs compressed painfully and pushed all the air from his lungs as they slid through the opening, but he didn't get stuck. Blacknail felt relieved as he slid outside, but then the back of his head smashed into the bottom of the windowsill. He collapsed bonelessly onto the ground outside. His eyes fluttered, and he twitched as he lay in a twisted heap.

"Hells, how the fuck did he manage that," a surprised Malthus swore as he lost sight of the hobgoblin.

Blacknail gave himself several seconds to recover and then picked himself up. He groaned and rubbed the back of his head until the shiny little stars had disappeared from his vision. He was very thankful he wasn't fat like a human and his bones were so bendy. They were supposed to be like that right?

Blacknail shook his head to clear it and tried to focus. He was far from safe outside. Malthus and the other assassins couldn't follow him, but the hobgoblin knew they had ordered most the men to watch the perimeter of the building, and that was where he was now. The yard outside this part of the structure wasn't all that wide and was bordered by a line of shrubs. The plants themselves were there to conceal the dirty wall of the building next door. Really, it was just a pretty alley.

There was nowhere for him to hide out here. Autumn had stripped most of the leaves from the bushes. Most importantly, the hobgoblin could already hear footsteps approaching. What was he going to do now?

"There he is!" a large man yelled as he turned a corner and came into sight. Several other people were right behind him, and all of them were armed.

The hobgoblin hissed in aggravation as he saw enemies begin to approach from the other side of the narrow yard as well. He was faced with walls on two sides and hostile humans on the other two. He'd known there would be lots of enemies outside but had been hoping to spot an escape route through them. There wasn't one though, and that left him with only one option.

Blacknail sprinted away from the window he'd come out of and then turned around and sprinted back toward it. Right before hitting the wall, he flared his Elixir and jumped as high as he could. His outstretched claws found purchase, and he managed to catch hold of a second-story windowsill. He had nowhere else to go but back inside. Blacknail smiled smugly as he pulled himself and began to climb up the wall. There was no way any of the big fat pink humans below would be able to follow him, so he was safe for a little while.

That was when a crossbow bolt slammed into the wood beside his head. The stunned hobgoblin stared wide-eyed at the vibrating projectile for a split second before his gaze automatically turned toward the shooter. Below him, a purple-vested guardsman was reloading a crossbow as other human thugs gathered around him.

"Damnation, you missed. Quick, reload. The slippery bastard is getting away," one of them yelled.

Blacknail gasped in shock. "Uh-oh."

If that human hadn't had such terrible aim, Blacknail could have died!It was time to leave. With panic and Elixir lending him strength, Blacknail quickly flipped himself up and over the windowsill and back into the building. Hopefully his second trip inside today went a lot better than his first.

# *Chapter 26*

The cloaked hobgoblin found himself in another bedroom that was a smaller version of Luphera's, and he wasn't alone. A blonde woman in a lacy red shift was standing not too far from the window. She was deathly pale and staring at him in horror. Blacknail slowly looked up and met her gaze. Her only reaction was a slight shiver; she seemed too scared to move. He had absolutely no interest in this woman, and she obviously wasn't dangerous, so maybe he could ignore her? The hobgoblin took one slow step forward.

Instantly, the blonde started screaming shrilly. The long, high-pitched sound ripped into Blacknail's sensitive ears. He winced in pain as a sharp ache developed in the back of his skull. Not only would the woman's screams attract too much unwanted attention, but it also was really annoying. He had to get her to stop.

"Shut up!" he yelled at her angrily.

She didn't stop, and Blacknail groaned. This called for desperate measures. The hobgoblin took a step forward and grabbed the woman. He drew his knife and waved it in front of her face.

"Quiet or I'll stab-ss you!" he hissed in her ear. Amazingly enough, this actually caused her to scream louder, which Blacknail hadn't thought possible. This human was too stupid and annoying to live. Why wouldn't she just shut up!

The hobgoblin couldn't take the noise any longer; something had to be done. He sheathed his knife, tightened his grip on the woman, and pulled. A second later, the woman was flying out the window, and much to the hobgoblin's relief, the screams finally stopped. There was a thud and a grunt of pain from outside. Blacknail giggled in satisfaction and amusement. It sounded like she'd hit one of the men standing out there on the way down. Hopefully, it had been the crossbowman.

Blacknail knew he didn't have a lot of time, so he hurriedly dashed out of the room and into another hallway. He'd lost his pursuit for now but probably not for much longer. He needed to find this Najget man and kill him quickly. Then, hopefully all his problems would go away.

However, before Blacknail could even figure out which way to go, he heard footsteps quickly approaching from both directions. He was cut off; there was nowhere to run.

"Cheese weevils," Blacknail swore viciously.

He really should have run back to Herad instead of going to see Luphera. She was nothing but trouble and lots of it. Especially her long legs...

Blacknail smacked himself along the side of his head to clear his thoughts. He couldn't think of anything else to do, so he dashed up to a random door and silently opened the door a crack. Maybe he could find somewhere to hide until everyone stopped looking for him, or maybe Najget would walk by so Blacknail could kill him. That would certainly simplify things.

The hobgoblin peeked through the door and into the room on the other side. The chamber wasn't empty; there were two women inside. A scantily clad woman, similar to the others Blacknail had run across, was cowering behind a more muscular woman who was holding a sword. The swordswoman looked like she'd dressed in a hurry; she'd thrown on a jacket but wasn't wearing a shirt beneath it. Both of them were focused on the door, one in fear and the other with determination. Blacknail didn't think it was a good idea to go in there, unless he wanted to get stabbed or screamed at again, so he hurriedly moved on to the next door.

The hobgoblin was unsurprised to discover it led into another bedroom. This one was thankfully empty though, so Blacknail quickly slipped inside. Seconds later, he heard a large group of people stomp out into the hallway. Why did this place have so many beds? Did people come here just to sleep? That didn't make much sense to him.

Other than the large, four-post bed with white hanging curtains, there were several other pieces of furniture in the room. A large, heavy clothes drawer stood against one wall, and a small side table had been placed beside the bed. There was also a closet and another window, but Blacknail didn't think it was a good idea to try and go back outside right now.

The sound of doors being opened and closed as men searched the nearby rooms reminded the hobgoblin he didn't have a lot of time. He couldn't see any better options, so he rushed over to the closet and pulled the door open. He was tempted to try hiding under the bed, but that hadn't really worked out all that well for him last time.

It was small and cramped inside, but Blacknail dove inside and closed the closet door behind himself anyway. Most of the space was taken up by clothes that were hanging from a rod. The majority of the clothes were dresses, but there were a lot of smaller, more frilly bits as well. There was also a large brown sack lying on the floor. Blacknail opened the sack and found it full of dirty clothes that smelled strongly of human sweat. He frowned at them and looked around the rest of the closet. There were no good hiding spots in sight. With a disgusted sneer, Blacknail reached up under his mask and pinched his nose shut before climbing into the sack. It would hide him for a few more seconds anyway.

As soon as he was discovered, Blacknail planned on jumping the closest human and making a dash for the window. Since so many men were now searching for him inside the house, there were probably fewer humans guarding the perimeter. The longer he hid, the more likely it became that he could slip through the remaining guards and escape.

He was beginning to think Luphera had tricked him and that he hadn't imagined sensing some hostility from her after all. He wasn't sure why she would be angry at him though. He'd done nothing but help her out. Even if a man name Najget existed, she must have known Blacknail wouldn't be able to get to him nearly as easily as she'd said he would. If she had tricked him, she was going to regret it. He might have to flee for now, but someday soon when she least expected it, he'd be back to get his revenge.

The hobgoblin had already drawn his knife, but for now, all he could do was wait and hope the humans looking for him were even stupider than normal. The clothes inside the sack really smelled bad. What had the woman been doing when she wore them that had gotten them so smelly?

The hobgoblin's thoughts were interrupted by the sound of the room's door bursting open. Several sets of footsteps rushed inside. Blacknail instantly went still and quieted his breathing. He'd been hoping there would be fewer of them; it would be difficult to get past so many.

"I got the bed, you check the closet," someone said from the other side of the closet door.

There was a ruckus and more than a few thuds as the men tore the room apart looking for Blacknail. Then the floorboards creaked as someone approached the closet. There was another creaking noise when the door was pulled open, and a flood of light illuminated the closet. Blacknail could make it out even from inside the sack.

"Anything in there?" one of the men asked.

"A lot of woman's clothes," the man by the closet answered as he looked around.

"Let's get going then. We got a lot of rooms to search."

"One second, I should check this sack."

The man's shadow blocked the light as he reached toward the sack. From within his hiding spot, Blacknail tightened his grip on his knife. The second the man looked in the sack, he was going to get a knife in his eye and an angry hobgoblin in his face.

"You think the Faceless Assassin is hiding in a whore's laundry sack? He's probably on the other side of the building by now," the second man chuckled in amusement.

The first man paused. His hand was hovering only inches from Blacknail. The hobgoblin's heart started pounding as he readied himself to attack.

"Malthus told us to be thorough and check everywhere," the closer man told his companion.

"Fine, whatever, just make it quick, you disgusting pervert."

The man began to reach toward the top of the sack again. Blacknail tensed and held his breath. If he could take the first human out before he could make any noise, then he should be able to make his escape.

"Stop! Everyone who is not an employee is to leave the premises immediately. All house guards are to stop searching and escort them out," a familiar female voice suddenly commanded from out in the hallway. Luphera projected her voice loud enough that it echoed through the hallway outside the room Blacknail was in and through all the adjacent chambers as well.

"What's this?" the man reaching toward Blacknail's hiding spot said as he froze again.

A moment later, he stepped back and away from the concealed hobgoblin. Blacknail was more than a little confused as well. What was Luphera doing? He hadn't killed the Najget person yet. Had she betrayed him and come to finish Blacknail off herself?

"What do you think you're doing? Stop interfering in my search!" Malthus yelled from another room. There was then the sound of heavy footsteps as he stomped out to confront the woman.

"There is no more search, and your services are no longer required," Luphera answered disdainfully a few seconds later.

"What? That hell-begotten assassin is still running around this place! There's no way Najget cancelled our contract now. You're going to be in a lot of trouble when he finds out about this foolishness, woman."

"What Najget wants also no longer matters to anyone but the gods. Your men failed to protect him, and now he's dead," Luphera calmly explained.

"That's impossible! I had two of my best men guarding him, and Herad's knifeman never went anywhere near them," Malthus replied with obvious shock.

Blacknail carefully nodded to himself. The annoying human assassin was right; he hadn't even seen anyone who looked anything like the man Luphera had described.

"Nonetheless, all three of them are now dead. I don't know how he did it, but this Faceless Assassin has made you and your guild look like fools, again. I understand this isn't the first time he's sneaked right past you and killed a man under your protection," Luphera pointed out.

"No, I refuse to believe the bastard escaped me. He must

have had an accomplice that struck at Najgetwhile he distracted us. That means he's still here somewhere, and I intend to find him," Malthus replied angrily.

Blacknail definitely hadn't killed a group of three people. He would remember that. Had Herad sent backup, or had the humans perhaps done something stupid and killed themselves? Blacknail knew from experience it was hard keeping humans alive sometimes. Half of Herad's band would be dead if he hadn't kept getting them out of trouble.

"I know there's more than one assassin here, and that's the problem. You're disturbing our business with all this violence, and it's unacceptable. The only reason the assassin came here to kill Najget was because he allied himself with you," Luphera replied coldly.

"We were just here to protect our employer. We can hardly be blamed for him having enemies. That's why he hired us in the first place," Malthus responded scornfully.

"Then why have so many of you knifemen been coming and going? I'm not blind. You've been using this place as some sort of waystation or hideout, and that's unacceptable. This is a brothel not a den of assassins."

"We'll leave once we've captured the masked assassin and not before. We'll be doing you a favor by getting rid of him anyway," Malthus countered.

"I'm not an idiot. Now that Najget is dead, the other assassin will have no reason to stick around. He was smart and skilled enough to completely outplay you, so he's probably already long gone. If I let you stay until you find him, then you'll never leave. I have no intention of letting you control me the way you did Najget," Luphera argued.

"That's not my intention! I want that bastard's head. He's here somewhere, and I'm going to find him!" the assassin growled with barely contained fury.

"No, you're not. This is my business now, and I'm telling you to leave! If you refuse, then these gentlemen behind me and the many others like them throughout this building will forcibly remove you in the most unpleasant method possible," Luphera ordered the man.

"We could offer you the same deal we gave your boss,"

Malthus pleaded.

"Frankly, even if I required your services, and I don't, I doubt you could deliver on any promises you made. Your track record lately has been truly pathetic," the new mistress of the house told him dismissively.

"You'll regret this."

"I doubt it. Now get the hell out of my brothel and don't come back, unless it's to spend your coin on our services," Luphera commanded him coldly.

Muttering and the sound of footsteps filled the entire floor as all the searchers started giving up and leaving. Blacknail was relieved when the man closest to him walked away and shut the closet door. The closet grew dark again, and the hobgoblin took a second to scratch himself now that there was no one around to see. He was getting kind of hot and sweaty. After a few minutes had passed, the building around the hobgoblin grew quiet.

"Go make sure they've all left. I want some privacy," Luphera then announced from where she was standing out in the hall.

"As you wish," a male voice replied before fading footsteps signaled his departure.

"That means you can come out, Blacknail. It's just me here now," Luphera then said aloud.

That didn't actually make the hobgoblin feel safe or like coming out. He was still more than a little confused as to what had just happened, but he knew he'd been tricked. He should never have agreed to help her out. She was a lying liar.

"I know you're there, and we have important things we need to discuss. I have a message for Herad that you need to deliver," the woman announced.

Blacknail sighed and reluctantly pulled himself out of the bag. It didn't smell very good in there anyway, and he couldn't stay there forever, so he stalked out of the closet and to the bedroom door. Silently, he peeked out into the hallway. Luphera was there, and she was alone. She also wasn't armed. He'd been half expecting her to be carrying a loaded crossbow or something. She was, however, wearing more clothes than Blacknail had ever seen her in before. A full-length purple frock with golden embroidery covered her. The clothes and her straight posture lent her a new air of authority.

The hobgoblin took a tentative step out into the hallway. Luphera turned toward the masked hobgoblin and smiled his way when she heard him approach. “There you are. For a second, I thought you were avoiding me.”

Luphera was a little unsettling most the time, but now Blacknail thought he heard something weird in her voice. It made Blacknail uncomfortable, but he really wanted to know what was going on.

“I didn’t kill Najget yet-ss, but I was totally going to-ss,” he told her as he carefully walked over.

Luphera smiled at him and winked conspiratorially. “Nonsense, I have several guards that will swear they saw you do it. I’m told it was very impressive too,” she responded with a chuckle.

Blacknail had no idea why she was making that weird eye motion, but compared to some of the other things he didn’t understand about Luphera, he supposed it was nothing. Also, the hobgoblin was also sure he would have remembered killing a man in purple with a mustache and two guards... Well, whatever. He would have killed the man if he’d found him first, so it was kind of like he’d done it.

“I’m very good at killing people,” he bragged, which caused Luphera to smile.

“So I’ve heard. It’s also very impressive how you led that idiot Malthus on such a merry chase and avoided him so effortlessly,” she said appreciatively as she stepped closer to him.

“Yes, I’m very stealthy; even when I’m right beside them, people can’t see me,” Blacknail replied. It was even technically true sometimes, like when it was very dark or when he was hiding in a sack.

All of a sudden, Blacknail felt Luphera’s hand on his shoulder. He flinched in surprise. When had she gotten so close? Wait, he was doing it again! He was letting Luphera’s words and smiles distract him. He had to focus.

“You lied about how easy the job would be. I think you tried to trick me. Why?” Blacknail asked her suspiciously. Luphera’s grin broadened and took on a slightly sinister look. Blacknail instinctively took a step back away from her.

"I owed you one, or it might be more accurate to say, you owed me one. I know it was you who killed Galive, and he wasn't the only one that died that night. There was a woman, and while I barely knew her, she was still one of mine," Luphera explained.

Blacknail frowned as he thought about her words. He did remember killing a woman who had been in bed with Galive. He hadn't really had a choice though. She would have messed everything up. Had she been of Luphera's tribe and not Galive's? Human tribes sure were complicated.

"Sorry, I didn't know she was-ss yours. She was just in the wrong place," Blacknail explained reluctantly. Did this mean they were enemies now? The hobgoblin's left hand crept closer to the dagger he kept hidden in his coat, but Luphera didn't make any hostile moves.

"That's all right, you didn't know, and you've almost paid me back now. There's just one more thing you can do for me," shetold him as she walked closer.

Now Blacknail was very uncomfortable. He took another step backward, but Luphera glided effortlessly after him. She was impressively nimble on her feet...

"Um, right, I need to go back to Herad... You said you had-ss a message for her?" Blacknail remarked nervously.

"Running away to another woman, eh? How mean. Well, you're not going anywhere until I get a chance to properly thank you. Why don't you take your mask off and relax with me?" Luphera smiled knowingly.

"I can't do that... I was told not to because um... magic," the hobgoblin replied nervously. The woman smiled at his response and took his hand. Blacknail flinched.

"I don't believe you. Could the real reasonbe because underneath it you're not human? Don't worry, a bit of green skin isn't going to scare me off. It sounds exciting, actually," Luphera told him excitedly with a hungry smile.

Blacknail's eyes went very wide. He'd been kind of hoping it would though... and wait, she knew he was a hobgoblin. He'd been found out! How had she figured it out? He was a great pretender and had acted exactly like a human at all times.

Someone else must have let the secret slip. It had probably been Khita, she practically never shut up.

"Why are you so surprised? Knowing things is my business or half of it anyway. I look forward to showing you the other half very shortly," Luphera explained flirtatiously.

Her closeness and the scent of her skin caused a shiver to work its way down the hobgoblin's spine and come to rest below his gut. He smelled a lingering trace of the perfume from before on her clothes, and it began to do strange things to his head.

# Part Four:
# Queen of Swords

# *Chapter 27*

The cloaked hobgoblin tiptoed silently down the shadowy hallway. The dull noonday sun shone in through the nearby windows, but he kept out of the light and in the dark. Since this passage was rarely used for anything but storage, it didn't get a lot of traffic, and the windows were the only source of light. Blacknail could hear the creak and thud of people's footsteps moving around him, but none of them seemed to be moving in his direction, and that was good. He wanted to avoid detection at all costs. He'd come fairly close to being caught earlier when a guard had walked by, but Blacknail had managed to duck aside and hide behind a shelf at the last second.

His heart still hadn't slowed to its normal speed and was thudding in his chest. It would be very bad if he was discovered, and Blacknail didn't even want to think about the consequences. He had to stay hidden from the humans no matter what! Of course, he was unlikely to be found. He'd proven over and over again that mere humans couldn't detect an amazing hobgoblin like him. He was the dreaded Faceless Assassin and Herad's undefeated sneaky killer!

"What in all the hells are you doing, Blacknail?" Saeter asked from right behind him.

The hobgoblin's heart exploded in panic, and he jumped several feet into the air. Oh no, it was master Saeter. Blacknail hadn't heard anyone approaching! When he hit the ground, he was already dashing away down the hallway as fast as his feet would carry him. He had to escape and quickly!

"Stop right there, you little green idot! Come back here, or I swear I'll go get my bow and hunt you down through Daggerpoint and all the lands beyond it," Saeter barked loudly.

Blacknail believed him; he could hear the stubborn certainty in his master's voice. When he used that tone, there was no arguing with him, and he always did what he said he would no matter how stupid or dangerous it was. The hobgoblin reluctantly stopped running, went completely still, and let out a pitiful whimper. This was the worst possible outcome. Why did it have to be his master that had found him? The urge to flee and hide was overwhelming, but he knew that wouldn't work. Saeter would find him soon enough. He was incredibly annoying like that.

"Right, now come back here," Saeter ordered impatiently.

The hobgoblin sighed and obeyed. With his head down, he walked sullenly back to his master. He didn't dare meet his eyes.

"Lose the hood, and look at me," his master ordered next.

He sounded very annoyed, so Blacknail reluctantly pulled his hood down and met the old scout's gaze. Saeter looked him over inquisitively for a few seconds, and his expression changed from an angry look to a concerned one.

The hobgoblin cringed and had to turn away a few seconds later. What if his master could smell something? What if it showed? His master spoke up.

"What bloody nonsense has gotten into you, Blacknail? You've been acting weird and avoiding everyone since you returned from chasing those assassins. You told Herad that they got away after a brief fight, and she didn't question it. She doesn't know you like I do though, and I'll eat my boots if that's what really happened," he asked the hobgoblin quietly so no one would overhear.

"Yes, it is. That totally happened," Blacknail nervously replied while his anxious eyes wandered around the room.

Saeter just glared at the hobgoblin stubbornly; he obviously wasn't convinced. Blacknail withered under his master's gaze for several seconds. The hobgoblin knew Saeter wasn't going to let up until he got an answer, so obviously he had to lie through his teeth. Blacknail looked up and met his master's eyes. He licked his lips with his long tongue nervously as his brain worked feverishly to come up with the greatest lie ever told.

"I got lost..." he muttered a second later.

His master crossed his arms and gave the hobgoblin an

unamused stare. Blacknail winced and groaned regretfully. Why had he said that? That was a stupid lie and totally unconvincing! Why hadn't he thought of anything better?

Overcome with shame, the hobgoblin flipped his hood back up to hide his face. He then crouched in order to make himself as small as possible. Maybe if he stayed like this, his master would eventually get bored and leave...

"Seriously?" Saeter remarked in disbelief. The old scout reached down and pulled Blacknail's hood off. He opened his mouth as if to say something but then froze.

"Are you... blushing?" he asked in surprise as he examined the hobgoblin. Blacknail did feel weird, like all his blood was rushing to his face, especially around the cheeks.

The hobgoblin opened his mouth to respond and deny everything, but he stopped. He did sort of want to talk to someone. Last night, his experience with Luphera had been very... different. The memory caused Blacknail to flinch, and he felt his face burn hotter. Luphera didn't act or look anything like a female goblin, so why had he let her drag him around by his handsome nose? He felt used, and he had no idea what he'd been thinking. That terrifying scent and her hungry smile had done something weird to his head... and other parts of his body.

Luphera had invited him back, but there was no way he was ever going to do that! He felt dizzy just thinking about it. At first his instincts had taken over, but once they'd died down, he'd had no idea what he was doing there. What if he'd done something wrong... No, there was no way he was ever going to go back! How was he supposed to be around humans now? What if they could smell her on him? Their noses couldn't be that bad, could they? He didn't want anyone to know.

Saeter coughed impatiently as he stood over the red-faced hobgoblin. Blacknail's mouth hung open, but he had yet to say anything.

"There's this woman..." the hobgoblin muttered a second later as the truth burst out of him unexpectedly.

Saeter's face went through several stages. First his eyes narrowed in confusion, then he frowned doubtfully, then his eyes widened with shock and worry, until finally his expression settled into a look that portrayed deep but sad wisdom. The old gray-haired scout reached out and put a hand on Blacknail's shoulder.

"There always is," he sagely told the confused hobgoblin.

There was a weird twist to Saeter's smile, and his eyes also seemed a little odd. Blacknail didn't care though, he was just relieved his master wasn't... overreacting. He grinned happily as he began unburdening himself. There was no way his wonderful and ever-so-wise master would make fun of him.

Blacknail began to explain. "You see—"

"Nope, keep it to yourself," Saeter interjected quickly as one eye twitched.

"But..." the hobgoblin exclaimed in confusion.

"Some things you need to solve for yourself," his master explained simply with a blank face. "Now come with me, Herad wants us."

Blacknail watched in confusion as his master turned around and headed for the door.

"Ugh, I don't even want to think about it," Saeter muttered quietly to himself a few seconds later as he shivered slightly.

What had just happened? The hobgoblin was glad his master didn't seem to care, that was obviously the best outcome, but he also felt more than a little slighted. Saeter should have at least listened a little bit. Not that Blacknail wanted to tell him anything, of course. Yet surely, the whole situation was interesting and worth talking about, right?

The confused hobgoblin was left there crouched on the floor of the hallway all by himself. He stared after his master for a second before his thoughts untangled themselves. Then with a start, he remembered Saeter had told him he'd been summoned by Herad. Quickly, he got up and hurried after his master. No matter how embarrassed he was, it would still be a terrible idea to anger the chieftain. He was fairly certain he couldn't actually die of embarrassment, but he couldn't say the same thing about being stabbed.

Blacknail quickly caught up with Saeter and followed him to the other side of the building. Their destination soon became apparent; it was the sitting room where they'd met with their chieftain after Galive's death. Saeter walked right in, but Blacknail took a second to peek around the doorway before entering. He was still feeling more than a little shy and didn't want to run into any unpleasant surprises.

Herad was lounging back on a sofa in the middle of the room and was scowling darkly at everyone she saw. The bandit chieftain definitely seemed to be in a bad mood. She was wearing a pair of long black trousers and a dark brown leather vest over a black shirt. She held a silver goblet up in one hand while her other hand massaged the pommel of a dagger sheathed at her hip.

Blacknail hesitated to walk into the room when she was so angry. However, Herad quickly noticed him standing in the doorway and glared at him, so the hobgoblin immediately straightened up and walked nonchalantly in as if he hadn't been hiding.

There were only a few other people in the room, and all of them were members of Herad's tribe. Blacknail headed toward where his master stood in a deserted corner of the room. Once there, he kept to his master's shadow and as out of sight as possible. He was still feeling a bit awkward about being around humans, and with Herad in such a bad mood, it was best not to attract attention.

It took a few moments for everyone invited to arrive in the sitting room, but no one said anything as they waited. Their boss' dark mood hung in the air, and no one dared break the silence. There were an awful lot of anxious glances being exchanged between the bandits though. When the last person arrived, Herad's personal guards sealed the room. Blacknail jumped a little as the doors were slammed shut; not having anywhere to run made him fidgety and nervous. It was only then Herad finally spoke up.

"I just got an interesting message from an information broker. It said they owed me a favor for services rendered by a subordinate of mine, and it was sealed with a lipstick mark," she announced coldly.

No one said anything as Herad slowly gazed around the room and at everyone there one by one. Her eyes lingered on some people more than others, and thankfully they completely overlooked Blacknail, who was still hiding behind his master.

"I don't know who exactly it was referring to, but I have my suspicions. Some people lack discipline, and have a bad habit of sticking their nose in things that don't concern them." Herad glared coldly at Saeter.

The old scout was stone-faced and kept his expression carefully blank, but when Herad looked away, he gave Blacknail a dark suspicious look out of the corner of his eye. The hobgoblin quickly turned away and tried to look innocent. He thought he managed to pull it off.

"That's not of immediate concern though. What's important is that the message contains a lot of details on Zelena's movements and plans. Some of it is easily verifiable, but most of it isn't. The sender also expressed concern about Zelena's schemes to control Daggerpoint and wished us luck in defeating her," the bandit chieftain explained.

"We get tips and word from all kinds of information dealers almost every day, so what makes this one stand out?" someone brave asked.

Herad nodded and smiled darkly at no one in particular. Blacknail thought she was trying not to look at Saeter, although he wasn't sure why.

"I've heard of this broker before, and the letter also contains information on my own movements. It lists things I'd thought I'd kept secret. Thus, I'm willing to believe most the information on Zelena is also reliable," Herad explained.

"I'm guessing it's not good news," an older female bandit commented reluctantly.

"No, it's not. As most of you know, I've managed to cripple or thwart practically all of Zelena's schemes. She hasn't been able to turn most of the other chieftains against me, or at least she hasn't been able to get their direct support for any sort of attack. They're too afraid of me to risk that," Herad remarked arrogantly.

"They should be afraid of you. You're the deadliest fighter in the city, and from what I've heard, you've been dispatching Zelena's pet captains left and right," another man replied proudly.

This time Herad's dark eyes were hard and cold as she responded. "All very true, but I can't do everything myself. According to the information I've received, Zelena has abandoned her plan to turn the other chieftains against me, and since her assassination attempt also failed, she's now planning to simply purchase enough men to launch a frontal attack on us."

Some of the bandits gasped in shock, and others blinked in confusion, but most didn't seem too concerned by the news. Blacknail himself understood what Herad had said, but he didn't really know what to think about it. He had no idea how many people there were in the city or how many warriors each tribe had. He just knew there were a lot.

"Even if she buys up all the loose scum and hired muscle in the city, and lures a fair number of hands away from other chieftains as well, she'd still have a very hard time defeating us in any direct attack. She didn't bring all that many of Werrick's men with her east," Saeter remarked thoughtfully.

"Without Werrick's veterans to stiffen their spines, anyone they hire is unlikely to be of much use anyway," another man added dismissively. Several of the other people in the room apparently agreed with him, because they nodded and made approving noises. Herad wasn't one of them.

"That's true, and Zelena realizes this as well. Only an idiot wouldn't, and while Zelena is many other things, she isn't an idiot. That's why she has purchased the services of a small group of mercenaries. According to the letter I received, they're due to arrive sometime next week," she explained grimly. The reaction to this news was more dramatic. Dark muttering and swearing filled the room.

"Where in all the hells is she getting all that bloody coin?" someone asked in surprise.

"Fuck," someone else cursed.

"It can't all be from Werrick's spoils out west. Even he couldn't be making that much from robbing and pillaging. Zelena's throwing gold around like it's well water," another bandit remarked in frustration.

"Are the other chiefs going to allow that? No one's ever brought a force like that into Daggerpoint. It's going to make a lot of people nervous, especially the governor," someone else added.

"She seems to think she can get away with it," Herad told

them.

"It's not that much different from hiring the normal thugs and riffraff. Half of them are deserters anyway. There are certainly no rules against it, and the rules around here are pretty fluid," Saeter commented.

"And if anyone complains about it, then she has a nice force of mercs at hand to silence them," a scarred bandit added with dry humor.

"What are you planning to do about it?" Saeter asked Herad calmly over the din. The old scout didn't seem too concerned, and so neither was Blacknail. He trusted his master to know what to do.

"There aren't that many options. Ideally, I'd just have Zelena assassinated, but word is, the assassins have her squirreled away somewhere secret. That also means we can't attack her before the mercenaries get here," the bandit leader replied.

"And we can't exactly start a fight with every chief whose minions might join her, or all the free agents in Daggerpoint," Saeter pointed out.

"So we're doomed?" another bandit asked nervously. Herad snorted disdainfully in response and threw the man a disapproving glare. He wilted under her attention.

"Having a group of mercenaries at her side hardly makes Zelena invincible. Bringing them into town will make her enemies, and we can use that," she told all her minions in a voice full of steady authority. Instantly, the room quieted and everyone calmed down. The panic hadn't subsided completely though, a hint of it lingered in the room.

"How?" someone asked expectantly.

"Simple, we build up alliances of our own and then crush Zelena's coin-bought soldiers. They're mercs, so they won't be sticking around. That means Zelena has to attack us, and that gives us the advantage. Now that we know they're coming, we can fortify the base and prepare our forces. When Zelena attacks, she'll be walking into a trap," Herad answered.

"Sounds like it could work. This is a nice defensive location," Saeter added in support of his boss.

"What do we know about the sellswords?" someone asked.

"They're an infantry company called the Leather Heels. The

broker didn't know much about them, except that they're from down south and that they've seen a few battles," Herad explained.

"Too bad Vorscha isn't around, she'd know more about this company," Saeter mused.

"It would also be nice to have her here for the fight. There's no one I would rather have at my back," another man added.

"She's needed where she is and couldn't get here in time anyway. We have more than enough men for this plan," Herad remarked confidently.

"I'm guessing you want us all to keep this to ourselves?" Saeter asked her.

"Obviously. A trap only works if the victims don't know it's a trap. None of you are to share this information with anyone, including your subordinates. I wouldn't even be telling all of you this if it wasn't necessary. Just remember, if you open your mouth, I'll find out about it, and then I'll seal your lips permanently. No second chances. I don't care if you're drunk or even being tortured," Herad told them threateningly as she gazed around the room.

There were grim nods of acknowledgement from most the bandits present. No one seemed to think she was exaggerating. Blacknail made a mental note to remember to forget this entire conversation had ever happened. He was taking no chances.

A few minutes later, after Herad started explaining the details of her plan, Blacknail began to grow bored of all the talking. He sighed quietly to himself and stifled a yawn. That was when Herad spoke up in an excited tone that immediately caught the hobgoblin's attention.

"Some of you might be questioning me, and thinking that I'm a poor bet, but that couldn't be further from the truth. It's Zelena that's desperate here, not me. I've knocked that bitch on her ass every time she has tried something, and this latest stupid ploy of hers will be no different. When her last desperate gamble falls apart, and we flood the streets with the blood of every petty thug stupid enough to accept her coin, there will be no one left to challenge me. I will be the undisputed ruler of my territory and the top dog in Daggerpoint and beyond. Then, a new age will dawn in the North, my age, and all of you here will reap the benefits!" she announced eagerly. Her voice was full of absolute confidence.

Loud cheering broke out in the room as the bandits' greed and pride got the better of them. All trace of their earlier fear and uncertainty had disappeared.Herad saw their reaction and grinned hungrily. Her ambition and bloodlust were plain as day. Blacknail giggled and licked his lips as he pictured all the fun things that were about to happen. It seemed like his tribe was about to go to war. It was about bloody time!

# *Chapter 28*

Now that all her minions were solidly behind her, Herad started organizing them. Her short black hair fell over her forehead as she leaned forward over the table in front of her sofa and gave out her orders. “Corveyn, you’re in charge of the defenses. I want work parties organized and this place fortified as much as possible. If you need funds, then you’ll have them.”

“Not a problem. I already have a few surprises in mind for our guests when they arrive,” a man who Blacknail assumed was Corveyn replied.

He was one of the men who had joined the tribe after they’d arrived in Daggerpoint. All these new hires were beneath Blacknail’s notice, unless they had something he wanted, so he hadn’t bothered to learn their names. He was Herad’s favorite after all, and they were just rookies.

“Saeter, I want you to get in touch with some of your old contacts. See if you can recruit a few more good men, or at least convince as many as possible not to join up with Zelena when she starts spreading that coin of hers around. They can’t spend it if they’re dead,” the chieftain told Blacknail’s master.

Saeter nodded calmly in acknowledgment, and Blacknail stepped out from where he’d been hiding behind him. The hobgoblin smiled hopefully at his mistress. He wanted a job too! However, Herad didn’t even glance his way as she issued orders to the other bandits. Blacknail pouted sulkily as he gazed Herad’s way. Why hadn’t she given him a job? He was far more useful than most of these lazy humans. Surely there was someone who needed killing, or maybe some pies that needed stealing?

Herad happened to glance Blacknail’s way, and she noticed his demeanor. The bandit chieftain rolled her eyes but then gave him a wicked grin. The hobgoblin returned her smile hopefully.

"Don't worry, Blacknail. I'm sure an opportunity will present itself and I'll find someone for you to hunt. It might even be someone in this room, if they disappoint me enough." She chuckled darkly and loudly enough that everyone in the room undoubtedly heard her.

Muted muttering broke out between the bandits as several people looked Blacknail's way, and the hobgoblin heard his master grunt in disapproval. He wasn't sure why Saeter wasn't pleased though. Blacknail was glad Herad trusted him to hunt her enemies for her, and he enjoyed the fearful looks he was getting. The new members were barely part of the tribe anyway. None of them had been around nearly as long as him! He'd joined the tribe a whole um... lots of months ago! That was practically forever. Also, in a tribe, it was natural for the weak to fear the strong and for them to be kept in their place. Everyone was certainly very afraid of Herad! The fact that the chieftain had mentioned Blacknail personally, obviously meant she considered him to be only one step below herself in position and toughness. Maybe his master was jealous?

"All right, that's enough gabbing from you lot. It's time to get to work. Get on out of here," Herad announced loudly. Her voice cut through the commotion around her, and everyone else instantly grew silent and jumped to obey her. Soon, all the bandits were walking through the doors and exiting the room.

Saeter let most of the other bandits leave, and get out of the way, before heading out himself. Blacknail followed him closely, and as soon as they were alone in the hallway, Saeter turned to him. "Listen, Blacknail, you shouldn't be happy about being picked out like that by Herad."

Blacknail frowned at his master's comment. He didn't understand why Saeter was upset.

"It means she trusts me and that I'm dangerous!" the hobgoblin bragged.

"Maybe, but it will also make your own comrades afraid of you," the gray-haired scout replied.

"They should be afraid of me; I'm much faster and smarter-ss than them. None of them could challenge me," Blacknail pointed out arrogantly.

"That's not the point, Blacknail. Herad's words were meant to set you against the rest of the tribe. If they're too afraid of you, then they will see you as a threat, and then they won't have your back later, or they might even try to take you out," Saeter explained.

The hobgoblin gave his master a confused look. Wouldn't most of them do that anyway? "Obviously I'm stronger than them, so I don't-ss need their help, and they won't dare attack if they're afraid of me," he replied as if he was stating the obvious.

"And if they gang up against you or simply leave you to die somewhere?" Saeter asked. Blacknail squinted and scratched his long green nose as he considered that idea. He didn't like it. Humans sure were a sneaky race. How was a poor hobgoblin supposed to keep himself safe?

"What do you think I should do?" he asked his master reluctantly.

"You need to show them you're more than just a killer, and that they're your comrades and friends," the old scout replied.

"So I need to outsmart and trick-ss them..." Blacknail mused aloud. "That should be easy; I'm a great actor!"

Saeter sighed in resignation and shook his head. "Sure, whatever works."

"You sure are tricky, master!" Blacknail replied happily.

"Go get your mask and gear, Blacknail. I may as well get started on recruiting for Herad right away, and that means you'll be coming with me," Saeter told him irritably as they moved.

"Where are we going?" the hobgoblin asked curiously.

"We're going to a bar. There's some people there I should talk to," Saeter replied.

"Why?"

"I need a drink. Talking to you has given me a headache. Also, I used to move between the smaller bands a bit before I joined up with Herad, so I know some of the people. The kind of coin Zelena has will seem awfully tempting to them, but most should listen to reason," Saeter explained.

"Bah, why is Herad worried about a few tribeless humans? She should just kill them all if they're going to become our enemies," Blacknail suggested.

"That's a bloody stupid idea! Try to actually use that skinny green head of yours, Blacknail. Fighting them would just hurt us, and we're trying to recruit some of them, remember?" Saeter replied heatedly.

"Oh, you're right. Sorry, master," Blacknail responded. "So first we recruit, and then-ss we make the new members fight for us. If they die, we don't even have to give them shinies!"

Saeter turned around and swatted the hobgoblin atop his head. Blacknail hadn't been expecting it, so he didn't manage to dodge the blow in time.

"Ouch," he whined, as he took a step back and rubbed his now sore ear.

Saeter glared at him furiously, and Blacknail wilted under his gaze. What had he said wrong? He'd thought that was a great idea...

"We're trying to avoid making more enemies, Blacknail. Daggerpoint is a pretty immoral place, but even here bloody killing sprees in the streets are frowned upon," Saeter explained.

"Why would anyone-ss care what we do to our enemies?" the hobgoblin asked with honest curiosity.

Saeter sighed in frustration and gave the hobgoblin a brooding look. Blacknail met his gaze with a confused expression. It seemed like his master was thinking deeply about something unpleasant. He hoped he wasn't about to be smacked again...

"You can't just go around killing everyone, even in the North," Saeter explained a few seconds later. "This piss-poor excuse for a city is still a city, and it needs to stay at least somewhat civilized. If everyone just started killing everyone else, then Daggerpoint would fall apart. No one would be able to buy food, clothes, or build shelter. Soon after that, almost everyone would be dead or have left."

"But the strongest would-ss hold the territory; it would all be his."

"So what? It's the people that make the city valuable," Saeter replied. "It's not like the wilds, were you can make most things for yourself. In a city, you need lots of people to buy, sell, and make things. An empty city is worth less than a mud pit."

The hobgoblin tried to wrap his head around that. It sort of made sense to him, maybe. "So, if I were to kill-ss the maker of tasty pastries, then he couldn't make any more-ss of them, and if I were to start killing too many people, he might run away."

Saeter rolled his eyes at the use of the pastry example. "Kind of, it's a bit more complicated than that though. If you scare away or kill too many other people, then who will buy his goods? If there's no one to sell pastries to, then he'll leave. The city is sort of like... an animal. It can take a few cuts and scrapes, but if you wound it too deeply or hit the wrong spot, then it will die."

Blacknail nodded at his master's words. He could picture that. All the people in a city were kind of like the different squishy bits inside a rabbit, they were even the right color. The hobgoblin frowned as another thought occurred to him. Were there green bits inside animals? He shook his head to clear his thoughts. That didn't matter. He should probably concentrate on Saeter's words for now. He could always search through the insides of a rabbit later.

"I think I understand, master, but I still think there must-ss be a less boring way to do this," Blacknail told the old scout.

"If you can come up with one, then knock yourself out," Saeter replied condescendingly.

Blacknail was a smart hobgoblin, so he knew his master didn't want him to actually bash himself across the head. His words were a weird way humans gave people permission, or so Khita had explained when Blacknail had woken up after the first time Saeter had used that expression.

"So we can't do anything too scary... I know! They're weak and alone without a tribe, so I'll come back at night and kill them from the shadows, where no one can see," Blacknail announced proudly as he rubbed his hands together in anticipation of a hunt.

Saeter eyed him critically. "I'm not sure you understand how many of them there are. We're talking about a good part of the people in the city. Even you couldn't pull that off, and some of them are very skilled. I used to be one, remember?"

"How about just their leaders then, so the others will flee in terror?" Blacknail mused thoughtfully.

"Sure, that sounds fine," Saeter replied.

"Really?" Blacknail asked hopefully.

"No, that's a bloody stupid idea! There's still far too many of them for that to work," Saeter answered scathingly.

"Fine, whatever. You said they all live in their own part of the city?" Blacknail asked sulkily. There had to be some way to solve this problem that wasn't as boring as talking. It wasn't like humans were usually all that hard to murder.

"Well, they can hardly live in an area controlled by a gang leader, and the governor's territory is too expensive for them," Saeter replied.

"Ha, it's simple then. We'll burn all their homes down in the middle of the night and kill them as they flee before us," Blacknail suggested gleefully.

"Creepily enough, that might actually work. We're not going to do it though. That would definitely count as too much damage to the city, and every time you kill someone, you might be making someone else your enemy," Saeter told him.

"...but the flames would be so pretty," Blacknail muttered to himself. This was very complicated. However, he supposed his master had a point. Killing that one woman who had been with Galive had made Luphera angry. There were just so many humans shoved into Daggerpoint, he supposed they all knew each other or something.

"So if we can't kill people, then what do we do?" the hobgoblin whined.

"I already told you. I'm going to go talk to some people, and you're going to follow me."

"That doesn't sound very fun," Blacknail commented darkly. In fact, it sounded very boring, and over the last few days, the hobgoblin had slowly come to realize that talking wasn't one of his strong points.

"Not everything is supposed to be fun. Think of this as a chore if you want. Personally, I think sharing a few drinks with some old acquaintances sounds bloody great right now, so get moving, and stop asking me these damned annoying questions," Saeter crankily replied.

Blacknail grumbled to himself but quickly headed to his

room to get dressed. A few minutes later, he rejoined his master, and together they left their band's base and headed out into the city. Saeter led Blacknail toward their destination. It was only just after noon, so Daggerpoint was busy, and the streets were full of its myriad of colorful inhabitants. Merchants hawked their wares from stalls or store fronts. The more successful ones had bodyguards at their sides, to prevent theft or other problems. The others simply glared suspiciously at everyone that approached and kept one hand on a weapon.

Small groups of thugs, and what passed for normal citizens, were also walking around. It could have been a scene from any other city, except almost everyone was rough looking and heavily armed. Knives and swords appeared to be the weapons of choice, but several people had clubs, and one man was even walking around with a spiked mace in his hand. The hobgoblin and Saeter weaved their way through the crowds while keeping their distance from most of the other people. The only interruption was when Saeter had to stop and drag an errant Blacknail away from where he was attempting to purchase an unidentifiable piece of meat on a stick, using money he had somehow acquired from another man's pocket after bumping into him.

Saeter then took them off the main roads, and into the less-traveled alleys and residential streets. The road there was only wide enough for a single cart, littered with junk, and blanketed in thick shadows. The pair walked for several minutes until they came to a tight street corner. That was when Blacknail realized something was wrong. The back of his neck was tingling. Alarmed, Blacknail looked around and spotted hints of movement among the shadows. They'd walked right into a trap.

The hobgoblin's ears went flat against his head as he hissed a loud warning to his master. Saeter flinched and dropped his hand toward his sword hilt. Before he could draw his weapon though, several figures burst out of hiding and rushed toward the pair—several very small figures. It was a group of street children. The urchins ran over and quickly surrounded the two bandits. They weren't stupid though. This was Daggerpoint. They were wary and kept a little distance, in case the pair turned violent. Their clothes were ragged and filthy. Blacknail could see their ugly pink skin through the holes in it.

"Please, sir, do you have any coins to spare? My sister is sick, and I can't afford food for us both," a taller male begged with wide, desperate eyes.

"My parents beat me unless I bring home enough coins, please help me," a smaller girl whined.

"I don't have any parents, they were killed by a gang of thieves," a third said, in a clear attempt to upstage the others.

Saeter sighed and began to pull out his coin pouch, but he wasn't as fast as Blacknail. The hobgoblin had also reached into a pouch, but he had pulled out a handful of stones.

"Away, tiny thieves!" he yelled as he hurled them toward several of the children. The youngsters saw the projectiles coming and quickly scrambled out of the way. The stones bounced off their turned backs and raised arms, or flew harmlessly past.

As the children recoiled, Blacknail raised his hands up above him menacingly and growled as deeply as he could. The urchins took one look at his masked form and turned to flee. They gasped and shrieked as they ran as fast as their little legs could take them. However, Blacknail didn't have the chance to gloat.

"What in all the hells do you think you're doing?" Saeter swore angrily at Blacknail as he pulled him backward by his cloak. The hobgoblin stumbled at the unexpected tug.

"Chasing away the little thieves! If you let the small ones close, they'll take-ss your stuff," Blacknail replied warily. His master seemed really angry.

"They're street children, you shouldn't attack them! They might be annoying, but if you give them a few coins, they'll leave," Saeter explained, glaring furiously at Blacknail.

"But if I just chase them away, then I don't need-ss to give them any of my shiny coins," Blacknail pointed out reproachfully. That was common sense.

"Listen carefully, Blacknail. I know you don't understand morality, but by the gods, you're going to understand this. You don't need your coins as much as those children do. You don't even spend most of them; you just hoard them!"

"I don't understand," a startled hobgoblin replied with wide-eyed confusion.

"It's called charity, Blacknail. You give some coins to others who need them more than you. Those children will starve or freeze in the winter without the money they get from begging, if they aren't murdered by a random thug," the old scout explained.

"They look fat-ss and healthy to me," Blacknail countered defensively.

"That's because you're a stupid hobgoblin. Humans aren't supposed to be dressed in rags or that thin," Saeter told him.

"But there's food everywhere-ss here. You humans pile it in the street. Look right-ss over there, there's a cat! They're tasty and not that hard to catch," Blacknail pointed out.

"Humans don't eat that stuff," Saeter explained irritably.

"Why wouldn't they, if they're hungry? They're just spoiled by human food," the hobgoblin replied dismissively as he glanced in the direction most of the children had run.

"They'd get sick, Blacknail! Human children aren't goblins. They can't eat garbage and hunt cats through the streets!" Saeter exclaimed.

"They could if you gave them slings, they're not that slow and weak," Blacknail replied.

Saeter sighed in defeat and gave Blacknail a hard, intense look. "Forget it, Blacknail. Just don't hit any more children, ever. If you do, then I'll give you the worst beating of your life, and then get Khita to nurse you back to health," Saeter told the hobgoblin.

"Fine, but I'm not giving them shinies... I mean coins," Blacknail replied darkly before shuddering at the thought of being stuck defenseless with Khita for days. His master was a very scary human.

Saeter grunted and continued walking down the now empty alley. Blacknail cast another suspicious glance back toward the way most of the small humans had fled before hurrying after his master.

# Chapter 29

Saeter led the hobgoblin through several more back streets before they emerged back into a more public area. The street ahead of them was wide andmostly empty. It was bordered by worn-down-looking homes. Everything had a well-used feeling to it. There were no crowds bustling about in this part of the city. Only a few tough-looking men and women could be seen walking together in small groups. The people here seemed to like to keep to themselves; there wasn't a lot of talking or noise. Saeter and Blacknail silently passed these people by as they made their way down the street.

After several minutes of walking, Blacknail noticed a building that was clearly not a home of any sort. It was much larger than the two houses on either side of it, even if it had the same worn-down aura. Most tellingly though, there was a sign that hung out above the door, so Blacknail knew that meant he was looking at a human tavern. Unsurprisingly, it also appeared that Saeter was walking right toward it. Blacknail sighed in resignation as they walked up the creaky wooden steps of the tavern. He could already smell booze, and the door wasn't even open yet. When Saeter opened the door, Blacknail sneezed wetly beneath his mask as the scent of alcohol and human sweat washed over him.

The inside of the building was uncomfortably warm and stuffed full of humans. Apparently, the reason the streets were so empty was because everyone was in here, and by the smell of it, none of them had bothered washing. The floor of the tavern was ruggedstone and totally uncovered. The walls were rough-looking wood and completely bare of decoration. There were a few tables and benches scattered about but not enough for everyone, so a lot of people were standing around in small groups. Almost everyone inside was dressed in rough workmen's clothing, including a lot of the women. Only a few women were wearing long, plain dresses and shirts instead.

Saeter and the hobgoblin got more than a few glances as they moved into the room. Unlike outside, no one here was hooded. Blacknail hissed nervously as he realized he stood out from the crowd. He didn't like being the center of attention. The hobgoblin's posture stiffened, but Saeter ignored everyone else and walked up to the bar. A second later, Blacknail hurried after him. He felt much safer beside his master.

The bald barkeep was round and fat, even for a human. He lazily turned to look their way as they approached, and then he scowled in irritation. Blacknail didn't think the man was reacting to them; it seemed more likely that he always grimaced like that at everyone. His thick face was certainly lined enough for it. As the barkeep glowered thoughtfully at Saeter and Blacknail, a flash of recognition suddenly appeared in the large man's eyes.

He grunted at Saeter. "Huh, I thought you were dead."

"I'm impossible to kill, you should know that," the old scout replied gruffly.

"You haven't been by in a few years. At your age, that usually means a man has retired or died, and you never struck me as the retiring type," the barkeep explained with a ponderous shrug of his shoulders. "I figured that you'd wandered north to the ruins of Coroulis in some glorious but utterly futile attempt to kill the Doom."

"Bah, I wouldn't give that overgrown lizard the satisfaction of chewing on my bones. When I meet that unholy monstrosity again, it will be because I know I can kill it," Saeter responded as he took up position on the other side of the long, crude wooden bar from the man.

"Almost everyone in this business has ghosts, old man. Even if yours are city sized, you still need to learn to let them go. Coroulis is nothing but rubble now, and even if you somehow manage to kill the most powerful monster of our age, it won't be coming back. The world has moved on."

"The world hasn't moved on. It has rotted, and it's all that monster's fault," Saeter replied in a cold voice that seethed with suppressed hate.

The old scout had turned to look off to one side, and an awkward silence hung in the air. Eventually, the innkeeper turned to Blacknail and gave him a once over.

“Who is your friend?” he inquired.

“He’s a comrade of mine. You don’t need to worry about him,” Saeter answered. The innkeeper didn’t seem convinced; he eyed the hobgoblin suspiciously. He also apparently wasn’t the curious sort though, because a few seconds later, he shrugged and changed the topic.

“Well then, what brings you back here? Don’t tell me you’re looking for work,” the innkeeper asked.

“No, I have a permanent employer these days. I’m just here to tickle some ears,” Saeter replied. He no longer sounded so upset.

“Well, the bulletin board's still over there. Feel free to post something,” the large, bald man remarked.

“I’m looking for something a little more thorough than that. Maybe you could help me spread the word?”

“Depends on what you want said,” the barkeeper answered. He looked past the pair at another group of patrons who were across the room. Saeter ignored his rude behavior and continued talking.

“I hear Zelena is going to be looking for some muscle soon. When her men come around, I want it known that it’s a bad deal, no matter what they pay. The kind of deal that puts a man in an early grave.”

The innkeeper huffed in annoyance and turned back to scowl darkly at Saeter. “Not likely. Not even for you. I find it healthy to stay out of local politics, and that’s what this smells like to me.”

“I’m not asking you to tell any falsehoods. It’s simple fact. Zelena will use up anyone she hires and throw them away. Her plan is already a failure, and it’s just going to get anyone she hires killed,” Saeter explained irritably.

“Oh, I trust your word, Old Raven. I can’t say that about many men, but I’ll say it about you. That doesn’t change nothing though. I’m still not going to get involved. Men die every day here in Daggerpoint, and everyone here knows the risks when they take a job," the barkeep responded grimly.

"I can pay up front," Saeter offered.

"I imagine so can Zelena. It's not about the coin," the bald man replied.

Saeter sighed and frowned. He looked around the room, and he didn't seem to like what he saw. He grimaced as he took in all the people staring at him and Blacknail. The hobgoblin had started to nervously clutch the hilt of the sword at his hip.

"I don't remember this place being so full before, and I can't say the atmosphere has improved either," Saeter remarked. The barkeeper turned to look at his other patrons and then grunted in acknowledgement. It was hard to tell what he thought, as his face seemed frozen in a never-ending grimace.

"People around here have become suspicious of strangers lately, especially ones that hide their face. There have been some unusual disappearances that have put people on edge," he explained darkly.

"What do you mean disappearances?" Saeter asked suspiciously.

"Missing beggars, loners, and sometimes people aren't making it home at night. People think it might be ghouls," the large man answered reluctantly.

Saeter turned to give Blacknail a thoughtful stare. Blacknail stared back blankly in return. He didn't like the look on Saeter's face. It usually meant he was about to tell Blacknail to do something annoying.

"I might be able to help you with that. If there are ghouls around, I should be able to track them down," Saeter offered.

"How are you going to do that, master?" Blacknail asked curiously as he leaned closer to his master. Saeter turned toward the hobgoblin and rolled his eyes.

"I'm not; you're going to do it," he answered dryly.

"Oh," Blacknail replied uneasily. The barkeep gave the hobgoblin a dismissive glance and turned back to Saeter.

"Last time I checked, ghouls are hard to track down, unless you have trained dogs. The governor is the only man in town with them, and he doesn't bother himself with unconfirmed rumors. I don't think your friend there will be able to do it," he said dismissively.

"Do you doubt my tracking skills?" the old scout replied coldly.

"No, but—"

"Well this... fellow here learned from me, and he's even better at tracking some things. You might even say ghouls are his specialty," Saeter explained boastfully.

"Don't expect any kind of reward for this. I'm not going to change my mind about interfering in the affairs of the chiefs," the barkeeper responded darkly.

"Bah, ghouls are everyone's problem. I'm not looking for a reward. I just don't want to have to worry about this crap later. Besides, I'm just going to find them, not exterminate them. That will be up to the governor," Saeter replied dismissively.

Blacknail groaned; he didn't think that was very likely. Experience had taught him that if there was trouble around, Saeter would inevitably drag him into the middle of it. He would be very surprised if they didn't end up in a fight or fleeing for their lives.

"Fine, do what you want then, old fool," the barkeep told him.

"I always do," Saeter replied.

The two men began talking about the details and other things that Blacknail didn't find very interesting. He scanned the inside of the tavern, but nothing caught his attention. Luckily, Saeter finished up his conversation after only a few minutes.

"Come on, Blacknail," the old scout said as he walked away, back toward the door.

Blacknail followed his master, but before he reached the door, he turned back toward all the men and women who were throwing him dark looks. There was no way he was going to let some grubby-looking, tribeless humans look down on him. The hobgoblin straightened his back and met their gazes. His face was hiden behind his mask, but that was frightening enough. Most of the locals looked away, but one or two glared back. The hobgoblin let his hand drop to the hilt of his sword, and he growled in their direction. Suddenly, no one was meeting his gaze.

Blacknail grinned wickedly from behind his mask. None of

these smelly humans dared to challenge him! The hobgoblin skipped happily outside, and the door swung shut behind him. Ha, of course no one dared confront him; he was far too scary for weaklings like these!

“Stop wasting time,” Saeter grunted as he looked impatiently back at Blacknail.

“I’m right-ss behind you,” the hobgoblin replied.

Saeter shook his head disdainfully and then proceeded to walk down the street. Blacknail smiled as he sauntered over to his master. What were they doing again? Oh right, they were tracking down ghouls...

“Why are we-ss doing this? I don’t want to go near-ss any foul black bloods,” Blacknail asked with disgust.

Some of his memories from when he’d been a mere goblin had grown fuzzy, but he still remembered Herad’s fight against the ghoul things perfectly. He was unlikely to ever forget it, so he didn’t really need or want any new memories of ghouls. They wouldn’t be good memories.

“I wasn’t planning on confronting any ghouls today. I just want you to sniff around and see if there are actually any around,” his master answered.

“Bah, why are we-ss even doing that?” Blacknail asked.

“Because we can,” Saeter grunted in reply. His reply didn’t really answer Blacknail’s question.

“I don’t do a lot of things I could-ss, usually because you won’t let me. ‘Don’t steal that’ or ‘don’t stab thems’ you tell me, and those things sound like much more fun than ghoul-stalking.”

“I meant we’re doing it because no one else but us can. Remember when I told you about cities and how they can fall apart?” Saeter asked.

“No,” Blacknail replied.

Saeter sighed again. “It was like an hour ago! Daggerpoint is like an animal, remember?”

“Oh right-ss, but we’re not killing anyone right now, so we’re not hurting the city or stopping pastries from being made,” Blacknail countered.

“We may not be hurting the city, but the ghouls certainly are. They’re a sickness, and if left alone, they’ll kill the city,”

Saeter replied.

"...and then-ss all the pastries and tasty treats will be gone." Blacknail sighed in defeat. Of course they were the only ones who could do this. Everyone else in the city was apparently useless and stupid! How had all these humans survived without him around to save them constantly? It was a mystery.

"Right. Anyway, we're here now. Most of the disappearances have happened on this street. Sniff around, and see if you can smell any ghouls." Saeter stopped walking and stood in the middle of the empty street.

Blacknail reluctantly nodded and did as he was told. He leaned over and began to smell random cobblestones. When he didn't detect anything that way, he moved over to the edge of the street and sniffed the barrels and alley entrances there.

"I smell nothing," Blacknail told Saeter after several minutes of wandering.

"Keep trying," Saeter grunted in reply.

The hobgoblin sighed and started over again. After several boring minutes of smelling the same untainted, but still foul, scent of humans, he decided to wander down into the nearby alleys. His master didn't seem like he was going to let Blacknail stop anytime soon, so he walked over to the nearest backstreet entrance. It was a fairly tight alley with two rough-looking houses on either side of it. The hobgoblin walked into the shadows and idly began sniffing random things. Then he froze and started sniffing one spot again. Saeter noticed the hobgoblin's sudden fascination with a broken piece of board.

"Did you find their trail?" he asked eagerly.

"No," Blacknail replied as he sniffed the piece of wood some more.

"Then what in all the hells are you doing?" Saeter shouted in frustration.

"I smell familiar people-ss."

"Who?" Saeter asked curiously.

"Two of the men-ss who serve the mage Avorlus," Blacknail answered.

"They probably live around here," Saeter remarked dismissively.

"They bled here, and so did someone else. If they hunt-ss

other men here, it would explain why their base reeks so much of human blood," Blacknail mused to himself.

"What!" Saeter exclaimed in alarm. "You should have mentioned that before!"

"All mages smell of blood, just usually only-ss their own," Blacknail replied with a shrug.

"Come on, we're going." Saeter suddenly growled and spun around.

"What about-ss the ghouls?" Blacknail asked in disbelief.

"There are no ghouls!" a furious Saeter replied as he began stomping back out into the street. "This might actually be much worse."

Blacknail let out a defeated grunt as he followed his master. Of course as soon as he was resigned to having to fight a pack of ghouls, he was told the situation was actually somehow worse. Did Saeter ever deliver good news? Why did Blacknail follow him around again?

"Are we going toward the worse things or away-ss from them?" he asked his master with morbid curiosity. Ghouls were more than dangerous enough for Blacknail, so he really hoped they were heading away from danger. He knew his master too well to believe that though. Saeter had some odd, and more than a little crazy, ideas about what could be considered fun.

Saeter grunted in reply. "Away. We're headed back to see Herad."

Blacknail felt a wave of relief wash over him at his master's words. Somehow, against all odds, Saeter had started to actually make sense! It must be Blacknail's lucky day.

"Good," the hobgoblin replied cheerfully. Hethen followed Saeter into a nearby alley.

As the pair walked into the shadowy passage, Blacknail heard something from behind him. He spun around just in time to see two men enter the alleyway behind them and draw their blades. Blacknail hissed loudly in alarm as he reached for his own sword.

"This better not be another group of street kids..." Blacknail's master turned around to see what had alarmed the hobgoblin and stopped talking when he noticed the two men. "I'm thinking you two aren't here to welcome us to the neighborhood," Saeter remarked as he studied the pair.

"You've been sniffing around where you don't belong, so now you're dead meat," the leader replied.

"That's a bad idea; we're part of Herad's gang, and she takes attacks against her people personally," Saeter explained threateningly.

"That never works," Blacknail muttered darkly.

"Well, then we won't tell her about this," the closer assailant told Saeter with cruel humor.

"See, it didn't work! It never does," Blacknail pointed out irritably.

Saeter turned and gave him an annoyed look. "What should I have said, then? Do you want to take over the negotiations?"

"Let's just kill them. They don't look so tough! The one in the front is too skinny, and the one in the back looks slow and stupid," the hobgoblin replied.

"What did you just say about me, you little bastard?" the farther of the thugs asked angrily. Blacknail sighed and shook his head. Human ears sure were pathetic if they couldn't even hear someone talking from that short of a distance away.

"Let's kill these assholes, quick," one of the thugs told the other.

His companion nodded, and both of them pulled a vial out of their coats. Blacknail's eyes went wide as he watched them chug the contents. Everyone kept telling him that Vessels were rare, but that didn't really seem to be the case...

"See, this is why you try to talk first," Saeter told the hobgoblin irritably.

Blacknail grunted vaguely in reply as his master turned to face their attackers. Saeter's face twisted into a grimace as he considered them. He looked as if he'd swallowed something unpleasant.

"So I was right. You two work for Avorlus," he commented darkly.

"How the fuck—" Before the dark-haired one could say more, his companion shut him up by punching him in the shoulder and giving him a cold glare.

It was the perfect opportunity to hit them with a surprise attack, so Blacknail stealthy reached into one of his pouches for ammo. His fingers frantically searched the inside of the bag, but he didn't feel any stones. Oh right, he'd thrown them all at the pack of little thieves that had ambushed them. He'd forgotten to retrieve them because Saeter had started lecturing him.

"Dog teeth," Blacknail muttered to himself.

If there had been only one Vessel, Blacknail could probably have fought him off, and if he'd been alone, he could have just run for it. With Saeter here, and with two Vessels as his opponents, he didn't know what to do.

# *Chapter 30*

Since he had no ranged weapons available, Blacknail drew his sword. Meanwhile, Saeter reached into his coat and took out a pouch of his own. The old scout threw a quick glance at the alleyway behind them. The hobgoblin saw the movement and knew what Saeter wanted to know.

"There are only two of them. I hear no one behind us," he told his master. Saeter nodded and turned back to watch the pair of thugs who were approaching. He eyed the two men warily.

"We're running. Follow me," he whispered a second later. Blacknail's eyes widened slightly in surprise. That was not what he had expected Saeter to say.

"They'll be fast-ss runners," he warned his master. Blacknail really hoped his master had a plan. Normally he was all for running away from danger, but he wasn't sure Saeter was fast enough to escape.

"Now!" His master grunted a second later as he started running. Instantly, Blacknail turned and sprinted away as well. He shoved his sword back into its sheath. Within a few short seconds, he pulled ahead of the old scout.

"Blasted cowards. Don't let them escape!" one of the Vessels yelled from behind them.

The pounding of heavy footsteps reached Blacknail's ears as the two thugs gave chase. The hobgoblin looked over his shoulder and winced when he saw how fast their pursuers were running down the alley toward them. The men were moving at a pace a non-boosted human would have a very hard time matching. They would catch up within seconds. Blacknail could increase his own pace, but Saeter probably couldn't. Desperately, the hobgoblin searched his pouches for something useful as he ran. If only he had been a mage, then he could have used magic or something against them! One of Blacknail's hands came to rest against his coin pouch, and he let out a resigned sigh as an annoying idea occurred to him. The hobgoblin quickly reached inside, scooped coins into his hand, and whipped them back at their pursuers.

"Eat-ss this, pinkies!" Blacknail yelled as the swarm of glittering projectiles flew through the air. The two Vessels barely had time to react before the coins showered over them. They both raised their hands to protect their faces, but not in time to stop the first few projectiles.

"Fuck," one of them swore as a coin smashed into his forehead and drew blood. He stumbled and slowed momentarily to wipe the blood from his face. The second pursuer winced in pain as a coin bounced off his kneecap, and he slowed as well. Behind his mask, Blacknail smirked smugly at them.

Idly, he wondered if this counted as charity. The two thugs had certainly needed the money, thrown at their ugly faces, more than he had. He would have to ask Saeter later, after they finished running for their lives.

Just ahead of Blacknail, Saeter rounded a corner and momentarily disappeared out of sight. When the hobgoblin caught up, he noticed his master was emptying the pouch he'd been holding onto the ground. It had been full of little spiky pieces of metal.

"Keep running," Saeter told him as he finished and picked up speed again.

"I never stopped! You're-ss the slow one, you run!" Blacknail hissed back.

"Bah, whatever." Saeter grunted in reply, and the annoyedhobgoblin had to suppress an urge to kick his master in the ass.

The two of them only managed to run a short distance before their pursuers rounded the corner as well. The thugs were moving very quickly, and thus, they didn't have time to notice the presents Saeter had left behind for them.

"Ugh, bloody hells! My foot," one of them screamed as he stepped on a spike. The other man instantly looked down, and his eyes widened in surprise at what he saw.

"Fuck, caltrops!" he exclaimed.

The first man stumbled and quickly hopped out of the way. He was limping, and his face was scrunched in pain, so he was clearly no longer in any shape to continue the chase. However, the second man had been warned. He was managing to awkwardly hop across the caltrops without stepping on any, so Blacknail picked up a rock off the alley floor and hurled it at his face. The thug was looking down at his own feet, so he didn't see it coming at all. There was a thud as the heavy stone bounced off the side of his head. He stumbled and stepped on a caltrop. As the hobgoblin watched, the man's leg gave out and he tipped over sideways to land on his side. As he hit the ground, several more spikes were driven into his body.

"Damn you to all the hells forever!" the man screamed shrilly in pain. Ouch, Blacknail was fairly sure that guywas no longer a problem either. Maybe he should go back there and finish them off...

"It's not worth it, keep running," Saeter suddenly remarked between heavy breaths. The old scout had clearly understood the hobgoblin's hesitation and body language. Blacknail sighed in regret and continued running. He'd been hoping to at least go back and get his coins, and he wouldn't have said no to having some fun with the two men who'd attacked them.

The pair burst out of the alley and onto one of the main streets. Without slowing, Saeter led Blacknail right into the middle of the crowds. Men and women pressed against the hobgoblin from all sides, but he ignored them. Several minutes later, after it was clear no one was still following them, Saeter slowed down to a walk and moved off to the side of the road. He was huffing and breathing heavily. His face was red and looked exhausted, but the hobgoblin had barely broken a sweat. All this easy city living was clearly making Saeter weak.

"I think we lost them," the gray-haired scout told Blacknail. "Now we need to get back and have a talk with Herad though."

It didn't take them long to reach Herad's compound. They passed the guards and stepped inside without a problem. Blacknail eyed his master warily as he walked. Saeter seemed to be growing more and more animated the closer they got to

Herad, and that made the hobgoblin nervous. When he got to the entrance to Herad's room, Saeter burst through and the door slammed into the wall behind him with a loud crash. His eyes burned with rage as he stomped into the chamber on the other side.

Blacknail stayed out in the hallway and cowered behind the two startled-looking guards that Saeter had blown past. All three of them gave each other shocked looks and then peered wide-eyed through the doorway to see what happened next.

Herad looked up from her desk. There was a look halfway between annoyance and amusement on her face. She was also reaching under her desk for something that was probably a weapon, but she relaxed and smirked when she recognized Saeter.

"Down boy," she ordered him loudly.

Saeter stopped a few feet from her desk and grimaced as he realized he'd unintentionally obeyed her. Herad smiled mockingly at him.

"Good boy," she remarked as her eyes glittered with amusement.

Saeter's scowl deepened. He didn't look happy. However, Blacknail let out a relieved breath. It didn't seem like they were going to fight. So his master would probably live.

Saeter grunted. "I'm not a dog."

"Then don't act like one, old man. Knock on the door before you enter, and don't slam it," she told him condescendingly.

Blacknail could hear Saeter grinding his teeth as he tried to hold in his anger. Luckily, this just seemed to amuse Herad.

"I'm here because there's something you need to know," he said a few seconds later. One of Herad's eyebrows rose as she gave Saeter an unsurprised look.

"Well, I didn't think you stormed in here to invite me to dinner, so please go on and tell me what bug has gotten up your butt this time," she remarked disdainfully as she leaned back in her chair.

"Avorlus is a blood mage," Saeter announced gravely.

The old scout met Herad's eyes and stared her down. Herad's mouth opened slightly, and she looked momentarily lost for words. Blacknail had no idea what a blood mage was, but it sure sounded serious!

"Well… that certainly makes sense and is useful to know. How exactly did you figure this out?" Herad calmly asked after a moment or two of thought.

"That's it? I just revealed there's blood mage in our midst, and that's all you have to say?" Saeter growled angrily.

"What is it you expect me to say?"

"I expect you to do something about it!"

"He's useful, so I don't really care all that much," Herad explained emotionlessly as her dark eyes narrowed.

"He's a blood mage!" Saeter exclaimed in outraged disbelief.

"And now that I know what he is, I can hold it over him to guarantee his cooperation, so thanks for telling me. Now shut your trap. You're not to discuss this with anyone," Herad ordered as she glared coldly at him.

Blacknail heard footsteps, so he turned to see Mahedium approaching the room. Herad's guards straightened and tried to look like they hadn't been listening in, but the hobgoblin gave the mage a friendly wave before peering back through the doorway.

"Don't you know how dangerous it is to be around blood mages? Not to mention, they kill people and harvest their blood!" Saeter pointed out.

Before Herad could answer, their conversation was interrupted as Mahedium walked into the room. They both scowled at him as he entered, but the mage didn't seem disturbed.

"I heard you wanted me, Saeter," the mage calmly said as he approached Herad's desk.

"Yes, I did! I wanted to discuss your friend, Master Avorlus. Did you know he's a blood mage?" Saeter replied angrily.

"That's a very serious accusation. I take it you have proof?" Mahedium asked. The young mage was still calm and composed. He held his staff in one hand and stood straight with military discipline. With his plain face, hazel eyes, and short brown hair he looked as unremarkable as usual.

"I know he's been abducting people off the streets and that his home reeks of people's blood," Saeter replied darkly.

"He's probably a blood mage then," Mahedium admitted

with a frown.

"Did you know?" Saeter asked threateningly.

"I had some suspicions but nothing more," the mage replied without concern.

"Why didn't you say anything?" the old scout exclaimed angrily.

"It's not something I care to accuse people of without proof," Mahedium answered coldly.

"More like you didn't care..." Saeter countered.

The mage met Saeter's angry stare without flinching. The old scout turned away from him after a second and looked back at Herad.

"You two aren't taking this seriously enough. Blood mages pollute the very earth, and they twist beasts into monsters!" he announced in frustration. His face was red and he was breathing heavier than normal. This was the most worked up Blacknail had ever seen him. However, Herad just gave Saeter a flat uncaring stare.

"As far as I'm concerned, blood mages aren't much worse than any other type of mage. I've never met a combat mage that didn't have the blood of dozens of men on their hands. All that garbage about blood magic causing mutants to appear is just superstition," Herad told him dismissively.

"That's different, combat mages are soldiers. Blood mages prey on people for their own ends," Saeter replied.

"As a combat mage, I also believe there's an important distinction there," Mahedium added. "Also, Saeter isn't completely wrong about the relationship between blood magic and crystal hosts."

A triumphant look appeared on Saeter's face, and he opened his mouth to say something, but Herad cut him off.

"Explain," she ordered the mage.

"Blood magic comes in several forms, but it's actually very simple. In fact, the first mages probably all used blood magic before modern alchemical magic was created. The type I imagine Avorlus is doing, simply involves harvesting the blood of people who didn't survive the transformation into a Vessel, and maybe some that did. He's probably dosing the people he's abducted and then distilling their blood to create Elixir," the mage explained.

"Why would he do that, and what does it have to do with mutants?" Herad asked.

"It's a way to create more of an Elixir, even if you don't know the formula for it. With such an endless supply of samples, it also becomes much easier to study an Elixir and discover its recipe. Unfortunately, refining the blood also creates a lot of waste products that contain active crystals. It's unlikely, but possible, that exposure to this waste could cause a creature to become a host," Mahedium admitted.

"So, a horde of savage mutants isn't about to tear its way through the city," Herad said with a glare at Saeter.

"No, most likely exposure would just kill the creatures it comes into contact with. It's very dangerous stuff to anyone not already a mage or Vessel. I wonder how Avorlus is disposing of it," Mahedium replied.

"One mutant would be too many. We need to stop him before it's too late!" Saeter said.

"Your paranoid fear of mutants is getting annoying. They die like everything else," Herad replied scornfully.

"You've never seen the havoc a truly dangerous crystal host can create. No man can stand against them, the empty ruins of Coroulis should be proof enough of that," Saeter countered. His face was still red from being so worked up, and he waved his hands as he talked. This clearly wasn't an argument he was willing to lose. Of course, Herad wasn't usually one to care what other people thought, only that they obeyed.

"Even if I wanted to do something about him, and I don't, I'm not in a position where I can throw away such a useful ally. Perhaps over your rather long and eventful career as a thief and murderer, you've noticed that people who play at being a hero, and who involve themselves in events that aren't any of their damn business, end up dead or as failures. That's not a mistake I intend to make," she replied harshly and with obvious scorn.

"Some things are more important than petty gains, and worth sacrificing for. Maybe, becoming murder queen of the cutthroats shouldn't be your first priority," Saeter told her.

Herad's chair slid back across the floor with a shrill screech. A dangerous look appeared on her face as she rose to her feet.

Her dark eyes narrowed as she regarded Saeter with hostility. Both Saeter and Mahedium took a step back away from her as she walked toward them.

"You overstep yourself, Saeter! Remember that I'm the chief here and that you work for me. You will do as I say, and nothing more, or I'll dispose of you like so much trash," she snarled as she stood in front of him.

The old scout stiffened, and his face went slightly pale, but he held her gaze, and his eyes were full of defiance. Blacknail hissed quietly in alarm. Why wasn't his master backing down? He was going to get himself killed after all! The hobgoblin held his breath as Saeter and Herad glared at each other. Blacknail's master seemed unwilling to submit and look away, and Herad's left hand began to creep closer toward the hilt of a dagger on her hip. The hobgoblin began seriously considering creating a distraction and dragging his master away in the chaos. Maybe he could pretend there was an attack or start a fire? As Herad's fingers closed around her dagger's pommel, Saeter finally spoke up.

"It's as you say; you're the boss," he answered flatly. Blacknail sighed in relief. Saeter started to turn away from Herad, and head toward the door, but the bandit chieftain stopped him.

"Where do you think you're going? I didn't give you permission to leave," she hissed.

Saeter froze and grimaced. It looked like he wanted to say something unwise. Blacknail held his breath again. If his master said anything stupid, and suicidal, then Blacknail was going to bash him over the head and apologize to Herad for him.

"I'm... going to go get a drink." Saeter grunted reluctantly a second later. The hobgoblin relaxed.

"Very well, go ahead. Just remember that I meant what I said about keeping this quiet," Herad replied smugly.

The old scout didn't respond. He just immediately walked out of the room. Mahedium threw Saeter a concerned look, but he also chose to keep his mouth shut.

Saeter walked out the door, and past the two guards and one hobgoblin who were now trying hard to look like they hadn't been listening. Blacknail moved to follow his master as soon

Saeter stomped out into the hallway, but he hesitated when he heard Herad address him.

"Blacknail, make sure the old fool behaves, or you'll both regret it," she told him coldly.

"Yes, mistress," Blacknail answered as he turned and lowered his head submissively.

"At least one of them knows who is in charge around here," the hobgoblin heard his chieftain mutter as he scurried quickly after Saeter.

Why couldn't Saeter keep his mouth shut? If he kept this up, one of these days Herad was going take offense at his actions and kill him. He'd come awfully close just now, and Blacknail would rather that didn't happen.

Saeter's feet thudded against the wooden floorboards as he stomped through the building. He was obviously still furious, so Blacknail hesitated to approach him. He should probably try to cheer his master up though.

"I could just kill Avorlus for you, or we could do it together, master. I've gotten very good at the sneaking and stabbing," Blacknail offered hopefully as he walked up beside Saeter.

"You're not helping, Blacknail. I've done a lot of immoral things in my life, but I'm not an assassin," the old scout replied.

"I am, so I'll do it for you!" the hobgoblin cheerfully pointed out.

"No," his master sternly replied. "Stay here, I need to be alone for awhile."

As Blacknail looked on, his master sighed tiredly and walked out the front door of Herad's base. The hobgoblin would normally have been more than happy to let him go, but Herad had commanded him to keep an eye on Saeter. With an exasperated sigh, Blacknail stealthily crept after his master.

Things would be much easier if Saeter would just not resist the chief or if he would at least launch a proper challenge. Of course, if he did challenge Herad, he would most likely be cut to pieces, but if Herad did spare him then he would at least learn his place. There wasn't much chance of Saeter winning. His master really needed to realize that Herad was a lot tougher than him, so he should do as she said. That was simply the natural order of things after all.

# *Chapter 31*

The air in the closet was dry and stale. It was almost pitch black inside. Only the tiniest hint of light managed to slip in under the door. Deep at the back, behind a pile of crates and a heap of musty old sheets, there was a quiet muffled shuffling sound as a shadowy figure stirred. Two long arms that ended in long jagged nails reached out and carefully retrieved something from under one of the sheets. There was then a sinister chuckle as Blacknail the hobgoblin brought the wheel of cheese up to his mouth and took a luxurious bite out of it. It was so tasty and yummy! He'd hidden his cheese wheel here several days ago, and now he was enjoying a quick snack. No one would ever think to look for his tasty treat here. As he happily chewed the strong tangy cheese, his revelry was suddenly broken by the sound of raised voices.

Last night, he'd followed Saeter out into the city, but nothing interesting had happened. Herad had ordered Blacknail to look out for his master, so he had carefully shadowed Saeter through the streets. The old scout had just wandered to the nearest tavern though, and spent the evening drinking.

Blacknail had slipped into the tavern as well and sat down at a table. He'd chosen a spot across the floor from Saeter that was tucked away in a dark corner. When anyone had tried to approach him, he'd simply hissed at them until they had gone away. If they hadn't got the message, then he'd drawn his dagger. Other than the fun he'd had scaring the occasional drunk or waitress, it had been a very boring night. Eventually, his master had stumbled drunkenly home, and Blacknail had followed him back. The hobgoblin had only needed to kill one mugger to keep his master safe.

It was now the next morning, and Blacknail's ears perked up as he detected unusual activity. Not only were a group of people discussing something rather loudly, but the sound of hurried footsteps now filled Herad's base. Something was happening...

The hobgoblin carefully placed his cheese back in its hiding spot and stealthily crept out of the closet. He was curious about what was going on, but also cautious. It was entirely possible Herad was just in a mood, and had decided to put everyone to work. It was also possible she'd simply started to kill everyone she saw. In either of those cases, Blacknail wasn't planning on going anywhere near her.

He silently made his way down the hallway and toward the speakers until their voices got clearer. One of them was definitely Herad, but she didn't sound angry. Rather, she sounded excited and cheerful. Blacknail flinched as he was suddenly overwhelmed by an urge to run back to the closet and crawl under something. If Herad was happy, then bad things were about to happen to somebody, and Blacknail didn't want it to be him.

"... just a few hours away. They weren't all that easy to count, but there are about a hundred and a dozen of them. They're definitely a foot company; only a few of the officers were mounted," a familiar-sounding bandit was saying.

"They're a little early, but we're ready for them," Herad replied.

"They were moving pretty quickly and seemed organized. Whoever these guys are, they know how to march," the other bandit explained.

"Did you get a good look at their equipment?" Herad asked him.

"Not really; they're transporting it in covered wagons. I don't think there was enough room in them all for too many pikes or crossbows though. They had shields on their backs, so most of them are most likely planning on fighting with sword and shield," he replied.

"I would prefer it if they didn't have shields, but crossbows would have been a bigger threat. You didn't ambush or raid them at all?" the chieftain inquired.

"No, as per your orders, we held back and remained out of sight. The mercenaries didn't give us an opening to go after anyway. Their officers and supplies were always well protected."

"Good, the element of surprise is worth more than the loss of a few grunts to arrows from the forest. It's important that they don't realize we're expecting them," Herad announced to everyone there. "I want every single member of the band accounted for and equipped within the hour. The men already here are to start rolling out the heavy defenses right away. It's time to dig in."

"Right away, boss," a new bandit responded before Blacknail heard him run off.

As Herad continued to talk, Blacknail slipped into the room. He wanted to be part of the action as well. Hopefully, Herad would give him a real job this time. The chamber was packed full of people, most of whom Blacknail couldn't be bothered to remember by name. He did see both Saeter and Khita though. No one looked his way as he walked over toward his master.

"Have you been able to round up a few more horses?" Herad asked a tall, lanky woman.

"No, there have been some complications there, boss," the woman replied nervously.

"What kind of complications?" Herad asked with more than a hint of anger.

The female bandit winced and paled slightly. Blacknail was glad he wasn't the one who'd annoyed the chieftain.

"A lot of the dealers are having problems with their stock. A lot of the animals in the city are sick. They think there's either a flu going around or that someone has been poisoning them. I don't know why anyone would do that though," she explained quickly.

Herad grunted in acknowledgment and some of the anger left her face. It was quickly replaced by confusion. She didn't seem to know why anyone would do that either. Blacknail went very still and tried to look as innocent as possible by forcing himself to smile. He wasn't sure it was working very well. Luckily, Herad didn't look his way. Saeter turned and gave the hobgoblin an irritated look though.

"They started it!" Blacknail whispered to him.

His master didn't seem convinced by this argument. The old scout sighed and shook his head until he turned back toward Herad a second later.

"Smelly stupid horses," the hobgoblin muttered to himself. How dare they get him in trouble! Next time, he was going to use stronger poison.

"What about Zelena? Is she moving?" Herad asked.

"Well, we still don't know where she actually is, but none of her men seem to be doing anything yet," a blond man replied. He was one of the bandits Blacknail couldn't be bothered to remember.

"Good, then we probably have some time. I want you to tell the guards to lock and block every door but the main entrance, girl," Herad said as she looked at Khita.

The young redhead pointed to herself uncertainly.

"Yes, you," Herad replied irritably and pointed to the door.

"I have a bloody name," Khita muttered darkly to herself. The young woman knew better than to disobey though, and she hurriedly headed for the exit. Blacknail watched her go, and when Khita noticed him, he stuck his tongue out at her mockingly. She scowled at the hobgoblin in return, but that only made him smile smugly.

Herad then turned toward the band's only mage. Blacknail hadn't noticed him at first because he'd been standing at the back of a group of people and out of sight. Also, while most humans looked the same, Mahedium was even more generic looking than most.

"Mahedium, I want you to visit your friend Avorlus and deliver a message for me," she told the mage.

The mage frowned in displeasure as he considered Herad's words. "Is he going to like this message?"

"Probably not." Herad chuckled as she threw Saeter a smug smirk.

The old scout's face muscles tightened and he clenched his fists, but he didn't say anything. Mahedium sighed in resignation, and Herad handed him an envelope. The mage then nodded and left the room.

"Blacknail and Saeter, I have a job for you two as well. Saeter, I want you to take some of the other scouts out and stop anyone who tries to approach the base. I don't want Zelena to know what she's getting into before it's too late," Herad told them.

"You're the boss, how could I refuse?" Saeter replied coldly.

"What do we do if too many enemies show up?" Blacknail asked quickly.

The hobgoblin didn't want to give Saeter the chance to annoy Herad. He also wanted to know exactly when it was all right to run away. That was an important thing to know if there were going to be lots and lots of angry humans around.

"Fall back to the first line of defense and help defend it. I want you to keep an eye out for assassins or scouts that try to sneak past though. That's your main concern, Blacknail. I expect Zelena to send them in when she realizes how hard a nut we'll be to crack, and I want you ready. It'll be your job to deal with them," the bandit chieftain explained.

Blacknail scowled doubtfully. If Malthus showed up, Blacknail didn't want to get in another fight with him. The annoying man was a much better sword fighter than him. Herad was giving him a very dangerous job. His expression didn't go unnoticed.

"If you manage to handle Zelena's knifemen, then I'll buy you all the food you can eat," Herad told him as she grinned sardonically.

The hobgoblin fidgeted as he considered the offer. It sounded interesting, but Blacknail wasn't an idiot. The job was going to be very risky, so he wanted something more than just a lot of food. He wanted quality food.

"You'll give-ss me all the expensive blue cheese and apple pies I want-ss?" the hobgoblin asked as he licked his lips. Herad rolled her eyes, and several bandits chuckled.

"Anything you want," she answered dryly.

"Then I'll do-ss it!" Blacknail replied as he grinned smugly to himself. He was obviously a master negotiator! Blue cheese was worth a little danger. It smelled so good but was very hard to find or buy.

The merchants wanted crazy amounts of coins for it and never left it lying around, which was very rude of them. Even the thought of eating as much of it as he could swallow sent shivers of joy down his spine.

"Do you think you can handle it?" Saeter asked him with concern. The hobgoblin looked at the ground and began to think furiously. A few seconds later, he looked up and met his master's gaze.

"Yes, I can do it. They might be sneaky and dangerous, but they're just humans. I also don't have to fight them fair," Blacknail replied with a vicious grin.

"Sounds like you have a plan," Saeter remarked.

"It's the best plan ever! This job will be easy," the hobgoblin bragged as he grinned smugly.

Saeter grunted dubiously and frowned at Blacknail, but he didn't say anything further. The hobgoblin knew his master was skeptical, but was sure his plan would work. The meeting continued on for almost another hour before Herad sent everyone away. Saeter immediately went off to gather men for their mission.

"Get ready to do some running and fighting. You'll want all your gear for this, including your bow. I have to wrangle up the other members of our little party, so I'll probably be a while. I'll meet you out front at the eleventh hour," his master told him.

The hobgoblin nodded and dashed over to his room to get his stuff. He would need all the time he could get if he wanted to prepare his surprise for Malthus and the other assassins. Blacknail quickly wound the bandages around his arms and legs, donned his cloak, and pulled on his mask. He grabbed his backpack and filled it full of some extra rope and stakes. Then, as his master had suggested, he strapped his bow to his back and pulled on his sword belt. When that was done, Blacknail quickly rummaged through one of his other bags. A second later, he pulled out a pair of sausages and scoffed them down. He didn't want to run on an empty stomach.

The hobgoblin dashed out of the building. When he returned around two hours later, his backpack was missing, and he was out of breath from running so hard. Saeter was right where he'd said he would be, just outside the front entrance to Herad's base, and he wasn't alone. Two dozen other men were with him. Blacknail recognized them all as scouts that had been with the band since before he'd joined. The rangers were dressed somewhat similarly to the rest of the band. If anything, their leathers and cloaks were more worn looking than usual. Unlike most the men in Herad's employ though, they had an aura of stillness about them. It wasn't that they didn't seem dangerous, it was that the danger was tempered by patience, which was good, because Blacknail was late.

"So the hobgoblin's finally here," one of them commented as Blacknail arrived.

"Good, I was beginning to think old Saeter was going to make us leave without him, and he's probably worth two or three men for something like this," another replied with a smile.

Blacknail gave the second man a friendly nod of acknowledgement. He had spent more time around the scouts and foresters than any of the other bandits and was thus comfortable being around them. He also respected their skill. They were hunters.

"More than that, at least ten," Blacknail bragged, which drew a round of chuckles.

A scattering of wispy, white clouds filled the sky overhead, but the noon sun was still visible most of the time. A cold heavy wind was blowing from the north, and it was pulling the dark clouds that lay thick on the skyline ever closer. Blacknail thought there was a good chance the day would soon grow dimmer.

"All right, we're all here, so let's get moving," Saeter told everyone. "Our job is to intercept anyone trying to get a good look at the compound. Gavius, I want you and seven others to watch the gap in the buildings to the west. I'll take these eleven and watch the main road."

There were nods of agreement from everyone present. The rangers started to form their parties, but just as the groups had started to split up, Saeter spoke again. "And remember, nobody here should try and play hero. If you see anything you can't deal with, then don't try, go for reinforcements. It's not our job to stop a serious advance."

"You remember it!" Blacknail muttered as he gave his master a dark look. If anyone here was going to end up putting themselves in danger, it was almost certainly going to be Saeter, and that meant Blacknail would have to put himself in danger to help him. This time, if the old scout tried anything stupid, Blacknail was going to drag him away, even if he had to knock him unconscious first.

Saeter led the hobgoblin and the other rangers over to the main road, and they started walking to their destination. As they moved, Blacknail observed their surroundings carefully for any signs of danger. This part of the city was mostly deserted. The fact that it had been claimed by Herad was common knowledge, and so was her violent nature. Not that a lot of people had lived here even before the bandit chieftain had moved in. Most buildings here were old warehouses. Right beside Blacknail, two large ones stood on either side the road. Their foundations were rough stone and mortar, but the rest of them were made of thick wooden planks. Saeter stopped and pointed to a window high up on the second floor of the building to the right.

"That spot has a good overview of the entire area. I want someone with a bow up there. If you see anyone that doesn't belong, then use standard birdcalls to tell everyone else which side of the street they're on," Saeter said.

"I'll do that," one of the scouts replied. The man exchanged a nod with Saeter and headed for the entrance to the warehouse.

"All right, you two are with me and Blacknail. The five of us will take the west side of the road. The rest of you will take the eastern side. Carvus, you're in charge," Saeter explained. There were nods of agreement all around, and then the group split into two. Scouts weren't the most talkative of people.

"Keep those big green ears of yours open, Blacknail," Saeter told the hobgoblin as they walked off the street and into an alley.

"I will-ss, no one will get past me!" Blacknail replied happily.

The hobgoblin was already scanning his surroundings with all his senses. Hunting like this always made him excited, and this time was no different. The act of sneaking around while looking for prey made him feel all tingly inside. There was nothing he would rather be doing, and he couldn't wait for some unexpecting enemy to stumble onto his path. Dealing with them would be so fun!

It had rained slightly that morning, so the loose cobblestones under Blacknail's boots were still damp and muddy. The sun had dropped low enough in the sky that it didn't illuminate the spaces between the buildings, so the alleyway was gloomy and full of shadows. Blacknail heard a slight noise from up ahead, and he instantly whipped his head around to stare intently in that direction. Was it an enemy? No, a rat had just scuttled out of hiding. The hobgoblin sighed and continued following his master as the vermin disappeared through a hole in a wall.

They continued trudging through the alleys for what seemed like forever to Blacknail, and it was boring! Why hadn't an enemy shown up yet? The hobgoblin was beginning to think he should be going on ahead by himself. There were supposed to be lots of enemies in the city right now, so he could just go grab one of them. The sucker would never know what hit him!

Suddenly, Blacknail heard a thumping sound from down a side street up ahead. There had been a few more false alarms since the rat, so at first he didn't think too much of it, but then the sound repeated itself several times. It sounded suspiciously like footsteps. A large group of unknown people were approaching. The hobgoblin's group was out here looking for enemies, and it seemed likelythat they'd found some.Hooray?

# *Chapter 32*

Blacknail hissed softly in warning as the sound of footsteps on wet cobblestone drew closer. Saeter quickly held up a hand and signaled everyone to stop, and he looked back at Blacknail to see what was the matter. The hobgoblin responded by pointing to the source of the noise and then making the hand gesture for people approaching. Saeter immediately gestured for the group to split up, take cover, and ready their weapons for an ambush. Blacknail was more than happy to obey. Finally, some prey had shown itself! He hoped they had lots of shiny bits and tasty things on them he could take as trophies, like pie.

The hobgoblin quickly dashed over to a rain barrel and hid behind it before drawing his bow. It had been a while since he had last used the weapon, but he remembered how. It just wasn't something he usually carried around with him in Daggerpoint, since a sling was almost as good and much less conspicuous. Experience had taught Blacknail that half the art of successfully hitting someone lay in making sure they didn't know you were about to take a shot at them, and that was hard to do with a bow unless you were very far away.

The other members of his party also took cover behind various obstacles and waited for the source of the noise to draw near. Blacknail could barely contain his excitement. He was shivering eagerly and had even started to drool in anticipation as he listened to the footsteps approach. The stupid humans didn't know what was about to hit them! Unless it was Malthus of course. If it was, Blacknail planned on running away as fast he could.

Soon enough, a man's head poked out from around the corner. His wild-looking hair was dirty blond, and he had a short beard. After a few seconds of staring down the street suspiciously, he turned around and looked the other way for a few seconds before stepping back around the corner and out of sight.

"It looks clear," Blacknail heard him tell someone.

There was a low rumble of conversation, and then the blond man stepped back out into the street. He was soon followed by several other men and a woman. Blacknail studied them as they walked closer. All of them were wearing rough, mismatched leather armor and were armed with short swords. They all looked like normal Daggerpoint thugs to the hobgoblin, but they clearly weren't just out for a morning stroll. They were far too nervous to be anything but intruders, and that meant they were fair game.

Saeter's hiding spot was the closest to the enemy because he had been leading the group. While still concealed, Blacknail's master flashed the signal for three, and then the one for two. Blacknail smiled eagerly as he realized it was a countdown. Just as the lead thug stepped in a small puddle in the middle of the street, Saeter gave the go command. As one, the scouts rose from their hiding spots and unleashed a barrage of shrieking arrows. Their targets barely had time to react before the arrows ripped into them.

Howls of pain filled the air, and three of the enemy fell with feathered shafts protruding from their flesh. Their bodies hit the wet ground with a splash and went still. Two more of the enemy had been hit but were still standing. Blacknail hissed in annoyance. His own arrow had missed and flown harmlessly down the street. The stupid human had moved at the last second! That wasn't fair. He had wanted to show off how great an archer he was!

"Damnation, you bloody bastards!" swore a large, brown-haired thug.

He had a deep gash across his arm that had been caused by an arrow grazing it, but the wound didn't stop him from drawing his sword and charging the closest target he saw. The three uninjured thugs behind him also drew their own weapons and charged as well. Blacknail hissed in irritation when he realized they were headed for Saeter. Why did that always happen?

The hobgoblin was relieved that at least the last two thugs weren't joining the attack. One was too busy cradling his arm because it had an arrow sticking out of it. The other was uninjured but decided to make a run for it. He dashed back the way they'd come but didn't get very far. A scout to Blacknail's left calmly put an arrow right between his shoulder blades.

Saeter saw the enemies bearing down on him and threw down his bow so he could pull out his sword. Blacknail hurriedly put his own bow down on the barrel in front of him and rushed over to support his master. Two other scouts were right behind him. They all drew their swords as they moved. Saeter took a step back as he warded off his opponents with a wide swing of his blade. This bought Blacknail enough time to close on the thug closest to him. The hobgoblin put on a dash of speed and ducked under the man's blade. He then stabbed the tip of his sword deep into the terminally surprised man's belly. There was a wet sucking sound as the blade sank into flesh, quickly followed by a choking noise as the man collapsed and vomited up blood. Blacknail hurriedly stepped out of the way of the messy red torrent and kicked the kneeling man hard in the ribs so he could pry his sword out of his guts.

That left four enemies that were still attacking Saeter. Blacknail's master didn't seem to be having any trouble keeping out of reach of their blades though. He calmly sidestepped any slash or stab that went anywhere near him, and soon the other two scouts reached his side. Instantly, the odds turned against the thugs; now they were the outnumbered ones. Saeter and the other bandits took full advantage of this. All together they pressed forward and attacked as Blacknail leaped to the side and threatened the thugs' flank. The hobgoblin didn't like attacking from the front.

Blades flashed through the air as Zelena's hirelings were encircled and pushed together. The clang of steel on steel filled the alley as blade met blade. As Saeter and the other scouts attacked and exchanged blows with their opponents, Blacknail leaped in from the side and slashed at one the thugs' feet. The hobgoblin's swing didn't connect, but it forced the man to lurch out of the way and caused a gap to open in the intruders' defense. Almost immediately, one of them stumbled, and a sword cut into his neck. He collapsed and the gap widened. Saeter and his men redoubled their efforts, and blood splashed against the ground as another of Zelena's thugs was cut down. Blacknail giggled excitedly as he circled behind the remaining enemies; he sensed victory.

"Halt," Saeter told his companions as he held out a hand.

Blacknail and the scouts stopped their attack. The hobgoblin threw a questioning glance at Saeter. He'd been having a lot of fun, and they were about to get to the best part, so why had Saeter made them stop?

"Throw down your weapons, and surrender. There's no point in fighting," the old scout told the last two thugs.

"We surrender," the remaining man instantly replied as he dropped his sword. The woman was quick to follow. Both of them looked relieved but still more than a little afraid. Their fear was understandable, since they were surrounded, and at their feet lay the bloody corpses of their former comrades.

The hobgoblin was still wound up from the fight. He shivered as he fought down the urge to pounce on his defeated foes. He really hoped this surrendering business was Saeter's clever way of disarming the enemy so that they were easier to finish off, but he doubted it. Annoyed, Blacknail distracted himself by studying the captives. The surviving male was a shorter man with a wide build. The hobgoblin thought he looked like he had quite a bit of meat on him. He had dark eyes and dirty brown hair. He also had a short scraggly beard that did little to conceal his fat cheeks and the pockmarks on them. The female was tall for a woman and gaunt looking. She also had messy, short brown hair and pale, washed-out blue eyes. Blacknail eyed her suspiciously. She seemed full of nervous energy and was constantly fidgeting. If one of them was going to try something, it would probably be her. Blacknail hoped she did. Both the captives noticed his intense stare, masked face, and agitated demeanor. The man blanched and took a step away from him, while the woman paled and froze. Their reactions simply excited Blacknail further.

"See, I told you the hobgoblin would come in handy. He led us right to them, and we caught them like fish in a barrel," the ranger from earlier remarked.

"That wasn't actually what you said," his companion replied dryly.

"Close enough. Thanks, Blacknail," the first man said.

"No problem; it was easy," the hobgoblin replied cheerfully without taking his eyes off the prisoners.

Saeter ignored the chattering going on behind him and was also focused on the captives. "Surrendering was the right choice. Now, what were your orders?" he asked them threateningly.

"We were just told to scout ahead and report back any activity," the male captive quickly replied.

"We're not Zelena's minions, we're just in this for the money. They offered us bonuses if we brought back good info. Please, don't kill me," the woman begged.

"Do you know anything about Zelena's movements?" Saeter asked them harshly.

"Yes, I do," the man replied eagerly. "She's planning on attacking you today and is massing her forces over at Second and Gilber Street."

Blacknail's master looked them over contemplatively for a few seconds before turning to his companions. "They're just throwaway hirelings, and probably a distraction for the real scouts."

"What do you want to do with them?" one of Herad's rangers asked. He didn't sound like he really cared all that much.

The old scout turned to look at the captives again and frowned. The woman gave him a hopeful smile. Blacknail took a step forward and eagerly voiced his opinion.

"You could let them go…" he suggested eagerly.

Some of the tension disappeared from the captives' posture, and they looked relieved.

"… and then I could hunt them down through the streets for fun," the hobgoblin finished.

Both the captives took a hasty step back from him, and a horrified expression appeared on the woman's face. It was a very quick reversal.

"That would take up too much time," Saeter replied dryly.

"I could catch them very fast," Blacknail remarked as he eyed the woman.

She smelled strongly of fear, and Blacknail detected a slight shiver to her movements. She was obviously more afraid than her companion, and her fear was exciting the hobgoblin. He would really enjoy hunting her. Blacknail licked his lips greedily.

"Nope, still not going to happen," his master answered sternly, and Blacknail sighed deeply in regret.

Saeter then turned toward the two captives. There was a sad look in his eyes. "You shouldn't have taken this job. I don't have time to lock you up, and you obviously can't be trusted."

"No, wait please!" the brunette woman wailed before one of the scouts silenced her with a swing of his blade.

The stocky man tried to flee, but Saeter stabbed him ruthlessly in the back. The old scout then sighed unhappily at the corpses at his feet.

"I wanted to do that!" Blacknail whined. His master obviously hadn't enjoyed doing it, so why had he hogged all the action?

Saeter looked up and frowned at the hobgoblin. His master looked sad for a second but his face quickly hardened. "I have another job for you, Blacknail. I'm betting there's another more skilled group of scouts around, and I want you to track them down. There should only be one or two of them."

"Sure thing," Blacknail replied happily. He would get to hunt some people after all! That was better than just stabbing them.

The hobgoblin immediately took off at a sprint down the dirty alleyway. He had plenty of energy to burn, and within seconds, he disappeared from Saeter's sight. Instinct told him that anyone using the humans from earlier would have wanted to make sure their distraction did as they were told, so Blacknailback traced the enemies path and soon stumbled on a scent that didn't belong to them. Someone had indeed been shadowing the first group of humans as they'd approached Herad's territory.

From there, it was simple for Blacknail to follow the new scent trail through the winding back alleys until he closed in on his prey. The man he was following wasn't bad at moving silently and keeping out of sight, so the hobgoblin had to proceed carefully when the trail grew fresh, lest he stumble into him. He didn't want the man to know he was being stalked, that would take the fun out of it.

Blacknail carefully scanned the shadows for any sign of movement, or anything that didn't belong, as he moved through the alley. His prey was close now. He saw nothing though, so he closed his eyes and concentrated on listening. The clatter of everyday activities echoed through the narrow streets from far away, but Blacknail tuned it out. A slight wheeze stirred the air somewhere to his right, and the hobgoblin's eyes shot open. He immediately stalked toward the source of the noise. There was someone nearby. It had come from the other side of a decrepit-looking building, so rather than expose himself by walking down the street, Blacknail chose a different way. Silently, the hobgoblin crept up to the wall in front of him and began to climb.

He swiftly made his way up the rough, uneven wooden exterior of the building and pulled himself up onto the roof. Ever so carefully, he stalked across the clay roof tiles until he reached the far edge, and then he looked down.

Below him, a man wearing the familiar hooded cloak of an assassin was pressed up against the building. The hobgoblin watched as the man peered nervously around a corner and down the street for signs of pursuit. He appeared nervous for some reason, and that annoyed Blacknail. Had he somehow detected the hobgoblin's presence? Blacknail was just about to drop down on the unsuspecting assassin and assassinate him, when he heard someone else approaching. Thinking it might be more enemies, he quickly rolled back over to the other side of the roof and out of sight.

When the new arrival turned the corner, the hobgoblin peeked over the tip of the building to see who it was, and his eyes widened in surprise. He recognized the man; it was What's-His-Face the bandit! He was one of the men that had joined Herad after Fang had died. Was he also looking for spies? Much to Blacknail's confusion, the assassin stepped out from the shadows and greeted the newcomer. What's-His-Face returned the greeting, and the hobgoblin's eyes narrowed suspiciously. The man wasn't looking for spies, he was a spy! Blacknail was definitely going to kill him.

“Do you have the information?” the assassin asked the traitor.

“I don’t know, do you have my gold?” he replied.

The assassin grunted, pulled out a small pouch, and threw it to the traitor. The bandit caught it and opened it so he could peer inside. He seemed satisfied with the contents because he smiled and tucked it into his coat. Upon hearing the word gold, Blacknail had instantly focused on the pouch, but he hadn’t been able to see inside of it when it had been opened. If there was gold in there though, then he planned on taking the shiny stuff for his own. He didn’t actually have any gold yet, just a bit of silver.

“It’s your turn,” the assassin remarked, and the traitor nodded.

“All the information you want is in there, including stuff about her defenses and the location of her camp,” the man explained as he pulled out a scroll case and handed it to the assassin.

“What about information on which merchants she deals with, the caravans she’s hit in the last year, and the details of her operation down south?”

“Ya, that’s in there too. I don’t know why in all the hells you want that though. It seems pretty bloody useless.”

The assassin nodded and then opened the case and looked the scroll over quickly. A few seconds later, he closed it again and tucked it away.

“Good, this will do nicely. Thank you for your efforts,” the assassin replied.

The traitor man snorted in response. “I know which way the winds are blowing. Herad’s no match for Werrick and the people behind him. Her days are numbered.”

“Very true, but then so are yours,” the assassin remarked with deceptive calm. He lunged forward and stabbed the traitor up under his ribs.

The man coughed and crumpled lifelessly onto the alley floor. The assassin quickly cleaned his knife off with a cloth and re-sheathed it. The corpse’s eyes were wide open in surprise, and the assassin gave it a smug smile. He picked the pouch up from where it had fallen on the ground and opened it. This time,

Blacknail clearly saw the glint of gold from within, and he purred softly to himself.

The man laughed. “I'll be taking this back for myself.”

Blacknail giggled as he dropped down on the man’s back. “Nope, it’s mine.”

“What, who?” the startled assassin gasped. He was stunned by the impact and started to fall.

The hobgoblin wasted no time; he began stabbing wildly at the man’s exposed sides. Before the assassin even hit the ground, Blacknail had stabbed him more than half a dozen times, and then Blacknail stabbed him half a dozen more. The grinning hobgoblin stepped off the man’s squishy body and started to loot the bloody corpses. He took the scroll as a gift for Herad, but he claimed all the assassin’s knives and the pouch of gold for himself. He’d earned them after all.

# *Chapter 33*

With his human prey laying dead on the wet cobblestones at his feet, Blacknail hurried back toward Saeter and the other scouts. He broke out into a quick run so it only took him a few minutes to find them. Thankfully, they hadn't gone far and were just around the corner from where they'd fought Zelena's hirelings.

When he turned the last corner and Saeter's form came into view, Blacknail let out a deep relaxing breath. He was relieved his master hadn't managed to get himself into trouble while he'd been gone. He'd sort of been expecting Saeter to have picked a fight with a troll or something. He had no idea how or why a troll would show up in the middle of the city, but if one did, he was sure Saeter would run into it.

"I'm back," Blacknail called out as he rejoined the rangers. He didn't want to startle them and get shot in the chest by an arrow.

"Did you find anyone?" his master asked with obvious interest.

"Yep, I found-ss two stupid humans—"

The hobgoblin was unexpectedly cut off by the shrill sound of a distant whistle. The first blast of noise was soon followed by several more, and they formed a pattern Blacknail recognized. It was the signal that enemies were coming down the road. Even the humans beside him, with their tiny useless pink ears, had apparently heard it because they turned to look in that direction.

"Time to go. Quickly, get back to the road!" Saeter commanded everyone as he broke out into a jog.

Together, the group of rangers dashed back toward the main street that led to Herad's compound and the lookout there that had signaled them. As they ran, Blacknail risked a quick look around.It was still cloudy overhead, so it wasn't all that bright out, but there was enough light to strip most the shadows from the tight corridors that Saeter's group were running through. The sunlight had also finally started to dry the wet ground, and all the puddles were evaporating.

The scouts soon arrived near the warehouse where they had stationed the sentry earlier, and they came to a cautious stop. One of the scouts peeked out at the street from around a corner, but the roadway seemed clear. Carefully, he led the others to the entrance of the building. Blacknail listened carefully for signs of an ambush as well. He didn't hear anything at first, until they got close to the doorway, and then he heard a slight shuffling noise. There was at least one person concealed on the other side of it. He was about to hiss a warning when he got a good whiff of their scent. It was familiar. Sure enough, a second later, a familiar face stepped out of the doorway and greeted them. It was one of the rangers Saeter had sent out earlier.

"Good, you're back. We need to get out of here," the ranger told them. "Zelena's men are moving in force now. There's easily a hundred of the scum coming down the road. The misbegotten bastards will be here in just a minute or two."

"Any word from Herad about how the preparations are going?" Saeter asked him gruffly.

"No, and I don't care. We're not here to buy her time, if she even needs it. We were just told to stop anyone trying to get a look at our defenses until the main attack comes, and it's bloody well here now," the other man replied impatiently.

Saeter grunted in vague agreement before replying. "Fine then, let's get going. Tell the sentry to get his ass down here so we can leave."

The other rangers soon arrived, and the entire group quickly retreated down the road toward the base. As they ran, Blacknail could hear a commotion behind them, and it made him more than a little anxious. The clutter of hoofs on stone and the thud of boots were very clear in his ears. It definitely sounded like people were chasing them, and he didn't like being hunted. He was a predator. Prey were beneath him.

Blacknail could also hear quite a bit of activity from up

ahead, and he really hoped it was the rest of his tribe. It would be awkward if it was a trap, because then he'd have to make a break for safety and leave everyone else behind. The reason for all the noise soon became obvious, however, and it wasn't a trap. The wide cobblestone road that led to Herad's base was full of bandits, and a tall wooden barricade now stretched all the way from the building on one side to the building on the other. It was a little taller than a human man and had been hastily constructed out of mismatched wooden panels. Herad herself was out front overseeing the work as her minions finished assembling the wall. Her idea of supervision seemed to involve an awful lot of screaming and insults.

"Move faster, you lazy vermin! If you don't start moving your fat asses, then you won't have to worry about the enemy because I'll kill you scum myself!" she yelled savagely at the workers. The bandit chieftain then noticed Saeter's group returning and turned toward them.

"I take it that your arrival means that Zelena's finally attacking?" she asked Saeter as they walked up to her.

"A large force of what certainly looks like Zelena's men is coming down the road right behind us. There's no sign of the mercenaries yet though. How are things going here?" Saeter replied.

"Well enough. The barricade isn't pretty, but it should do the job. The demolition crews have also finished collapsing buildings across the other ways in," Herad answered.

"We sure are making a mess," one of the other scouts murmured to himself.

Before Saeter could respond to Herad, her expression hardened and her hand dropped toward her sword. Thankfully she was no longer looking at Saeter but gazing past him instead. Both Blacknail and his master hurriedly turned to see what she was gazing at. It was probably important. The hobgoblin growled softly as he took in the figure of a lone horseman on the empty road behind them. The rider had come to a stop well out of bowshot, and he was too far away for the hobgoblin to see details, but he seemed to be scrutinizing Herad's barricade.

"The first enemy has arrived. Looks like you two got here in time for the big fight," Herad remarked.

“Oh, joy-ss,” Blacknail hissed sarcastically. He had seen human battles before, and being stuck in the middle of one was among the last places he wanted to be.

The bandit chieftain whistled sharply to get everyone’s attention. Blacknail winced as the noise painfully pierced his skull. Ugh, he hated it when humans whistled. How did they even do that?

“All right, everyone, get to the other side of the wall. The pathetic fools we’re about to slaughter have arrived!” Herad yelled loudly enough for all her nearby minions to hear.

There was no gate in the barricade, so Saeter’s group followed Herad into a nearby building. The door was shut and locked behind them, and a large bookcase was jammed up behind it for good measure. With that done, they stepped out of another door and into the area behind the barricade where they would supposedly be safe. The hobgoblin was glad they had a wall, but he thought it would probably be safer to be somewhere that wasn’t about to be attacked.

A slight smile appeared on Herad’s face as she surveyed the scene before her. Her men were rushing around to put the finishing touches on the wooden barricade that loomed before them. Blacknail thought this was a good time to give her his gift, because it looked like things were going to get very busy soon, and he didn’t want to forget. He found that when people tried to kill him, it was usually very distracting.

“Oh great-ss mistress, I have a present for you!” he announced loudly to catch her attention. Herad turned around and scowled at the hobgoblin. He gave her a hopeful grin in return.

“You’d better not be about to lay some dead rat you caught on the way back here at my feet,” she remarked coldly.

“He’s a hobgoblin not a cat,” Saeter interjected dryly.

Herad huffed impatiently for Blacknail to get to it. The hobgoblin hurriedly pulled the scroll case out from where he’d tucked it into his belt and held it out in front of himself where she could see it.

“I don’t think you’ve started writing or even reading, so what in all the hells is that?” she asked curiously as she reached out and took it from him.

"Maybe it's hobgoblin poetry," one of the scouts whispered to the man beside him, which caused him to snicker quietly. Blacknail ignored them.

"The vile and smelly traitor gave it to the stupid human assassin I killed. So I offer-ss it to you as proof of my kills," he told Herad excitedly.

"What traitor?" Herad asked with sudden anger as her eyes narrowed dangerously. Her expression didn't get any better when she opened the scroll case and started reading. In fact, it got much worse.

"Umm, you know… the man. The um… pink one with the tiny ears and nose," Blacknail stuttered in reply. The traitor may also have had hair of some color.

Herad looked up from her reading and scowled at him again. Blacknail cringed under her scrutiny. Why was she angry at him? Maybe he should learn people's names after all. Why did all humans have to look so similar?

"He's the one who smelled kind of rusty all the time-ss," the hobgoblin added hopefully.

He was disappointed; Herad's scowl grew deeper, but thankfully she turned away from him and toward his master. Surely he hadn't been the only one to notice that smell? Humans sure had bad senses.

"Saeter, I don't suppose you happened to see the bastard Blacknail is talking about?" Herad asked.

"Um no, sorry," Saeter replied carefully. Herad groaned in uncharacteristic frustration and eyed Blacknail irritably again. The hobgoblin gave her a nervous smile back.

"Fine, whatever. Don't worry about his bloody name then. Tell me exactly how you got this scroll!" she commanded the hobgoblin.

Blacknail immediately launched into a rambling explanation on how he'd tracked the super dangerous eight-foot-tall assassin through the streets and then killed both him and the traitor in an extended knife fight. There may have been a vicious pack of dogs, or harpies, as well. He left out the little unimportant details though, like the pouch of gold.

"Well, it seems like you handled the situation right," Herad told the hobgoblin. "I can figure out who in all the hells the traitor was after I deal with the small army that is about to attack us. Now get back to work. I want you both to join the defensive line, but don't forget to keep an eye out for anyone trying to sneak around it."

"Yes, oh great-ss mistress," Blacknail replied respectfully. He thought it was a good idea to make sure he was back on her good side. Herad wasn't impressed though.

"Shut your flapping trap and move. I'm busy." She turned away dismissively.

"You heard the boss; let's get going," Saeter told the hobgoblin.

The pair hurried away from the irate bandit chieftain and went to find a good position. Blacknail started to head directly for the barricade, but Saeter stopped him and pointed out a nearby roof with easy access by an exterior stairway. It was off to one side of the barricade, was within easy bowshot of it, and had a clear view of the street. The building was also tall enough that anyone below would have trouble scaling it to get at them, so they made their way over to it. By the time they reached the rooftop balcony, the horseman had disappeared. The road in front of Herad's barricade was now empty.

"Maybe he got-ss scared and went home. I'm very scary; people run from me all the time," Blacknail remarked hopefully.

His master chuckled in reply. "Not likely."

Saeter and the hobgoblin weren't the only ones getting into position; dozens of Herad's bandits were also nearby and getting ready. The barricade was too thin to at the top to stand on, but platforms had been set up behind it for people to climb.

Most of the platforms were stacks of crates or barrels that had been piled up behind the wooden wall. There were also one or two carts that had been dragged over. The makeshift footing looked effective though; the bandits standing on it could easily hit anyone that tried to get over the wall in front of them.

Men armed with a variety of weapons, including spears and bows, were positioned all along the barricade to defend it. As Blacknail looked down, the last few bandits got into position and the sounds of activity died down. A sudden stillness then fell over the area as everyone waited for the enemy to show themselves. They didn't have to wait all that long. Within minutes, there was a clatter of hoofs as several riders appeared at the end of the road. One of them held a long banner. There wasn't quite enough wind for it to unfurl, so Blacknail couldn't make out the symbol on it, but it still looked more than a little impressive.

As all of Herad's minions watched, the horsemen talked among themselves and observed the barricade that blocked their way. They didn't seem very impressed by it. A deep keening noise suddenly rippled though the air as one of the riders raised a horn to his lips. The eerie wail washed over Blacknail and caused the hairs on his skin to rise. When the noise died down, Blacknail didn't feel any better, because it was quickly replaced by the sound of pounding footsteps, and quite a lot of them.

As Blacknail watched, the horsemen cantered off to the side of the road, and a rough-looking mob of men came down the street past them. Blacknail gulped nervously as he gave up trying to count. There must have been hundreds of them! Certainly, there were more of them than he had fingers and toes anyway.

"They look like normal Daggerpoint riffraff. Zelena must be holding her real soldiers in reserve," Saeter remarked matter-of-factly.

Blacknail eyed his master skeptically. There were even more enemies than he could see? They already outnumbered Herad's band!

"They look more than scary enough to me. Let's find somewhere safer to be, like the forest!" Blacknail whined.

"Bah, stop being a coward. Fighting isn't all about numbers," Saeter replied scornfully.

As the wave of armed and angry-looking humans descended upon the barricade, Blacknail got a better look at them. They did seem to be nothing special. Most of them wouldn't have stood out if Blacknail had seen them walking down the street. Of course, this was Daggerpoint, so that just meant they weren't armed with anything larger than a short sword or a large club. By contrast, Herad's men were better armed and shinier. Almost all of them had helmets, and many of them had weapons larger than short swords. A few of them even had chainmail shirts and shields. None of the attackers had that sort of equipment, but there were still a bloody lot of them.

Blacknail was brought back to reality by the sound of Saeter pulling his bowstring back. He looked over just in time to see his master release an arrow at the approaching enemies, and a loud twang sound echoed past him as the bowstring vibrated. The projectile sailed over the heads of the first few advancing attackers, and slammed into the throat of an unlucky man several ranks back. Instantly, the man collapsed and disappeared as he was trampled underfoot by the rest of the mob.

A victorious roar went up from the rest of Blacknail's tribesmen as they celebrated the kill. It was quickly matched by a chorus of bloodthirsty cries from the wave of heavily armed thugs that were bearing down on the wall. Now that they were within bowshot, the mob picked up speed as one by one they started breaking into full out sprints.

The attackers looked eager to strike back and spill some blood of their own. Blacknail was going to have to do his best to disappoint them. He clenched his fists nervously as the violent maelstrom of noise from the young battlefield below washed over him.

The first shot had been fired. The first death had been dealt. The battle that would decide the fate of Herad's band and all of Daggerpoint had begun. Blacknail's stomach grumbled. He wished he'd brought more snacks. Maybe he could loot something...

# Chapter 34

The wave of attackers bore down on the barricade. The thugs and bandits screamed as they ran and waved their weapons. Blacknail and his master looked down over the battlefield from a balcony on the side of a building beside the makeshift wall. Both of them had bows and full quivers of arrows.

"Don't just stand there. Help me out!" Saeter growled at the hobgoblin.

Blacknail smiled eagerly as he took up his bow and fitted an arrow to it. He gripped it steadily and pulled the string back all the way to his face. Then he carefully selected a particularly stupid-looking, red-haired human from among the advancing crowd, aligned his sights on the man's chest, and let the arrow loose. The unleashed projectile sprung forward with a deep twang and bit deep into the knee of a man standing several feet to the left of Blacknail's target. The accidental victim screamed before collapsing onto the ground. The hobgoblin grimaced at how far off he'd been. He was a great archer; that arrow should have gone where he'd aimed! The wind must have shifted or something... stupid wind.

"Huh, not a terrible shot," Saeter remarked as he let loose another arrow of his own.

"Yes, now he can't run-ss away," Blacknail responded guardedly. He'd do better next time. The last shot had been a fluke after all.

The hobgoblin selected another arrow and target. This time he chose to aim at the chest of a tall lanky man with a small steel helmet. If the man didn't want to be shot, then he shouldn't wear such a shiny hat. Maybe Blacknail would take it as a prize after the battle. The hobgoblin let go of the bowstring, and the arrow zoomed forward and straight toward the unsuspecting man. The hobgoblin grinned happily as he watched it fly true. The grin slipped from his face though, when the arrow ricocheted off the surprised man's helmet and spun into the face of the man next to him. They both went down in a confused tumble of limbs, but then a few seconds later, they both got back up again.

The first man looked pale and unsteady on his feet, and there was a large uncomfortable-looking dent in his helmet. He staggered and blinked uncertainly for a while before rejoining the charge. The second man had a large gash across his face that was bleeding heavily, but he appeared to still be able to fight as well. Both definitely seemed like they would live...

"Dog breath-ss," Blacknail hissed angrily.

"Ha, that was an unlucky shot! Just keep on shooting. They've almost reached the wall," Saeter yelled.

Blacknail grunted unhappily in reply as he squinted at the mass of moving humanity below. As he watched, the front runners reached the wall and stalled before it. The hobgoblin was more than a little curious as to how they planned on actually getting over it. The hurriedly put-together wooden barricade was only about as tall as a human, but there were dozens of armed men behind it who were extremely motivated to stop anyone from climbing it. It was too high to jump over, and to climb it, someone would need both hands, which would leave them more than a little vulnerable to being stabbed or hit over the head with something heavy.

The hobgoblin's next arrow missed completely and slammed harmlessly into the ground. He growled in frustration at his latest failure. The shaft must have been bent! In fact, if Blacknail turned his head just so and glared at the arrow a certain way, then it definitely looked curved. It wasn't his fault he'd been given defective weapons!

As more and more attackers reached the wall, their intentions became obvious to Blacknail; they were planning to simply overwhelm the defenders with the force of their numbers. As the mob rushed forward, they left a trail of dozens of dead and wounded on the ground behind them. More than a few of them had already been brought down by Herad's archers, but there were still plenty more. Groups of Zelena's soldiers began throwing themselves at the barrier. They aimed for any spot that looked undefended and easy to climb over. Some tried to go over alone while others worked together to try and distract the guards and protect the climbers. Blacknail was happy to see it didn't work very well. Almost all the climbers got a blade shoved in their face as a reward for their efforts, but some made it and the fight started in earnest. Fighting began to break out on the other side as attackers scaled the barricade and found themselves face-to-face with Herad's men. The defenders tried to overwhelm the initial attackers before more of Zelena's hirelings could make it over, and the desperate attackers tried to survive long enough for reinforcements to scale the wall behind them.

Blacknail was very glad Saeter had chosen a position that was nowhere near any place that was under attack. The melee below him didn't look like a lot of fun. He liked it up on the balcony where he was safe and could shoot people without being distracted. Blacknail noticed one of his tribesmen along the wall cut down a climber and get dragged from his perch by several other attackers for his trouble. Immediately, more men began to scale the barrier where it was now undefended. The hobgoblin quickly chose one of the men and shot an arrow at him. Blacknail held his breath expectantly for the short seconds it took the arrow to hit its target, and hit it did. The projectile slammed into the man's ass, and he howled as he fell from the wall.

"Aha, that one-ss hit!" the hobgoblin laughed triumphantly. Blacknail raised a fist into the air and gave a little jump as he celebrated his glorious kill. He really was a great archer! He'd been aiming for the man's back, but that was really close.

"Get down!" Saeter suddenly roared. The old scout hurriedly grabbed Blacknail's sleeve and yanked him to the ground. The surprised hobgoblin's wrist jammed painfully as he tried to catch himself and stop his fall.

"Wha?" he hissed in pain and confusion.

Blacknail's bewilderment was dispelled as an arrow whirred through the exact space his head had been a split second ago. The hobgoblin felt his throat tighten from the shock, and he gulped nervously. That had been very close...

Saeter growled as he held the hobgoblin down. "Pay bloody attention to what's going on around you, you damn fool."

"Yes, master. I will. I just-ss didn't think they had any archers," Blacknail replied submissively. His master had just saved his life. He was fairly sure getting an arrow in the skull was fatal for a hobgoblin.

"Well, now you know they do!" Saeter answered heatedly as he let go of the hobgoblin's sleeve. The old scout peered carefully over the edge of the balcony they were on. A few seconds later, he quickly rose to his feet, aimed, and shot his bow in one smooth motion.

"There, I got the bastard," he crowed proudly as he smiled.

Blacknail was more than a little impressed. Since they'd left the forest, his opinion of his master had started to slip. He thought Saeter was... sort of useless in the city, but now he knew he'd been foolish to believe that. He still had a lot to learn. As Blacknail admired his master's skill, Saeter suddenly tensed. The gray-haired scout then threw himself to the ground as a flock of arrows ripped through the air and smacked into the wall behind him and Blacknail. The hobgoblin flinched at the noise and dropped onto his stomach with his arms covering his head. Above him, several still-quivering and humming arrows protruded from the wooden side of the building. Apparently, Saeter had missed an archer or two...

"It seems we've attracted some unwanted attention," Saeter remarked as he grinned at Blacknail from where he lay next to him on the balcony.

"Yes, so let's leave," the hobgoblin hastily replied. He didn't like being shot at nearly as much as he did shooting at people.

"Just a second." Saeter crawled over to the balcony's edge and peeked over it. He then scanned the battlefield below them thoughtfully.

Blacknail crawled up beside him, while keeping an eye out for incoming projectiles, and followed his gaze. He quickly noticed what his master was looking at. In the center of the street, among the chaotic masses, a small disciplined group had appeared. They stood out from the others and were clearly more than normal Daggerpoint thugs. Their formation included several men with shields surrounding a group of archers. As

Blacknail eyed them nervously, the bowmen resumed shooting. Arrows began to rain down on the defenders that were still struggling to hold the barricade, and the occasional unlucky attacker as well. The climbers redoubled their effort to make it over the barricade, and the sounds of fighting intensified.

"So, Zelena has finally made her next move. I wonder what Herad will do. They're both playing their cards close to their chests," Saeter mused to himself.

As Blacknail peered over the balcony railing, he noticed movement at one of the windows of a building across the street. He tried to see what it was, but it was too far away and all blurry.

"There's something there," he told his master as he pointed to it.

"Ah, here we go; there's Mahedium," Saeter replied.

Blacknail had no idea how his master could tell who was at the window, the hobgoblin's own eyes had trouble making out things that far away, but Saeter was soon proven right in a dramatic fashion. A heavy pulsing noise washed over the battlefield as a wave of rippling air shot forth from the window. The violent distortion slammed into the center of the shielded archers, and the street beneath them exploded. Sharp stone fragments flew off in every direction, and Blacknail was practically deafened by the blast. Mixed in among the dirt and rock of the explosion were shields and other pieces of equipment, as well as several torn limbs. Bodies were sent rolling across the ground as the impact threw them aside. Only a few of the men anywhere near the blast site managed to keep on their feet, and they looked worse for wear.

The battlefield seemed to pause as everyone took in this new development. As the roar of the blast died down, the sounds of steel on steel, and screams of pain and rage, seemed muted and less frequent. A weird veil of quiet fell across the fighting.

Then, Mahedium unleashed another barrage upon the largest concentration of attackers near the wall. Screams filled the air as men were torn apart by the magical force, and the tide of battle shifted once again. Blacknail grinned savagely at the beautiful destruction that filled his eyes. It was moments like this that made him really want to be a mage. The rest of the thugs attacking the wall faltered and began to panic. Men trying to climb the wall froze as their companions below them took a nervous step back. Blacknail even saw one shorter female fighter, who had successfully made it over the barricade, abandon her position and leap back across. She was obviously very smart for a human.

Herad's men were quick to take advantage of this opening, and they regrouped. Her bandits surged up to the wall and began to cut down Zelena's stunned men. Soon, no attackers were left on the defenders' side of the barricade, and Herad had taken complete control of the wall back. That was too much for the remaining attackers at the foot of the barricade. They still outnumbered the defenders, but now they were disorganized and at a serious disadvantage. As one they seemed to waver, and then one of them screamed in surprise and pain as Blacknail's latest arrow slammed into his left butt cheek. Why did that keep happening? That wasn't where he had aimed...

As if the wail had been some sort of prearranged signal, the attackers broke and started to flee. Groups of them began dashing away from the wall and down the street. Within seconds, the fighting stopped and only the sound of panicked footsteps remained. Soon, even that was gone, and the last of Zelena's soldiers disappeared down one of the many shadowy side streets.

"Aha, we won! Run-ss stupid humans, run. I'll find you though; you can't hide-ss from me!" Blacknail cheered triumphantly.

The hobgoblin then quickly turned away from the battlefield and headed for the stairs that led down to the safe side of the wall. He wanted to beat the rush and get the best loot for himself.

"Where do you think you're going, Blacknail?" Saeter asked.

"I'm going-ss to go find some prizes. Some of the people in our band are really greedy and will take all the good stuff for themselves, unless I get-ss there first!" the hobgoblin responded.

"The battle is far from over!"

The hobgoblin turned around and gave his master an uncomprehending stare. Below him on the street, the last of the attackers had already fled. Only blasted rubble and a scattering of corpses remained. It certainly looked like his tribe had won...

"Really?" he asked his master doubtfully.

"Yes, that was just the first wave. They were disposable. Zelena's commanders threw them at us hoping that they would weaken us. Their main force is still to come, and now they've tested our defenses," Saeter explained.

"... and that's bad?" Blacknail asked with wide eyes.

"It might be. We'll have to see what they do next," Saeter replied.

The hobgoblin sighed and walked back over to his master. He leaned over the balcony and tried to peer down the street to see if anyone was coming. He couldn't see very far though, because another tall wooden warehouse was in the way, but after several minutes spent leaning precariously over the railing, he finally heard something. It was quiet enough that he almost dismissed it. It wasn't the sound of a large group of people, but rather, it sounded more like just a few. Was the enemy trying to be sneaky? If so, they wouldn't be able to get past him. No one was as sneaky as Blacknail; he was the sneakiest of them all.

As he turned to look in the direction the sound had come from, a sudden burst of movement caught Blacknail's eye. A small group of men burst out of the entrance of one of the nearby side streets and took up position outside it. There were about a dozen of them, and they stuck close to the nearby building for cover. They didn't seem very threatening to Blacknail. What were they doing? Several of them had bows, but what could half a dozen archers do, especially at that range? Unless they were all very good shots, they would have trouble hitting anyone from that far away.

As he watched, another man stepped around a corner and into sight with a lit torch in his hand. Blacknail tilted his head to the side in confusion. That was weird. Why did they have a torch out in the middle of the day? Maybe they were cold? A few seconds later, his question was answered and his eyes widened in surprise. One of the men drew an arrow and held it up to the flame. Instantly, the oddly thick head of the arrow caught fire. The archer then wasted no time in taking a shot at the wall with his bow. The fiery projectile arced through the air and slammed into a wooden panel on the barricade before bouncing off and falling harmlessly to the ground. It was quickly followed by others though, and several of those hit the wood and stuck.

"Oh, fire!" the hobgoblin remarked in fascination as he stared at the flames that writhed around the enemies' arrowheads. He wanted some of those. Imagine being able to light fires from a distance. The possibilities were endless, and you didn't even need magic!

Those of Herad's men that had bows of their own shot back, but the new attackers were quick to scramble behind cover where they were hard to hit. A steady rain of fire arrows began to fall on the wooden barricade that protected Herad's forces.

Slowly but surely, the flames began to spread and consume the wooden barricade. Cries of alarm went up from the defenders as their protection burned. Blacknail winced as he heard Herad start yelling at the top of her lungs.

"Get those fires out now! You know what to do," she commanded her men. Blacknail knew things were serious because she hadn't even had time to swear.

Saeter joined in the defense. The old scout drew an arrow from his quiver and took a shot at one of the saboteurs. This time, however, he missed his mark by a few inches, and his arrow bounced harmlessly off a wall behind one of the attacking archers. The close shave startled the man, and he dropped the arrow he'd been about to shoot. It clattered onto the ground and went out. The archer had to go back and have it lit again.

"Damnation!" Saeter swore as he reached for another arrow. "They're too far away. I really hope the fools don't burn the entire city down. Why is that damn barricadeso flammable?"

A mental picture of all of Daggerpoint burning suddenly sprung to life in Blacknail's head. It was almost all wood so it would burn quite nicely, and it would sure make for a huge spectacle. He kind of wanted to see that, just not from the inside.

"Uh oh," Blacknail exclaimed nervously as he studied the panicked activity below him.

# *Chapter 35*

The wooden barricade that Herad's minions were hiding behind was burning in several spots now. Suddenly, the front door of a building next to the barricade swung open and a force of Herad's men started pouring out. The armed bandits immediately raced toward the archers who had shot the fire arrows. However, the saboteurs didn't stick around to fight. They took a few seconds to fire off one last volley and disappeared back into the alleyways. Some of the lead members of the bandits tried to give chase, but they were soon called back.

"You bloody idiots, get back here! Unless you've got a death wish, get back here," their leader yelled.

Before Herad's men could start to retreat, a new group of archers appeared on the other side of the street and loosed another volley of fire arrows at the barricade. A few of the saboteurs shot at the bandits out on the street instead of the wall, and one of Herad's men went down with an arrow in his side. The leader of Herad's men froze for a second and looked around hesitantly before springing into action.

"Grab the injured, and let's get back to the wall. We're not doing any good out here," he yelled as he started organizing his squad's retreat. By this time, the flames from the first enemies' arrows had started to spread across the wooden barrier. There was a loud crack and a shower of sparks as a particularly dry section caught flame.

"We should get down there and help," Saeter told the hobgoblin as he started down the stairs.

Blacknail nodded happily in reply. He wanted to see the fire from closer anyway. The dancing reds and oranges were always so pretty, and he liked the crackling noise the flames made. The hobgoblin and his master quickly rushed back down to the road behind the barrier. It was a mad bustle of activity there. Bandits were running around everywhere as they tried to fight the fire, keep a lookout for the next attack, help the wounded, and move flammable supplies out of the way. Herad was in the very middle of the street shouting commands. At her direction, the barrels by the wall that some of the bandits had been standing on were opened, and water was scooped out into buckets. Blacknail was impressed. Apparently, Herad had predicted the enemy would use fire.

Saeter immediately headed for the chieftain to get orders, but before they got there, Mahedium stepped out of a nearby crowd and drew her attention. The mage was carrying his usual staff, and Blacknail eyed it with new respect. He'd seen the damage it had inflicted on the enemy. The mage wasn't alone this time though. A scared-looking boy was at his side. The lad was carrying what looked to be a spare mage's staff and had short blond hair. Herad grinned excitedly as she noticed the mage.

"Are you ready?" she asked him.

"Yes, a blaze this size should be no problem. I'm well prepared for much worse," Mahedium replied. The boy at his side shied away from Herad.

"Then get to it! The flames aren't getting any smaller, and my barrier isn't getting any stronger," the bandit chieftain told the mage dryly.

"Just make sure there aren't any snipers hidden anywhere nearby. I'd hate to get an arrow in my back as I'm working. That would be inconvenient for both of us," Mahedium replied coolly.

"Blacknail and I will take care of that, if that's what the boss wants," Saeter explained as he joined the other two bandits.

"That's fine with me, just hurry up," Herad told them.

"Good, you two are the best," the mage commented as he calmly, but vigorously, started walking toward the barricade's entrance.

All four of them hurriedly passed through the building that led to the other side of the wall. The boy following Mahedium stayed as far away from Blacknail as possible. Blacknail was curious why the boy was with them, but every time he so much as glanced at him, the boy hid behind Mahedium. The hobgoblin made a mental note to try again later when he wasn't wearing his scary mask.

"My staff, please," Mahedium told his aide as soon as they got back outside.

The boy immediately handed the staff he was carrying to the mage, and the mage exchanged it with his own. Mahedium then stared at the staff head for a few seconds before making a few quick adjustments by turning a metal knob on the side of it. When he appeared satisfied with the result, the mage aimed the tip toward the wall. There were bandits atop the barricade throwing water down, but they were barely keeping the flames under control. Flaming arrows would occasionally appear from an alleyway or rooftop down the street and hit previously untouched spots on the wall. These new flames distracted the men trying to quench the fires and were preventing them from getting things under control.

As Mahedium leveled his staff at the wall, Blacknail felt the air swirl around him, and everyone's clothes began to stir as newborn air currents pulled and tugged on them. Blacknail had to reach up and grab his hood to keep it from slipping off. The hobgoblin jumped in surprise as a white icy spray burst forth from the mage's weapon and slammed into the wall. Frost formed instantly wherever it hit, and within seconds, every flame had been extinguished. The wooden barricade was still charred in quite a few places, and covered with patches of ice, but it seemed mostly intact. Saeter raised a surprised eyebrow as he regarded the mage's work.

"That was no measly magic trick. I don't think I've seen that before," Saeter remarked.

"Huh, I'm not surprised. A staff like this isn't something many combat mages get their hands on, outside the navy anyway. It's delicate and requires three different stones to power it. There's no better way to put out fires, but the guilds don't like handing out staffs with more than one stone in them to combat mages," Mahedium replied.

"Where'd you get it from, then?" Saeter asked curiously.

"Avorlus had it, as well as the stones to power it. I didn't ask where he got it from though, because I'm not sure I'd like the answer," the mage replied.

"And he just gave it to you?" Sater eyes hardened at the mention of the blood mage.

"Herad sent him an eloquently written letter asking him for his aid, and so he graciously agreed to help us in our time of need, as any gentlemen would," Mahedium explained sarcastically.

"Ah," Saeter replied as he scowled darkly. Blacknail didn't get it.

"He also gave me several other crystals and the use of half a dozen of his men," the mage added.

One of Saeter's eyebrows rose and he gave the mage an incredulous look. "Herad must really have him by the balls. That sounds like a small fortune."

"Indeed, it is. Avorlus has his own reasons for wanting Zelena's plans foiled though Herad's rather... direct letter certainly motivated him further," Mahedium explained. This conversation was making Blacknail more confused. He didn't really understand what his master and the mage were talking about.

"Ha, I imagine it did," Saeter replied. "She certainly knows where to stick the knife. Although, I imagine you're right about him not liking the idea of Werrick taking over, or anyone else for that matter. Chaos suits people like him much better than order."

"I don't get it. Why is Herad grabbing Avorlus's balls?" Blacknail suddenly interjected.

Saeter wheezed loudly and began coughing hard enough that he had to bend over. The fit only stopped after he hit himself in the chest a few times, and even then, he still looked pale. The corner of his mouth was also twitching. Mahedium blanched, grimaced, and seemed to be struggling to keep a spasm that had developed in his left eye under control. The boy at his side just looked shy and scared, so basically the same. None of those responses answered the hobgoblin's question. In fact, they raised several more.

Blacknail's master threw a quick glance over his shoulder, and when he saw no one was there, he gave a quiet chuckle and smiled at the hobgoblin. "It's just a saying, Blacknail. It means she's threatening him, and he has to do as she says."

"Ah, all right-ss," Blacknail replied uncertainly. Any further conversation was interrupted by someone yelling down at them from the wall.

"You four may want to stop gabbing and get back on this side of the wall. We've got incoming," a bandit that was leaning over the top of the barricade told them.

Immediately, they all looked down the street. Blacknail's ears went back against his head as he saw what was there. It was a lot more enemies, and they looked meaner than the last ones. Coming down the street toward the wall—and the hobgoblin standing in front of it—were two formations of soldiers. Unlike the last attackers, these men weren't a mob; they were organized into ranks. They were also far better equipped. The smaller group on the left looked a lot like Herad's own men. They had rough-looking armor and an assortment of wicked-looking weapons. The group on the right was even more dangerous looking. Each man in it was equipped in exactly the same way, with a brown tabard, chainmail shirt, metal cap, short sword, and a small shield. They were also walking in step and moving all together, like some sort of gigantic bug with a hundred little legs. Blacknail had never seen anything like it. On one hand, it seemed sort of pointless to him, but on the other, it was more than a little terrifying.

"That'll be Werrick's regulars on the left and the mercenaries to the right. Now the real fight starts," Saeter mused aloud.

"We should head back inside," Mahedium quickly replied. The mage then started for the door without waiting for a response.

Blacknail eyed the incoming troops anxiously. They didn't look weak, and together they outnumbered his tribe by a fair bit. "We should-ss run away. It's stupid to try and fight them like this," he told his master.

"Herad knows what she's doing, Blacknail. We can win this. The chief has a plan, and if it doesn't work, well she's never been too proud to run before. Probably, she even has an escape plan all laid out just in case," Saeter replied as they both headed off the street.

"You wouldn't happen-ss to know this escape route, would you?" Blacknail asked him curiously. Herad wasn't known for sharing.

A derisive snort from Saeter was the only answer the hobgoblin got. The pair then quickly hurried after Mahedium and back through the building to the other side of the barrier.

"Are we going back to the uh... place we were before?" Blacknail asked his master.

"It's called a balcony, and we may as well; the other option is to take a spot on the wall," Saeter answered.

"No thanks," Blacknail remarked quickly. That seemed like a horrible idea; a lot of the people that had been protecting the barricade had gotten themselves killed! What kind of idiot would want to go there?

The old scout and the hobgoblin then made their way back to the balcony where they had overlooked the first part of the battle. As Blacknail was climbing the last stretch of the creaky wooden stairs that led up the side of the building, he caught another good look at the approaching enemy. The two enemy formations were still moving separately and advancing slowly. A small group of horsemen rode between them, and they seemed to be the leaders.

"It's too bad none of those riders are stupid enough to get within bowshot. I wouldn't mind putting an arrow in someone more important than a grunt," Saeter remarked as he gazed toward the enemy.

"Yes, then I could-ss shoot those horses," Blacknail replied viciously.

Saeter rolled his eyes and sighed in exasperation but didn't say anything.

"What-ss? They're mean ugly things that trample-ss and bite people!" Blacknail explained.

"Let's just concentrate on the battle," his master replied dismissively.

The hobgoblin scowled in frustration. Why couldn't all these humans see that horses couldn't be trusted? Blacknail knew that one day he would be proven right! Then everyone would know how smart he was, and all the horses would be slaughtered. What a glorious day that would be.

"So we're just going to stand here and shoot people like before?" Blacknail asked his master. The hobgoblin didn't mind doing that. Except for the part at the end where the enemy had started shooting back, it had been both fairly safe and rather amusing.

"Pretty much," Saeter answered as he readied his bow.

"Why doesn't Mahedium just-ss blow up all these idiots like before? Then-ss we could all go back to base and eat," the hobgoblin remarked.

"Maybe he will. We'll have to wait and see," the old scout answered distractedly.

The first rank of soldiers entered the edge of bow range, and Saeter aimed and drew his weapon back. There was a familiar twang as he released an arrow, and seconds later, it pierced the shoulder of one of Zelena's men.

"Stop showing off, Saeter! We get it, you're a good archer. Why don't you come down here and shoot with the rest of us?" a laughing man yelled up from below, which was quickly followed by amused snorts and chuckles from the rest of Herad's men.

Blacknail leaned over the edge of the balcony, spotted the laughing man, and threw a small rock at him. How dare he make fun of Blacknail's master! The stone bounced off the bandit's steel cap with a noisy clang.

"Ow, that hurt, you blasted green wretch!" the man cursed in response. There was more muted laughter, and Blacknail smirked smugly to himself.

"Save it for the enemy, they're almost here," Saeter ordered the hobgoblin, but Blacknail noticed he was grinning slightly.

A sharp clear trumpet blast drew everyone's attention toward one of the horsemen, and as Blacknail watched, Zelena's men stopped moving. The mercenaries quickly marched ahead and all together they raised their shields. The first rank of soldiers held them in front of themselves, and the ones further back lifted them above their heads. The round shields were unpainted wood with thin steel bands around the edges.

"Well, that will help protect them against archers, but how are they planning on dealing with our mage and the wall?" Saeter mused aloud.

The enemy was within easy bowshot of the balcony now, so

Blacknail loosed an arrow their way. Unfortunately, it slammed harmlessly into one of the soldiers shields and stuck there. The hobgoblin growled in frustration. More of the defenders started shooting and a shower of arrowsdescendedupon the advancing enemy. Almost all the arrows failed to find a soft target though, and only a few mercenaries fell. Meanwhile, the enemy's quick march brought them ever closer toward the wall.

"Cease fire," the hobgoblin heard Herad yell.

Immediately, her men stopped firing, and the rain of arrows ceased falling. The hobgoblin saw Mehdium climb up onto the barrier and level his staff at the enemy. Blacknail watched wide-eyed as a wave of force once again appeared at the end of the mage's staff, and then like a massive invisible snake, it shot hungrily forth. Within seconds, it would collide with the mercenary formation. Blacknail waited eagerly to see these new enemies get smacked violently aside like rats hit by a boot. Their fancy shields wouldn't stop them from being blown up!

The mercenary formation finally stopped, and their shield wall suddenly parted. A tall, armored man stepped out from the front rank and raised a steel amulet on a chain.

"Fuck," Saeter cursed unexpectedly from beside Blacknail.

The hobgoblin was then surprised further when his master hurriedly fitted an arrow to his bow and took a shot at the tall man. Herad had told them to cease fire, so why was his master ignoring that order?

As both the magical blast and the arrow raced toward him, purple light flared forth from the mercenary's raised amulet. The air began to churn, and a vortex of light burst into being. It began sucking up everything in front of the mage. The air churned and whirled as dust and grime from the street was picked up and pulled into the amulet. Mahedium's blast and Saeter's arrow were also tugged aside and sucked into the unnatural vortex. There was a flash of purple light and then the other mage dropped his amulet, and the vortex disappeared. Mahedium's spell had disappeared without a trace, and the enemy formation was completely unscathed.

"That's not good-ss, even if it was sort of pretty," Blacknail remarked nervously.

"No, it seems Mahedium has some competition, and this

battle will be uncomfortably close," Saeter replied darkly as he scowled at the figures below.

"At least that guy isn't throwing any magic back at us," Blacknail remarked hopefully. That hope didn't last long. The enemy mage gestured, and one of the men behind him passed him a staff. It looked exactly like Mahedium's own weapon. The enemy mage then leveled it at the barricade that blocked his company's progress, and a familiar-looking ripple shot forth.

This new blast slammed into the wooden wall and smashed through it. Splinters and bits of wood filled the air as a large section of the barricade exploded noisily. Mahedium and several other bandits were thrown off the wall and disappeared as a loud crash roared across the street. A few seconds later, cries of alarm and pain filled the air. At least a few of the hobgoblin's tribesmen had been wounded, and a huge, easily traversable hole had been punched through Herad's barricade. As Blacknail watched with wide eyes, the tall enemy mage stepped back into rank, and the mercenaries began to march inexorably forward again as wreckage rained down from above.

"Huh." Blacknail grunted as he felt a sinking feeling in his gut. This wasn't good...

# *Chapter 36*

The thud and crunch of heavy boots on cobblestones filled the air as the large wedge of shield-bearing mercenaries pressed forward through the hail of arrows. The enemy soldiers were headed right toward the large, gaping hole their mage had created in the barrier that Herad had ordered built across the road.

"What do we do?" Blacknail asked his master frantically.

The roar of the barricade exploding had sent the hobgoblin's heart into overdrive, and it was beating a hundred times per minute. The feeling was uncomfortable, and he twitched nervously as his every instinct urged him to run somewhere safer or to find somewhere dark to hide. Any place that hostile magic men were blowing up stuff was a bad place to be. The only thing stopping him from fleeing was a desire not to abandon his tribe, in case he couldn't find them again later, and Saeter's reassuring presence beside him.

"Keep shooting," his master barked as he let loose an arrow at the nearest enemy soldier. The old scout had aimed low, so his arrow hit the man below the shield and sliced through the side of his leg. The mercenary didn't look critically wounded, but he stumbled and cried out as he fell.

Blacknail did as he was told and sent another arrow at Saeter's target. It hit the collapsed man in the center of his now exposed back, and the mercenary twitched and then slumped loosely onto the ground. He looked dead. Unfortunately, there were plenty more mercenaries left, and they had now almost reached the shattered wall. Saeter took another shot, and Blacknail was about to do the same, when the sound of a horn rang out from behind the barricade. The hobgoblin froze and turned to see what was going on.

"That's the retreat signal," Saeter exclaimed.

"Did we lose?" Blacknail asked. He hoped the answer was yes so they could all go back to the forest.

"No, this fight's not over. Herad isn't out of tricks yet. It's just time to withdraw and reorganize," his master answered. That sounded like it meant they were allowed to run away, so it was good enough for Blacknail.

"Time-ss to go then," the hobgoblin replied as he hurriedly started down the stairs.

Saeter followed him, and when they reached street level, the last of Herad's men were jumping off the back of the barricade. The long stretch of rigged-together pieces of wood stood empty as its builders hurried away and left it behind. The only people still near the wall were two small squads of bandits who seemed to be keeping watch over the gap in its expanse and the mercenary company that was quickly closing in on it. The rest of the bandits were running farther down the street, but they weren't panicked or moving aimlessly. Orders were being shouted by lieutenants, and everyone was being organized into squads.

"Where's Herad?" Saeter yelled at the nearest squad leader.

The man pointed back toward the abandoned barricade, so both the hobgoblin and his master turned to look. Blacknail didn't see the chieftain, but now that he was looking closer, he did recognize three of the larger bandits. They were part of Herad's personal guard.

"Shit, what now?" Saeter grumbled anxiously as he started running in that direction. Blacknail sighed in exasperation as he followed his master toward the most dangerous part of the battlefield. Because, of course.

Ahead of them, there was a loud clatter as the pile of rubble beside the hole in the barricade shifted, and two more of Herad's bodyguards straightened up and rose into sight. They were both holding up the end of a heavy-looking panel of wood that had been lying atop the rubble. A second later, two other figures appeared between the guards. One of them was Herad, and as they watched, she pulled Mahedium up from off the ground. Once he was standing, if unsteadily, Herad wrapped an arm around the limping mage's shoulder and began dragging him behind her.

"Here, let us take him. I'm sure you have better things to do," Saeter offered as he ran over to help. Blacknail assumed he was also being volunteered.

"Damn right I do! Just don't fall behind, old man. I need that mage in working condition," Herad replied as she passed Mahedium off to him.

With her hands now free, the bandit chieftain raised her fingers to her lips and whistled sharply. Instantly, all her minions near the barricade began to fall back and join the others down the street. They didn't seem to want to stick around, and Blacknail didn't blame them. Bad things were coming. He could feel it in the tips of his ears. The hobgoblin moved over to help his master by supporting Mahedium's other shoulder. The faster they got Mahedium moving, the more distance there would be between them and the enemy. The mage shook his head and blinked before turning toward Saeter.

"Thank you. Just give me a few moments and I think I can walk on my own. Nothing appears to be broken. I just had the wind knocked out of me," Mahedium told them.

"And half a mountain of rubble dropped on you," Saeter dryly replied.

"We should-ss probably walk faster," the hobgoblin interjected nervously as he looked back over his shoulder.

Just as Blacknail finished speaking, the first group of mercenaries marched cautiously through the gap in the barricade behind them. The trio had almost reached the rest of Herad's men though. They were only a few dozen feet away from the closest thing to safety around.

"Good thing they aren't in any rush to attack. You're heavier than you look," Saeter remarked.

"Yes, but what happens if the bad-ss mage decides to throw exploding magic at us right now?" Blacknail replied uneasily. This was apparently something that hadn't occurred to Saeter yet, because he tensed up and gave the enemy behind them a nervous look.

"I don't suppose if that mage there decides to blast us into human paste you could stop him?" Saeter remarked expectantly.

Mahedium coughed in reply. "Maybe." He didn't sound very confident.

"Bloody wonderful." Saeter sighed.

"Hopefully they don't recognize me as the mage from before, and all they see is some walking wounded. There's no way they would waste any mana crystals on us then," the mage explained.

Blacknail eyed him thoughtfully. That meant if the enemy did recognize Mahedium, they could be about to blast all three of them into little bits. He didn't want to die that way, or any other way really.

"We should dump him. We can say he tripped," Blacknail suggested quietly to his master as he covered the still somewhat stunned mage's ears with his hands.

"Herad needs him, and besides, we're already here," Saeter answered dryly.

The hobgoblin stopped staring back at the enemy and looked ahead. Saeter was right; they had already reached the rest of Herad's men. He gave his master an unabashed grin and uncovered Mahedium's ears. Saeter and him let go of Mahedium, and the mage managed to stand by himself. Herad was watching from out of sight of the enemy at the back of a nearby squad, and she called the mage over. He seemed unsteady at first, but after a few seconds managed to start walking without their help.

"Thanks, you two, for your help," he told them.

"No problem, you can pay me back-ss later. Now I'm just going to go stand over there and um... guard that very important barrel," Blacknail replied wryly. He took a few steps away from the mage and cast another nervous glance back at the enemy.

Saeter smacked him across the back of the head.

"What? If we stay near him-ss then the other mage might set us on fire or turn us into little pieces," Blacknail hissed quietly to his master.

"This is a battlefield. Nowhere is safe," Saeter replied as he led them over to a small squad of men off to the side of the road.

During this time, the enemy hadn't been idle. They weren't attacking, but soldiers had continued to stream in through the gap in the barricade, and now almost half the mercenaries had taken up position on the same side of it as Herad's men. The two sides glared at each other. On one side were over a dozen loose squads of bandits in mismatched gear, and on the other was a solid formation of uniformed soldiers that was slowly growing as more of them slipped through the wall. The expectant stillness was broken by Herad's voice.

"Show these poor bastards what happens to my enemies, mage," she yelled.

At her command, Mahedium stepped forward and once again leveled his staff. Instantly, a purple glow sprung into being above the enemy's front rank as the enemy mage raised his defenses. However, Mahedium didn't do as anyone expected. No shimmering air or invisible force appeared. Instead, a pillar of roaring flame burst from his staff and raced across the battlefield. However, the flames didn't head for the enemy. Mahedium had purposely aimed several dozen feet to their left.

The column of raging fire slammed into the wooden barricade and hungrily consumed it. Within seconds, that section of the wall had been transformed into a roaring bonfire. Its flames reached as high as the nearby roofs, and it was still spreading and growing with incredible speed. The crackle and hiss of burning wood filled the air. Mahedium then unleashed another blast of flame at the barricade on the other side of the gap. The enemy combat mage was powerless to stop the second blast as well. Apparently, his purple magic wind sucker thing only worked on attacks headed toward himself.

Blacknail giggled happily to himself as a soothing wave of relief washed over him. So that was what the plan was! He liked it; it was a nice little trap. More traps should involve fire.

The mercenaries' position was now less than optimal. They were stuck halfway through the barricade, and flames were rushing toward them from both sides. There was no way they could turn around and retreat quickly enough to avoid the flames completely. So the tall enemy mage did the only thing he could; he went on the offensive. He dropped his amulet, grabbed his staff, pointed it in Mahedium's direction, and unleashed a blast of force. Immediately, there was a chorus of angry shouts as the mercenaries around the enemy mage started rushing forward at Herad's men and away from the fire. Blacknail was happy to see that their formation wasn't quite so neat anymore.

As the wave of magic raced toward Mahedium, he reached under his shirt and pulled out an amulet of his own. In imitation of his counterpart, he raised it. The crystal didn't glow purple, and no whirling vortex appeared. Instead, a small, circular, transparent shield appeared in front of him and quickly expanded until it covered not only him but all the men around him.

The force blast smashed into it with a loud crashing sound that Blacknail felt in his teeth, and a wave of dusty wind blew outward from the impact site. In the middle of the blast zone stood a completely unharmed squad of bandits with Mahedium standing tall at their center.

Herad's voice suddenly rang out. "Charge, and push them back into the flames!"

At her command, every bandit squad attacked. They flowed together as they raced toward the enemy. The mercenaries' forward march faltered as their morale took a serious hit. Not only were they now cut off from reinforcements, but their mage seemed to have been bested, and their backs were up against the wall. Not to mention, the wall was on fire.

Both mobs of fighters were racing toward each other now, but they hadn't met yet. Both mages used this time to quickly throw some attack spells back and forth. The mercenary mage sent a ball of kinetic energy into a squad of Herad's men that were too far away from Mahedium for him to protect. It smashed into them and scattered them like leaves in the wind. In a split second, a dozen men had been blown off their feet, and several didn't get back up. Mahedium took advantage of his opponent's distraction and blasted the edge of the mercenaries' formation with a wave of curling flame. Screams filled the air as men discarded burning shields or fell, smoking to the ground. The enemy mage cursed loudly and raised his staff to counterattack, only to take an arrow in the neck and keel over before he could do anything. It was only one of many arrows that began to rain down on Zelena's hired soldiers as archers hidden on rooftops on both sides of the street opened fire.

Herad had revelaed another of her hidden tricks.

Now the mercenaries really started to falter. The death of their mage clearly demoralized them, and their advance ground to a halt. Herad's men didn't stop their charge though, and battle was soon joined as the lead combatants from both sides crashed together. The still somewhat disciplined enemy shield wall was hit by the first rank of Herad's men. A wave of bandits wielding swords, clubs, and spears began battering at the mercenaries and quickly started bending around the enemy formation. Herad was now the one with the numbers advantage.

The mercenaries were a tough nut to crack though. They were better equipped and more disciplined than their foe, and they were too close now for archers or magic to be used. Hand-to-hand combat would now decide who would be victorious. The clash of metal on metal, the thud of blades biting into wooden shields, and human cries of rage and pain filled the street. Behind it all was the crackling of wild flames as the wooden barricade burned.

Blacknail and Saeter kept to the back of their squad. Neither of them was too eager to enter the melee. The hobgoblin was only as close as he was so he could keep Saeter out of trouble. He kept an eye on the old scout as he darted around the edge of the fight and halfheartedly exchanged blows with the occasional opponent. It wasn't really his job to fight on the front lines. That was what rookies were for.

Even with so many things set against them, the Leather Heels Company stood their ground. They kept their shields high and their blades swinging. Bandit after bandit fell before them, and it looked like they would manage to hold, but then Herad herself joined the fray. The bandit chieftain charged out from among her minions with her bodyguards at her side and slammed into the center of the enemy's formation. Her silver blade flashed through the air and cut down two mercenaries as her hulking guards slammed themselves into soldiers. They were wearing heavier armor than most the other bandits and carrying heavy two-handed swords or pikes. Herad's men rallied around her and drove into the gap she created. As she whirled into the enemy formation, more and more mercenaries fell, and their formation began to dissolve. The sound of Herad's vicious laughter rang out as she batted a blade away and slashed its wielder across the face. She looked like she was having fun. A mercenary stabbed at her chest, but she sidestepped the blow and ended up with only a shallow cut across her ribs. Herad then stabbed low. Her blow cut her attacker's leg just below his groin. He collapsed as blood poured from the wound.

Suddenly, there was a loud cry of despair, and the enemy's resolve broke. Their formation dissolved into chaos, and Herad's men started pushing them back, but there was nowhere for them to go. The roaring flames of the burning barricade blocked their escape. Step by step they were pressed backward until one of them stumbled and fell into the blaze. His screams rent the air as he caught fire, and he lunged forward in a futile attempt to escape the flames that now covered him. Of course, there was nowhere for him to go, so all he managed to do was throw himself on top of his startled comrades and spread the flames before one of them panicked and cut him down.

This distraction only served to weaken the mercenaries further, and soon another man was pushed into the flames, and then another. The smell of roasting human flesh wafted over the battlefield. Blacknail really wished he'd brought more to eat now; the scent was making his stomach gurgle with hunger.

Enemy soldiers began to drop their weapons, either in hopes of surrendering and being spared or just so they would die a clean death at the end of a blade instead of burning to death. Herad didn't take any prisoners. She and her men cut into the mercenaries until they had all been slain and the more stubborn ones pushed into the flames of the barricade. A triumphant cheer went up from her men when the last of the mercenaries had fallen.

As a bloodstained Herad strolled over the corpse-littered street, her men started looting the bodies. They were safe from any counterattack for a while and they were eager to get their hands on some valuables. Blacknail took a few minutes to try and find some boots and socks that fit him. He tended to go through them quickly because of his long sharp toenails. After he'd found a satisfactory pair, the hobgoblin glanced around the battlefield. The butchered or burning remains of his tribe's enemies were scattered everywhere, and most of Herad's men were still busy looting the bodies for weapons or valuables. The flames that wreathed around the barricade itself were finally starting to die down as the last of the wood it was feeding on blackened and crumbled.

"Have we won yet?" Blacknail asked Saeter hopefully. He was fairly sure they'd won, but then again, he'd thought that after the first enemies had run away, and it hadn't been true.

Saeter grunted in reply. "No, we're just getting to the hard part."

# *Part Five:*
# *The Hunter's Feast*

# Chapter 37

"This battle is far from over. We've just reached a brief lull," Saeter told Blacknail. "Even if the rest of the mercenaries decide to call it quits, we'll still have only taken out Zelena's gold-bought thugs and soldiers. We still haven't gone up against Werrick's own men."

The old scout had to speak loudly in order to be heard over all the background noise. Bandits were still stomping around and cheering their victory as the remains of the wooden barricade burned. All in all, it put Blacknail in a festive mood. It certainly smelled like a party; the air was thick with smoke and the iron scent of blood. The cackling flames of the burning wall also prevented the enemy from launching another attack, for now. The fire wouldn't last all that much longer though.

"Zelena's a sly one. She'll have kept something up her sleeve. Werrick's regulars will be harder to deal with than the others," Saeter added.

Blacknail scoffed. "If they're so tough, why did she need-ss to hire so many other fighters?"

"To wear us down so we're easier to take out," Saeter replied.

"Ha, they didn't do all that much, and they probably cost a lot," the hobgoblin countered.

"She doesn't have to pay them if they all die," his master explained darkly.

"Oh, that's tricksy. This Zelena lady is smart-ss. Who is she again?"

"You don't know who Zelena is?" his master asked in surprise.

"She is the enemy. That was all I needed-ss to know before. It's hard to remember the names of so many humans, so I don't worry about the ones that will probably die soon," the hobgoblin replied with an indifferent shrug.

"Do you know who Werrick is?" Saeter asked.

"The enemy," the hobgoblin replied with another indifferent shrug.

Saeter sighed in frustration before replying. The lines on his face under his gray bangs looked deeper than usual. "Most people consider Werrick to be the most powerful of the northern bandit chieftains because he has the most men, and Zelena is one of his lieutenants. A while back, people started calling him the Wolf because of the ruthless way he raided caravans."

"Why are we-ss fighting him?" Blacknail asked curiously. It didn't seem very smart to pick a fight with the strongest enemy possible, but maybe it was a Herad thing.

"Herad and Werrick hate each other. They've met here in Daggerpoint a few times, and Herad ended up killing one of his lieutenants in a duel. The arrogant prick thought Werrick's name would allow him to do anything he wanted, but it didn't," the old scout answered.

"Ah, makes sense," the hobgoblin replied with a knowing nod. The same type of thing could happen if there were rival gangs of goblins in an area, just with less walking about and more poo throwing. Humans were weirdly indirect sometimes.

"The battle isn't going too badly though. Herad thought Werrick would be too busy to come to Daggerpoint for the winter this year, and she was right, but he sent Zelena in his place. Zelena's personal forces are smaller than Herad's, and even without the barricade, we still have a strong defensive advantage," Saeter explained.

The hobgoblin rubbed his chin as he thought his master's words over carefully. From what he'd just heard, it seemed likely that Zelena would attack soon, so he needed a plan.

"Let's go join the archers on-ss the roofs. Once there, we can shoot all of Zelena's men-ss because they don't have shields," Blacknail suggested. That seemed like the safest plan. However, before Saeter could reply, there was a scream of pain and a hollow thud as something fell from the top of a nearby building and hit the ground. Blacknail looked over to see a twisted corpse lying there, and it had a crossbow bolt sticking out from its chest. A quick flash of movement drew the hobgoblin's eye upward, and he glimpsed a familiarly dressed figure dash across the roof and disappear. It had been one of Malthus's assassins.

"Or maybe we should stay here," the hobgoblin remarked warily as he scanned the nearby roof tops.

"Blacknail get over here, now!" Herad suddenly roared from across the street.

"That doesn't seem to be an option," Saeter remarked dryly with obvious amusement. The hobgoblin winced in reluctance. He had a feeling he knew where this was going, and he didn't like it one bit.

"You'd better do as she says," Saeter told him.

Blacknail sighed and started dragging himself over to where his mistress was waiting. There was another scream of pain from across the street, and the hobgoblin sighed as the sound of running footsteps on a nearby roof reached his ears.

Herad was yelling at a pair of nervous-looking subordinates and gesturing toward where the first archer had fallen from, but when Blacknail approached, she looked over and the rage in her eyes died down slightly. She still looked very angry though. The hobgoblin just hoped she wouldn't direct that anger at him. He was still her favorite, right?

"There you are! You're supposed to be taking care of those assassins, so go over there and kill them," she commanded Blacknail.

The hobgoblin grunted vaguely in acknowledgement. She made it sound so simple...

"What are you whining about? I thought you had a plan all worked out so that mere humans wouldn't stand a chance," Herad told him impatiently.

"I do, and it's a great plan. There's no way it will fail," Blacknail replied crossly.

"Then go do it before I lose any more of my men," the chieftain ordered him.

"Ugh, fine, but don't forget my blue cheese," the hobgoblin muttered darkly in reply.

Herad eyes narrowed dangerously at being talked back to, but she nodded in acknowledgement. "Don't worry about that. Do as I say, and you'll have all the rewards you could ever want."

It was Blacknail's turn to nod now. He then turned away and headed over to one of the nearby homes. Saeter walked up to Herad. The old scout had a concerned look on his age-lined face as he confronted his boss.

"You're depending on Blacknail for quite a bit. He might be in over his head, you know," Saeter told her with obvious concern. Herad's reaction was to laugh in his face. Her sharp barking laughter unsettled the old scout, and he shuffled nervously. He wasn't the only one either. Most of the other nearby bandits threw her surprised or anxious looks.

"You just can't see it, can you? I'm not betting on your pet or your partner, old man. I'm betting on the monster we created, one the likes of which has never walked the North before," she explained with vicious amusement.

"That's a tad dramatic. He's just a hobgoblin, and not a terribly old one at that," Saeter countered.

"There has never been a goblin like him, and you know it. He will kill those men because that's what he is, a predator. Wolves need not fear the lamb," Herad replied coldly.

"Those are some well-armed sheep." Saeter turned and looked in the direction Blacknail had gone.

The hobgoblin himself was now walking toward one of the fallen archers and scanning the rooftops for any sign of enemies. He slipped between squads of Herad's men as he moved in order to keep out of sight of any watchers. When he was sure no one hostile was looking, he dashed off the main drag and into a shadowy alley that was squeezed between two large warehouses. Once there, he started creeping farther in as he listened for any signs of his prey. He might not know where the enemy was, how many of them there were, or what they were planning, but he did know where he needed to go. He had made a perfect plan of his own earlier for dealing with the assassins after all. Now, he just had to adjust the plan slightly and figure out how not to get shot by the assassins' crossbows. They were an unwelcome addition to his scheme but one he was sure he could work around, or at least dodge at the last second.

Blacknail decided to head toward the closest location Herad had placed archers. Trying to chase assassins through these dark side streets seemed like a lot of work, but if the enemy was here to get rid of the archers then they would serve as the perfect bait. The suddenly eager hobgoblin rushed through the dirty alleyways toward his target. It only took him a few moments to find one of his tribe's archer stations. From behind a pile of crates, he observed five men who were standing on a rooftop above him. Two of them were on watch while the other three were resting.

However, Blacknail immediately noticed several blind spots that he, or an assassin, could use to approach them unseen. The hobgoblin shook his head in disapproval. These members of his tribe weren't very good sentries. It was a good thing Blacknail was here to protect them, or most of them anyway...

The hobgoblin circled around the area until he found somewhere he could watch the two best ways to sneak up to the archers. The building was right on the edge of the battlefield, and a large section of it had been collapsed to serve as part of the barrier that funneled attackers toward the main street. The northern side was still standing though, and it made a good lookout spot. Blacknail climbed up and perched at a window on the second floor. If he waited there, he was sure the assassins would soon show themselves. They were after Herad's isolated archers, and this group had made themselves vulnerable. These enemies moved like predators, if not very good ones, so they would without a doubt be drawn to weakness, and that made them predictable. As Blacknail waited among the rubble and shadows, the voices of the archers reached his long green ears.

"Are you sure we're just supposed to be sitting around here?" one of them asked.

"Do you see anymore enemies coming down the main street? No? Then that's what Herad told us to do," another bandit replied.

On one hand, Blacknail wanted to smack them for being so loud and drawing attention to themselves, but on the other hand, that was exactly what he wanted them to do. Maybe he could smack the survivors after the battle was over. The hobgoblin's thoughts were interrupted by a rustling noise, like heavy cloth rubbing up against something. A second later, a trio of cloaked figures pulled themselves up onto a nearby roof.

They crouched there for a few seconds to make sure no one had noticed them and started to slowly and quietly make their way across the shingled roof.

Blacknail smiled wickedly as he watched them from his perch. It was time for him to get moving. He quickly turned away from the window and climbed down the pile of rubble he'd used to get to the second floor. The assassins were using one of the routes he had scouted out earlier to approach the archers, so he knew exactly what he had to do. It was too bad he hadn't had time to set any traps. Silently, Blacknail dashed across the street and started climbing the side of an ivy-covered building. The thick vines allowed him to easily make his way up to the roof. He was then positioned perfectly to ambush the assassins. As Malthus's men crossed the last stretch of roof, Blacknail peeked around a brick chimney and observed them. They were focused on sneaking up on their targets. The idea that someone might be stalking them in turn didn't seem to have occurred to them, and that made Blacknail feel all tingly inside.

The slate rooftops in this part of the city were squeezed close together. It was easy enough to jump between them. Any trace of the morning's dampness had been erased by the hot rays of the midday sun that hung overhead. The squad of five archers was still positioned on a rooftop that overlooked the battlefield and the now smoldering remains of Herad's barricade. On the roof next to them, the trio of assassins were creeping ever closer by using the slant of the roof to conceal themselves. On the next building over, a hobgoblin lurked behind a chimney stack and was eagerly awaiting the fun that was about to start.

One of the assassins had a crossbow strapped to his back. He looked up over the peak of the roof at his targets and then pulled the weapon off his back and began loading it. His two companions began unsheathing their blades. The first assassin rose and sighted on the back of one of the archers' lookouts. He didn't take the shot though. Instead, the other two men crept out of hiding and started creeping closer. In just a few moments the two swordsmen would be upon the archers. They might have been outnumbered, but with the element of surprise on their side, they would make quick work of Herad's men. Blacknail would almost have been impressed by the maneuver if they hadn't left themselves completely open to a counter ambush. That was undoubtedly all you could expect from a bunch of fat city humans.

The hobgoblin quickly pulled his own bow off his back, drew an arrow, and aimed at the crossbowman. As the first of the enemy swordsmen made the long step over to the other roof, Blacknail let the string go. There was a sharp twang as the arrow zoomed through the air and slammed into the back of the crossbowman. As the man gasped and crumpled, the hobgoblin yelled out a warning to his unprepared tribesman.

"Oh, no! The enemy is attacking. Quickly, protect-ss yourselves!" he screamed shrilly at the top of lungs.

The two swordsmen instantly froze and threw startled looks back at Blacknail and the corpse of their companion. The sentry also spun around, and his eyes widened in surprise when he saw Blacknail. He quickly noticed the attacking assassins as well.

"Hells, an attack!" he cursed loudly.

At the sound of his voice, the two swordsmen jumped back into action and charged the sentry. The bandit took a scared step backward and tried to draw his sword. He didn't have enough time though, and he had to give up and dodge out of the way of a slash from the lead assassin. However, the sudden evasive movement caused the lookout to lose his balance, and Blacknail winced as he toppled over the side of the roof and disappeared from sight. Hopefully, that was going to hurt later.

The attackers didn't waste any time in racing after the other archers. They clearly wanted to reach their foes before they were ready. Blacknail decided to intervene. He dashed across the tiled roof after them. The tiles threatened to come loose beneath his feet, but he had to keep the enemy in sight, or they might get away. The sounds of fighting rose from the other rooftop as he moved. Blacknail jumped across the gap between the buildings and ran up the side of the roof. Below him, on the opposite slope, the two assassins who were left were fighting the three remaining members of Herad's band. Judging by the bleeding corpse lying prone on the roof, one of the archers had already fallen.

Now though, the remaining archers had discarded their useless bows and drawn their close combat weapons. Two of them had short swords, and one had a small hand axe. Unfortunately for them, they didn't seem very good at using them. The two assassins still clearly had the upper hand in the fight. Their blades flashed through the air and forced the bandits back. It was all the archers could do to defend themselves as they flailed about with their own weapons. The clay tiles of the roof also made the footing treacherous. It was a sloppy mess of a fight.

As the hobgoblin ran toward the closest enemy, he jumped over the tip of the roof and then kicked out with both feet. His boots slammed into the shoulder of one of the assassins, and the impact knocked him sideways with more than enough force to send him right over the edge. There was a surprised yell and a smacking noise from below as the man hit the ground. This was quickly followed by a series of crashes as a section of clay tiles came loose and slid off the roof. Blacknail landed next to the last remaining attacker, but the tiles below him came loose from the impact and started to slide. The hobgoblin scrambled to find his balance and get a solid grip on the roof.

"Oopsie." Blacknail hissed in annoyance as his footing shifted beneath him. This wasn't good.

The last enemy was startled but quick to react. He lurched around and swung down at Blacknail's head with his sword. The hobgoblin's eyes widened in alarm as the silver flash descended toward his face. A surge of panic jolted through him, and Blacknail instinctively reached deep inside himself to burn a bit of residual Elixir. With lightning speed, he twisted to the side, found solid footing, and drew his own blade to parry the blow. The impact knocked the assassin off-balance for a second, and he didn't get time to recover. An axe slammed into his back, and the man's eyes went wide with shock. His legs gave out a second later, and he toppled over.

"Thank you," Blacknail told the bandit who had finished the last assassin off.

"Ha, we're the ones that should be thanking you. If you hadn't yelled out that warning, they would have gone through us like Ritchet Oil through a sick sheep," the axe wielder replied.

Blacknail gave him a blank stare. Like what through a what?

What was this crazy human talking about?

"Er, no problem," the hobgoblin replied as he brushed himself off. He then took a small sip of Elixir to replenish himself.

All that fighting had gotten his clothes dirty. Stupid assassins and their running around on unsafe rooftops! He snorted in annoyance and kicked the corpse of the assassin off the roof. It fell in a clatter of shattering tiles. Why did humans put such dangerous things on their roofs? Anyway, the first part of Blacknail's amazing plan was complete. The second part was for him to get the rest of the assassins' attention. The third was for him to kill Malthus and all his annoying cloaked minions. He wasn't quite at the third step yet, but he was getting there, and he was really looking forward to it! The hobgoblin walked over to the peak of the roof and coughed to clear his throat.

"Malthus, you stupid-ss fat pink bastard! I just killed three of your little friends, and I'm going-ss to keep killing more of them until you fight me! So come here and face me, unless you're-ss as cowardly as you are ugly!" he yelled shrilly at the top of his lungs.

The sound of his voice echoed over the city. The remaining archers that were standing beside him gave the hobgoblin shocked looks. They seemed more than a little nervous.

"Oh, right. You may want to find somewhere-ss else to hang out. Things are probably going to get-ss exciting here soon," Blacknail told them thoughtfully.

# Chapter 38

The bandit archers Blacknail had saved from the assassins took his advice and decided to leave. It would have been pointless for them to have stayed to help him fight, but it would have also been nice of them to offer. Humans sure were an ungrateful bunch. Before they left, Blacknail borrowed some of their rope. The hobgoblin was a little concerned that Malthus would get lost and not be able to find his location, so he wandered back over to the first assassin he'd killed. He then picked the corpse up and hung the cloaked body by its neck from the tallest nearby chimney. There was no way Malthus could miss that helpful sign! Now all he had to do was be patient. Wait, what if Malthus didn't come because he suspected an ambush or something? That would ruin Blacknail's perfect plan.

"This isn't a trap. I just want-ss to kill you, Malthus!" Blacknail yelled out to clarify things.

The sound of his voice echoed loudly over the nearby rooftops and through the dark alleys between them. The hobgoblin was more than a little disappointed when no one yelled back to thank him for the explanation. Standing around on the rooftop was definitely getting boring. Why couldn't Herad fight people who were more interesting and talked more?

Blacknail impatiently strolled along the rooftops as he waited for his enemies to show up. He would occasionally stop to throw out a few more insults—apparently Malthus was the son of a goat—but the hobgoblin kept his head down and eyes open. The fact that the assassins were running around with crossbows hadn't slipped his mind. A few minutes later, Blacknail finally heard the sound of someone trying to sneak up on him. He quickly looked over his shoulder to see a flurry of movement in an alley below him as several cloaked figures dove for cover.

"I think he saw us," one of the men whispered.

"That's impossible," another replied quietly.

"I can hear you too!" Blacknail answered back helpfully. He wanted them to stop sneaking around and attack him already. There really was no point in them trying to sneak up on him.

"Damnation, how in all the hells can he do that?" one of the assassins cursed.

"Maybe he just guessed what we said, and he didn't actually hear us," another suggested. There was a moment of silence as the assassins thought this possibility over.

"I'm not-ss just guessing. I can really hear you," Blacknail yelled back.

"Rot and ruin! It must be some sort of magic," one of them cursed from where he was hiding behind a pile of trash.

"He could have guessed that we'd think he was guessing," the first assassin added thoughtfully. There was another second of silence. Then the hobgoblin heard a smacking sound like someone had gotten slapped or punched, and Malthus spoke up.

"Shut up, you idiot. It doesn't matter how he's doing it! Everyone just stay silent. We're switching to hand signals from now on," he commanded his men.

"Just hurry up! You're taking forever," Blacknail impatiently shouted their way.

"Shut your vile trap, you freakish bastard!" Malthus yelled back angrily.

"You're not supposed to be talking!" the hobgoblin pointed out cheerfully.

Blacknail may have been imagining it, but it almost sounded like he could hear Malthus grinding his teeth all the way from the roof. Was he angry for some reason? Blacknail was just trying to be helpful, so the assassins would stop wasting so much of his time. He waited for Malthus and his men to approach him. After a few seconds, they tried to slip around the other side of the building and flank him. Blacknail sighed in annoyance at their snail-like pace. Well, if they wouldn't come to him, he would go to them! The hobgoblin broke out into a dash. The thump of his footsteps as he ran knocked the tiles beneath his boots loose, and they started to slide and fall off the roof and onto the ground below. Blacknail jumped the gap between ledges and landed on the next roof over. He scrambled to catch his balance for a second and then continued running straight for Malthus and the assassins, or at least toward the roof that hung over their heads.

After another quick leap, he passed them right by and kept on running. There was muttered swearing from the alley below as the hobgoblin zoomed by, and Blacknail smiled in self-satisfaction. His plan was perfect. All he had to do was get Malthus to follow him, and he had a fairly good idea about how to do that.

"You idiots are too slow. I'm just going-ss to lose you in the city and then go kill Zelena," he yelled as he ran by. The muttering from below intensified, and was quickly followed by a stampede of footsteps. It definitely sounded like all the assassins were chasing him.

"Quick, after him! Don't let him escape, but keep an eye out for ambushes. This is probably a trap," Malthus ordered his minions as he took off after the hobgoblin.

The rooftops were treacherous and harder to run on than the streets below, and that slowed Blacknail down somewhat. They also allowed him to take more than a few shortcuts though, and more importantly, he was a hobgoblin Vessel, so he was easily able to keep his lead. In fact, he had to slow down several times so he didn't get too far ahead. At the brisk pace he was keeping, Blacknail soon led his pursuers out of Herad's territory in the warehouse district and out into the city proper. The roofs under his feet and the buildings that supported them grew smaller. The occasional citizen of Daggerpoint also appeared below, now that they were away from the battle.

As a Vessel, Malthus was by far the fastest runner in his squad, but he seemed reluctant to leave his men behind, and that slowed him down. All the assassins were also on the ground below Blacknail, and he was above them on the rooftops, so they couldn't attack him no matter how close they got. Or at least that was true for the first few minutes of the chase. Suddenly, there was a series of odd thumps from below, and a curious Blacknail looked over the edge just in time to see Malthus launch himself off a pile of crates, grab a post that protruded from a wall, swing himself up, twist through the air, and then roll onto the roof. However, the maneuver slowed the assassin down and left Blacknail with a strong lead, so he wasn't too worried. Even though Malthus was a Vessel, he was still human, so Blacknail was confident he could outrun him.

The hobgoblin grinned smugly at the assassin without concern, until there was a shout from below and Malthus reached over the edge of the roof just in time to catch a crossbow one of his subordinates had thrown up to him. Blacknail's smile quickly faded after that.

"Uh oh, that's bad-ss as bugs," he swore to himself.

The still-running assassin leader pulled out a bolt and started struggling to load his crossbow while he was still moving. Unfortunately, Blacknail was fairly sure he would get it right soon. He was proven correct a few seconds later when an ominous clicking noise rang out behind him. All of a sudden, Blacknail wasn't left with very many good options, so he jumped off the roof. A second later, a crossbow bolt whistled over his head and flew off into the city. The still-crossbow-bolt-free hobgoblin now hung in the empty air over the street that ran beside the edge of the roof. A split second later, he began to drop inexorably toward the rather hard-looking cobblestones below, so he twisted around and grabbed a clothesline that hung over the road. His weight dragged the line downward, and he began to slide down its length toward the center of the street, until the line broke with a sharp snap.

"Piss on crossbows!" Blacknail hissed as he flailed in the air and fell uncontrollably toward the ground again.

There was nothing else nearby he could grab, so he tucked himself up and rolled when he hit the ground. The rough stone and gravel of the street dug into his back as he careened across the street and smashed into a stack of crates. Luckily, the crates weren't solidly built. The thin wood shattered easily when the cart-wheeling hobgoblin hit them to reveal they were stuffed full of packing straw. Bits of broken wood jabbed painfully into his sides as he slammed suddenly to a stop, but the cloak that he was now tangled up in stopped any of them from drawing blood.

"Ow," the hobgoblin whined as straw rained down around him. The only part of him that was visible was his feet. They stuck up into the air while the rest of his body was hidden by shattered crates and their contents.

"He's down, get him!" Malthus yelled from a nearby rooftop as he reloaded his crossbow.

Blacknail's head poked out from the pile of wreckage he was buried in, and he spat out a mouthful of straw. He didn't feel so great. The city seemed blurry and to be spinning around him for some reason. There was something else that felt wrong too... His face felt oddly exposed. His mask! Blacknail quickly pulled his mask back on. It must have come loose when he'd crashed. Luckily, it didn't seem like anyone had seen his face. Herad had told him to keep his identity a secret. Blacknail shook his head to clear it and quickly rose to his feet, just as the first of his pursuers ran around the corner of a nearby building and came into sight. It was time to go!

"There he is!" one of the assassins yelled as he pointed to Blacknail.

The hobgoblin immediately broke out into a sprint toward the nearest alley. He almost tripped as he struggled to untangle his cloak from his feet but caught himself at the last second. He had to get out of sight before Malthus reloaded that crossbow! He apparently made it because no pointy objects slammed into his back as he dashed for cover. The good news was that he was almost at his destination now. The bad news was that every bone in his body hurt and his vision was still a little blurry.

The assassins entered the alley only moments after Blacknail, but he had already sprinted a fair distance ahead. Since Malthus was still more than a bit behind, the hobgoblin took gleeful advantage of his absence. He pulled his sling out and sent a hail of stones at the men chasing him. They whirred through the air and smashed into the unsuspecting assassins.

"Bloody bastard," one of them swore as a stone slammed into his shin. He dropped to the ground, and he wasn't alone. Another assassin took a rock to his stomach and fell. That left... five more assassins plus Malthus that were still chasing him.

One of the remaining pursuers dove for cover and pulled a

crossbow off his back, so Blackail hurriedly fled down the alley. Rotten contraptions, why did all his enemies seem to have them? This would be a lot easier if he didn't constantly need to worry about being shot! Blacknail threw himself around the corner of a building and out of the shadows of the alley. He burst at a full sprint out onto a wide sunlit street.

"Ah, which way-ss now?" Blacknail hissed to himself. All that dodging had gotten him turned around, and he had to take a second to figure out where he was. He didn't dare slow down though.

Homes made from wood and white plaster lined the edges of the road, and the running hobgoblin drew curious glances from several people who were walking by. It was far from crowded here, but there were several dozen rough-looking men and women scattered about. This was Daggerpoint though, so he was mostly ignored. No one wanted to get involved in something that didn't concern them.

The assassins ran out of the alley a few seconds later, and Malthus had already gotten off the roof and caught up to them somehow. Blacknail veered left to place a small crowd of six people between him and his pursuers as Malthus raised his crossbow.

"What in all hells!" a woman swore as she noticed the weapon that was seemingly aimed toward her. The rest of her group flinched, and two of the men drew their swords. Malthus tossed his bolt thrower to the assassin on his left and then drew his own blade. He dove forward with an angry growl, and his sword flashed through the air.

The assassin's blade knocked one of the men's weapons aside, and he slashed through the other's exposed wrist. The second man shrieked in pain, and his sword dropped from his now bloody, mangled hand. Malthus dove through the remaining unresisting members of the crowd and continued after the hobgoblin. Shouts of surprise and alarm rang out as the assassin leader scattered people in his wake and they fled from him. Blacknail started running a little faster. He was almost there now!

The street was now almost completely empty of pedestrians as everyone fled from the ruckus, but now Malthus himself was between Blacknail and the crossbowman. They couldn't shoot through their leader. The hobgoblin suddenly turned right and vaulted over a small waist-high wooden post fence that stretched the short distance between two homes. He landed on packed dirt with sparse grass sprouting from it. Malthus was hot on his heels, and the hobgoblin had to run as quickly as possible to stay ahead of him. A tall stone wall blocked his way, so Blacknail jumped up on top of a barrel and then flipped over the barrier. He landed in a cluster of bushes on the other side and quickly scrambled to his feet.

There were no buildings on this side of the wall. Thick scrubby bush and gangly trees filled the area. The ground was dry and cracked, but it showed obvious signs of flooding in the spring. That was probably why no one had built anything here. It was a forgotten little corner of Daggerpoint that had been allowed to run wild. While exploring the city, Blacknail had discovered several places like this, but this was the closest one to Herad's base. Blacknail grinned as he ducked out of sight behind a tree. This is where he had decided to prepare his fun little surprises. It was time to see how these fat city humans did in Blacknail's natural environment!

As the hobgoblin watched, Malthus appeared atop the stone wall. The man grimaced and cursed quietly to himself as he scanned the bush below him. He seemed hesitant to chase his target into the thicket. Blacknail was tempted to taunt him again, but he knew that wouldn't help. Not knowing where his target was and whether he had doubled back toward the battlefield was undoubtedly bugging the assassin. After a minute or two, Malthus's cloaked subordinates climbed up onto the wall next to him. They also seemed less than happy when they saw what lay ahead of them.

"What do you think?" Malthus asked.

"I think he led us here on purpose," an assassin remarked.

"There's no way he's led us into an ambush. It would take a half a company to secure this bush, and we'd see signs of them," another man replied.

"Not to mention there's no way Herad would throw away that many men during a battle," Malthus added.

"What if he just wants to waste our time while we search this foul mess for him? He could be long gone," one of the other assassins asked.

Malthus scowled darkly and stared into the bush and trees for any signs of Blacknail. He appeared to be deep in thought and conflicted about what to do. "No, he's in there. He's alone, wounded from his fall, and cornered. I'm not losing this chance to take him out. I don't care if Zelena wins her little battle. I want this bastard dead. Daggerpoint is our territory; there isn't room in it for both us and this freak."

There were reluctant nods of acknowledgement from the other five assassins, and together Malthus and his men jumped into the thicket below. They landed among the bushes and spread out as they pressed forward. From where he was lurking and watching, Blacknail purred quietly to himself in pleasure and his eyes flashed with malevolent joy. The chase had ended, and the real hunt had now begun. His perfect plan had reached the final stage.

The hobgoblin carefully turned and began to silently creep away from his pursuers. He then purposely stepped on a large twig. The piece of wood broke under his weight and made a loud snapping sound. Instantly, the assassins turned toward the noise, but they couldn't see him through the heavy brush. They thus began to move toward the source of the noise. Blacknail giggled to himself as he led them deeper into the shadows of the trees.

# *Chapter 39*

As Blacknail slipped through the trees and around the nearby thorny bushes, a bird sang out from above and drew his attention for a second. It had been a while since he last remembered hearing such a sound. There weren't a lot of songbirds among the dirty streets of Daggerpoint. He could reminisce later though. Right now, he had people to hunt. Or were they hunting him? It was a little confusing...

The rustling of plants reminded the hobgoblin that Malthus was chasing him. Blacknail threw a quick look over his shoulder and saw nothing but living green plants and a canopy of leaves fading to red and autumn gold. He could no longer see the shaped stones and squat buildings of Daggerpoint. The hobgoblin stretched and straightened his posture as he felt an unseen weight leave his shoulders. It was good to be back among nature and away from the places humans had made their own.

He reached up toward his face with a clawed hand and pulled his smiling mask off. The hobgoblin then tossed it aside into a bush where he could retrieve it later. This was not a place for wearing masks. His green angular face broke out into a wide toothy smile as it was exposed to the world. In the wild, even in this little isolated patch of it, things were different, purer. There was nothing to hold him back or make him question himself. His thoughts could run free without restraint or the weakness that came from hesitation.

A branch snapped off to his left and the hobgoblin's long green ears twitched as they picked up the noise. Without a doubt, it was Malthus and his pack. The assassins were making quite a bit of noise as they moved through the woods, much more than Blacknail. The area here was more brush than true forest. The trees were small and spread apart enough that there was no real canopy to block the light. That just made the undergrowth thicker though. There were bushes and tall stands of plants everywhere for him to hide in, and walking in a straight line was difficult.

The hobgoblin had assumed the assassins would be unaccustomed to wilder places, and it sounded like he'd been right. He was having no trouble keeping track of them and slipping ahead of them unseen. He wasn't even trying to conceal his trail, but they didn't seem to be able to follow it regardless. Thus, he would have to remember to make some noise every once in a while. The humans couldn't be allowed to believe he had escaped. It was a delicate game he was playing with these hunters of men. There was an uneasy balance that had to be kept. To win and claim his prize, Blacknail would have to prey upon their instincts and shape their desires to his own end. He had to appear weak and vulnerable to lure them in, and yet he couldn't allow them to draw in too close. He had to get them to walk into his trap and believe it had been their own idea. Luckily, most humans were very stupid.

As he approached a cluster of thin, white-barked trees, the hobgoblin heard movement off in the bushes from a fair distance behind him. A second later, he heard the rustle of leaves from out of sight and over to his left. Blacknail took a second to look over his shoulder and scan the forest behind him. It really was quite easy to track Malthus and his men in here. He could hear their untrained footsteps crunching twigs and leaves as they pushed their way through the brush. The assassins were spread out, but it sounded like they were keeping in sight of each other as they combed through the grass and bushes for any sign of him.

Right now, his prey was falling too far behind for his liking. Blacknail coughed and sputtered loudly, as if he was in pain and couldn't help it. He wanted them to think he was wounded and vulnerable, and not thinking about how stupid of an idea it was to have followed him in here. The more they underestimated him, the easier it would be to trick them. The coughing wasn't really fake though, he had fallen off a roof after all. That had hurt a lot.

A loud twang-like noise suddenly split the air behind Blacknail.

"Eep!" the hobgoblin squeaked in alarm as he dropped to the ground and covered his head.

A crossbow bolt ripped through the greenery with a whipping sound. There was then a loud crack as the projectile sunk deep into the bark of a tree trunk that lay several feet ahead of him. The forest behind Blacknail suddenly echoed with the crashing and snapping of plants as Malthus and his men shot forward and pushed their way through the forest toward Blacknail. It was time to get going! The startled hobgoblin jumped to his feet and dashed forward, deeper into the trees. As he ran, he snuck a look back and saw Malthus's form burst out of a thicket of bushes and throw an angry look around. Blacknail quickly stepped behind a tree and out of sight. Okay, maybe he had let Malthus get a little too close that time. Blacknail was glad the assassins only had one crossbow...

"Damn that bastard to all hells! I thought we had him this time," Malthus hissed angrily.

The master assassin was standing next to where Blacknail had been a few seconds ago and staring hatefully at the crossbow bolt stuck in the tree.

"Do you want to turn back?" one of his men asked with more than a hint of nervousness in his voice.

"No, we're right behind him," Malthus replied angrily.

"I still think this is a trap," the other man replied.

"Of course it's a trap; we know that, and it doesn't matter. Stop letting a little patch of bushes and trees unnerve you, and let's get after him," Malthus commanded his men.

Blacknail took advantage of their discussion to slip away to the side and put some distance between him and his pursuers. He really needed to take care of that crossbow. It was too much of a wild card, and being shot would probably hurt a lot. The hobgoblin crouched down behind a bush and squinted as he watched the assassins. All six of them had been close together while they talked, but now they were spreading out again. It was the one on the far right that held the crossbow.

There was no way he could charge the man before Malthus intervened, and even using his sling would involve getting dangerously close and revealing himself. It also wasn't guaranteed to take the man down in one hit, and it might convince Malthus to turn around and leave. Well, it was probably about time to begin anyway. He had lured them deep enough. He would just have to position everything just right so the crossbowman got taken out first.

The hobgoblin slowly got up and crept further away from the assassins. When he was far enough away that a screen of bushes and leafy tree limbs concealed him, he stopped. Then he looked down, selected a fairly large twig, and stomped on it. The twig snapped beneath his boot, and a loud cracking noise echoed through the forest. Blacknail was already diving behind a tree. A second later, another crossbow bolt tore through the greenery and sliced through the air where his chest had been mere moments before. Blacknail picked himself off the ground and peered around the tree he had used as a shield. One of his eyebrows rose in surprise at how accurate the shot had been. That assassin was really good with a crossbow. The hobgoblin was definitely killing that guy first.

Blacknail hurriedly got up and began dashing through the forest. He made absolutely no attempt to be quiet about it, and instead focused on keeping ahead of his pursuers. Underneath the sound of his own footsteps, he could hear his pursuers. It was also important to keep the crossbowman too busy running to reload. A large tree with droopy branches appeared on Blacknail's left, and he recognized it. With a cunning grin, he ran up to it and threw himself onto the ground beside it. He coughed again loudly and moaned dramatically.

Seconds later, Malthus and his men burst out of the bushes and saw him. Blacknail picked himself off the ground slowly as if he was in pain and had tripped. The hobgoblin had discarded his mask, but his hood was still up. It wasn't quite time to drop that yet.

"I've got you this time! You can't escape now, and no one will be coming to your rescue," Malthus gloated smugly as he smiled.

Blacknail ignored him and stepped around the tree. Which way would each assassin go? There was a click as the crossbowman began reloading, and Blacknail's heart skipped a beat. The trick here would be to predict exactly what the assassins would do. He needed to be careful though, Malthus had fooled him before by pretending to be too angry to think properly.

The master assassin signaled to his men using a quick series of hand gestures that Blacknail didn't understand. Immediately though, two assassins—including the crossbowman—started circling around to the left. Malthus and the other three men headed straight for Blacknail. The hobgoblin turned to face them and drew his sword. The crossbowman raised his weapon so Blacknail took a quick step backward. The gnarly trunk of the large tree was now in the way of a good shot, but the crossbowman and his guard just started flanking Blacknail to cut off his escape as the rest of their companions descended on the lone hobgoblin. Blacknail had them exactly where he wanted them.

"So much for the Faceless Assassin! When you die at my hands, it will be just another chapter added to my legend. You weren't even much of challenge, although I have to admit you're a lucky fool and not half bad at running away," Malthus bragged as he drew his own weapon.

"Things are not-ss always as they seem, Malthus. Perhaps you are the one that-ss is about to die," Blacknail replied.

"I am the best killer in all of Daggerpoint, and you're just a creepy little freak. No man is my equal. I'll take great joy in ripping that hood off your face and seeing what lies beneath it," the assassin leader responded angrily.

Blacknail began to laugh, and he didn't bother trying to sound human. His shrill malevolent laughter rolled over the assassins and they flinched in surprise. Even Malthus looked startled by the sound.

"Stupid human, you are right but so wrong. Herad is not a man and you ran from her. Soon, you will see my face, and then you shall run from me as well," the hobgoblin cackled.

"Shoot him!" Malthus roared impatiently but with a hint of fear. He had clearly been unnerved by the strange laughter.

The crossbowman aimed his weapon and began to take a step to the left to get a better shot at Blacknail. The hobgoblin leaned around the tree and gave him a toothy grin. The assassin stared in shock, and his eyes widened in horror at what he saw beneath Blacknail's hood. That was when the spear took him in the stomach. The weapon was a long, sharpened branch that had been tied to a forcibly bent-over sapling. It had been concealed in a bush and been triggered by the assassin's foot hitting a trip wire. Saeter had taught him how to make them to hunt deer or wild boar, but it worked on humans just as well.

The crossbow fell from the man's slack hands and hit the ground. He gasped as he looked down at the wooden spear that was stuck in his guts and started shivering uncontrollably. The rest of the assassins gaped in confusion as they tried to make sense of what had happened. That was when the sling stone smashed into the forehead of the assassin standing next to the crossbowman.

There was a loud crack and a spray of blood as the stone tore through his flesh and slammed into his skull. Before either of the assassins' bodies began to crumple, Blacknail was already burning Elixir and dashing forward. The hobgoblin laughed again as he ran toward the fallen man's weapon. It had worked! That was two men down. The first piece of the puzzle had fallen into place, and now all Blacknail had to do was follow the rest of the plan. He was truly a sneaky super genius!

"Shit, what in all hells!" a surprised Malthus cursed as he sprinted after the hobgoblin. The man was fast but not as fast as Blacknail. He may have been closer to his fallen companions but surprise had slowed his start as well.

Blacknail reached the weapon first and scooped it up. He spun around and grinned as he aimed it at the master assassin. Malthus reacted quickly this time and dodged away to the side, but Blacknail had predicted this. The hobgoblin shot the assassin that had been following in Malthus's footsteps instead. That was three down. The man shrieked in pain as the bolt punctured his chest and then collapsed a second later. Blacknail quickly tore the string off the crossbow. He then threw the broken weapon straight at Malthus's charging form. The assassin flinched and batted it aside with his blade. Blacknail jumped to the side and dashed away. The last two of Malthus's minions that were still standing tried to intercept him and cut off his escape.

"No, don't chase him. There are more traps!" Malthus roared suddenly.

His cloaked subordinates froze in their tracks and warily scanned the ground at their feet while trying to keep one eye on Blacknail. They didn't want to be caught off guard by a shot from his sling. The hobgoblin himself ran to the edge of the bushes and then turned back around. He was a safe distance away now.

Malthus slowly and carefully walked over to his companions' side. He looked calm but Blacknail could see rage smoldering behind his eyes. It amused the watching hobgoblin. He liked pissing off Malthus. The master assassin suddenly whipped a throwing knife at Blacknail's head, but he easily leaned out of the way. He was too far away for such knives to be much of a threat. Malthus growled as he stared at Blacknail.

"Do you think that just because you managed to take out a few of my men that you've won? Nothing could be further from the truth, Faceless One. As long as I live, your days are numbered, and it will take more than a few traps made from pointy sticks to kill me," he said angrily.

Blacknail laughed again. The time for hiding who and what he was, was over. Now it was time to spread delicious fear and panic.

"I have just gotten started, arrogant man. You won't leave this forest alive. It was so very stupid-ss of you to follow me here. Also, my name is Blacknail, and I have a face," the hobgoblin replied haughtily.

He grinned broadly and reached up slowly to pull down his hood. His enemies froze as they got their first view of his green skin, pointy ears, long nose, and sharp jagged teeth. Blacknail could see the blood drain from their cheeks as they took in his inhuman visage. It made him laugh again. This was so much fun!

"Cor-Dius's cloak shield us. He's not human," one of the assassins whispered in horror. Blacknail took a step forward and stared into the eyes of the closest enemy. The man stared back with wide-eyed dread.

"Rawr," the hobgoblin yelled as he lurched forward a step.

The man shrieked and fell over backward as he tried to

stumble away. Blacknail chuckled darkly at the stupid human and licked his lips in anticipation of what was to come. He then turned to the still-frozen Malthus and gave him a brief bow, before stepping into the bushes and out of sight.

"Soon..." the hobgoblin's eerie voice promised as he walked away. He shivered in excitement as he crept through the forest and circled around his prey. The humans had yet to move. They stood there for several seconds without saying anything.

"We should never have come here. We're going to be killed and eaten!" one of the men whispered fearfully.

"Shut up, or I'll kill you myself," Malthus told him as he stared his subordinate down.The man was shivering in fear, and he couldn't meet his boss's eyes. Malthus snorted in disgust.

"So he's not human; it changes nothing! It won't stop me from cutting his head off with my sword, and it actually explains a lot," Malthus exclaimed.

"He's right about one thing though. We should not have walked into these woods," the last man added fearfully.

Malthus grunted darkly in reply as he scanned the nearby greenery for signs of Blacknail. He was still looking more than a little pale and jumpy. "That was definitely a mistake, but we're far from finished. I'm not scared of a little green freak that likes to hide in bushes," the master assassin told his men, but judging by their skeptical expressions, they didn't seem too reassured by his speech.

As Blacknail watched from his new hiding spot next to a pile of rocks and thorny plants, he smiled. Malthus was clearly lying. The air reeked of blood and terror, and those delightful smells were only going to grow stronger.

# *Chapter 40*

Blacknail the hobgoblin stalked through the dense forest scrub with a merry spring in his step and a huge grin on his face. He had just killed three human warriors! How amazing was that? Incredibly, super, unbelievably amazing is what it was! When he finished off Malthus and his last two minions, it would be a total of... six human warriors! He couldn't wait to tell everyone about how awesome he was. Saeter would be so impressed, Herad would give him more cheese than he could possibly eat, and everyone else would finally realize how much better at everything he was than them. It was important they knew that.

Up ahead, across a few dozen feet of thick bush, the three remaining assassins were slowly trudging back toward the city. They were slowed down by the need to check for traps and watch for ambushes. Much to Blacknail's disappointment, they'd already found and disarmed one that had been in their way. The hobgoblin was keeping his distance from his prey for now and waiting for an opportunity to appear. At the pace they were going, they wouldn't be able to escape from the forest any time soon, so he could afford to be patient. Rushing in would be stupid; Malthus wasn't a human he intended to underestimate again.

After a few more minutes of watching, Blacknail stealthily moved up beside his quarry and narrowed the distance between them. The assassin to Malthus's left was beginning to slow. Instinctively, the hobgoblin's eyes picked out the fact that the man's legs were dragging and his shoulders had started to slouch. Blacknail's heartbeat sped up and his mind focused. Distractions and other thoughts were pushed aside as he studied his prey. He sensed weakness, and that was an opportunity waiting to be taken advantage of.

He tore his eyes away from the man and turned to study the terrain. If the assassins kept their current course, they would soon pass next to a small ridge. It was the perfect place for an ambush. Now he had both a place and a target. It was time to put his latest brilliant scheme into action! The hobgoblin picked up his pace and moved through the underbrush to cut off his quarry's path. He quickly crept through the trees until he reached the ridge. He then looked out from behind a large moss-covered rock that sat at the very edge of the ridge. Malthus and his men were approaching, so Blacknail quickly ducked back out of sight.

The trio of men were looking very nervous as they carefully moved through the brush. One of them flinched and jumped slightly when he was startled by the cry of a blackbird. He wasn't Blacknail's target though. The hobgoblin was aiming for the other assassin, the one that hadn't reacted at all and looked tired. As Malthus and his men drew closer, Blacknail took out his sling and silently loaded it with a stone from one of his pouches. He peeked ever so slightly out from his hiding spot and watched hungrily for the right time to strike.

Below him, Malthus turned away to look off into the opposite side of the forest, and the fatigued assassin slouched and looked down toward his feet. Blacknail made his move. There was a quiet rustling as the unseen hobgoblin rose to his feet and then a loud crack as his spinning sling unleashed its payload. All three assassins flinched at the noise. The stone zipped through the air toward the off-guard man's chest, and instead of ducking or dodging, he froze. Malthus acted quickly though. The master assassin's cloak whipped around him as he moved with lightning speed and tackled the other man to the ground.

Blacknail clenched his fists and hissed in annoyance as his projectile sailed harmlessly off into the trees. He didn't have much time for regret though; Malthus was back on his feet within seconds and headed Blacknail's way.

"Come face me, you cowardly abomination!" the knifeman roared as he dashed toward the earthen ridge the hobgoblin stood atop of.

"Maybe later!" Blacknail yelled back. He quickly ran away and disappeared into the trees.

It took Malthus several seconds to climb the small cliff that lay between them. The soil was loose and wet, so by the time he got to the top, the hobgoblin was long gone.

"Hells and damnation," the master assassin cursed loudly to himself as he looked around. He didn't give chase though. Instead, he reluctantly turned back around and rejoined his men in heading out of the bush.

"You're just going to let that thing get away?" the anxious assassin asked.

"For now. There's no bloody way I'm chasing that thing through its own territory. As far as I know, the entire purpose of that attack was to try and lure me away and into more of those traps. No, all we need to do is get out of this damn bush, and then we're the ones with the advantage. I'm not going to underestimate that creature. It must be a hobgoblin, and I've heard stories about them," Malthus replied.

Not far away, Blacknail was hanging halfway up a slender tree and watching the assassins. Its thick leaves hid him from below, but its thin gray trunk was still swaying slightly from his hurried ascent. It probably wasn't the best hiding spot, but he was stuck there now. When he saw Malthus lead his minions off into another section of bush, the hobgoblin carefully climbed down and began to creep after his prey.

As he moved, the hobgoblin's eyes narrowed and his forehead grew lined. He had a problem he had to think through and solve. His ranged attack from the ambush moments ago had been an obvious failure. He hadn't managed to even wound anyone, and he'd even had to flee for his life. He was going to have to get closer if he wanted his next strike to succeed. That would be difficult though. He would need a new plan.

The assassins were terrible woodsmen, but they weren't blind or stupid. They knew what he looked like and would see him if he got too close. Hmmm, what if he changed his appearance though? Blacknail giggled and rubbed his hands together gleefully as a fun idea popped into his head. It was time to get down and dirty!

It had rained a bit earlier that morning, so there were still a few scattered puddles and patches of wet ground around. The hobgoblin quickly headed over to the closest one he remembered and took off all his clothes. It had been quite a long time since he'd last run around naked, and it felt quite liberating, if a little cold. The hobgoblin hastily and enthusiastically jumped into the muddy puddle and began rolling around. Mud and dirty water splashed up in to the air as he shifted his weight around. It had also been quite a while since the last time he'd done this, and he'd missed it. The mud felt wonderful and cool on his skin and so much better than wearing itchy clothes. Humans were so weird about covering themselves up. They'd probably enjoy the occasional mud bath if they tried it.

When Blacknail got back up, the green skin that was stretched over his lanky frame was covered in muddy smears. The result was shifting patterns of green and dirty brown that blended in with the forest around him. After bundling his gear and discarded clothes, the hobgoblin headed back after his quarry. The mud on his skin was already starting to dry and flake off as he ran.

Once again, Blacknail circled around the assassins and got out ahead of them. Luckily, they had been slowed because they'd run into a noose trap. The trap had done little more than snag one of the assassins' feet and trip him, but it had prevented them from getting very far. From a safe distance away, the very dirty and naked hobgoblin watched as Malthus cut his subordinate free and helped him back onto his feet. The third man was keeping watch in case Blacknail tried anything while Malthus was distracted. Up ahead, a thick hedge of thorny bushes cut off the way forward. There was only one real path through it. The tall briars had a gap in the middle of them that a human could easily walk through. It was probably some sort of game trail.

"Hmm, perfect-ss," the hobgoblin murmured happily to himself when he saw it.

With one last look backward, to make sure the assassins were still occupied, Blacknail stalked through the trees and over to the pathway. A quick inspection of the area revealed a leafy depression that would conceal him, so he climbed in. He was only a few feet from the edge of the trail. It was at moments like this that Blacknail really appreciated how bad a human's sense of smell was. It almost made things too easy.

Soon his prey was moving again, and the hobgoblin grinned in delight when they headed his way. From his hiding spot, Blacknail waited for Malthus and the other men to pass by. He was both nervous and excited. All three of the assassins were keeping close together, but the thin trail was only wide enough for one person at a time to walk comfortably, so they were strung out in a line. Malthus was leading the other two and thus the first to walk by. The master assassin made his way warily down the trail. He carefully studied the heaps of thorn bushes and other thick plants around him as he walked. Then he stepped right next to Blacknail's hiding spot and looked in his direction, but his eyes passed right over the hobgoblin. Nonetheless, Blacknail's stomach twinged, and he felt a flash of nervousness as he held completely still. He could have reached over and touched the master assassin.

Then Malthus was past the hobgoblin and walking away from him. There were still two more assassins left, but Blacknail relaxed and calmed down. Malthus was the one he was worried about. The first of the two remaining enemies walked by without seeing anything either. The cloaked man didn't even really bother to check his surroundings, most likely because Malthus already had. He just strolled along after his master. Now there was only the rear guard left. The last of the assassins followed his companions through the gap. The nervous-looking man was mostly focused on keeping an eye out for people sneaking up from behind, so he only looked in Blacknail's direction for a split second before turning back around to stare anxiously at the forest behind him.

The assassin stepped next to Blacknail, and this time the hobgoblin reacted. The second the man's back was turned, the almost invisible hobgoblin silently stood up and stretched out his long, thin arms. One clawed hand instantly snapped down over the unsuspecting man's mouth and sealed it, while the other reached around with a small dagger and quickly sliced open his pink throat. The hobgoblin's victim tried to struggle and cry out, but it was futile. His throat was gushing blood, and

Blacknail had him locked in a tight embrace. He couldn't even fall over.

Malthus and the other man continued forward; they hadn't heard a thing. As he carefully watched them walk away, Blacknail kept his victim's mouth covered and slowly lowered him to the ground. He had to keep very quiet. The noise of the forest would only cover up a tiny bit of noise. The man's now unmoving corpse touched the earth without making a sound, and the grinning hobgoblin took a few quiet steps backward. The other two men still hadn't noticed anything, so he wasted no time in dashing away around the tall thorn bushes and out of sight.

He'd done it! He'd snuck up right under that arrogant fool's nose and killed his companion. Blacknail giggled to himself smugly. Who was the best assassin now? He was, that's who! The hobgoblin giggled again as he dove behind the bush where he'd stashed his pants and the rest of his gear. Mere seconds later, yelling broke out from behind him as the dead man's companions noticed his absence and his corpse was discovered. Oh, how Blacknail wished he could see their faces right now!

"Shit, he got Janus! The monster was right here, and we didn't even notice. He must be flaming invisible. We have to make a bloody run for it now!" Malthus's subordinate yelled with a voice full of fear.

He sounded one step away from full-blown panic, which made Blacknail feel really special. Even fully grown human warriors were terrified of him! He was so amazing.

"Be quiet, he's probably still somewhere nearby," Malthus replied sternly. "You know why we can't make a run for it. Not only are there traps scattered around this accursed place, but do you really think we could outrun a hobgoblin in a forest? One trip over a root or slip on some mud and we'd be done. We need to keep our heads together and make for safety slow and surely."

"That's not working though! That thing... is out there, and it's just playing with us! It's going to creep up behind us and slit our throats, and we won't even see it coming. We have to run!" the other man stuttered loudly in response.

"If you run, then I'll kill you, and then you won't have to

worry about the hobgoblin," Malthus told the other man coldly.

"Fine, you're the boss, Malthus. You know what's best, so I'll stay with you. That hobgoblin is probably no match for you anyway," his nervous subordinate replied.

"Make sure you do, because I'm watching you," Malthus remarked threateningly.

Over on the other side of the thorn hedge, Blacknail had finished putting his clothes back on and was considering their words. He scratched his bald head as he considered Malthus's behavior. The man sure was mean. He had threatened to kill his own companion if he tried to run. The poor man was obviously terrified!

Blacknail pulled his sling back out and sent a stone arcing over the bushes toward the assassins. It sailed through the air and tore its way through the greenery next to them. It went nowhere near the humans, but that wasn't the point. The last of Malthus's minions yelped and jumped up into the air when he heard the unexpected noise. A second later, he took off like a shot away from the bushes and Malthus.

The master assassin sighed deeply in annoyance and there was a whirring noise that sounded suspiciously like a knife being thrown. Oddly enough, it was followed by the sound of a blade sinking into flesh and a heavy thud. Blacknail grinned smugly; that was another one down.

"It's just you and me now, hobgoblin! Are you ready to fight?" Malthus roared in challenge.

Blacknail didn't reply. He wasn't quite ready yet, so Malthus would have to wait. Right now, any confrontation between them would be far too much like a fair fight for his liking.

When no one replied, the master assassin began trudging through the forest again. The hobgoblin followed closely behind him. Malthus was on his own now. He'd gotten rid of all the assassin's minions, but Malthus was by far the most dangerous of them all. The man was a far better swordsman than the hobgoblin. Blacknail knew he would need a special plan to best the man. It was too bad he didn't really have one... Oh well, something would probably pop into his head before too long.

Several minutes later, Malthus was getting dangerously close to the edge of the vacant land to return to the city.

Blacknail was running out of time. He'd been kind of hoping that Malthus would trip over a trap and kill himself, but that hadn't happened. No dangerous forest creatures had inexplicably appeared and eaten him either.

As the master assassin walked out into a small clearing that Blacknail recognized, the hobgoblin realized he had no choice. This was his last chance to stop the man from returning to the battlefield, and if that happened, Herad would get very mad. With a regretful sigh, the hobgoblin walked out of the bushes and into the grassy clearing.

"Here I am, Malthus. Let's fight," he announced halfheartedly as he pushed a branch out of his way.

"So the monster shows itself. What's wrong; have you run out of tricks? I told you that I wouldn't be done in by such petty traps or schemes," Malthus replied angrily as he glared at Blacknail. The assassin's blade was already in his hand, and he looked completely uninjured. He didn't even seem that fatigued, although his cloak and clothes had become stained and dirty.

"I got-ss tired of your smell. You've been upwind this entire time," Blacknail replied as he drew his own sword and strode forward.

Malthus smiled and carefully began to walk toward the hobgoblin. He didn't seem ruffled by the loss of his men or the events that had happened in the forest. Blacknail couldn't tell if it was an act or if he had been pretending earlier. It probably didn't matter though.

"I admit that I misspoke earlier when I said my victory over you would be one small part of my legend. Instead, it shall be among my crowning achievements. In fact, I think I'll have your head mounted and put on display," the master assassin said as he took a fighting stance in the center of the clearing.

The hobgoblin raised his own blade and cautiously went to meet him. A gust of wind blew through the forest and into the clearing, knocking autumn leaves loose from the trees and sending them swirling to the ground. As the killers eyed each other and began to circle one another, both their cloaks caught the wind and rippled. Then there was a flash of silver as Malthus struck first.

# *Chapter 41*

Blacknail ducked as the master assassin's sword sliced through the air toward the hobgoblin's head. As a result, the blow passed harmlessly above him. He then raised his own blade to protect himself as he lunged forward to stab Malthus, but the assassin laughed and easily sidestepped the blow.

"You're fast but too predictable," Malthus told Blacknail with an amused chuckle.

The hobgoblin grunted in annoyance. He raised his guard again and silently stared his opponent down. Neither one of them looked away as their eyes met. Without warning, Malthus struck again. Blacknail hissed angrily as he burned Elixir for speed. A hot wave of energy ignited within him as he jumped backward. The tip of Malthus's blade cut though his shirt and drew blood, but it was only a scratch. The master assassin immediately stepped forward and followed up his last attack with another one. This time, it was a horizontal slash aimed at the hobgoblin's chest. Blacknail stepped forward to meet the blow and swung his own weapon. There was a loud clang as the blades collided, and Blacknail felt the pommel vibrate in his hands. A second later, the blades slid down against each other until the swords locked. Both fighters eyed each other as they fought to keep their balance and their swords up.

"That's very hard on a sword, you know. They—"

Before he could finish, Blacknail's left boot shot up toward the man's groin.

"That's not very sporting," the assassin joked as he easily twisted his hips out of the way of the low kick. However, his move forced him to shift his balance and push his locked blade up higher.

Deep within the hobgoblin's mind, instinct and experience

sparked. Blacknail lunged forward as he instantly acted on the sudden thought. With lightning-like speed, the hobgoblin's open mouth snapped toward Malthus's hands. The assassin's eyes opened in surprise as he was caught off guard by the move. Apparently bite attacks were rare in human sword fights. Blacknail's teeth grazed the man's knuckles as he jerked his hands, and the sword in them, back.

The quick movement caused Malthus to stumble, and the hobgoblin mercilessly pressed his advantage. He stepped forward and battered the man's sword aside. As Malthus struggled to get his guard back up, Blacknail's blade sliced toward his exposed shoulder. Blood wetted the edge of the hobgoblin's sword as it cut into the assassin's skin, but Malthus was already dodging to the side. The attack failed to cut deep enough, and Malthus spun away without any real damage. The assassin tucked himself into a ball, and the long grass of the clearing was flattened beneath him as he rolled away.

The hobgoblin wasn't about to let him get away that easily though. He charged after the assassin with his sword raised above his head. The distance between them rapidly shrunk. Just as he was about to catch up, a pair of slender projectiles flew from the assassin's form while he was mid roll. Caught off guard, Blacknail could only flinch to the side to avoid the first one and flail wildly at the second. He got lucky, and there was a muted clang as his blade safely knocked the spinning knife from the air. Malthus used this time to spring to his feet and retake his fighting stance. Blacknail hissed in annoyance. He had been so close to killing the bastard! Now they were right back where they started.

"You're certainly a creative fighter, but you're not the only one with a few tricks up his sleeve," Malthus bragged as he grinned smugly.

"You talk-ss too much," Blacknail replied with a scowl.

"Whereas you apparently have better uses for your mouth," Malthus observed aloud irately. "I suppose I should expect such things from a savage beast like you."

The assassin scowled and wiped the small cut on his hand against his pants. Blacknail hoped it got infected. No wait, he hoped Malthus died way before that could happen.

"You taste like-ss a weakling and smell worse," Blacknail grumbled in reply as he spat off to the side. Looking carefully, the wound on the assassin's shoulder was a sticky mess of torn cloth and blood, but it seemed to have already stopped bleeding. It didn't seem to be slowing him down either. Malthus's sword was still held out in a high guard, and it looked steady.

Blacknail only had a superficial wound as well. He took up a basic stance of his own as he stepped forward. Both fighters had come out of the first exchange on even ground. The next clash of swords would determine who the better swordsman was, so Blacknail wasn't going to do that. That would be really stupid, and he wanted to live. Thus, he was going to keep trying to cheat! In fact, he already had a plan in mind. He just needed to figure out how to set it up. The hobgoblin let his gaze slip away from Malthus. He scanned the surrounding brush.

His opponent didn't give him time to think though. Malthus advanced on Blacknail. He looked eager to resume the fight, and that was another reason for Blacknail to avoid it. There was a crunching noise as Malthus stepped forward and crushed a twig beneath his feet. The hobgoblin readied himself as the assassin moved into striking distance. Sure enough, his opponent immediately attacked. Blacknail blocked a flurry of quick strikes from Malthus, but every blow forced him backward. The clang of steel on steel filled the clearing as their swords clashed.

Blacknail found himself slowly retreating as he desperately struggled to keep the assassin's blade at bay. The sword in Malthus's hand flowed like water through the air and had a grace Blacknail couldn't match. The hobgoblin could only burn Elixir and muster as much speed as possible in an attempt to keep up. The bushes at the edge of the clearing were getting very close now. He couldn't back up forever. Not unless he wanted to risk tripping over something and then getting stabbed as he flailed around on top of a thorn bush.

Blacknail batted aside one slash that was aimed low, but Malthus's blade twisted back around toward his face in a quick fluid motion. The hobgoblin hissed in alarm and threw himself to the side. Instead of following up though, Malthus took the opportunity to brag.

"I've got your measure now. I suppose you're not a bad swordsman, all things considered. You're better than you look anyway, but far from a master. This next pass will be your last," Malthus remarked disdainfully.

The assassin then lunged forward again with a confident smirk on his face. His blade whistled through the air toward Blacknail. The hobgoblin stepped back to lessen the power of the blow and block it, but Malthus grinned. The assassin's dark cloak rippled as he spun around to the side. His blade twisted around like a snake, and suddenly an alarmed hobgoblin found his sword being knocked from his hands. Desperately, Blacknail managed to keep a grip on the hilt, but the tip of the blade was forced down. However, Malthus's technique wasn't finished. His own sword slid forward and stabbed toward Blacknail's gut. The hobgoblin hesitated for a moment before letting go of his weapon and jumping out of the way. The sword hit the ground with a muted thud as Malthus stepped passed it. The assassin quickly descended upon the now unarmed hobgoblin.

"And now you're mine," he gloated as he raised his blade above his head.

A panicked look appeared on Blacknail's face as he cringed away from the blow. He threw himself backward and to the right, but there was nowhere for him to go. The thorn bushes were behind him and Malthus's charge was too fast. The razor-sharp edge of Malthus's sword sliced down toward the hobgoblin, but Blacknail wasn't worried. His mouth split open to reveal a wide, toothy grin. Malthus noticed the change and he hesitated, but it was far too late. As his sword swung downward, his foot hit the trap. Leaves and other debris exploded into the air as the rope concealed beneath the grass sprung into motion. It wrapped around Malthus's foot and pulled it savagely up into the air as the bent-over sapling it was tied to unfolded with a loud snap.

"Ahhh, hells," the assassin yelled as the slithering rope wrenched him off his feet.

The sapling wasn't tall or strong enough to get him completely off the ground, but it didn't have to. Malthus was dragged roughly across the grass, and his head hit the ground with a loud thud. His sword slipped from his hands as he was pulled away. When he came to stop, the stunned assassin was lying on his back next to the still-swaying tree. His clothes were disheveled, and he was covered in bits and pieces of torn-up plants. It wasn't the best look on him. Blacknail grinned smugly to himself as he appreciated his handiwork. It had taken a lot of work to place so many traps everywhere, but it had been worth the effort. It was a good thing he had spent so many hours learning to make rope...

As Malthus groaned and blinked in confusion, the hobgoblin skipped happily over to his side. The fun part was finally here!

"And now you're mine, stupid human," Blacknail gloated as he loomed over his prey and grinned wickedly. The hobgoblin wanted to take his time and enjoy this. What should he do to his catch? Should he skin him like a rabbit, cut off all his fingers and toes, or set him on fire? All three options had pluses and minuses. It was so hard to choose...

Oh, he knew! He could combine all of them and make Malthus jerky! It probably wouldn't taste all that great, but it would be very satisfying in other ways. Blacknail reached down to pull one of his knives out, but was interrupted when he felt Malthus grab his leg. What was the man up to? He wasn't strong enough to do anything with his bare hands. As the hobgoblin looked down in curiosity, he felt an odd tingling sensation. He frowned and then was thrown sideways as pain burnt its way up his leg. He landed on the ground several feet away and yelped as every muscle in his body started to spasm.

Blacknail writhed painfully on the ground. What had Malthus done? Some sort of magic? Whatever it was, it hurt a lot!

"Ha, as if you could defeat me! I'm the greatest knifeman in Daggerpoint, and you're just a jumped up beast. My master selected me to succeed him and trained me to be undefeatable. I have all his skills and the power of a Vessel at my fingertips," Malthus exclaimed as he cut himself free and slowly stood up. For all his bluster, the assassin sounded pained, and he made no move to approach the fallen hobgoblin. He seemed unsteady on his feet and barely capable of standing.

The pain running along Blacknail's nerves suddenly died

down. He coughed and quickly rolled into a defensive crouch. As Malthus watched, he stood up and met the man's eyes. Both of them stared hatefully at each other as they caught their breaths and cleared their heads.

The nearby songbirds had been startled by all the noise, but they resumed singing now that things were quieter. Around the two combatants, colorful leaves continued to drift lazily down from trees onto the knee-high grass. Blacknail hissed softly to himself. His entire body hurt, especially his leg, and the pain focused his thoughts. He now was utterly focused on killing his opponent. He would rip the man apart with his bare hands and enjoy the squishy feeling of his wet flesh between his fingers.

"Your pants are on fire," Malthus dryly pointed out.

The hobgoblin's first instinct was to ignore the man and assume it was a trick. However, his leg did sort of feel funny... Blacknail looked down. There was a large hole in the cloth below his knee where he had been grabbed, and it was smoldering.

"Eeep," Blacknail yelped as he hopped up on one foot and began trying to put out the flames. He slapped his leg repeatedly with his hands until it stopped smoking.

"It would be far too embarrassing to die by your hands, so I'm going to have to go all out now," Malthus remarked with a pained sigh.

As Blacknail calmed back down, Malthus unwrapped a thin short chain from around his waist. It was no longer than a man's arm and ended in a weighted hook.

It didn't seem like that threatening of a weapon, but Malthus wouldn't have drawn it without a reason. Something told Blacknail it was connected to the burning attack from earlier, and that could only have been caused by one thing.

"Magic, but you're not-ss a mage," Blacknail hissed in annoyance as he drew a pair of daggers and stared Malthus down.

"Indeed," Malthus chuckled. "Not all Vessels are created equal."

The assassin raised a hand up to where Blacknail could easily see it. As the hobgoblin warily watched, little tendrils of lightning danced between the man's fingers.

"That's cheating!" Blacknail exclaimed annoyance as he scowled.

"It's a flashy trick, but it consumes a lot of very expensive Elixir. Stabbing someone is almost always easier anyway," Malthus added in explanation.

Blacknail hadn't known Vessels could do magic tricks. How come he didn't have a power like that? He wanted a fancy magic trick, and he didn't care how much it cost! It wasn't like he paid for his own Elixir anyway. Also, Mahedium was definitely going to get an annoyed visitor later. How dare he not give Blacknail the best magic possible!

The combatants were only a dozen feet from each other and had both recovered enough to move. Malthus took a step forward and began to spin his chain. It made a whirring sound as it cut through the air. Blacknail raised his daggers and took up a knife-fighting stance Saeter had taught him. He knew the chain had to have some sort of trick to it. Most likely it could somehow shock him like Malthus's touch had. If that was the case, this fight was going to be very bothersome, and more than a little painful.

The hobgoblin kept his guard up as Malthus suddenly lunged at him. The man's spinning chain shot out toward Blacknail's chest. He didn't try and block it. Instead, he dodged left and slashed over the chain toward Malthus. The assassin simply stepped back out of the way. His chain had a lot more reach than a dagger.

"Crunchy maggots," Blacknail cursed.

Knives weren't the best weapon for this, and his sword was too far away to get at. Maybe he should have kept that crossbow... Malthus suddenly swung the chain around toward the hobgoblin's head, and Blacknail was forced to duck out of the way. The assassin kept attacking without a break. The chain rattled as it swung toward its target over and over again. Blacknail managed to dodge every blow, but he couldn't get near his opponent. Malthus had too much of a range advantage.

As he fought, the hobgoblin furiously tried to come up with a solution. He needed a new plan. What tools did he have on hand? What could he use? Suddenly, Blacknail remembered some of the preparations he'd made earlier. There was something nearby he could use!

As Malthus continued his assault, Blacknail sidestepped another attack and circled around to the left. With one eye on his opponent, he hurriedly started backing away. The assassin immediately followed him, and his chain slashed out at the hobgoblin's legs. Blacknail jumped over the weapon and continued his retreat. Then Malthus lunged forward again, and his chain smashed into the hobgoblin's upper arm. Blacknail felt a crunching sensation as the weapon impacted his flesh and bone, but no shock. He reeled to the side but managed to keep on his feet. Ow, now his arm hurt too!

"Huh, your clothing must have been too thick. I'll have to hit somewhere else next time, or just beat you to death," the assassin remarked as he resumed spinning his chain.

"No, you won't-ss do any of those things," Blacknail hissed angrily back.

He had grown tired of this fight. He was exhausted, in pain, and really wanted to kill this stupid, stinking human bastard! The hobgoblin kicked the ground at his feet. The tip of his boot hooked a branch that was lying there and flipped it up into the air. Immediately, Blacknail burned Elixir, and he felt the magic energy drive away some of his aches and pains. With inhuman speed, he grabbed the long heavy branch out of the air and swung it at Malthus's head. The man's eyes widened in surprise as the improvised club closed the distance between them. There was a loud thud and cracking noise as the branch slammed into his face and knocked the man over sideways.

Malthus crumpled onto the ground, and Blacknail didn't give him any time to try any more tricks. He stepped forward and continued his savage assault. The clearing was filled with wild growling and heavy thuds as Blacknail ruthlessly beat the assassin to death. Soon, there was nothing left but a wrecked and bloody corpse. The assassin's skull had several dents in it, and one of his eyes had been knocked loose from his head. From experience, Blacknail knew humans couldn't survive nearly that much damage.

"Ha, I win!" The exhausted hobgoblin moaned as he dropped the club and turned around.

He was breathing heavily as he started slowly walking back

to the battlefield. Both his leg and his shoulder hurt, but his mission had been accomplished. It was time to return to his tribe, so he could demand extra cheese and take a very long nap. He'd earned it.

# Chapter 42

Feeling exhilarated after his victory over the assassins, Blacknail exited the brush and began running through the city. He had to get back to his tribe so he could brag! Almost immediately, he heard a shrill scream. Down the street, a blonde woman that he hadn't seen ran into her home and slammed the door shut. Oops, Blacknail had forgotten to fix his appearance. At this point, he was wearing nothing but dirty rags that completely failed to hide his face. With no other choice, he quickly turned back to loot some clothes from his fallen enemies.

None of Malthus's stuff was salvageable; nothing was left of them but bloody scraps. It had been totally worth it though. He regretted nothing. However, Blacknail found intact clothes and a useable cloak on the other fallen assassins. Once he had managed not to look like some sort of murderous drifter, even if he kind of was one, the hobgoblin stepped back into the city. He slipped out of the bushes at the edge of the scrubland and into a nearby alley.

The cool air in the shady alley was a welcome change from being out under the hot sun. All the clothing he wore got very hot when he did strenuous activities such as fighting off squads of assassins and dueling their leader. It didn't take Blacknail all that long to trace his way back to the edge of Herad's territory. He kept his head down and his distance from any crowds as he walked the city streets. There weren't a lot of people around anyway, and those that Blacknail did see were moving quickly and looked nervous. Word of the battle taking place had undoubtedly already spread. All the magical explosions from earlier had probably gotten people's attention as well. Like rabbits or mice that had heard an unexpected noise, the citizens of Daggerpoint were seeking shelter and finding other less dangerous places to be than out on the streets.

As he drew closer to Herad's base, the sounds of fighting became more and more obvious. The cloaked hobgoblin stopped at the entrance to an alley and looked up over the city. As his eyes roamed over the rooftops, he listened to what was going on around him. It sounded like the battle had started up again. Zelena must have attacked again while he was gone. Blacknail's chest tightened painfully as he felt a sudden sense of urgency. He picked up the pace and started to jog. He didn't really want to join the fighting, but what if something bad was happening?

Quickly, Blacknail scuttled up the side of a nearby building and pulled himself onto the roof. Once up in the sunshine, he looked over to where Herad's barricade had been built. Nothing remained of it but ash, and the stone around it was stained black. The flames had scarred the city. Farther back from the blaze, the cobblestone streets were red with blood. Ha, Herad really had dyed the streets of Daggerpoint with the blood of her enemies, and more than a few of her own minions as well. Saeter had told him she wasn't being literal, but he'd been wrong!

The killing was far from over though. Below Blacknail, the struggle for control of Daggerpoint was still ongoing. Blacknail frowned with concern as he realized Herad's men were making a fighting retreat back toward their base. If the enemy reached the base, then all the hobgoblin's things would be in danger, even his cheese!

Zelena had finally committed her own forces, and they'd been joined by what was left of the mercenaries. A small solid square of shield-bearing infantry were pushing their way down the center of the street. On both sides of them were loose mobs of Zelena's bandits. The attackers were steadily pushing the bandits of Blacknail's tribe back, and they also had them outnumbered. They looked to have a man and a half for everyone in Herad's tribe. However, the battle was far from over. Herad may have lost her wooden wall, but Blacknail knew she'd made other preparations. He'd spent a lot of time avoiding having to help set them up after all.

The advance of Herad's enemies was slowed by layers of obstacles such as overturned carts and piles of sandbags. Blacknail's tribe made ready use of the cover as they fought. Before they could be overrun, they abandoned their barricade and moved to the next one. As the hobgoblin watched, a group of archers appeared on a rooftop down the street and opened fire. After several volleys had fallen on Zelena's men, the archers quickly disappeared before the enemy could muster a counterattack.

After looking around for a few more moments, Blacknail climbed back to the ground. The safest place to be where he could still keep an eye on things would be next to Herad and his master. At least it would be, as long as Saeter wasn't doing anything too stupid. Blacknail hurried through the empty side streets that ran parallel to the battle. He ran until the sounds of battle were behind him. It was then he noticed the sentries. There were two of his tribe posted at the corner of the street, and they were doing a terrible job because they hadn't noticed his approach. He wasn't even trying to be all that stealthy! Something really needed to be done about how terrible humans were at watching and waiting. After all this was over, maybe he should start attacking sentries at random. That ought to get them to pay attention, and all the really bad ones would end up dead.

As the hobgoblin studied the two men in front of him, his first thought was that he should just slip past them unseen. He decided against it a moment later though. That would take effort, and he was too tired and sore for that sort of thing. Instead, he slowed down to a non-threatening walk and headed their way. The pair of sentries quickly noticed him and their shadowy forms tensed, finally. One of them stepped forward and drew their sword.

"Stop, who goes there?" he shouted as he brandished his blade in what looked like a poor attempt to look intimidating.

"It is I, Blacknail the faceless assassin and the greatest killer in Daggerpoint," the hobgoblin bragged in answer. He'd gotten the last title after he'd killed Malthus. He was fairly sure killing the old greatest killer made you the new one. If that wasn't case, then he'd just kill anyone else who tried to claim it. There was no response for several seconds. Both the sentries started whispering to each other.

"That's the hobgoblin, right?" a thin man with a scruffy beard asked.

"Ya, tell him to drop his hood so we can be sure," the shorter bald one replied.

"Drop your..."

Blacknail had already flipped his hood down. The bearded bandit squinted through the shadows at him

"Well, he's definitely a hobgoblin," he remarked in relief. He seemed glad that a fight wasn't about to break out.

"Are we sure it's Blacknail though?" the bald bandit asked apprehensively. His eyes were wide, and his voice shook with anxiety. He obviously didn't like being in a dark alley with a hobgoblin. His companion turned and gave him an irritated look. Apparently, Blacknail wasn't the only one who thought that was a really stupid question.

"No, it's some other random hobgoblin that has decided to play dress up and wandered over to see what's going on. As if anyone but Saeter could ever tame a hobgoblin, or want to!" the bearded bandit replied with biting condescension.

The two men then started to argue and bicker heatedly amongst themselves. Blacknail ignored them and walked right past. They were too preoccupied to stop him. Clearly, Herad wasn't expecting a flanking attack and was putting her less intelligent minions where they could do the least amount of harm.

After a quick peek around the corner to make sure it was safe, Blacknail stepped out onto the main street. Before him was the rear of Herad's forces. Bandits were running everywhere as they rushed to and from the front lines. A nervous energy permeated the air, and Blacknail could smell both fear and excitement. Herad stood in the center of all the activity. She was only a few dozen feet from the fighting and was yelling orders as she waved her short sword around. At her command, bandits abandoned cover or held their ground and counterattacked. When a group looked like it was about to be overrun, she and her bodyguards would dive in and join the fray themselves. Enemies fell by the dozen when that happened.

Blacknail couldn't help but notice two unfamiliar faces next to her that were also racking up quite the body count. Judging by their physical prowess and the dark look in their eyes, Blacknail was pretty sure they were Sloshers sent by Avorlus. Mahedium had mentioned something about that earlier, hadn't he? The fear she and her bodyguards inspired among Zelena's men was obvious. They hesitated to approach her and were quick to retreat when she advanced. Only the mercenary formation was unaffected, and Herad seemed to be avoiding them.

Suddenly, there was a shift in the way the enemy was moving. The ranks of Zelena's men parted, and three humans stepped out into the now empty space in front of Herad. One of them was obviously a mercenary. He was wearing their brown tunic and armed and armored the same way as them. The second was a huge human male in crude leather armor with a large round belly and a long black beard. He had a huge mace over his shoulder that looked to be the size of Blacknail's entire body. The third was a tall woman with a chainmail shirt, steel helmet, and a long spear in her hands.

The hobgoblin was willing to bet that they were all Sloshers. Herad must have thought so as well, because she instantly focused on them and ordered most her men back. Only Avorlus's Sloshers stayed by her side as she marched forward to meet these new foes.

Blacknail looked away from his chieftain for a second and tried to find Saeter. He scanned the nearby crowds but didn't see him anywhere near the rear. With a frown of annoyance and concern, he started looking along the front line. There, a flash of movement caught his attention, and he spotted his master's face. Ack, Saeter was doing something stupid! Why was he fighting on the front lines? That was for dumb people and disposable members of the tribe! His master wasn't replaceable. Did he want to get Blacknail killed?

Immediately, the frantic hobgoblin began pushing his way through the crowd of bandits that lay between him and the front line. He had to make sure his master was safe. Who else would feed and train him? For reasons beyond Blacknail's understanding, Saeter had his sword out and was fighting one of Zelena's henchmen. He was holding his own, but he looked exhausted. His shoulders were slumped, and his movements were slower than usual. Blacknail's heart started beating faster, and a sick, uneasy feeling grew in his gut. He picked up his pace and shoved a nearby bandit out of his way.

As the hobgoblin drew nearer, Saeter managed to parry his opponent's blade and deliver a deep slash to his chest. The enemy fell as blood poured from the wound. For a moment, Blacknail almost felt relief, but it didn't last long. Another enemy fighter stepped forward to challenge his master, and this one was bigger and had a larger sword! Saeter raised his blade defensively, but he was too slow. The larger man's sword swatted it aside and sent the old scout reeling. As Blacknail watched, his master collapsed onto the ground and didn't get back up.

The hobgoblin was sprinting now, and not so much pushing people out of the way as picking them up and throwing them. The uneasy feeling pulsating in his gut was being subsumed by a new emotion, a burning wave of all-consuming fury. It raged through him like a storm of fire. Blacknail's clawed fingers tightened and curled. His eyes narrowed, and his lips curled up into a snarl to reveal his long pointy teeth. He was angry, very, very angry.

The thug standing over Saeter raised his sword high in preparation to strike. There were still people in the hobgoblin's way, but he didn't care. Blacknail flared Elixir. It mingled inside of him and seemed to drive his rage to new heights. He was so empowered, he jumped and landed on the shoulders of a surprised bandit. The man wobbled, but Blacknail had already lunged away toward the target of his now intense and focused hatred. He hit the unsuspecting thug like a sack of bricks thrown by an ogre. The man gasped painfully in surprise, dropped his sword, and lurched sideways as the speeding hobgoblin smashed into him. A second later, he was falling over, and Blacknail had his hands around the man's neck. A second after that, Blacknail's claws sank into the man's throat, and the hobgoblin tore his windpipe out in a small gory red explosion.

Several of Zelena's henchmen stepped forward to deal with

the new threat, but they all froze in terror a second later. The jump and following impact had thrown the hobgoblin's hood back, and Blacknail was far too enraged to give a damn. He rose from atop his victim's body with a vicious snarl on his face and blood dripping from his hands. A loud menacing growl echoed up from his chest and out through his lips as he turned to stare malevolently at his closest enemies. He would rip them all apart and bathe in their blood!

Some of Zelena's men flinched away from his gaze, others paled and remained frozen in fear, and one blond, tall, powerfully built man stepped forward to attack. Blacknail ducked under the blow and killed him with a knife through his groin. The man fell and bled to death in seconds.

The hobgoblin's bloodlust was far from satisfied; feeding it had just made it stronger and the cravings more seductive. Blacknail went for the weakest and easiest prey next. He grabbed the fallen man's sword and swung it toward the closest of his stunned foes. The hobgoblin Vessel's inhuman speed took everyone by surprise. Before anyone could react, the blade had sliced off the man's hand. Blacknail was already spinning toward the next target. He slashed up toward the thug's face but was stopped by a clumsy block. This barely slowed the hobgoblin. He pushed his blade forward to knock the man off-balance and then stepped forward. As quick as thought, Blacknail's hand shot out and his fingers sank into the man's exposed eye sockets.

More screaming filled the air. It seemed to synch with the hobgoblin's frantically beating heart and was music to his ears. Blacknail withdrew his hand and gave it a quick lick. The taste of iron, blood, and brains felt wonderful on his lips. It tasted like belonging.

A blade sliced through the air toward him, but Blacknail dodged to the side. He laughed gleefully as the claws on his left foot tore through the front of his boot and into the groin of an attacker. Then, another thug stepped forward and right into Blacknail's blade. The edge bit into his neck with fatal precision. Blacknail laughed as bloodlust overtook him. All these stupid humans were so slow, and their moves were so obvious. He could kill them all day, and he would, because it was such great fun! He ducked under a wild, panicked swing and gutted the idiot who had attacked him. A space had cleared around Blacknail now. Both friends and foes had fallen back from him and the pile of mangled corpses at his feet.

The hobgoblin frowned as the sound of a yelling voice penetrated the red haze that surrounded him. One of his enemies was trying to summon some crossbowmen. Damned crossbows, Blacknail was so going to kill him next. He took a step forward to do just that when a hush fell over the battlefield. Almost everyone was suddenly looking toward the center of the battlefield as Herad's voice echoed over it.

"Your Vessels are dead, Zelena. They couldn't stand against me and neither can these pitiful drags you call an army. Now, do you dare challenge me personally, or will you run like a coward?" she yelled loudly enough for everyone to hear.

There was no response from anyone on Zelena's side, so Blacknail took this opportunity to murder the man to his left while everyone was distracted. Unfortunately, he didn't die as quietly as the hobgoblin had hoped, and his screams filled the air for a few moments before Blacknail could finish him off. Blacknail met the eyes of his next victim and stepped forward. The man's eyes widened in terror as he returned the hobgoblin's gaze, and a second later, he turned and ran. The thug to his left followed him, and then running away suddenly became the popular thing to do.

All around Blacknail men began to flee for their lives. Soon, it wasn't limited to those few men near the hobgoblin. The rhythm of pounding boots on cobblestone rang out repeatedly as all of Zelena's men broke formation and turned to run. Even the mercenaries started to march slowly backward. As they fled, Blacknail took a step forward to chase them but then stopped. As hungry as he was for new kills, he couldn't help but notice that none of his tribe were in pursuit. Going after all of Zelena's men alone might sound fun, but it was also probably unhealthy.

The hobgoblin stood all alone on the blood-covered street. As the red rage of his bloodlust slowly drained away, he remembered he'd come here for a reason. His master had been hit! How could he have forgotten that? Blacknail spun around to find out what had happened to Saeter. He desperately needed his master to be all right. No amount of blue cheese could replace the man who had taught him so much!

# *Chapter 43*

There was ragged cheering from Herad's band as Zelena's forces fled for their lives. The shouts of dozens of tired but joyful men and women rose into the air as they celebrated their victory. Everyone still standing was glad just to have survived the long day of fighting. With the battle now over, the anger and the energy that had come with it quickly started to drain from Blacknail's body. Suddenly, he could feel all his injuries again, and if anything, they hurt more than before. The hobgoblin couldn't rest yet though. He immediately began limping around in search of his master. Blacknail needed to know if he was okay and not dead or anything. What was he going to do if Saeter was hurt? His chest felt unpleasantly hollow just thinking about it, and so did his stomach. His master was the one that fed him most the time!

Thankfully, it didn't take long for Blacknail to find Saeter. The hobgoblin winced when he saw his master lying up against the side of a building. Immediately, Blacknail ran over to his side and poked him in the arm.

"Are you alive? It's not-ss my fault if you died," he asked as he crouched over his master. Saeter coughed, opened his eyes, and glared angrily at the hobgoblin.

"I'm fine, stop poking me, you overgrown goblin!" the old scout growled weakly.

"You don't look fine," Blacknail replied in an unconvinced tone as he tilted his head to the side. Now that he was closer, the hobgoblin noticed someone had wrapped some bandages around his master's chest and left arm.

"Bah, I'm just taking a brief rest. I'm not so weak that a blow like that could do me in. I'm out of shape is all. Now leave me alone," Saeter said and closed his eyes again.

Blacknail sighed in relief as he stood back up. Well, his master was apparently going to live, so that was good. The curious hobgoblin decided to ask around and find out what exactly had happened while he'd been fighting. A few minutes later, he got his answer. Apparently, the blow from the now very dead thug had merely stunned Saeter, and when Blacknail had charged in, one of his nearby tribesmen had taken the opportunity to drag the old scout back away from the front lines. The rescuer was a young blond man. He was one of the new recruits that Herad had hired in Daggerpoint. Blacknail walked over to him. The young man paled slightly as he warily watched the bloodstained hobgoblin approach. Blacknail smiled reassuringly, but that didn't seem to help for some reason.

"What's your name-ss?" Blacknail asked him.

"Eylias," the man stuttered in reply. Obviously, he was awestruck being around an amazing bandit such as Blacknail. The hobgoblin wasn't surprised, he was really amazing.

The hobgoblin stepped up in front of Eylias and looked him over carefully. The blond bandit froze, and his eyes widened in utter amazement. Blacknail thought he looked smarter than the average human, although that wasn't saying much. With snake-like speed, Blacknail leaned forward and wrapped the man in a huge hug. Eylias's panicked attempts to escape were futile, but cute.

"Thank you for saving Saeter! I like you," the hobgoblin exclaimed happily.

"You're very welcome!" the man squeaked in alarm as Blacknail squeezed his ribs together.

"You can be my minion. I'll show you how to make rope and kill people you don't like," the hobgoblin announced cheerfully. All the important bandits had subordinates, so why shouldn't Blacknail? He was pretty much the second or third most important bandit in the entire band!

Eylias gasped. "I don't think..."

"Most humans don't. It doesn't matter; you just have-ss to do what I say," Blacknail explained as he let the man go. Eylias stumbled unsteadily as the hobgoblin stepped back.

"I mean... I'm already part of Richter's crew, so I can't be in yours," the man quickly said after sucking down a long breath.

"I'll just ask-ss Herad to fix that. Then we can go out into the woods!" Blacknail replied.

"The woods?" the man asked with dawning horror.

"Sure, you need-ss to learn to hunt, and knowing how not to get eaten or torn apart is important too."

"No thanks, I don't really want to learn that stuff," Eylias quickly blurted out. Blacknail shook his head and sighed; he had expected this reaction. Humans were really lazy after all, so they needed motivation.

"Don't worry! You just have-ss to do as I say, and then nothing bad will happen to you," Blacknail said with a dark look and a meaningful nudge. For added emphasis, he then made a few stabbing motions with his hand. You could never explain things too clearly to humans.

"I see," the young bandit replied a few seconds later. He sounded more than a little shocked and overwhelmed. The right side of his face also seemed to be twitching slightly. Well, it wasn't every day a nameless disposable grunt like him managed to get such a great new position in the tribe!

Off in the distance, the sound of Herad yelling could still be heard. Even though the battle was over, there was still tons of work to be done. Men were rushing around to help the wounded, load all the corpses and body parts on wagons, loot the fallen, and finish off wounded enemies. The hobgoblin wanted to join in the fun, but he was too tired and sore. He didn't have the energy left to wander around the battlefield and look for loot to take home. Oh well, most of his tribesmen would undoubtedly grow tired of their prizes and leave them lying around somewhere Blacknail could pick them up anyway. Most of the things the hobgoblin wanted ended up in his possession one way or another. He just had to keep an eye open for all the despicable thieves that wanted to steal his stuff.

Just then, a pair of men arrived with a stretcher. Blacknail watched with interest as they loaded his master up and began to carry him back to base. That stretcher sure looked comfy, and Blacknail was really sore from all the fighting. A few dozen feet away, another man was carrying a stretcher and looking for wounded to carry. Blacknail decided to help him. With a cheerful smile on his face, he grabbed Eylias and dragged him over to the porter.

"I want to ride-ss on this. Carry me back to base," he told the man with the stretcher.

"It's um... only for wounded people," the porter replied uncertainly.

"I'm very wounded. I can barely walk-ss, and I feel like I'm going to fall over. Now carry me back to base, or my new minion Eylias will show you-ss how wounded I am by hurting you the same way," the hobgoblin replied threateningly with narrowed eyes.

The porter gave Eylias a confused look. The young blond just stared back with a bewildered look on his face. Blacknail drew his knife and started to pick his nails clean with it in a very conspicuous manner while he stared intently at Eylias. He got the message.

"Right, you'd better do as he says," the young bandit reluctantly said.

The porter looked between Eylias and Blacknail before shrugging and setting the stretcher down on the ground. The hobgoblin then cheerfully jumped on, and the two men started carrying him down the road. It was as comfy as Blacknail thought it would be, so he laid back and enjoyed the ride. He should travel everywhere like this.

However, they didn't get very far before their trek was interrupted. Blacknail heard the sound of familiar light footsteps approaching, and he opened his eyes to see Herad headed his way. At first she gazed toward Saeter's prone form and scowled in dissatisfaction, but then she turned toward Blacknail. Her eyebrows rose slightly in surprised amusement as she took in the sight of the hobgoblin sprawled over the stretcher being carried by the two men.

"Ah, there's my favorite hobgoblin. I heard that you'd walked back here on your own without any obvious injuries, but the sentries clearly must have not been paying enough attention. You're obviously wounded, so I'll have to punish them later," she told him.

Blacknail grinned uncertainly and stifled a lazy yawn. The two men carrying him froze at their boss's attention. The hobgoblin noticed his chieftain looked unusually... happy. It made him uncomfortable, like being in the calm center of a storm. Apparently, all it took to put her in a good mood was the deaths of hundreds of her enemies.

"Yes, I'm very wounded; it hurts-ss everywhere. Bad sentries, they're terrible at their jobs. Ow, the pain-ss," he whined dramatically as he collapsed back onto the stretcher.

"I see. Well, since you're obviously not too wounded to talk, I need a report on what you've been up to. I gave you a mission," she told him with a trace of her usual sternness.

The hobgoblin quickly began telling his boss all about his plan to take out the assassins and how it had worked perfectly! He grinned and made suggestive hand gestures as he recounted the daring escapes and close fights that had taken place as he'd dealt with Malthus and the other two dozen assassins with him. There might also have been a trio of enemy mages.

"...but now I'm so wounded. Ow, the pain-ss is everywhere inside of me," Blacknail finished melodramatically. The bandit chieftain rolled her eyes, and a small grin appeared on her lips as the hobgoblin spoke. When he was finished, she shook her head in disbelief.

"Since you're so wounded, I guess you won't be able to get your reward for a while," Herad remarked. Visions of blue cheese and meat pies flashed through Blacknail's head, and his stomach grumbled loudly in response.

"I can still eat!" Blacknail exclaimed quickly as he sat back up.

"Somehow, I thought that might be the case," Herad remarked dryly as she started to walk away. After a second, she seemed to hesitate and then spoke again without looking back.

"Oh, and Blacknail... good job pulling Saeter's ass out of the fire," she told him before leaving. When she was gone, Blacknail relaxed and collapsed back down onto the stretcher in relief.

"What-ss are you two waiting for? Get moving!" he growled at the porters.

After returning to base and getting his own injuries patched up, Blacknail curled up on his big comfy bed and took a nap. When he heard the sound of someone trying to wake him, he did his best to ignore it. Unfortunately, that proved difficult, and he soon had to roll over and open his eyes so he could glare at Khita.

"Wake up, Blacknail. You've already slept for over a day, and Herad wants you," the young woman said as she reached over to shake the hobgoblin.

"Touch me, and I'll bite you." Blacknail hissed as he rolled away from her.

"She wants you to follow her to a meeting with the other chiefs in Daggerpoint," Khita explained.

Blacknail grunted vaguely in reply but didn't move. That sounded really boring. He was in no hurry to get off his wonderful bed and out from under his soft sheets.

"She wants you there to scare everyone and intimidate them," Khita added.

The hobgoblin's eyes opened again as he thought her words over. That actually did sound like fun. He could practice making scary faces. With a deep sigh, Blacknail sat up and looked back at Khita. "Fine, I'm getting up. Go away."

"Hurry up. You don't want to keep Herad waiting," Khita replied as she walked out the door.

A few minutes later, Blacknail was dressed in his usual clothes but without his mask. He was fairly sure he wouldn't need it, and it was still in the bush where he'd thrown it anyway. He would have to remember to get it later. He then dragged himself out of his room and joined Herad and her hulking bodyguards at the main entrance to the base. Herad was dressed in a fancier version of her usual black leathers, and the shadows under her eyes seemed darker as well, but she smirked when the hobgoblin arrived. Either the effects of winning the battle had yet to wear off, or she was really looking forward to this meeting, because she was still looking unusually cheerful. She wasn't even glowering, and it didn't look like she was about to kill anyone at all! Weird.

With Blacknail in tow, the two dozen bandits headed out toward the central district. They passed by the guards that stood watch over the border without incident and entered the better part of the city. After a brief walk past increasingly better maintained and larger homes, they arrived at the mansion at the center of the city. More sentries like those that guarded the central district stood outside of it, but Herad ignored them. She strolled right past them, and they quickly shuffled out of her way without comment. A few of them noticed Blacknail and scowled, but the hobgoblin just threw them a toothy smile, and they didn't say anything.

As they approached, the doors to the mansion were thrown open, and they marched inside. The room on the other side impressed Blacknail. It was the fanciest room he had ever seen. It was much fancier than even Luphera's or Avorlus's homes. The walls were smooth, pearly white plaster and long, wispy white curtains framed the large glass windows. Intricate silver chandeliers hung from the roof to provide lighting. Even the tables and chairs looked like pieces of delicately crafted art.

"Greetings, mistress Herad. If you would please follow me, I will take you to the conference room," a sharply dressed servant explained with a bow.

Herad nodded in reply, and the man immediately led them through a side door and into a short hallway. He then pulled open another door and motioned them inside. The room on the other side of the door was dominated by a large round table. A dozen men and women were seated around it while a few dozen more stood around the edges of the room. Herad motioned for her minions to take up position along the wall behind her as she swaggered over to a chair and sat down at the table.

Once again, Blacknail drew a lot of attention, and no one seemed happy to see him. The hobgoblin ignored them. He was busy trying to find somewhere to sit down. Whoever had set up this room had been very inconsiderate in not including chairs for everyone, so Blacknail had to do a bit of problem solving. There was a small stand up against the wall, and the hobgoblin simply took all the junk on top of it and placed it on the floor before sitting down. During the process, a few of the decorations, including a silver candleholder, may have somehow inexplicably ended up in his pockets.

"Ahem, now that everyone is here, let's get this meeting started. As you all know, several important and unusual events have recently taken place in this city," a well-dressed, older man with a gray goatee announced. Blacknail was fairly certain the man was studying him out of the corner of his eye.

"That's a bloody understatement, Governor," one of the

rougher looking men at the table replied as he threw Herad an annoyed look.

"It's a small miracle that most the city's still standing. Some people have a lot to answer for," someone else added.

"Ha, who are you referring to, Raelan?" Herad replied with a scornful chuckle. "I was simply defending myself, and I wasn't the one that brought a mercenary company into the city with the intention of conquering it. Also, anytime you want me to answer for something, you can feel free to challenge me to a duel. I'll gladly accept either that or a larger fight. With Zelena gone and Fang dead, I have the largest force in the city."

"Indeed, we are not here to reprimand anyone," the governor interjected. "While I have no say in what you do amongst yourselves in the outer parts of the city, I myself don't consider Herad to have broken any of the rules we agreed to when I invited all of you into the city. However, Zelena's actions require some... discussion."

"What do you mean by discussion?" another chieftain asked.

"I mean that I'm hoping we can agree to some clarifications about the rules. In particular, I'm talking about Zelena's use of mercenaries. There is presently no rule against hiring such forces, but I think we can all agree that in light of recent developments, that it's unacceptable," the older man explained.

"I have no problem with that. While everyone is here, I'd also like to remind them that most of my band is operating down south right now, and anyone else who enters my territory will be handled without mercy," Herad added.

"And what about Herad's new pet there? That thing should be put down. It certainly shouldn't be roaming the city, let alone allowed in this room!" a large ugly-looking female chieftain exclaimed.

Blacknail turned and glared at the speaker. He was pretty sure she was talking about him. He wasn't a pet though. The woman was obviously not that smart, but Blacknail still didn't like being insulted. Well, Herad had brought him here to be scary, so he doubted she would care if he spoke up.

"Like that weak fool Malthus, you insult-ss me. I'll be seeing you later," he growled in his most sinister voice as he glared at the woman. The woman flinched away from him as he spoke, and she wasn't the only one. Several other people in the room appeared more unnerved by his ability to speak than his looks. Herad laughed.

"I'd like to see you forbid Blacknail from anywhere or anything. Several people who used to sit around this table learned the hard way that he goes where he wants. Even running would be futile. If you think he's dangerous in this city, then you haven't seen anything yet. He was trained to hunt and track by Saeter himself, and he's a bloody hobgoblin! There's nothing he enjoys more than hunting people through the forest. I'm sure that if you apologize he'll forgive you though," she remarked cruelly.

Blacknail did his best to look threatening. He scowled at the men and women at the table and around the edges of the room. If that didn't get a reaction, he smiled at them and licked his pointy needle-like teeth with his long, agile tongue. That seemed to be what disturbed them the most.

The chieftains soon started to argue amongst themselves, and eventually, even acting scary started to grow boring. The humans just kept talking and talking! Blacknail was about to get up and wander around the room when the meeting finally came to a close. After what seemed like hours of arguing, the only thing the bandit chieftains had agreed upon was the governor's proposal to ban mercenaries. If Herad had to deal with people like this all the time, it was no wonder she wanted to kill everyone.

After a brief walk back to their base, Herad was greeted at the entrance by Saeter. Blacknail was glad to see his master up and about. The bandit chieftain dismissed her guards and turned to the old scout as they walked deeper into the building.

"What do you want, Saeter?" she asked him.

"I thought I should inform you of a discovery I made while looking over the loot Zelena left behind when she fled the city," Saeter explained forebodingly.

Herad frowned at his words and tone of voice. "I take it that this isn't the kind of discovery that can be converted to cash?"

"Depends on what you mean. One of the things in the storeroom was an oak chest," he told her.

"I remember it," Herad replied impatiently.

"Well, I thought it looked familiar, so I tried to open it. The good news is that there were several small bags of silver inside. The bad news is that I opened it with this. Blacknail took it from Persus when the man's caravan visited our camp." Saeter held up a familiar golden key. There was an ominous silence as Herad absorbed the old scout's words, and then her lips tightened into a scowl.

It took a few seconds for Blacknail to remember what Saeter was talking about. Persus had been that crooked merchant who had visited Herad's camp back when Blacknail had been a goblin. He had belonged to a tribe called the Broken Wheel Company, or something.

"Maybe they just buy chests from the same locksmith," Herad replied a second later as she stared menacingly at the key.

Blacknail's master opened his mouth to say something, but Herad cut him off.

"Shut up, I was being sarcastic, Saeter," she hissed at him.

The old scout closed his mouth and looked grim.

"Demons and damnation, that fucking weasel! Well, at least this explains why Werrick seems to have unlimited funds," the bandit chieftain exclaimed darkly as she glowered. "The Broken Wheel Company owns half the border lords and has more money than any of the southern kings."

Blacknail had no idea what they were talking about or why they were upset. It was just a key. He kind of wanted to ask for his cheese now, but it seemed like a bad time.

"Yes, if they're backing Werrick, then our war with him has just gotten started," Saeter told Herad as he met her gaze. There was silence as the old scout and the bandit chieftain stared at each other. The usual animosity they shared was completely absent, and they both looked grim.

"Oh, good! That sounds like fun," Blacknail exclaimed happily. He walked over, threw an arm around Saeter's shoulders, and beamed at Herad. He couldn't wait for the next battle! This Werrick fellow wouldn't know what hit him. All the shiny coins in the world wouldn't save him from Blacknail.

# *Chapter 44*

The plain-looking man passed his coat off to the waiting servant. He was middle-aged, and his brown hair had begun to recede. His jacket was of the finest quality, but you wouldn't have noticed at first glance. It was tailored in a subdued style and had a simple design. As the servant stepped away, the man calmly adjusted the collar of his shirt and walked down the mansion's hallway. He didn't bother to say anything to the servant or even acknowledge his presence. He even ignored his surroundings as he moved, even though the inside of the building was lavishly decorated. His face remained absolutely expressionless.

A long, red carpet muted the sound of his footsteps as he walked. Night had fallen hours ago, and it was pitch black outside, but an abundance of bright oil lamps lit the man's way. The light from them glinted off the expensive silver and bronze items that were on display around the room. When he reached the end of the hallway, he unhurriedly pulled the door there open. There was a lavish but cozy room on the other side, and it had three occupants. They were all seated around a small, intimate table in the center of the room. All three of them looked up as the newest arrival entered and closed the door firmly behind himself. It clicked shut as the mechanism within sealed the room.

The man gave each of his compatriots a quick look-over, but his thin face revealed nothing of his thoughts. There were two other men and one woman at the table. One of the men was older than him and had a neatly trimmed beard, graying hair, and a smug twinkle in his eye. The other was younger, clean-shaven, and didn't look to be in good shape. He had a pudgy cast to his features and looked like he was carrying extra weight.

"Thank you for joining us, Ressarus," the gray-haired gentleman said as the man pulled out a chair and took a seat.

"Thank you for hosting this meeting, sir," Ressarus replied politely but emotionlessly.

"I hope your journey here was less eventful than mine." The matronly looking woman was wearing a long plain dress that gave her a frumpy look and her long blond hair was carefully braided. All together, it made her seem older than she actually was.

"I ran into no surprises, and I'm glad to see that you're fine and still capable of continuing to fulfill your responsibilities to this company," Ressarus told her.

"Your concern touches my heart," the woman told him dryly as she tinkered with a wine glass.

"None of us are responsible for your travel plans or how spectacularly they went wrong. Maybe next time you won't skimp out on hiring the necessary protection. We don't control the North yet," the younger man told her scornfully.

"I never said you were," the woman replied coldly. There were no servants in the room, and only a single bottle of wine on the table. Nor were there any windows in the walls. All the light came from a silver chandelier hanging overhead.

"Wonderful, now that the formalities are done with, let's get down to business. I have ventures of my own to get back to and a throng of lesser nobles that need to be kept in line," the bulky man suggested impatiently as he reached for the wine bottle and poured himself a cup.

He then set the bottle back down and took a sip from his glass. His comment earned him scowls of disapproval from the woman and Ressarus. The older, gray-haired man simply smirked as he folded his hands in front of himself on the table.

"Oh, what's with that stupid look on your face, Ressarus? You're even less of a stickler for formalities than me," the youngest member of the group remarked irritably.

"Perhaps, but impatience is not something I approve of either, especially in business partners. I believe that the fact we went rushing in without proper preparation is the reason our plans have been recently delayed," Ressarus explained.

"Ah, you're talking about that mess in Daggerpoint. That

was unfortunate, but I would hardly even call it a real setback," the older man replied.

"But you're probably right that our impatience is to blame for our failure there. We saw an opportunity to expedite our plans and took it. However, Zelena's failure simply means we are back to our old schedule, and all it cost us was a small chest of silver," the woman added as she shrugged without apparent concern.

"Ha, even we don't have unlimited funds. We shouldn't get in the habit of accepting such losses. Investing so much money in that fool Zelena was a mistake on our part. We should have waited until Werrick could take things in hand personally," the bulky man remarked.

"Now now, we all knew this would be a complicated endeavor and we would face setbacks. Let us simply move forward from here," the older man interjected calmly.

"Agreed," Ressarus commented. There were mutters of agreement from the other people at the table as well.

"So, we underestimated both Herad's pride and her competence, but that won't happen again. Based on what Persus told us, we assumed she wouldn't make a good... employee, so we chose to ignore her until it came time for Werrick to eliminate her. However, these latest events have shown that we must deal with her directly," the bearded man observed aloud.

"Yes, the next time we move, we must leave nothing to chance. For Werrick to control the North for us, the Black Snake must be eliminated. I propose we spare no expense when we move against her; she must be crushed with overwhelming strength!" the younger man told his partners.

"Winter is almost here, so we can't do anything until spring. I'm not sure if you've ever seen a proper northern winter, but it shuts almost all travel down," the woman remarked.

"That works both ways. Herad's movements will be restricted as well. She will be stuck in Daggerpoint all winter. Come spring, she will assuredly then move south to reunite with the rest of her band. We simply have to get ready to strike once that happens," Ressarus explained.

"Won't that kind of manpower draw attention to ourselves?"

the woman asked.

"From who? The nearby lords are the next best thing to destitute. Hulgaron is kingless and Eloria preoccupied by a myriad of other concerns. We also have agents in place that can make sure anyone looking is distracted if necessary. A group of merchants paying to exterminate some bandits is hardly suspicious anyway. Anyone who even notices will probably applaud us!" the younger man explained.

"Indeed, it would even set a useful precedent. Since no one else is willing to stand up to all the nefarious bandits in the North, why should we not protect ourselves? When Werrick pushes south, none of the powerful lords will care if we raise a small army of mercenaries to protect our interests, and once that happens..." Ressarus drawled on suggestively.

The older man laughed and smiled cheerfully at his companions and poured himself a glass of wine. He then raised his glass up into the air in front of himself. He looked like nothing more than someone's favorite elderly uncle.

"Then it's official; I don't see any need for a formal vote. When the snows start to melt this spring, the Broken Wheel Company will destroy the Black Snake and her band. Cheers!" he happily announced.

The others all raised their glasses, even Ressarus's empty one, and a chorus of cheers and the sound of chinking glass filled the room. None of the participants had any doubt in their minds that they would succeed. The resources they controlled were simply far too great for a mere bandit chief to stand against.

# About The Author

I'm just a normal everyday guy by the name of Scott Straughan. I also go by the moniker Clearmadness sometimes. Like a surprising number of authors, I'm Canadian. These days I live in the province of Ontario, and contrary to the rumors, I am not actually a goblin.

I started writing because I love world building and reading. I started reading at a young age and never ever stopped. My teachers had to confiscate my books. Eventually, all those ideas and characters took root in my brain and I had to start writing, so here we are.

***Coming Soon!***

**The Iron Teeth: Book Three**

**More Information at:**

**www.ironteethserial.com**

Made in the USA
Lexington, KY
09 December 2018